CANYON

OF THE

HAUNTED SHADOWS

CANYON
OF THE
HAUNTED SHADOWS

KIRBY JONAS

Cover design by Clay Jonas

Howling Wolf Publishing
Pocatello, Idaho

Howling Wolf Publishing
1611 City Creek Road
Pocatello ID 83204

For more information about Kirby's books, check out:

www.kirbyjonas.com
Facebook, at KirbyJonasauthor

Or email Kirby at: **kirby@kirbyjonas.com**

Manufactured in the United States of America—*One nation, under God*

Publication date in electronic format for this edition: August 2016
Jonas, Kirby, 1965—
Canyon of the Haunted Shadows / by Kirby Jonas.

ISBN: 978-1-891423-23-9
Library of Congress Control Number: 2018912166

To learn more about this book or any other Kirby Jonas book, email Kirby at kirby@kirbyjonas.com

Dedicated to Steve and Teri White, whose faith in me was never-ending, and to Lynsi, Kelsi, Cara and Natali

CHAPTER ONE

With eyes and mouth stretched open in terror, a haunted, rusty moon and shreds of tortured cloud obscured the glitter of the Arizona stars. Shades of sleeping Titans ghosted among the bleak, broken castles of the Santa Catalina Mountains, and the shadowy corridors of granite and black-timbered canyons echoed with the eerie wailing of their terror.

From a far-off land they came, they looked over the countryside, exploring its crevices and its musty nooks, and they coveted its riches. In cruelty seldom surpassed, they enslaved the native people and set them to work in deep, dark mines. But as all such peoples do, they set in motion the wheels of their own doom. And in time, like the mightiest of trees, they fell.

And when they were gone, only the wind mourned their passing . . .

Alone, one man born of their seed remained, and the Santa Catalina Mountains, outside Tucson, Arizona, were his realm. Through their shadows, over their narrow ridges, across their forested slopes and glades, he moved like the shadow of a giant tree, and where he walked, the world bowed around him. He was one with the mountains—in his own way a mountain himself—and those from the valleys below were as insects. Nothing but ants, grasshoppers, to be trodden beneath his feet, to be brushed aside like reeds rustled by a cold, bitter wind.

No man who came here, who found the secret of these wild canyons, would ever leave the same . . . if he left here at all.

Here, deep in the Santa Catalina Mountains, echoed the moans of mighty men. Here wandered their lonely ghosts—forever . . .

And in loneliness and age untold, he alone remained—the man whose name of far-away youth had long been forgotten and who was now called by the handful of native people who knew him He-Who-Lives-with-the-Shadows-of-Death.

Death-Shadow . . .

CHAPTER TWO

Sam Coffey wiped at his huge salt and pepper mustache and spat to one side, well off the trail and away from his horse, Gringo. He gave a sideways glance of mock reproval to his partner, Tom Vanse.

"Someday God's gonna spit on you too, big boy."

Tom looked over at him and laughed. "What? It's just a scorpion."

"Seems like my mama used to tell me there's somethin' in the Good Book about God noticing the fall of the tiniest sparrow, too."

"Exactly. Sparrow—not scorpion." Tom looked down at the straw-colored scorpion, just three feet away from the right front hoof of his horse, Cocky. The arachnid squatted defiantly, its tail held aloft, like a pendulum, in hopes that some foolish human—or at this point probably *any* living thing—would make the mistake of getting within striking range of its venomous sticker. Spattered on the side of the game little creature were gobs of tobacco spit, but the largest portion of it streamed across the soil, like an arrow pointing the way.

Tom shrugged and spat again, but once more it was off, this time even farther to one side.

"You can't even aim," said Sam, one side of his face wrinkling up in a half-grin. "You spit like a girl."

Tom grinned, oblivious to the mushy flakes of tobacco now caught in his teeth. "Maybe the girls *you* go with. My girls don't spit. Hell, they don't even chew."

"What do they do, swallow their food whole? That'd figure."

Tom laughed again, his deep dimples creasing his face. "You're a funny man, Sam. Real funny." He looked down again at the scorpion, started to pull a plug of tobacco from his shirt pocket, then thought better of it and let it slide back in.

"You oughtta get down and lick that poor thing off," suggested Sam. "Or shoot it and put it out of its misery. How'd you like to go around with that dirty spit on you until the next time it rains?"

"Is that worse than clean spit? I'm sure he'll survive," said Tom. "Come on, supper's gonna be waiting."

With that, he squeezed his knees, leaving the scorpion angry, alive, and forgotten, and Cocky started forward again, his breathing having quieted down after a five minute breather. "Wait!" Tom drew in just as abruptly as he had started, and Sam did the same after pulling up alongside him.

After watching a faint cloud of dust for a moment, Tom said, "Looks like Cholla." By now, the rider who was making the dust was only two hundred yards out, not in the direction of the ranch, but on toward Tucson.

Cholla was a small-built Pima Indian Tom had found under a cantina awning in Tucson several months ago. He was gaunt as a calf with porcupine quills in its snout, and Tom took mercy on him and bought him a meal. He was just being Tom, expecting nothing in return, but Cholla, whose Pima name they had never been able to pronounce, had become Tom's faithful shadow. They hired him out of desperation, tired of him dogging their tracks.

Cholla slowed a dusty brown, scruffy mare with two eagle feathers in her mane to a walk before making it all the way to his bosses, giving his dust a chance to settle.

He was dressed in white cotton shirt and trousers, with sandals woven of yucca fiber on his feet. A narrow-brimmed, dirty black hat shaded his dark eyes and the canyon-cut skin of his desert rider's face.

"Señor Tom!" the Pima hailed. "Sam!" His breath came a little short, and without waiting for further pleasantries he waved a hand excitedly back behind him. "It is good you come back now. Cholla finds big problem."

"Slow up a little and take a breath, amigo," said Sam. "That little bronc is on her last legs."

Cholla shrugged. "I am apologize for that, my frien'. I ride hard tell you. Injuns, they steal your cows."

Tom and Sam threw a glance at each other. Sam felt an old dread creep up inside his chest.

"You need a drink, Cholla?" Tom offered. "Take my canteen." He reached down and threw his canvas-covered quart canteen toward the Indian, who caught it deftly and took a long swallow, thanking him in Spanish, which he spoke almost as well as his own tongue, and better than English.

"Now tell us the rest," said Tom. "You said Injuns. Are you sure?"

"Sure! Sure, I sure. Many Indians—men, women, also some childs. They drive two cows with them, cows they push from herd of Señor Sam and Tom."

"Did you see them?"

"No—tracks only. Cholla not big for trouble. No gun." He waved generously about his person, as if to verify his lack of a weapon.

Tom cleared his throat, spitting into the brush. "How far, Cholla? Do you want to go back with us?"

Cholla shook his head adamantly. "Not far. A ride for you— how do you say it? Three, four miles? But I no go, big boss man. Big trouble there. I take the mules back home." He pointed his right index finger, which was missing from the middle knuckle, at Sam. "Mr. Sam, you follow trail of Cholla. You find place I tell you. You watch close, amigos. I think is bad medicine you find."

It was easy for Sam and Tom to agree with their little Indian friend about not taking him along. They had no idea of his skill with firearms, even if they were to loan him one, and as he was obviously not anxious to fight it was a poor time to test him. A scared man could only threaten trouble in a tight spot. Wishing they had one or two of their more savvy hands with them, Tom waved the little Pima on.

"All right, Cholla, you just head back home. Maybe swing around to Nadia's house and tell her we'll be back home later." Tom threw a glance at his partner to make sure he approved.

Sam nodded. "Don't tell her about the Indians though. Just tell her we're still out with some cows. I don't want her to worry. *Sabe?*"

Cholla nodded with a nervous smile. "Sí, I understan'."

After Cholla headed back toward the ranch, Tom and Sam started following his backtrail. Sam saw where his tracks cut off the main road. After that, it wasn't difficult to follow the sign.

Any cowhand worth his salt could read a trail, and in spite of Sam's knack for that game Tom would not have needed him this time, at least not until they reached the stand of sycamores.

Here, among this grove of ten or twelve half-dead trees that had grown up around what was now a dry spring, the tracks nearly disappeared. They found first where Cholla's trail was cut by what appeared to be somewhere between a dozen and thirty travelers. Some of them, mostly the larger ones, wore moccasins. Most of the smaller tracks were left by bare feet. They saw where Cholla had followed them a ways toward a rocky defile that sliced through a ridge three hundred yards off. Then his tracks had stopped and turned back, and the thieves', which went on for twenty yards or so, suddenly disappeared.

Tom turned to look at Sam. With a little work, his trained eye could probably have picked the trail up again, but with Sam there it wasn't worth the trouble. This was not the time to practice his skills. "Your turn, pard. Work your magic—if you think it's worth it."

Sam frowned. As far as he could see, Cholla was right—the Indians were pushing two head. Whether they belonged to the Yaqui Gold was another question, but even if they didn't, in open range country a man didn't let a fellow rancher's stock get rustled any more than he would his own. It was expected for fellow ranchers to look out for each other, and most would have done it for Sam and Tom. It wasn't the loss of two cows that troubled Sam, either. It was the knowledge that if whoever had stolen them got away with it they might come back for more, and the gold he and Tom had acquired from their trip to Mexico would only last so long if they let every wandering stray drive away a cow or two.

Sam didn't have to reply. Tom knew they had to stick to the trail. Slipping his rifle from the scabbard, Sam gave his partner a long, hard look, then turned Gringo and squeezed him with his knees, pushing him on.

*   *   *

They smelled the smoke before they saw it. They had ridden only a mile or so beyond the sycamore grove, back up into the rough and rocky fore-range that skulked beneath the mighty Santa Catalina peaks. On some silent signal understood by partners who have ridden hundreds of miles of dangerous country side by side, they stepped off their horses and tied them in the shelter of an ironwood tree. From here, they continued uphill on foot, keeping away from the Indians' trail, and climbing through the scattered boulders and desert scrub. They were paralleling the path the thieves had taken, a path made obvious by the fact that the surrounding country was too rough and overgrown to push cattle by any other route.

There was no more smoke scent for more than a hundred yards, but then it came again, a brief waft of air smelling of mesquite. Stopping to scan the terrain, the partners spent more than twenty minutes there, barely moving anything but their eyes. They caught no sign of a scout, and with his heart thudding in his chest Sam started on. Tom followed wordlessly.

At the crest of the nearest ridge, they crouched low. They moved into the cooling desert breeze that had gifted them with the telltale smoke. Hearing a muffled voice, Sam stopped. His eyes sought out and marked the nearest cover—a cluster of boulders overgrown by catclaw eighty feet to their left.

Less than a minute later, another voice, then the ring of laughter. Sam felt Tom's glance, but he didn't meet it. Instead, he crept on. At the top of the ridge, he sank to his knees, then raised his head, so slowly that no one could have detected the movement unless they had already pinpointed his location.

Seventy yards below, in a cove among granite boulders, fifteen or more Indians surrounded a small fire. Two ribby longhorns stood nearby, guarded by a couple of teenage boys.

Cholla had been right; there was danger here. The government claimed they had done a thorough job in removing all hostiles and sending them off to prisons out of the territory. But they had missed the mark.

These people were Chiricahua Apaches.

After a long study of the layout below, Tom finally turned his head and met Sam's gaze. The look on his face was one of resignation. "I'd love to have you tell me I'm an idiot, but are they what I think they are?"

Sam gave his partner a wry half-grin. "All right—you're an idiot. But yeah, they are. I guess Miles got cocky too soon."

The "Miles" Sam referred to was General Nelson A. Miles, who had used Apache scouts to track down the infamous Geronimo, whom most officials believed to be the last of the hostile Apache leaders on the loose in 1886. After Geronimo gave himself up, Miles broke every promise he had made the war leader and sent not only him and all of his supporters off to prison, but the Apache scouts who had lent their aid to help run him to ground as well. It would forever be a shameful footnote in the history of white relations with the native people of the country.

Sam Coffey caressed the hammer of his rifle as he gazed down on the little band. Even from the distance, he could make out the nearly naked, emaciated torsos of the children, whose ribs protruded horribly. The women wore tattered dresses, and the men dressed only in breech clouts and knee-high moccasins, with a lucky few wearing loose shirts whose tails hung to mid-thigh. This Apache band had somehow escaped capture, but it was plain they were living out the last of their days if they didn't soon make it to friendly ground.

Tom looked over at his friend. "What do we do? Them people are starvin'."

With a curse, Sam looked down at his rifle, then over at Tom. "They're your cows as much as mine."

Swiping at a trickle of sweat that ran down the side of his nose into his mustache, Tom replied, "Sam, I'm just a kid compared to you. You're the wise old man of the woods with all the answers."

Sam returned a sarcastic smile. "Yeah—*kid.* I'm three years older than you. Well, if they know they've been discovered there's likely to be trouble. They can't afford to have anyone see 'em and turn 'em in to the Army. You prepared for shootin'?"

Tom gave the band another brief sweep with his eyes before looking back at Sam. "They don't look to have any firearms. Maybe a spear or a bow or two. Wouldn't be much of a fight, would it?"

"Reckon not, if you don't mind shootin' a few kids—and women. Well, we've gotta let 'em know they've been seen. It's for their own good. They've gotta get to Mexico if they're ever gonna find any peace."

With a sigh, Tom looked down at his rifle. "Your call. I'll cover you."

Sam grunted. "Thanks." With no more discussion, he rose to full height, gave his partner one last searching look, then started down the hill.

His life had been in his partner's hands before. If today was the day he must die he knew Tom would go down with him.

CHAPTER THREE

With eyes well-tuned to the slightest movement, the Apaches spotted Sam two steps after he stepped out of his hiding place.

Rifle hanging at his side, he clenched his jaw and continued down the hill, his step unfaltering. Even among Apaches as poorly armed as these, to waver in his show of courage was to invite attack.

Sam had already pinpointed five men as the likely leaders of this group—perhaps not the decision makers, but at least the most likely to lead a fight. These five stepped forward, but it was one wizened woman whose short-bobbed white hair drooped thick and parted on either side of her face who broke from the others and walked to meet him as he came out of the rocks onto the flat.

Fifty feet from the old woman, he shifted the rifle to his left hand and raised his right in an offer of truce. She watched him through slitted eyes, then finally raised her hand. The five warriors had lined out behind her. Their weapons remained loose at their sides, but they appeared ready to spring to the fight.

Sam and the woman stared at each other, gauging intentions. At last, she looked around her, and her gaze fell upon a boy of about twelve. She jerked her head to motion him forward.

The boy, whose coarse hair hung just below his shoulders, was one of the ones he had studied from up in the rocks. As he came close, and their gauntness became even more apparent, their ribs deeply etched in their torsos, it might have brought tears to

Sam's eyes if the situation had been less deadly. This boy in particular had limbs that resembled the legs of a crane although his thick-jointed elbows and knees spoke of one who might be a large man if he lived that long. He stood barefooted, his knees dark and scarred, with scabs over the scars. His cheeks were hollow, and his cheekbones protruded like sharp rocks. But in his eyes gleamed defiance and pride.

The boy came to stand beside the old woman, and she spoke to him. Then she turned to Sam, continuing to speak to the boy but watching the white man.

After her voice went still, the boy cleared his throat. "My mother, she says you are a brave man. We could kill you easy. Why you here?"

"My name is Sam," he said, and motioned behind him. "My friend Tom watches from the rocks. I come here because those are my cattle." He spoke in very plain English, trying to enunciate his words, although it was obvious this boy had been schooled by Americans and spoke as well as half the white people Sam knew.

The boy translated Sam's words, listened to the old woman, and turned back to Sam. "I am Sad-Boy-With-A-Stick. At your mission, they call me Dove. This is Weaving Cradles, the giver of life to my mother. She who held me in her belly is dead. Her husband, my father, is dead. My brothers and my sister—all are dead. Mexicans kill them. My mother says we are hungry. We are trying to go to our home in the *Cima-Silq*—your Sierra Madre. The soldiers try to stop us. White men try to stop us. The *Nakai-yes* try to stop us—what you people call Mexicans. Everyone wants the *Tinne-ah* dead, but we will not die easy. If you have come here to kill us, my mother says for you to start killing. We would rather to die than go where they took our people."

"I ain't gonna kill nobody, kid." Sam let his eyes scan the group behind the old woman. One of them held a beat-up old Springfield rifle, one a lance, and the other three clutched short bows, with arrows already nocked. If he so much as raised his rifle he was going to die, and although Tom might kill the Indians, or at least scatter them into the brush, Sam would be just as dead. But beyond the reality of his fear was his compassion.

What Weaving Cradles and Dove said was true. These people were starving, destitute. All the other children, like Dove, were barefoot. Some were naked. Sam had never been one to let people starve, even if they were stealing from him. He would have done the same himself, and no one could deny the terrible way the United States government, and many of its citizens as well, had treated these people. Often the killing had been mutual, but the government never tried very hard to stop it. They were only out-shadowed in their brutality toward Apaches by white and Mexican citizens and other Indian tribes—and, often, by the Apaches' brutality in return.

"All right," Sam relented. "You take these two steers and go. You have maybe a hundred more miles 'til you reach Mexico. But I ain't a rich man. I can't afford no more cattle. Don't come back to the United States. My cattle are scrawny. They ain't worth it. And soon there are others who will see you, and they ain't like me. They'll kill you."

Dove translated this to his grandmother, the woman he called his mother. In the Apache custom children called all matrilineal forebears "mother."

The old woman, Weaving Cradles, stared long and hard at Sam after the last words were spoken. Even as she stared, Sam saw a skinny old man make his way out of the group brandishing a spear. He walked over to where the steers were being restrained and ran one of them through with his spear. Before it had even stopped struggling there were several more Apaches swarming it, cutting into its back and flanks, some of them taking hunks of the gore-dripping meat and biting into it.

Sam's eyes watered, and he turned back to the old woman. She too had observed the carnage, and now she met his eyes and spoke. Dove watched her solemnly, then turned to Sam. "My mother says this. You see our people are starving. You see how we were the wolves of the desert and have come to this at the hands of the Long Knives and the people who moved to our land. Someday others will come for your land, too, and tell you you must give up your weapons. Then you will see. You will have to fight, or you will become like the animals."

Sam swallowed hard. "Keep your people safe, Dove. Go from these mountains and find peace in your Cima Silq."

With that, he started to turn, but from the corner of his eye he saw one of the five warriors raise his bow, shouting angrily. Sam whirled back in time to see the old woman charge the warrior, screaming at him in Apache. The warrior backed away from her, eyes wide. She was shaking a knife at him, and he stared at it, unable to remove his eyes from its blade. At last, she spun away, still brandishing the knife, and motioned for Sam to leave, yelling words of warning at him.

Dove translated. "My mother says you should go fast from here before she has to kill one of these men. They want for you to die so that you will not go to the Long Knives about us."

"Tell your mother there will be no Long Knives, son. You people have suffered enough. Tell her also that the Long Knives believe Geronimo was the last loose Apache. They don't even know you're out here."

With that, he turned away once more, satisfied that he would be allowed to depart in peace. He climbed the hill to where Tom waited, his rifle barrel cradled in the notch of a boulder.

When Sam was twenty feet away, Tom stood up, letting out a long breath. "That feller doesn't know how close he came to dyin'."

"I know, pard. But they're all close to dyin'. He probably would have preferred it."

"What about the steers?" Tom asked.

"Hell, Tom, the two of 'em together would only bring maybe twenty-five or thirty bucks on today's market. You willing to see fifteen people starve to death for that?"

Tom gave one of his wide, dimpled grins. "That's my Sam," he said. Side by side they walked over the ridge and headed for their horses.

*   *   *

It was four days later when Sam and Tom rode into the streets of Tucson to pick up supplies. Cuidado, their young Mexican helper, had gone in before them with one of the American punchers, Jeffrey Reese. Reese, the only cowhand on the spread who was married, had hauled his wife Trisha along to pick out some curtains for the bunkhouse. That was not something a man could be expected to do right. As the two partners rode into dusty Congress Street, they spotted Jeffrey and Trisha Reese headed toward them at a fast clip, with Cuidado standing on the porch of the Shoo Fly restaurant and pointing toward them. Around him was clustered a small group of men dressed in town clothing.

Jeffrey Reese, a heavy-set man some fifty years of age, with a silver-streaked beard, stopped beside his wife as they came up to Sam and Tom. "Hey there, boss men!" he hailed.

Tom grinned, and Sam spat off to one side, reining in his buckskin, Gringo. "Kinda formal, ain't you, Jeff?"

The bearded hand laughed, always full of good humor. Sam saw Trisha looking back over her shoulder toward Cuidado and the men gathered on the porch of the Shoo Fly. "Maybe I should be even more formal," said Reese with his grin still splitting his whiskers in half. "See them gents over to the Shoo Fly? They seem to think you two are somethin' mighty special."

"What's it all about?" Tom asked. He was a bit leery of strangers who came looking for him. He had been ever since going down into Mexico after the Yaquis' gold.

"Well, ride on over," Reese suggested. "Sounds like some friend of yours from up around Phoenix pointed these Easterners in your direction, namin' you as some great shakes as guides."

Tom guffawed, and Sam said, "Phoenix? Well, I reckon we'd best ride over there and get 'em shut of any such notion."

They nudged the horses over to the front of the Shoo Fly and climbed down. By now, the cluster of strangers had pressed to the edge of the porch, and Cuidado walked down and took Gringo's reins. Cuidado didn't very often ride horses, as he was intimidated by them, particularly ranch horses. But he and Gringo had made fast friends.

"Hola, jefes," greeted the Mexican. "You just in time. These men, they would to talk to you."

Sam looked beyond Cuidado to see four men in the group, all dressed in a way that set them apart from men of Sam and Tom's station in life. Each of the men, Sam noticed, was unique in his looks, from a gentlemanly sort in a narrow-brimmed gray derby; another of suave appearance with a well-trimmed mustache and beard; a third very young man; to the last one, a brawny, wide-set fellow with a brown derby hat and ham-like appendages some might call hands.

It was the first of them, the one with the looks of a gentleman, who stepped up to Sam, standing four inches shorter but holding himself with an elegant bearing that made him seem a man of some importance.

"Might you be the Sam Coffey and Tom Vanse we have heard so much about?"

Sam eyed him up and down, cautious of his reply. "I don't know if I'm the one you been hearin' about, but I'm one Sam Coffey."

"And I'm one Tom Vanse," his partner added.

"Well, my good men, my name is Preston Ashcroft," replied the stranger, seeming to miss their mild attempt at humor. Ashcroft pulled a light-colored doeskin glove from his right hand and thrust it forward. When the partners had taken it, the man went on. "I am a professor and one of the curators of the American Museum of Natural History, in New York City. I'm in charge of certain scientific explorations, one of which has brought me to your area of the globe. Your scouting and... shall we say *survival* abilities were recommended to me by a man up in Phoenix who tells me he is a good friend of yours, a man by the name of Abraham Varnell."

"Old Abe," said Sam. "I wondered. Sure didn't know he was in Phoenix. I reckon we should be a bit worried if he's got his rooster in this ring."

This time, Professor Preston Ashcroft laughed, and the good humor glowed from his eyes, while wrinkles cropped up around them and around his mouth. "He is quite the character. He tells me that you are undoubtedly the best trail guides in these parts. Particularly if a man wished to be taken through the Santa Catalina range."

Sam chuckled. Abe knew they had bought a ranch at the base of the Catalinas, but he could have no idea how well they knew the country. Fact was, he and Tom had worked on several ranches in the area, and there were some parts of the range they knew better than the average man. But then, it was a large range. "I reckon that depends on the part of the Santa Catalinas you want to explore. What did you have in mind?"

"That's the spirit," Ashcroft said. "Why don't we step over to the Cosmopolitan? I'll buy you some drinks—or dinner—or both. And we'll discuss my proposition."

Sam shrugged. "Suits me. Tom?" He turned and looked at his partner, who had a mistrusting glow to his eyes but agreed to go along. They bid so long to the Reeses and Cuidado, and together the six of them started across the street toward the Cosmopolitan.

The Cosmopolitan Hotel was a two-story building whose balcony and lower porch ran its entire length. It was not only the finest, but the only decent hotel in Tucson, a town long infamous along the highway called the Camino Real, or Royal Road, for its lack of lodging or decent food. They served drinks at their bar, along with lunch, and in their dining room could be found some of the best fare and wines in the territory, a close second to the Shoo Fly itself. This hadn't always been the case, to which any old timer could attest. Not many years before, Tucson had been one of the rudest of frontier communities, its streets a quagmire of filth and discarded garbage.

As the group ordered and waited for their dinner, engaging in light conversation, Sam and Tom had a few minutes to study Preston Ashcroft more closely. He seemed to be a straightforward man, elegant in dress and manners. Except for a closely trimmed brown mustache, graying throughout, he was clean-shaven. His closely cropped hair was thinning way back past the remains of a widow's peak. He had a nervous habit of pulling a pair of spectacles from an inside pocket of his green corduroy suit coat and putting them on, then pulling them back off and fiddling them around between his fingers. Those fingers were long and soft and slender, not attached to a working man's hands.

The Professor took a moment to introduce the other men with him, and they shook hands all around. The man with the well-kept mustache and beard was Stuart Baron. He was every bit as suave and polished as Ashcroft, perhaps even more so. But there was a calculated look to every smile he offered, and his hard blue eyes had no give to them. He wore a flat-crowned gray hat with a four-inch brim, an immaculate, pin-striped black suit, and polished riding boots that laced up nearly to his knees.

Delbert Moore was the young man, striving valiantly but unable to cultivate more than a wisp of mustache. His face was soft and pink, his fine hair blond, and his eyes an innocent blue of a much softer shade than those of Baron. He wore a suit coat of brown corduroy and a pair of tan canvas hunting pants tucked into riding boots much like Baron's, a style often seen on foreigners who came to the West on hunting expeditions.

But the man who drew more of Sam's study than any of the others was Viktor Zulowsky. Tom Vanse stood a good six-foot-four, and in any room, or on any street, he made quite a presence. Yet Zulowsky's sheer brute mass made Tom seem a touch delicate. He stood perhaps an inch shorter than Tom, but the height made little difference. Zulowsky must have outweighed Tom by thirty or forty pounds, and very little of it was fat. His hat was a low-crowned brown bowler, which in his case gave him the look not of a polished gentleman, but of a New York thug. His face was scarred, his right eyebrow finely divided by one of the more notable ones, and a jagged one perhaps an inch in length adorned his left cheek. He carried an impressive bulk of dark mustache that halfway covered the largest of his scars, which ran down from the corner of his lower lip to the bulge of his dimpled chin.

Zulowsky's hands were even more scarred than his face, tattooed, no doubt, by the bones and teeth of all the men he had driven to the ground. The big man had shoulders the width of a whisky drum turned on its side, and a neck near as big around as a normal man's thigh. Even dressed in a brown wool suit—which fit him loosely across the back and shoulders, the way a fighter would dress—Zulowsky looked nothing like the gentlemen he traveled with. It was pretty obvious the big bruiser had a special purpose here with them, one that didn't involve secretarial duties.

Once they had their plates in front of them, Professor Ashcroft insisted on everyone eating before talking business. They dug in, and conversation was sparse, unlike their conversation prior to being served, which had been mostly of the country, its traditions, its history, weather and recent news. Finally, Preston Ashcroft stabbed the last piece of his well-done steak, took the dainty bite, chewed and then swallowed it. He laid his fork and knife back to either side of his plate, and looked first at Tom, then at Sam, studying their eyes.

"Gentlemen? Let's get down to business," he said. "We are here on an archaeological expedition—something which could turn out to be extremely important to the scientific community. I'm prepared to pay you two hundred dollars to lead our party far up into the Santa Catalina Mountains."

Sam sat back in his chair, glancing cautiously over at his partner. "What exactly are you looking for?"

"Well, my friends, it is there where we run into something of a dilemma. You see, what we seek I am not totally at liberty to reveal at the present time. I hope it will suffice to say that we are in search of certain ... *artifacts* which we have reason to believe exist in one or more caverns in the Santa Catalinas. I would be pleased to reach an understanding with the two of you. I will provide you with a detailed map of our destination and you will take me there with no expectations of being told in any detail what we are after until the proper time arrives. I realize that you, being men of intelligence, may struggle with your own curiosity, but it is my hope that the sum of two hundred dollars will be enough to curb your inquisitive natures."

Pondering this for a moment, Sam looked at Tom. There was no sign on his face to tell what he thought of the offer, so Sam pushed a little further. "What would we be expected to do? You only need us to read a map?"

"No, gentlemen, I expect that you are too astute to accept such a simple pretense. Your duties will include these: guide us to a certain canyon deep in the mountain range, and a cave possibly buried along its side; bring in wild game for our sustenance; speak on our behalf with any native people we should encounter; deal with anyone who may stand in the way of our expedition—including any troublesome predators or other animals. We had also hoped, and it was suggested by your friend Mr. Varnell, that you might have some knowledge of using dynamite."

"Ahhh." It was the first time Tom Vanse had made much of a sound. "So it comes down to you expectin' trouble and you need us to Moore it off. We made a similar trip last year—a trip our very own Abe Varnell got us into. It near got us killed."

Ashcroft was not a man to let silence go unfilled, particularly if it gave them a chance to think their way out of working for him. "My good man," he said, "I would not inten-tionally put you in harm's way, at least no more so than you must be in each day doing your duties on a cattle ranch. The truth be known, we expect and of course hope for no trouble whatsoever. I truthfully believe that you will end up earning a very easy two hundred dollars for nothing more than following a map and providing us fresh meat for perhaps two weeks—three at the most."

"I assume you're talking two hundred each," Sam chimed in.

"Umm... actually, the two hundred is for both."

"I like two hundred each." Tom said.

Stuart Baron let out a laugh. It wasn't a friendly sound, and the look in his eyes was likewise not one of mirth. "Meaning no offense, but that's a ludicrous counter, Mr. Vanse. At least give us the courtesy of not insulting our intelligence. There must be fifty men around here who could accomplish what we're asking of you. What justifies the exorbitant amount?"

"Like you say, there must be fifty other men who could do this," said Tom. "A better question might be, why us?"

"Now rein in a minute, Tom." Sam eyed his partner, perplexed by this sudden change in roles. He was usually the one acting leery, while Tom liked to forge ahead.

"Smart man," nodded Baron.

Sam gave the man a look, and his was no friendlier than Baron's had been. But the plain truth was they could use this money. He wasn't willing to turn these men away just yet. "How about one fifty each?" he said. "We're makin' at least that at the ranch, and we may have to pay another hand or two to help out while we're gone. It ain't a question of just ridin' out. We both have responsibilities."

Baron and the Professor looked at each other, something meaningful passing between them. Professor Ashcroft glanced back at both Sam and Tom. "I can offer you each one hundred twenty—no more."

There was a derisive grunt from big Viktor Zulowsky, and he jerked an unlit cigar from between his teeth. Before he could say anything Stuart Baron's hand came up. "Gentlemen, again I ask you—what is it about you two that it should be worth our paying you even one hundred dollars each instead of going to the nearest saloon and hiring the first trapper we meet?"

"That's something I assumed you got from Varnell," Tom countered before Sam could form any words. "You went to all this trouble to find us. Must've been on pretty good advice."

"The advice of a retired prospector we know very little about. There must be a dozen people in this area with your qualifications."

Tom shrugged. "There may be, Mr. Baron. I won't deny that much. Maybe you should ask around. This is a pretty busy time of year for us." He pushed back his seat and started to stand up.

Preston Ashcroft raised his hand. "Don't be too hasty, Mr. Vanse. I didn't intend for us to step on one another's feelings." He frowned at Stuart Baron. "Please, be seated."

Sitting back down, Tom kept his eyes away from Baron, looking only at Ashcroft.

"Would one hundred thirty dollars each secure your services?" Ashcroft asked.

"One hundred forty would," Tom countered immediately. By this time, Sam had sat back in his chair to watch his partner dicker. He had been happy with the idea of one hundred each. If Tom could get more, then let him run.

"One hundred forty it is."

"What?" Viktor Zulowsky loomed up out of his chair. "I'll do it myself for that! And probably just as good as these two."

"Viktor..." When the big man looked over to meet Baron's eyes, the bearded man gently shook his head, motioning the big one back into his seat with a calming hand.

The Professor looked at Sam and Tom. "There you have it, gentlemen. I guess you've found yourselves a job."

"I'd still like some time to think about it," Tom said.

"But you said—" Sam cut the Professor's protest short with a raise of his hand.

He stood up and grabbed Tom's arm, making him stand up with him and looking back down at the Professor. "If you don't mind, I'd like to have a few words with my partner outside."

"You walk out of here now you can forget the job," Viktor Zulowsky growled.

"Viktor!" This time Stuart Baron's voice was sharp. He eyed Sam for a moment before letting his eyes run Tom up and down. "That would be fine, gentlemen. Please feel free to talk it over. But we can't wait forever. This expedition needs to be on its way by the day after tomorrow to keep within our schedule."

Sam nodded, his eyes surly. He didn't like Baron and had a feeling he never would. But two hundred eighty dollars was a little too much to pass up without at least thinking it over. With that in mind, he steered Tom toward the door.

The Professor's voice stopped the partners and made them turn back around. "One more thing for you to think about, gentlemen. If this expedition goes as I have high hopes it will, and if you perform to our expectations, I am prepared to offer you each a sizable bonus upon its satisfactory completion."

The partners looked again at each other, and Sam said, "We won't be long," then guided Tom on outside.

"What's your beef with this, Tom?" he asked the moment he had him out at the corner of the hotel. "Do you realize what we could do with that money?"

"I do," Tom said. "I also heard what we could do with that Yaqui gold. They're hidin' something from us, Sam. I don't like it. I'm tempted to say we go back out to the ranch and forget the whole idea."

It was at exactly that moment that the girl rode into view.

CHAPTER FOUR

She was riding a sorrel gelding with a golden mane and a grayish yellow, flowing tail. As sleek as the animal looked to Tom Vanse, his beauty was no match for his rider.

Riding along with the woman, on a dark bay horse, came a tough-looking man in faded blue kersey pants with a darker blue stripe down the outside seam where, judging by its width, the gold cloth stripe designating a sergeant of the Army once had been.

Even sidesaddle, the girl held complete command of her horse. She sat with her back straight, her shoulders to the rear and her chin up, guiding her horse by the use of her own head movements and the subtle signals of her legs and body. Tom had to chide himself for thinking of this rider as a girl, for she was at least in her mid-thirties.

But it was plain that she had not been raised in the Arizona desert. Her features, although not delicate nor fragile, were fine and soft, her skin unblemished. Her hair was braided and coiled on top of her head beneath a wide-brimmed straw hat lightly fastened down with a dark green scarf knotted beneath her chin. Her riding skirt and jacket matched the scarf, and her russet-colored lace-up boots appeared to be of the finest calf leather, almost as fine as the thin goat skin gloves that protected her hands from the sun and from her reins.

With the slightest of motions, a leaning backward of her body and scooting forward of her hips, augmented by a quiet, "Whoa," she brought the gelding to a stop in front of the Cosmopolitan Hotel. Before she could begin to climb down, her companion reined in, dropped down at the hotel's corner and came to her side, helping her out of the saddle.

"Reel up your tongue there, Curly, and poke your eyes back in the sockets."

Sam's voice fell on deaf ears until he shoved playfully at Tom's shoulder. Shaking himself, Tom turned to look at him. "Cut that out!"

"*You'd* better cut it out, Curly," Sam countered. "That old boy with her looks like a soldier from way back. He's liable to take a saber to you if you don't ease back on your oglin'."

"I wasn't oglin'!" Tom said, watching from the corner of his eye as the lady and her companion stepped into the cool shadows of the hotel.

"All right, then—leerin'."

Tom spat a stream of tobacco into the dust, clearing any leftover from the edges of his mustache with an expert lower lip. "You're inventin' that to cover your own wanderin' eyes. That girl's half my age!"

"What girl?" asked Sam. "I didn't see no girl."

"Well, the—" Tom stopped when he saw his partner's mischievous gaze. "The youngster that went inside the hotel with her daddy," he finished. "*That* girl."

"Well, I apologize, Tom," Sam said with feigned sincerity. "For a minute there I thought I saw your eyes shinin'. Must have been the sun. I won't say no more about her, since it's plain you weren't moved by her beauty one way or the other."

"That's right," Tom chimed. But inside his heart was still thudding a little. The young lady had strongly resembled his long-dead Beverly, if in nothing more than the bridge of her nose, her dark, arched brows and strong, dimpled chin. Maybe she had high cheekbones like Beverly, too, and the same well-defined jawline and well-formed body. He had hardly noticed.

Taking a deep breath, Tom said, "You ready to go back in there and tell those Easterners we don't need their money? Or do I have to do it?"

"That'd be fine—except we *do* need the money. You've seen yourself how much graze that ranch has on it. It's hardly even touched by our herd, and even our neighbors' stock ain't makin' a dent. We have plenty of grass, and we need some more cows if we're gonna make anything of that place. It's comin' up fast on the date I told Nadia I'd be ready to get hitched. But I ain't lettin' her marry a broke saddle tramp."

"Well, then maybe you oughtta go by yourself," Tom said, setting his jaw stubbornly. "You gotta have me babysit you everywhere you go?"

"*You* babysit *me!* Who pulled who out of that Yaqui mine, Curly? I got you beat by three years, and you're already goin' senile!"

"Yeah, and you've *gone,*" said Tom. "But if you're so all-fired set on makin' this trip, I'm puttin' my foot down. You're a grown man. Go by yourself. I'll just hang around home, do some work on a couple of those broncs, maybe help fix up the bunk-house a little. Maybe finish that big bed you started for Nadia. You obviously won't be home long enough to get it done."

"You don't touch that bed. You wanna stay home, that's all right. You can just sit there on the porch and knit or somethin' to pass the time. I know you're afraid some little bear cub or cata-mount kitten might pounce on you if you go back up in them mountains anyway."

Tom laughed. "Makin' cracks like that sure ain't gonna make me go up there gallivantin' around when we got so much to do on the ranch. You just go on, play your little games up there, and I'll handle the ranch by myself. I do better without you hoverin' over me like an old woman all the time anyway."

All of a sudden, Sam had a thought. "Or is you decidin' to stay something to do with that little filly we just saw? Damn, Tom—for all you know she's going to get on a stage and be gone tomorrow morning. And for all you know, she's probably mar-ried—maybe to that gent she was with."

"You need to stop jumpin' to conclusions. I never gave that girl a second thought."

"Uh-huh. What are you scared of?" Sam said, growing a little more serious.

Tom held his eyes for a long minute. "I almost got you killed last year, Sam. I'm not sure I have a good feeling about us goin' up there."

"It's settled then." Sam sighed and gave a brisk nod of his head. "Git on down to the store and pick up the supplies, and I'll see you when I get back."

"Now don't get hasty," said Tom, holding up his hands. "I'm still in the mood for one more drink before I take much more of this heat. I'll go back in with you, just don't try to talk me into goin' on the trip."

"Yeah, I can see where this is goin' in a hurry." Sam grunted with disgust. "A lot of work you'll get done around the ranch without me proddin' you. You'll be in here drinkin' the place dry the entire time. Curly, you never change."

Tom laughed and clapped Sam on the shoulder. Truth be known, while Sam was in his confab with the professor and his cronies, Tom intended to sit idly drinking a tall, cool glass of beer and filling his eyes with the young lady he had seen go inside, if indeed she had not already retired to a room. It wasn't as if he would ever be unfaithful to Beverly, but... well, he was just curious to hear her name. He was starting to think maybe he knew her from somewhere.

With that lie to himself firmly imbedded in his head, Tom followed Sam back into the hotel and started to make his way toward the bar, studiously avoiding any glance toward the Professor's table. Where was that girl?

As he made his way around a table, the voice, like honey butter, came drifting musically across the room. He couldn't help but turn, and there she stood—with Professor Preston Ashcroft.

The girl— Mentally, Tom kicked himself. He might be able to make someone else believe that, but he knew better than to think she was a girl. That was a woman standing over there—a woman through and through. She had her hat off now, and her fine hair shone dark in the lamplight, with a strong reddish cast that caught the flame-glow. Her skin seemed silken in the yellowish shadows, and it glowed with such healthy appeal he felt a sudden, compelling ache to touch the backs of his calloused fingers to it.

As he forced himself to turn back toward the bar, he heard the sound of the Professor's voice. "Oh, Mr. Vanse."

Turning, he forced his eyes past the woman and met Preston Ashcroft's eyes. "Yes sir?"

"Could I please have one more moment of your time?"

Sighing, Tom turned and walked to the table. "Sir?"

"No need for the 'sir'," Ashcroft chided. "We're all equals here. Tom Vanse, I would like you to meet my long-time assistant, Miss Melissa Ford. And this gentleman is ex-Sergeant James Ross. We all know him as Dowdy."

Somehow the last two sentences registered on Tom, but he found himself unable to draw his gaze away from Melissa Ford once he looked into her eyes. They were like two desert wells of clear, blue-green water, sparkling in the sun—which in this case was a sun made of lamplight. They took him inside them, held him, won his heart in an instant, and refused to let go.

Tom felt, more than saw, the woman's bare hand come out between them. He was still lost in her eyes, but not so much that he couldn't stick out his paw, more like a buffoon than a gentleman of any character. Her small but firm hand folded inside his own, and its warmth left him almost speechless, a state he was not intimate with.

"Pleased to meet you, Miss," he managed to say. "Miss Ford, was it?"

"Yes, Mr. Vanse. Miss Ford. Will you be accompanying us into the Santa Catalinas?"

"No, Miss Ford," said Sam from off to the side. "Tom won't be able to make it."

Tom's eyes flickered over to his partner, and almost without thinking he blurted out, "Now, Sam, I've had a little time to think it over, and... Well, it wouldn't be right for me to let you go up in that wild country without your partner. What are friends for?"

He returned his gaze to the woman, once again enthralled with the absolute, wholesome beauty of her. It had been years since a female had affected him this way. "Yes, Miss Ford. Sam and I were just discussing how we needed to go up there and scout out the country for suitable summer graze."

Sam grunted, a sound which he would have made much more vocal if not for the presence of the lady. Tom looked over at him, expecting him to make some wisecrack. Instead, he just sat there looking at him, one side of his mouth tilted up in a smile.

Tom managed a look of feigned confusion at Sam, but his dimples deepened with a smile when he looked back down at Melissa Ford. His eyes remained on the woman as he spoke to the Professor. "When do we leave, Mr. Ashcroft?"

*   *   *

Anyone could be star-struck, but with Tom it never lasted long. He was used to feminine charms, and although he didn't often see women like Melissa Ford it didn't take him long to get his wits back about him. He took a lot of ribbing from Sam Coffey as they ordered, paid for and loaded their supplies into the wagon. But it was all worth it, to be able to go on this expedition. It wasn't as if Sam wouldn't find something to tease him about anyhow. It might as well be Melissa Ford.

After they sent the Reeses and Cuidado on their way back to the Yaqui Gold, Sam took his leave to go visit Nadia, and Tom mentioned that he had found a new knife in the hardware store which he had been admiring for a few weeks. It would come in handy on their trek, so he parted ways with Sam and walked back into town.

Once he had made sure Sam was well on his way, anxious to visit with his fiancée, Tom headed back to the Cosmopolitan. There, he found Stuart Baron, Viktor Zulowsky, Delbert Moore and Dowdy Ross involved in a friendly hand of poker. The young woman was nowhere to be seen, but Tom expertly hid his disappointment as he nodded at the card players while walking past their table.

Taking a seat on one of the lobby couches, he picked up a copy of *The Citizen* and pretended to read that local rag while waiting and hoping Melissa Ford might wander down. Tom's luck with women had always been good, and he waited no more than ten minutes before hearing faint, delicate footsteps on the carpeted stairs. He looked up to see her descending with the Professor holding her protectively by the elbow.

Preston Ashcroft raised his eyebrows. "I'm surprised to see you, Mr. Vanse. I thought you would have returned to your ranch to prepare for the trip."

Tom dipped his head in acknowledgment as he pushed up from his seat. "Actually, I got thinkin' it might not hurt for me to stay in town tonight. You all might could use some help locating stock, wagons, pack saddles and what-not."

"Most thoughtful of you, Mr. Vanse. And most appreciated. Oh—and I also meant to mention to you that if you know of anyone else, perhaps two or three men, who might be in need of some extra cash we are interested in taking on a few more men—just to chop and carry wood, set up camp. You know, that sort of thing."

"I'll ask around," replied Tom.

"Good. In the meantime, perhaps you would like to accompany me and Miss Ford to the dining room. She had to freshen up a little before dinner, and now I believe she and Mr. Ross will take a bite to eat."

Tom shrugged, his eyes casually scanning Melissa's face. "Well, sir, that's right neighborly of you. I think I'll take that offer. They serve a mighty tasty apple pie down there, made by Aimee herself."

Melissa Ford's eyes flashed over to Tom. "Aimee?"

"Yes, ma'am. I thought you might have met her. Aimee's the cook here at the hotel."

"Oh." Miss Ford smiled and let her eyes glide away from the big man, sweeping the shadows of the dining room.

As they passed by the poker players, they stopped across from Dowdy Ross. Ross came quickly up out of his chair and jerked off his hat, and the others followed suit, with big Vik Zulowsky a little slower, more deliberate than the others. "Uh, howdy, Miss Melissa. Professor," said Ross. "You going to eat something, Miss Melissa?"

"Yes, Mr. Ross," she replied. "You're hungry, aren't you?"

"Uh..." He turned his hand of cards over secretively and studied them. "Well, yes, Miss, but..."

"It seems Dowdy is taking us for every penny in the game," said Stuart Baron with his most professional smile, which passed as fleetingly as it came. "I think he is loath to leave us while his streak of luck is running rife."

Dowdy Ross chuckled. It was the first time Tom had taken a moment to really look at the man, and he couldn't help but be impressed with what he saw.

Ross, although likely in his late fifties, was a well-built man, with the narrow hips of a man who had spent years in the saddle. Almost all of his clothing, along with his square-shouldered stance, spoke of his obvious cavalry background, and he wore a huge handle-bar mustache that even put Sam Coffey's to shame. Around his face Ross showed the only serious signs of wear and aging and plain hard times, from his balding pate and creviced forehead and jaws, to his longish eyebrows, to his left ear, which was missing its top fifth, corresponding with a scar that cut horizontally through his hair at that place.

Ross took a moment to make what for him seemed to be a decision of some importance as his calculating gray eyes looked Tom up and down, then at last settled on his face. He seemed satisfied with what he found there, for his eyes swung to Melissa, and an almost undetectable warmth came into them.

"Mr. Baron is right," Ross said. "I got a pretty good hand. Think I'll sit dinner out this time." He gave his belly a couple of sound pats. "Don't really need it, as you can see."

Finding his eyes drawn to Ross's midsection, Tom had to give a little lopsided smile. Ross's belly had a slight slump to it, all right, but judging by his big hands, strong shoulders, and the narrow hips he had noted earlier, this Dowdy Ross had been and probably still was quite a man.

After giving their regards, the trio trooped off to the dining room, where they seated themselves near a window facing Congress Street. Like a true adventurer, Melissa ordered the special of the day, which was grizzly bear steaks and chili. The order was something Tom would not have expected of an eastern woman of any gentility, and his estimation of the woman's spirit took a notch up, ever closer to his opinion of her good looks. Himself, he chose to wait until she was through with her dinner before ordering his pie.

When Melissa's meal arrived, Tom watched as she cut into and then took her first bite of the grizzly bear meat. Even though he had already eaten, the juices looked tantalizing. Without any forethought, he commented, "A few weeks ago a grizzly almost had one of my horses on his menu."

The woman paused in chewing and searched his eyes. The statement was enough to stop anyone. "A grizzly? You saw one? Alive?"

Tom laughed. "Ain't that scarce yet, Miss. But I'll admit we saw this one a little closer than we wanted to."

He told her about the incident involving his horse, and about how that particular bear had tried to live up to the grizzly's Latin name, *Ursus horribilis*. That name was one of many useless facts he had gleaned from curious conversations with two scientists he had stumbled into in his wanderings of the West.

After listening to the story with fascination, Melissa continued to meet his eyes. "Will there be grizzlies where we're going?" She managed to ask the question without any fear in her eyes, but she certainly watched Tom closely for his answer.

"You bet, ma'am. Just as likely there as anywhere. They used to be a plains animal, but humans have drove 'em up to the hills."

"It's a good thing we'll have horses," the woman said, trying to act casual. "We can outrun them if we have to... correct?"

"No, Miss, I'm afraid not. It's pretty even money between a horse and a grizzly up to a quarter mile—maybe farther." He suddenly realized what his words were doing to the woman, and to the Professor, who had sat there silent but mesmerized through that entire part of the conversation. "I wouldn't worry, though," he said quickly. "A grizzly's not likely to attack a bunch of folks together—or even one, unless he's cornered." This seemed to satisfy the woman's growing worry, for she went back to eating the bear meat and potatoes thoughtfully.

Tom and the Professor had sat there in conversation for several minutes as Melissa ate, with the Professor dominating with talk, as at dinner, of local weather, history, and anything but specifically what he had come to the Santa Catalina Mountains to seek. Suddenly, Ashcroft let out a little gasp and jerked his watch from the pocket of his vest by its gold chain. "Oh—I'm sorry, but I must leave the two of you for a few minutes. I need to make a stop at the bookstore before it closes, and the tobacco store as well. Would you like to go with me, Melissa?"

The woman looked over at Tom, and his heart seemed to skip. He was crossing his fingers, and he heard her give the answer he wanted to hear. "No thank you, Professor. We'll be fine here. In fact, don't give us another thought. I'm almost finished."

Even as he started toward the door, the Professor arrested himself by holding to the back of a chair and turned back to them. "You're certain? I can stay if you'd prefer." But in his eyes he was begging them to release him of the responsibility to remain.

"Don't you worry, Mr. Ashcroft," Tom concurred with Melissa. "We'll just have a bite of pie, and then I'll make sure Miss Ford makes it back to her room safe and sound."

After the Professor had gone, Tom sat for a moment as Melissa was eating, congratulating himself on his great fortune of being left here alone with her. He watched her eat in silence, a pastime which seemed to bother her more than it did him.

"So what is it that you do for a living, Mr. Vanse? Are you a full-time guide?" she asked, then took a small bite of the juicy bear steak.

Tom laughed. "No, Miss, I'm a rancher. Sam and I recently came into some money and bought a little spread west of town. Out toward the Catalinas, in fact."

"Oh! Imagine the coincidence. So then no doubt you're very well acquainted with those mountains."

Tom nodded. "We've been around some." The fact was, they had been "around" way too much—just not as much around the Catalinas. He could honestly say he knew one half of the range as well as anyone, but the other half he didn't know at all.

Nevertheless, he and Sam could read a map as well as the next man, and he figured they needed them more for their other abilities than their knowledge of that particular terrain anyway. Besides, the Professor had asked for other men, and he planned to insist that they bring along one of their hands, old Alfredo Sanchez, who probably knew the Catalinas better than any man in Tucson.

After chewing for several moments, then swallowing, Melissa followed up with a sip from her glass of claret. "Do you know what I find most fascinating about this part of the country? It's the flora here."

"Beg your pardon?"

Melissa laughed. "I'm sorry—my scientific background keeps jumping up to bite me. I mean your plant life. It's so varied, seemingly so dead in many ways, yet vibrant and full of life in others."

Tom chuckled. "They say everything in this country will scratch, poke, puncture, bite or claw you to death if you let it. But you're right—it's got a charm of its own."

"You wouldn't happen to know the names of some of the plants?" Melissa pressed on hopefully. "I would very much like to learn more. I bought a book at the bookstore, but I can only tell so much from the drawings."

"I've got a pretty good handle on most of them," Tom said. "The local names, anyway. Would you mind if I looked at your book?"

"No, not at all." Out of the reticule she had hanging from the back of her chair, Melissa produced a book about five by eight inches, with a tan cover marked by dark brown writing and a design meant to resemble engraving. It was entitled *The Plant Life of the Desert Southwest of America*.

Tom laughed. "I own that same book. Most of the plants around here have different names, maybe some local nicknames. Between the two of us we might be able to figure out what's what—if you have the time."

"If I have the time! Oh, Mr. Vanse, I would be most delighted. Learning local plants is one of my passions, and especially in a country as strange and charming as this."

"Charming? Well, miss, I sure never heard it called that before. But I reckon beauty is in the eye of the beholder."

Melissa smiled. "Well, Mr. Vanse, this country is rough, to be certain, but I do find it charming. We have nothing like your variety where I come from. Cacti is almost unheard of, except perhaps in the arboretums."

Tom squinted up his eyes. "Arbor what?"

"Arboretums," she repeated with a patient laugh. "They're like a plant museum, with living plants marked with signs that give their common names, and usually their Latin names as well."

"I didn't know they even had Latin names until I bought that book," Tom admitted. "Most people around here just know the different plants by cuss words."

For a moment, Melissa's eyes went round and quizzical, and then suddenly their edges crinkled up in merry laughter. "Do all Westerners talk like you, Mr. Vanse?"

He paused in thought. "No, ma'am. Only the smarter ones."

Again the woman laughed, and Tom laughed with her. He had never imagined that it would be so much fun learning the names of the local "flora."

*   *   *

After telling the others where they were going, Tom and Melissa went outside and untied Tom's horse from beside the hotel. He was riding a big palomino that day, a horse known around the Yaqui Gold not only for its beauty and stamina, but for a mean streak as long as a dry sermon. As Tom was drawing his cinch up, the horse, which he called Nicker, not because of the noise it made but because it liked to leave nicks in the hides of unsuspecting horsemen, tried to take a bite out of his hip. Almost as if he didn't even see it coming, he slammed an elbow into the horse's nose. Nicker swung his head away indignantly, shaking it as if trying to dislodge a lizard from his nostrils.

"Gotta watch this plug, Miss," said Tom as if nothing had happened. "Give 'im a chance, he'll take a notch out of you. He used to be what we'd call an 'oily bronc' until I took him in and taught him manners."

"An oily bronc?"

"Yeah—a bad horse. Oily, like Sam."

Melissa laughed musically, her eyes taking in all the details of Tom's face. He straightened up from the latigo and met her gaze. "What?" he asked innocently.

With a little shake of her head, she said, "I am delighted by the way you talk. You mesmerize me."

"Mesmerize you?" Tom repeated with a feigned frown. He knew what the word meant, but he got an odd kind of delight out of the image the woman seemed to have that he was some kind of uneducated backwoodsman. "Is that anything like memorize?"

"No, no, Mr. Vanse," she said quickly. "Mesmerize. It's sort of like... enthrall. Or captivate. I am simply intrigued by your... idioms and your sort of... 'homespun' drawl."

"Well, if idioms has anything to do with idiots, you got me pegged about right."

For the first time, Melissa blushed. "No! Idioms are just your sayings."

"You sure know a passel of words, Miss Ford. And you just might stand some memorizing at that."

He offered his big grin, flashing straight white teeth and those dimples the women all seemed to get such a kick out of. He had the sudden feeling he was getting to like this eastern society woman way too much. And there was something about the way he held her gaze that made him believe she might feel the same.

Once they had collected her sorrel from the stable where one of the hotel employees had put it away, they rode together into the desert. Melissa Ford sought to commit to memory the names of the desert plants. They were so varied and, in her words, enchanting, not only in their looks but in their names, that she found her mind more than occupied with this task.

Surrounding them were such odd desert denizens as cholla, ocotillo, saguaro, agave, ironwood, bur sage, desert broom, fishhook and barrel cactus. They found creosote bush, burro bush, salt bush, desert broom, marigold, yarrow, lupine, owl clover, paloverde, mesquite and jojoba. It wasn't long before the woman's head was swimming with her daunting task of memorization.

As for Tom, he had only intentions of memorizing her.

When they returned to the hotel, Tom stopped at the bottom of the stairs, and she turned and looked at him.

"I sure enjoyed the ride, Miss Ford. An awful lot." He glanced over at the table of poker players, still deeply engaged in their game. "I won't go up with you. It wouldn't look right. Besides, I promised Professor Ashcroft I'd help him out with a few things, so I'd best get busy."

She gave him a warm smile. "I understand. And he'll appreciate that. I will see you tomorrow then."

"Yes, ma'am, I'm sure you will."

He watched her walk up the stairs, so graceful and well-formed it made his head spin. She slowed down at the top, and with her hand on the banister she turned and met his gaze. Knowing he had been caught, he blushed fiercely and reached up fumblingly to tip his hat.

A laugh escaped her, merriment at the knowledge that she had embarrassed this man who seemed so strong and sure of himself. She smiled at him for several seconds, gazing into his eyes. Then she said, "Good night," turned, and was gone down the hall.

CHAPTER FIVE

Later that evening, Sam Coffey enclosed Nadia Boultikhine in his arms and breathed the rich fragrance of her hair.

Her ten-year-old son Nikolai had already gone to bed, and Sam and Nadia stood on the porch of her boarding house enjoying the moonless night and star-filled sky.

The woman hadn't been keen on seeing Sam leave on the archaeological expedition, but she understood the need of a few good bulls and some additional breeding age cows to keep their ranch alive. In time, she could sell the boarding house and put the proceeds toward the improvement of the Yaqui Gold. But currently they were in need of solid capital, and it would be foolish to turn down such a sum for the simple task of leading a bunch of archaeologists into the mountains.

"Will we ever get to settle down in peace together, Sam?"

He looked down at Nadia, seeing her eyes shine in the darkness. "Honey, this will be the last time I have to leave you this way. I feel it in my guts. I don't know what those folks are after, but I do know one thing: Those mountains are pretty clean of Injuns—Apache or otherwise. Sure, there's always a bear or a cat around, and enough bad men to keep things lively. But I'll be spanked with a cactus if it's not a dang sight safer than Mexico. Don't you worry. I'll come back, and I'll bring enough cash to buy a five-legged elephant."

Nadia laughed at her man's twisted sense of humor. She did not live her life by the promise of money, but Sam was right. That kind of cash would take a working cowhand a good many months to come by. It was nothing to scoff at, especially if, as the Professor had told Sam and Tom, the work could be finished in two weeks.

"I don't need any five-legged elephants. I only need one two-legged man covered with rough bark."

Nadia leaned close and hugged him again, and Sam kissed her forehead. He tried to make his breath come easy, but there was a strangling sensation creeping up in his throat. A strange, cold feeling had come over him, and he raised his eyes and stared up at the looming silhouette of the Santa Catalinas. Tonight that giant hulk of a mountain range seemed to have a pulse of its own...

*   *   *

The fore-range of the Santa Catalinas seemed to jag on and on. A distance which in more hospitable country could have proven an easy jaunt took the entire morning for the archaeological party. At noon, Sam drew Gringo to a halt. Slowly, as if the party were a line of rail cars, they came to a stop, until the very last mule, a little bally-faced sorrel, halted inches away from the half-shaved tail in front of him. At the back of the line, a young Mexican named Juan Sanchez pulled back on his reins and drew in his own little mountain horse.

A devil's playground, the mountains folded and pitched and buckled around them, millions of years of molded, shattered, eroded stones forming a tortuous bed for the myriad desert plants that called Arizona home. Although the distant gray-green shadows making a dark cape on the shoulders of Mt. Lemmon and the range's other high peaks marked the forests of spruce, fir and pine they would eventually climb to, here below they were still among the harsher desert plants, where thorns were the normal adornment, and oak and juniper made up the greater part of the large vegetation. The vicious points of agave made all travel treacher-ous along the spine of the ridge where they wove their way, and among the tangled boulders the century plant thrust its giant stalks and spiny leaves skyward.

The party consisted of eleven people. Near the lead rode Sam, with Tom beside him when the trail allowed. On their heels came old Alfredo Sanchez, father of Juan. He rode a dun mule that was possibly the smartest of all the four-legged creatures trekking that ridge, and most definitely the oldest, at twenty-four years.

Big Vik Zulowsky rode an ugly barrel-bellied bay behind Al-fredo, with Stuart Baron, Professor Ashcroft, Melissa Ford and Delbert Moore behind him, most often in that order. The mounts had established their pecking order within the first few hours of heading out. Only Sam, Tom and Alfredo allowed their animals out of that sequence, and that was because as guides they had to force their horses to the fore. Each of the other animals had learned its place, and it took some effort to get them to break out of it and only relaxation on the rider's part for them to slip back in. So far the morning's only casualty stemmed from a contest of wills between a chestnut mare Professor Ashcroft had rented at the stable and Melissa's beautiful sorrel. The sorrel now wore a swollen spot on his left knee, his constant reminder that the Pro-fessor's mare had proven to be his better.

Behind Delbert Moore, and just in front of the train of ten large mules and thirteen loose horses, rode Dowdy Ross, sitting tall and square-shouldered in the saddle, a beat-up Colt .45 on his right hip—standard Army issue. Young Juan Sanchez, at the rear, kept an eye on the mules and the cavvy of horses, making sure none of them dropped too far back in foraging for food.

The mules, like the horses, knew their place in line. The only difference was that these mules had journeyed over many trails together, and the order they walked in today was the same as they had respected over a thousand miles. Each mule wore a halter, but they made their way with no means of guidance. This was the way it was and always would be for them—a way of life. The one shave-tail who walked second from the back of the mule train was the only newcomer in this bunch. Following military custom, his tail had been shaved by the stable owner so that people would know not to trust him too much and make the mistake of walking behind him until good temperament had been proven.

Within the human ranks there was also a pecking order that could take days to establish. But it did not manifest itself in any particular order on the trail. One person preceded Sam along the mountain ridge. This one often went on foot, but alternately rode a sorrel pinto, mostly white with a large spot rolling over the top of its mane and onto both sides of its neck, and another one over its rump, which gave color to the tail. The animal's mane and tail were long and untrimmed, not unlike its hooves, which unlike those of most white-legged horses were as hard as rock and rang against the stones—a mountain-bred horse.

The rider who sat this pinto, on a saddle tall of horn and cantle, made mostly of rawhide and covered with a wool blanket, was one known only as Quiet Wind. Her presence gave Sam and Tom both the same eerie feeling. Because they had been told that morning that she had spent her entire youth in these mountains, neither of them seemed to be truly needed as guides on this excursion. This lent fuel to Sam's hunch that there must be some more dangerous reason for having them along...

She was long in years, this Quiet Wind. Her hair, although still mostly black, was coarse and lifeless and streaked with dark gray. She wore it long, down near her waist, in one braid that may not have been taken out in weeks. The lines of her face were severe, her mouth narrow and down-turned. Her nose was blunt, not sharp, yet still, because of her intense black eyes and deep copper skin she had the appearance of an old, battle-scarred hawk. Perhaps because of her eighty-some years she could not soar like a youngster, but her talons would be even more deadly with her years of experience. She walked the ridge in calf-high moccasins and seemed never to tire. When she rode the pinto it seemed more to keep him company than because she needed to rest.

Hanging about Quiet Wind's neck were a number of necklaces, mostly strings of matched beads. Down below all the other beaded strings swung a cast piece of what appeared to be old copper, in the form of a hawk with its wings spread and its talons reaching dangerously forward.

The party members stepped down from their mounts and dug into their saddlebags, eagerly seeking the sandwiches their cook, Dowdy Ross, had prepared for them before departing early that morning. They had taken breakfast when the new Tucson sun was fresh and yellow and rendering the town in bright colors. Since then, they had chewed on jerky or sucked on hard candy, drinking plenty of water and watching the looming mountains around and before them.

Now they slumped on boulder chairs and set to devouring the meat and biscuit sandwiches, washing them down with lukewarm water from their canteens.

Sam looked over to see Stuart Baron scanning their surroundings with a pair of field glasses. There was a time that careless use of binoculars would have been strictly taboo, but because almost all of the hostile Indians were gone from Arizona, Sam let it go. Any flash made by the lenses now would warn only animals, and if they were smart they were already leaving a wide corridor for this bunch. Viktor Zulowsky seemed awfully anxious to use the Ballard rifle he had been packing on his saddle all morning. It had a barrel-length brass tube telescope mounted on top, the same type some bison hunters had used to help them clear the plains of those wooly cattle. A deadly weapon the Ballard would be, in trained hands.

Stuart Baron was dressed in tan canvas riding pants, the strange-looking eastern type with room in the thighs enough for two. He wore a light gray shirt mostly covered by a brown wool coat with a heavy leather shooting patch on the right shoulder. It was the first time Sam had seen him wear a sidearm, and this was a nickel-plated Merwin-Hulbert pistol high on his hip. Baron tipped back his flat-brimmed gray hat and looked through the glasses one more time, then lowered them and turned to pick his way over the rocks toward Sam and Tom.

He stopped in front of them, wiping a gloved hand across his brow, then bringing his hat back down low over his eyes. He gave the partners a stiff, practiced smile. "Quite the country. Have you done much hunting up here?"

"Time to time," Sam said.

"I imagine there's a good population of those desert bighorn sheep I hear so much about. What about deer? Would a man expect to find more of your 'mule deer,' or is it whitetails up this high?"

Tom shrugged. "Some of both. But more likely you won't see either. These lower hills are hunted pretty hard by the market hunters. There are a few smart old bucks and some old does in here, but most deer are gonna be up higher." There were no seasons on game, and around any large population center of those last decades of the century it was uncommon to run across sign of any but the most wary of animals—bears, cougars, wolves, and the wiliest of the deer and javelinas. This close to Tucson, an animal that didn't have instincts for hiding didn't survive long.

Tom explained all this to Baron when asked the obvious question. "That's a shame," said the New Yorker. "So close to a magnificent hunting ground like this, and nothing to hunt."

Sam nodded and frowned, standing up to survey the country himself. "It's a shame, all right. And it ain't just the market hunters. If it weren't for them that come up here to shoot animals an' leave 'em lay it probably wouldn't be to the point it is."

"Surely you don't bother to carry it all out with you," said Baron. "That's what your cattle are for, to provide you with a healthy diet."

Sam and Tom exchanged a glance, and Tom dipped his head. He knew what was coming. But Sam managed to stay outwardly calm.

"That's the attitude that emptied out these mountains," Sam said in the most polite voice he could muster. "Me and Tom, and anybody else that has a lick of responsibility, we eat what we shoot. No tellin' when you'll come across good meat again."

Baron nodded. Instead of offended, the look in his eyes seemed somewhat amused to have touched a nerve. Behind him, the deep voice of Viktor Zulowsky chimed in. "I ain't packin' out every jackrabbit I shoot, I'll tell you that much. Sometimes you shoot an animal 'cause you need the practice. Plinking at targets ain't like shooting a living thing. Sometimes you just gotta keep your eyes and your trigger finger sharp." The big man walked over and stood beside Baron, taking a long drink from his canteen, then raising challenging eyes to Sam.

Sam was going to answer him, but he thought better of it. Zulowsky wouldn't have liked what he had to say. But by the hard look he gave Sam and Tom he didn't much care for the thought of being ignored, either.

"I greatly admire the distances you can see across out here," said Baron. "In our part of the country there is little use for long range weapons in the hunt. Most shots are taken under fifty yards."

Sam grunted with good humor. "That's how it was down in Texas. Out here you can take an animal as far as you can trust whatever rifle you're shootin'—and your own eyes."

With a nod, Baron snapped his fingers and held out his hand toward Viktor. The big man handed him the Ballard rifle. "Do you know firearms, Mr. Coffey?"

Sam nodded. "Some."

Whether Sam knew firearms or not, he had a feeling Baron's response would have been the same. By the looks of the big rifle it was one that Baron liked to brag up.

"This toy Vik's been packing around is mine. It's one I bought specifically to bring out here with me. The Ballard Number Six Schuetzen. Generally, they come in a thirty-two and a thirty-eight caliber, but this was a special order in forty-five one hundred—.45 caliber, one hundred grains of powder. I installed the telescopic sight myself—accurate to well over eight hundred yards, to a man with a steady hand and eye. I've hit a man-sized target with it at seven hundred. I had sorely hoped to be able to take one of your desert sheep with it."

"You may see one yet," Tom said. "So that's *your* rifle. I thought it was a little on the spendy side."

Viktor's eyes narrowed, and he squared himself on Tom and hooked his thumbs behind his waistband. "What do you mean by that?" he asked around the fat, unlit cigar between his lips. "You think I can't afford a good rifle?"

Tom looked over at Viktor and blinked. After a few seconds he said blandly, "I didn't mean a thing by it."

Viktor stared for a moment, seeming a little disappointed at the peaceable reply. Finally, he just nodded and looked away. On a whim, he reached into his suit coat and pulled out a match. He struck it on the rough wool of his trousers and stood puffing the cigar into life. The task accomplished, he threw the smoking match into the rocks. Sam and Tom both followed it casually with their eyes, making sure it hadn't landed where it would be likely to catch any brush on fire.

"No offense, mister," Tom commented, "but the brush around here is like kindling. You'd be surprised to see how fast an Arizona mountain can go up in smoke."

"There's nothing there," growled Viktor after taking a moment to get over Tom's gall at preaching fire safety to him. "If I need my grandma to follow me around and keep me safe I'll let you know."

Baron turned and looked closely at Viktor, frowning. After a moment, he said, "A bit of civility, Vik. He is only trying to keep us safe, and he *is* talking sense, after all."

"Yes sir." Uttering those two words seemed to cause Viktor Zulowsky great pain.

"Look it over, if you like," Baron said suddenly. Sam looked down at the big rifle the easterner was holding out to him. Never one to pass up a chance at handling a fine firearm, he took it.

He had to admire the incredible workmanship that had gone into it. Women could have their fancy hats and shoes, their bright evening gowns and diamond rings. It was a fine rifle like this which sent shivers up a man's spine and made his heart race.

From the tip of its thirty-two inch barrel to the butt stock, it was a piece of fine art. The barrel, part round and part octagonal, was exquisitely blued. To back up the telescope it boasted a vernier rear peep sight and spirit level front sights. It had the loop and spur type lever and double set triggers, which would serve a man well on those over-five-hundred-yard shots. Its stock was in the classic Schuetzen style, high-combed and with a heavy cheek piece, all done on an impeccable stock of English walnut. It was checkered flawlessly at the wrist, and the Swiss type butt plate bore a nickel finish that set off the entire work, with black horn on its forend tip as a further mark of excellence. To complete the piece, it had been engraved with a floral scene surrounding two bighorn rams on the left side, and elk on the right.

"That's some rifle, Mr. Baron. Thanks for the look-see."

Baron took the rifle back with an aristocratic nod, then turned and sighted through the scope at some imaginary ram across the canyon.

Tom Vanse happened to look over and caught Melissa Ford pulling something from her saddlebag, which he quickly recognized as the plant book she had shown him the day before. While her hands were busy with that work, she was watching him, and her gaze didn't waver when their eyes met. Instead, she gave a quick little shake of her head, and her eyes held a warning. They darted to Viktor Zulowsky, then fell away.

With that silent exchange troubling him, Tom stood up to go to his horse. Viktor was staring him down. A challenge. Wordless, without motion, but a challenge, pure and simple. Tom Vanse had the feeling it was going to be a long trip.

CHAPTER SIX

The high, dry mountains of the southwest, shadeless and close to the sun, can burn a man until his skin looks like raw meat during the day. But in the night, with little moisture in the ground to hold the day's heat, they can be bitterly cold.

They made their camp in a coulee, at whose head a small spring trickled out of the rocks. While they still had light, they dug out the rocks to create a little pool that within half an hour had filled to over a foot deep with cool, clear water.

They replenished their barrels and canteens and watered the horses. Some of them took the opportunity to wet a bandanna down as well, and to sponge off the dirt and grime and sweat that had accumulated through the day.

Sam didn't bother. A night sleeping on the ground in dusty blankets would put it all back anyway. Besides, part of his bedding was generally the blanket he had used under his saddle during the day, so a little more dust wasn't going to make a whole lot of difference in how he smelled in the morning. He smiled knowingly when Tom was one of the first to step up to the water hole and preen himself. Not long after, Melissa Ford—obviously Tom's reason for the spit-bath—visited it herself.

The sun swam down behind the mountains, oozing like a liquid pumpkin into pools of orange and yellow and crimson, and with it evaporated the warm air. Sam went from shirtsleeves to a heavy, blanket-lined coat in a matter of an hour. Tom did the same. Melissa Ford was already huddled under a woolen poncho by a fire Dowdy Ross had nourished into a good-sized flame. Anyone else who wasn't keeping warm by busying themselves caring for their horse or answering the call of nature was either wearing, or digging for, something to hold in their body heat.

Ross spent a lot of time fussing over Melissa, Sam had noticed, bringing her coffee the moment it was ready, sometimes offering her jerky, a peppermint stick, or a biscuit, and always a smile. This was a significant fact, because Sam had noticed that the rough-talking ex-cavalryman didn't smile much around anyone else. It wasn't the kind of doting that a man did who had romantic interests, however. The way Ross treated Melissa was more the way a father or an older uncle would have done. Sam lived his life reading other people, and he had never caught a hint of romantic notions behind Ross's eyes.

Sam guessed he and Ross had to be pretty close to the same age. The only difference was that a saggy belly had caught up to

Ross; Sam's way of life and means to buy fine food weren't such that the same fate had befallen him.

In time, all of them found their way to the fire, after the horses had been cared for and picketed out in the shadows with their nosebags full of grain. This low in the range, they had to rely heavily on whatever feed they had packed in, as many of the horses were not used to foraging in thorny undergrowth in the dark. Besides, they would need the energy granted by a diet of grain to continue the climb into the high, rugged Catalinas.

A cool breeze curled down off the mountain rims, and an elf owl made its pathetic call from the rocks overhead. A kangaroo rat bounded into the very edge of the firelight, paused a moment, then disappeared in another leap.

The Professor surprised Sam by pulling out a mouth organ, and started to work out a few tunes on it. He didn't seem like the type to wile away time on a frivolous pursuit, but he was good at it. It probably helped him unwind after the mentally grueling days that such a life must offer him. A time or two the harmonica seemed to loosen Ashcroft up enough that he even allowed himself to crack a joke.

Young Delbert Moore seemed overly ready to laugh at the Professor's slightest humor, stopping only if he noticed that Melissa didn't share the laughter. Even Stuart Baron, when he wasn't staring off into the shadows like a restless dog, laughed now and then.

In fact, the only one who didn't was big Viktor Zulowsky. Sam noticed that a surly frown was still frozen to his face, and more than once he saw him staring Tom down. He had a feeling Tom was going to tangle with that big boy before the end of the trip. And if appearances meant anything, Viktor would be a tough nut to crack. In Tom's younger days, there weren't many men he couldn't match blow for blow. But he had years on Viktor Zulowsky. In a face to face fight those years were going to tell. And

Sam had never seen Tom as big and muscular and obviously full of raw power as Zulowsky.

In campfire tradition, each man who had something to offer in the way of entertainment did so. Dowdy Ross unleashed a veiled sense of humor when he went into a story that everyone took serious from the outset.

"As the story goes, a stranger walks into a saloon up Kansas way, has him a drink, and goes out to get back on his horse. Now, this stranger has a mighty fine horse of Kentucky breeding—a famous racehorse. But when he steps out the door that horse is gone. So he walks back into the saloon and gives the whole room a real serious look. He says, 'I'm not going to bandy any words here. I'm just going to tell you that somebody in this town stole my horse. Now, you're a pretty close-knit town, I figure, and I'm sure somebody here knows who took that horse. I'm going to stand here for just a half hour and have two more drinks. I'm not going to pay any attention to who walks in or out this door. But then I'm going back out there, and if my horse isn't at that hitch rail where I left it, I'm going to have to do what I had to do down in Texas. And I sure hate to do what I had to do down in Texas.'

"Well, this is a tough Kansas town, but this fellow is a stranger to them, and they really have no idea what kind of a tough hombre they're dealing with. He talks pretty confident, and truth be known, he worries them a bit. So when he gets done drinking those drinks and steps outside, there stands his horse. He nods with some satisfaction and steps up on that horse to ride away, but the bartender just can't handle not knowing, so he walks out after him, and he says, 'Mister, I think you owe us something. Just what exactly did you have to do down in Texas when somebody stole your horse?' The stranger looks down at him and says, 'Why, I had to walk home, of course.'"

There was a general groan of good humor through the crowd, and Melissa laughed with glee. Old Alfredo Sanchez followed with a Mexican folk tale about how the horse got its long nose, and then it came to Tom Vanse.

Tom was a showman from way back, although he would deny it to the grave. He let the suspense build, while others around the fire—particularly Melissa—waited to see what he would come up with. Then he launched into a long poem about how two men went down into Mexico, to Yaqui country, searching out a hidden treasure. It was a poem he had never shared with Sam, and one that gave Sam chills.

It ended thus:

"Deep where the Yaquis cache their gold, live the dreams of men, as the story's told. Gold and jewels make a poor man proud, for he walks the streets with his head unbowed. So a man rides deep into Yaqui land; against all odds he'll try his hand. But the Yaquis bold make him rue the day; strong men come, but dead men stay."

Sam shivered and caught himself staring into the night beyond the fire. The bottoms of his feet, where the Yaquis had skinned them, were aching with the memory.

"What about you, Mr. Coffey?" he heard the Professor saying. "A story? A song?"

Sam scoffed. "Hell, Mr. Ashcroft, you wouldn't want to hear anything out of me. Believe me. I once tried out to sing with a choir, but the other mules voted me out. The lead mule in particular told me, 'Coffey, you can't believe any of us mules are gonna allow you to contribute to this music, not with a voice like that. I may be a half-ass, but if you think you got a singin' voice, you're a dumb ass." The words had no sooner left his mouth than he looked over at Melissa. "Uh, sorry, ma'am."

It was too late. The immediate shock had worn off, and Melissa Ford burst out with laughter, the sound drowned by Delbert Moore, Tom, the Professor, and Stuart Baron. Even Viktor Zulowsky busted out with a laugh, although he quickly cut it off as if caught in a shameful act.

"No apologies necessary, Mr. Coffey," said Melissa after the din had subsided. "I live in New York City, remember?"

Professor Ashcroft cleared his throat loudly. "The fire seems to be dying down, and we're about out of fuel. Is anyone ready to turn in?"

Tom was quick with his reply. "Seems a shame to waste a peaceful night like this. You all keep on visiting. I'll go get some more wood."

When he stood it was like he and Melissa were attached at the hip across the fire, for she came to her feet as well. "I'll go with you, if you don't mind," she said. "I need to get the blood moving in my feet."

Viktor Zulowsky started to rise as well, but then he quickly played the move off by bending to pick up two stick ends that had been burned off of firewood and threw them into the coals. Sam watched his scowl deepen as his brooding eyes followed Tom and the girl into the dark.

Off in the shadows, Tom twisted a half-dead juniper limb away from the rest of the tree and pinned it under one arm. Melissa stepped up alongside him. "I'll just tag along with you. I'm still accustomed to the lights of the city. My eyes haven't seemed to adjust to this kind of dark."

Tom smiled. "That'll come. Just be careful not to gaze at the fire if you can help it. It's not so important now, but back in the days when the Apaches roamed out here that kind of carelessness used to get people killed."

Melissa hugged her arms tight to her, shivering. "That seems so unreal," she remarked. "Was it really like that? Were the Indians that bad?"

"What have you heard?" Tom asked.

"Well, in the East some people make the claim that Westerners made it all up—that the Indians wanted peace and simply wanted to be left alone."

Tom looked over at her, trying to pick her features out of the dark. "Ma'am, I hope you'll excuse me for saying it, but the folks back east had their heads in the sand. No doubt it's true the Indians all wanted to keep their land, and I'm sure it's true that they would have loved being left alone, too, when it suited their needs. But there were plenty who were happy to have white men and Mexicans, and other, *peaceful*, tribes around when they needed them for something. Some tribes made a good living stealing from others, a lot like ants raiding other ants. And some of the things they stole were people—for slaves."

"Did the Apaches really do all those things to people? The things men came back from the West talking about?"

"Well, I don't know what you heard, but there ain't much the Apaches didn't try, in the way of causin' pain. They weren't much for takin' scalps, but torture... Injuns have a different set of morals than we do. They don't believe in hurting or stealing from a member of their own tribe, but they did some fearsome things to white men and Mexicans—and other tribes."

"And women, too?" Melissa asked.

"Women, too," he said with a nod. "And when it came to torture, *their* women were the worst. But don't ever get the idea that white men were innocent. Some of them were just as bad. I don't want you to think I'm against the Apaches. I'm just tellin' it like it is."

Melissa's glance darted back to camp, and then she changed the topic. "I suppose they'll expect me to bring some wood. Why don't you let me carry what you gather?"

Tom smiled. Melissa was quite a woman. Wordlessly, he handed her the length of wood he was packing and tore another one loose, handing that one to her as well.

"I have identified a number of plants from the book," Melissa said suddenly. "It's really quite fascinating, particularly where they talk about the different uses for them. The author must be an interesting man."

"I reckon so," agreed Tom. "Probably somethin' like Sam would be if he were more into literature and such. I doubt he could give you white man names for all the plants out here, but he knows what's good to eat and what ones to use as medicine. The ones that are poisonous, too."

"You admire him quite a lot, don't you?" Melissa asked.

Tom straightened up, snugging up a loose glove. *Admire him?* He hadn't thought much about it. "I guess I do, now that you put it that way. He's the best partner a man ever knew."

"He doesn't talk much. Does it ever get lonely for you?"

"No, ma'am. I do enough talkin' for the both of us."

Melissa laughed, and for a long moment their eyes rested on each other. At last, she said, "More wood?"

He cleared his throat, shaking his mind free of thoughts he didn't dare have about this woman. Quickly, he turned away, speaking over his shoulder. "A couple more like that and we should be good 'til bedtime."

The woman followed him, picking her way along in the dark by watching him. "Aren't you afraid of stepping on snakes out here?" she asked.

"What for? They won't break."

She laughed. "You don't seem to worry about much."

"Only about what I don't know—like what you folks are really doing out here."

The comment stunned Melissa into a long silence, and the two of them stood there without moving for what seemed like several minutes. "Mr. Vanse, I would tell you this very minute if I could. There's nothing I would rather do. But Professor Ashcroft has his reasons for the way he's doing things, and he intends to tell you and Sam everything soon. Try to be patient with him. This project means the world to him. Just know that it is nothing that would bother you if you knew. I would tell you if it was something bad."

"Fair enough, ma'am." He leaned down and jerked at a large branch, having to pry it back and forth until it tore free. "That oughta do it," he said. "We'd better get back to camp before they send a posse out."

Back in camp, even with the new wood on the fire the feeling in the group seemed to have grown darker. Juan Sanchez was telling a story in his shy, halting voice, seldom meeting anyone else's eyes as he spoke. Viktor Zulowsky sat whittling a stick with short, harsh strokes, once in a while looking at Tom, then Melissa, his glance malevolent. Baron occupied himself cleaning his rifle, and Delbert Moore had taken out a notebook, in which he was making some kind of notations. Old Quiet Wind sat by herself, off in the dark. She was gazing at the sky.

Sam was hunched forward, elbows on knees, smoking a cigarette and listening to the night.

When the scream began he was startled, and he almost dropped his cigarette. It came from up in the timber above them, perhaps no more than thirty yards distant, perhaps a hundred. It was the kind of eerie, throaty sound that filled space and seemed to come from everywhere. The only thing it could be compared to was the scream of a rough-voiced woman in pain, and it hung in the darkness long after it had ended, then at last was followed by one spiteful snarl.

CHAPTER SEVEN

Sam didn't think to look at Tom or the Mexicans. Instead, he glanced quickly around at the others. Echoes of the scream had died away, leaving the camp silent for several seconds.

Melissa was staring at Tom with her hand up to her chin. Delbert Moore was standing up, looking around with his eyes large and shining in the dark. Viktor Zulowsky tried to look tough and calm, but without realizing it he was furiously chewing on the stub of cigar in his mouth. The Professor and Baron were looking from each other to Sam and Tom, as if waiting for an explanation, and Dowdy Ross sat the way he had been, leaning up against his bedroll while he quietly puffed on his pipe.

It was Melissa who spoke first, directing her question to Sam. "What in the world was that?"

Sam let out a little chuckle. "A cougar."

Since Sam wasn't inclined to long explanations, Tom jumped in. "Out here they're sometimes called a painter or catamount—a mountain lion."

"Will he cause us trouble?" queried Delbert Moore.

"Nah." Tom waved the notion off casually. "I don't know why they do that, if they're mad we're in their territory, or just showin' off or what. Maybe they're just havin' fun tryin' to scare city folk."

Viktor swore. He looked an apology at Melissa but didn't offer any out loud. "I'd like to get a shot at him. Worthless cuss."

"Not exactly worthless," countered Sam. "They cull the sick and wounded deer and other critters. They have their place here—more than we do."

*   *   *

With a grunt, Viktor pulled the stub of cigar from his mouth and stared for several seconds at Sam, then looked away and shoved the soggy lump back between his lips.

Viktor was a big, strong, confident man back in New York and on the docks. He knew how to throw a roundhouse punch, an uppercut, a jab. He knew a dozen different ways to send a tough man to the ground and then kick him into unconsciousness. He wasn't afraid of the thugs and blackguards who hid among the stacks of freight on a midnight wharf. But that sound, now... He would never admit it to anyone, but he had been scared. And rightly so. It was beyond eerie. He hated knowing it, but here in these mountains he was lost. Here he knew nothing. He felt like a child again—nothing more than a pawn of the gods.

Viktor had lived a hard childhood. His father, also a stevedore, had died when he was only two, beaten to death on the docks by thieves. His mother took to going away nights, leaving him in the care of neighbors who acted like they didn't want him around. He didn't know back then what his mother was doing, and to the day she died they had never discussed it.

But then one late night after Viktor had taken to staying home by himself she had come home with a big brute of a stranger she said she had married. This new man stated in rough language that Viktor was not his son, and he had better stay out of his way. More times than Viktor could remember, when he forgot that warning, he lived to regret it. The man beat him mercilessly. Finally, Viktor left home, somewhere around the age of thirteen.

Already a young man of good size, he took to running with a rough crowd. At the age of fifteen they strong-armed a pair of businessmen strolling through Central Park on their way home from a late supper. One of his partners in crime was caught, and the police, in their typically brutal way, forced not only a simple confession out of the partner, but the identification of all his cohorts. Viktor would have ended up in jail, but Stuart Baron came to his rescue.

The big man looked over at Baron, remembering fondly. At first, he had treated the businessman with belligerence, even though the man was paying the policemen handsomely to turn him over to his care. But Baron seemed to understand him, and he gave him some indication that although he had become a man of some means and importance he had not been so different from Viktor at his age.

Baron had seen something special in Viktor. A quality. At least that was what he told him. Viktor had never believed he would hear words like that from a man of Baron's standing.

That had been years ago. Although Baron wasn't more than ten years his elder, he had come to serve as a father figure to Viktor. It was something they never talked about, of course. Those were tough times, when men seldom even hugged each other and were looked down upon for crying. But there was an understanding between Baron and Viktor that would last as long as they lived.

*   *   *

In the morning, Dowdy Ross had a fire crackling long before the sun came up, and sourdough cakes frying in bacon grease before even Quiet Wind rolled out of her antelope skin robe to face the east and offer her prayers.

Tom was up next, and after going out into the brush and rocks on the eternal errand, he came back into camp, took a warm cake from the plate with Ross's blessing, picked up his rifle and moved up the canyon in the soft gray light. He had lived with Sam Coffey long enough to know he could expect nothing worthwhile in the way of companionship or scouting until the sun was at least close to coming up and he had downed two or three cups of strong, black brew.

From where she sat in her blankets, Melissa saw Tom ghost out of camp. She watched him go and pulled the covers up about her neck to bask in their warmth and in her own scent. Finally, taking a quick glance around, she picked up her plant book and other essential items, then went to Ross and asked him to see that no one followed her. When she returned to camp several minutes later, Viktor Zulowsky had rolled out of bed and was kneeling near his blankets oiling the six-gun he carried in his shoulder holster. He looked over at her, his eyes dull. She avoided that glance, walking with practiced calm in the direction Tom had taken. She missed Viktor's sour frown and missed him pulling a second, much smaller, pistol from the inside of one of his boots as he stared after her.

Turning to sit, big Viktor Zulowsky finished cleaning his pistol and returned it to the shoulder holster. Then he gave the boot gun a once-over with the oily rag and looked around to make sure no one was watching before he slipped it back into its hiding place. He pulled on his riding boots, then walked over to the fire, holding out his hands to warm them. He couldn't help looking after Melissa, and again the frown slashed his features.

Melissa stepped lightly on the granite boulders, making her way with caution through the growth of yucca, agave and prickly pear that under-laid the oak and juniper. She stopped to scan the country around, and soon she could discern Tom, about two hundred yards up the slope, squatting with his rifle across his thighs and studying the gaping maw of the canyon. Casting a glance back toward camp, she started up through the treacherous rocks and spines, clutching her plant book tightly.

Tom turned his head when Melissa was yet fifty yards away. She must have scraped her boot across a rock without knowing it. He started to pivot his rifle, but when he recognized her he let it fall back to rest on his legs. Watching him, sensing his alertness, his awareness of all that surrounded him, she couldn't help but be awed. Being accustomed to the ways of the big city, men like Tom Vanse and Sam Coffey were still fascinating to her. There were plenty of tough men in New York, but tough in the ways of brawlers, knife fighters, and workers of the docks. Not tough and wary and in tune with the dangers country like this must hold.

She could not help but be enthralled by Tom, not simply because of his mastery of this vast and untamed land, but because of his intense good looks—the deep green eyes that could turn suddenly so hard, the broad, chiseled face that might seem as solid as these granite and limestone cliffs and canyons, then could in a moment be full of dimples, sparkling white teeth beneath a well-trimmed mustache, and the charm of a self-confident man who knew every single thing he wanted from his world. Both Sam and Tom represented a breed of man Melissa had only dreamed of and read about in tales of the wild western lands which she had once found so foolish. Tom had shaken her once secure world.

Taking a deep breath, Melissa glanced behind her one last time and then moved on up the broken ridge to Tom. The big man watched her close the gap, his face mild, musing. Their eyes held for a long time before she reached him. It was an exhilarating feeling to hold the gaze of such a man, not to be able, even with her most steady stare, to make him look away. Tom was afraid of nothing—not even a woman like her.

She stopped twenty feet off. Finally, unable to stand the silence, she raised her book. "Are you still studying?"

Tom smiled without showing his teeth. "Studying the country." He raised a pair of field glasses and held them out toward her. "If you're quiet and don't move a lot, you might see one of the largest bighorn rams I've ever laid eyes on."

Melissa's heart thrilled. Stuart Baron had spoken so much of the bighorn sheep that were supposed to reign in these rocky reaches that she was dying to see one with her own eyes. After a quick scan of the opposite canyon-side, and seeing nothing, she moved in soft, fluid motion to Tom and accepted the glasses. She followed where he pointed, and after a couple minutes' worth of patient coaching by the big man she honed in on the sheep—not just one, but four rams. But it was obvious to her who the crowned ruler was, even without being told. One of them had horns that appeared as thick as a big man's thigh, and they curled around and split on the ends as if they had outgrown their sheaths and were trying to break free. Within the curl of the horn was a circle the size of a dinner plate.

Melissa gasped. "Oh, Tom!" she exclaimed without realizing she had used his first name. "Mr. Baron will be very excited when he sees this. You don't know how he has waited for this moment." She lowered the glasses and looked at Tom, her eyes aglow.

"He won't have the chance," he said. "If we show him, one or two rifle shots will shatter the peace up here, and that big old ram will die for Baron's butchering satisfaction. We can't even get over there to get at the meat and use it. Is that really what you want?"

The woman searched his eyes. Her lips parted. "I... You're right, Tom. I mean—"

He grinned. "All right—Melissa. So you broke the mores of society and said my name. It'll be our secret."

She felt her heart pounding against the inside of her chest. Even in the cool mountain air a light sweat filmed her forehead, and so close was she to this man of the mountains that she could smell his musky scent. Her head felt as if it were full of air. "Mr. Vanse, I truly apologize. I hardly know..."

"That's not true, ma'am. You know me well enough. And it sure would hurt my feelings if I thought you really meant that apology. Now suppose you head on down the mountain before

Ross or Viktor or the Professor comes huntin' you and you get me fired. I'll be along."

Her heart still pounding, Melissa stood up from where she had taken a seat on the rocks beside Tom and moved almost in delirium back down through the rocks. She dared not look back, but she could feel him watching her.

Tom squatted in his place of advantage, seeing the canyon take on the day's light and feeling a pinyon-scented breeze whisper down from the sporadically timbered cliffs far above, almost pungent enough to taste, and cool against the sweat on his neck.

He looked with musing down the ridge, watching Melissa make her careful way back to camp with her book. What that woman did to him! He couldn't explain it. He had sworn many times that his long-lost Beverly was the only woman he would ever want or need or love. But Melissa Ford was a woman like he had never known, and it was as if she had released the manhood in him that he had so long guarded.

He sucked in a deep, sweet breath and looked again at the bighorns, which he could pick out now without the glasses. Like melted honey, the eastern sun exploded across the tops of the peaks above him, and within fifteen minutes more it spilled over the distant Rincon range, touching and warming his already flushed cheeks. He looked down the ridge. Of course Melissa was long-since gone. But he still felt her presence on that rugged ridge that she had too briefly warmed with her light.

*   *   *

They rode in silence, each person mulling over his own thoughts. Sam rode not far behind Quiet Wind, and this time Tom, riding his palomino, Nicker, took up the far rear, behind Juan Sanchez. They had both decided it best to follow this order, at least for the day, because they were worried that Juan might disappear before the trek had gone on much longer. It was obvious by the look in his eyes that the Mexican boy was scared out of his wits, still badly spooked by the sound of the cougar. It felt good to Tom to notice that with him riding in the rear the boy seemed to take a measure of courage, and so onward they journeyed through the mountains.

It was mid-evening, and with a great sense of relief they neared the spot on the ridge where Sam and Tom had decided to pitch camp. Sam threw a hand into the air, causing the party to draw to a confused halt. Tom gigged Nicker in the ribs and rode cautiously up to his partner. Far below, they could see a line of Indians moving, most of them on foot, but with three horses among them. Sam glanced quickly at Tom, and Tom responded by drawing his field glasses from a bag that hung on his saddle horn. He raised them to his eyes, and Sam lifted his own pair. While they silently studied, the others waited behind them.

Finally, Sam looked over at Tom. Tom was already watching him, his eyes expectant. "Well? I'm afraid you're gonna tell me that what I think I saw is what I really saw."

Sam grunted, hiding a laugh. "Well, Curly, if you think you saw what I think you think you saw, be real afraid, because that's what I'm gonna tell you."

Tom stared. "I didn't understand a word you just said."

This time Sam laughed, in spite of the fact that it was the last thing he wanted to do. "They're Apache."

"Could they be the same bunch that stole our cows?"

Sam shrugged. "Three horses down there. That bunch didn't have any horses. And I'd say there are at least ten or fifteen more people than the ones we ran into, and a lot more of them full-grown men."

"Then what now?" Tom asked. "You reckon they saw us?"

Sam had returned his eyes to the Indians, and even as Tom's question was registering on him the last of the Apaches disap-peared up a side canyon. He would have liked to answer Tom's question in the negative, but he knew the Apaches enough to feel it would be a lie.

"They'll have to be pretty desperate to buck the whole bunch of us. They just might whip us in a fight, but it'd be at a high cost. I've never known Apaches to want a fight they knew would cost 'em bad."

Tom sighed. "Let's hope they didn't see us."

Sam met his partner's eyes. Neither of them was stupid enough to believe that could be true.

CHAPTER EIGHT

At the same moment that Professor Ashcroft, Stuart Baron and Viktor Zulowsky jogged their horses up to the front of the column, Quiet Wind led her pinto from where she had been sequestered in the rocks ahead. The look she gave to Sam and Tom was a hard one, but she said nothing. She, like the white men, was an enemy to the Apache. Meeting them in battle meant the same to her as it did them.

"Why did you stop us, man?" Baron demanded. "We only have a hundred more yards before we camp."

"Problems," said Sam, giving the Professor most of his attention.

Angry, Baron jerked his reins and forced his mount in front of Gringo, glaring at Sam. "*I'm* talking to you, Coffey. Not the Professor."

Sam's steel gaze bore into Baron, and the city man did not like what he saw. "I don't like your tone of voice, mister," growled Sam. "You may be king turd back east, but out here we show a little more respect for each other. Last I remember, it was the Professor that hired me."

His face turning livid, Baron stared at Sam, standing up slightly in the saddle as his nerves tightened. "It looks like you'd better have a talk with the Professor, *Mister*. Apparently there are a few things you don't understand about this expedition and who is in charge of what."

Sam's eyes cut to the Professor. He was about to respond when Ashcroft spoke up. "Gentlemen, gentlemen, please. I'm afraid I am to blame for this misunderstanding. Mr. Coffey, Mr. Vanse, please let me explain. Although you will occasionally be expected to take orders from me, and I will make certain requests for your help or ask advice of you, it is indeed Mr. Baron who has charge of the expedition. He has final say concerning all that we do. Mr. Baron represents those who are financing this endeavor. He does the hiring and, if he deems it necessary, the firing. Once again, I apologize, and I hope this clears the air."

It was not an easy bit of information for Sam to swallow. After watching the Professor closely as he spoke, Sam finally cast Tom an unhappy but meaningful look. At last, he turned his eyes to Baron and after gritting his teeth for a moment, he ran his tongue along the inside of his lower lip as if to clear the way for what he wanted to say. "I reckon I owe you an apology."

For a moment, Baron's lips remained drawn in a tight line as he looked from one to the other of their faces. At last he drew a breath, his facial muscles relaxed, and they could see his chest swell out with air. Slowly, he settled back into his saddle.

"Thank you, Professor. Coffey, your apology is accepted—as long as we understand each other. So let's move on. Tell me—why did we stop and what is the problem you mentioned?"

"Indians," Tom cut in. His eyes slid to Sam, then back to Baron and the Professor. "Probably Apache."

"Apaches?" Delbert Moore repeated. The looks on the faces of the easterners, who had ridden up and surrounded them in a tight group, were both incredulous and stunned. Only the Sanchezes looked on without surprise. Tom and Sam's encounter with the other Apache band was common knowledge back at the Yaqui Gold Ranch.

"That's a lot of bull!" Viktor Zulowsky almost shouted as he stared at the two cowboys with blatant contempt. "We read the news back east. Everybody knows the last of the Apaches were sent to prison."

Sam corralled an angry reply. Tom, on the other hand, eyed Viktor coolly. "Well, there's a band of Apaches down that canyon that apparently don't read the same newspaper you do."

"Don't get smart with me, Mister *cow-boy,*" Viktor said with a sneer.

"Viktor!" came the sharp voice of Baron. "We hired these men as guides. This is their country, and there is no reason to doubt what they're telling us." He turned his attention to Sam and Tom. "Well, gentlemen, what would you suggest we do now?"

"We'd better get on up the ridge if we're gonna use this daylight," suggested Sam. "There's nothing for it now. I don't know how they couldn't have seen us. If trouble's comin' we'll have the high ground. Tom and me chose a place that would be good ground in a fight." Ross nodded his approval.

Viktor had stopped glaring at Tom and was scanning the landscape below. Melissa looked at Tom with worry etched deep around her eyes, but she didn't speak. Dowdy Ross reined close to her as if somehow to shield her from danger. With little more talk, they all began to file upward. It was less than fifteen minutes before they reached a flat area of yellow, crumpled grass surrounded by large granite boulders. It was here the weary travelers climbed down.

With Baron's permission to set up the camp as they saw fit for security purposes, Sam and Tom began lining everyone out. Only Viktor, predictably, would have none of their orders. He watched them for a moment, then took half a cigar out of his pocket. Looking at it briefly, he stuck it in his mouth and without betraying his thoughts went to set up the part of camp he and Baron would share.

The partners had planned the camp carefully, and mostly for protection rather than comfort. Being on high ground, there was no natural source of water, and all they had was what they had carried in barrels.

Sam arranged for two guards at the edges of camp, to trade off at two-hour intervals. They had a fire, but it was dim, only enough to cook with and sheltered by large rocks and dirt. It was to be extinguished as soon as everyone had finished eating.

Each person would sleep with any available weapons close at hand, and the horses and mules were to be grained and picketed in three separate locations, with four of them to be secured with chains close to their riders. Two of these were Gringo and Cocky, who would be picketed nearly on top of their riders and were well-trained to stand still throughout the night. With these conditions met, the troop settled in for a restless layover.

The Professor called Sam outside of camp the first chance he had and again apologized for not making matters more clear at the beginning of the trip. Finally, he said, "I would understand if you decided to back out of this expedition, Mr. Coffey—under the circumstances. But I would appreciate it if you stayed."

Throughout the Professor's speech, Sam stood listening in silence. Finally, he took in a long breath and blew it out. "Good to know where we stand, Professor. I'll stay on, since I hired out to do a job. But I'm sorry you're not the man I'm answering to."

Later, Tom and Sam stood looking out over the rough, moon-lit country that surrounded them. They listened to the night birds and insects that chirped on the ridge and along the canyon walls. In camp, they could hear the clang of tin cooking implements as Dowdy and Melissa worked on supper, and the dim sounds of conversation came to them now and then when the wind was right. The alluring scents of the Santa Catalinas swept up the slope on the soft breeze that cooled their faces. To the outdoors-man there is no finer scent than the desert mountains at night.

Sam chewed tobacco, not wanting the glowing tip of a cigar-ette to give away his location to anyone who might creep up on their camp. He spat into the dark and said, "I sure don't like taking orders from Baron. But he's the boss, so I guess that's it."

Tom nodded agreement. "Well, it could be worse—it could be Viktor." They both laughed.

Finally, Dowdy's rough voice called them back to the fire.

With a dish of stewed tomatoes and beef, enhanced by sour-dough dumplings, Tom nestled his back against a granite boulder, Marlin rifle across his lap. Unabashed, Melissa came to sit beside him, and Tom didn't miss the malevolent look Viktor threw their way. The big man hunched his shoulders and stalked off down the ridge to the place he had chosen to stand first guard. Sam had named himself the man's partner for that two hours, and he al-ready stood somewhere in the shadows quietly eating his meal.

"Will they attack us?" Melissa questioned Tom.

"Hard to say, ma'am." He studied her face for a moment, wondering if her cheeks were as smooth and soft as they appeared. "This is their country. It was stolen from them—about the same way they stole it from whatever tribe was here before them." He chuckled. "I reckon if they attacked I could understand it. We'd do the same thing if somebody tried to take it back from us now.

But there's women and children in that group. If they attack they'll go hide them somewhere first."

Melissa shivered and hugged her bowl of soup closer to her. Her moist eyes met Tom's glance, and she managed a smile.

*   *   *

The night passed without event. But in the morning Sam was up early, contrary to his custom, and he and Tom stood at the edge of the camp looking down-canyon. As the first soft light appeared and the canyon shadows began to gray, the Apaches appeared below them, clustered together. The women and children were still among them. Also with them were the three horses, and behind one of them trailed a travois. There were a large number of warriors visible in the group, and that concerned Sam. But the presence of the women and children was a good sign.

The morning's first raven gargled from a perch below, and the last star hung bright in the east. Little songbirds could be heard here and there among the rocks and bushes. Sam lifted his field glasses. For some time, he studied the Indians. Finally, he handed his glasses without comment to Tom, who had left his own back at camp. Tom made his own careful scrutiny. Like Sam, he felt no need to speak.

Viktor Zulowsky appeared beside them without warning and raised Stuart Baron's fancy Ballard rifle to his shoulder. "So they're back, huh? Well, I'll show you two *cow-boys* how to handle an Indian."

Sam turned and looked at him for half a second. Then, realizing what he was up to, he spun fully around and shoved the barrel of the big rifle into the air, grasping it with both hands.

"What the bloody hell!" exclaimed the New Yorker, anger flooding over his face. "Get your hands off. *Now!*"

Sam wasn't about to let go, and his own face was full of the same anger as Zulowsky's. Gritting his teeth, he growled, "You wanna get us all killed? You shoot one of them Injuns and it's damn sure gonna be the end of this expedition."

"I said get your hands off the rifle!" Viktor repeated, emphasizing each word. The big easterner was so consumed with rage he didn't appear to have heard anything Sam said. His eyes wild, face flushed and nostrils flared, with the veins on his neck starting to distend, he looked like an enraged bull. He let go of the rifle with only his right hand and doubled up his fist, raising it high.

Just then something appeared in the corner of Viktor's vision. The blue steel was Tom's Colt revolver. It was poised like a rattlesnake ready to strike.

"Do it and I'll bend this barrel over your skull," Tom said. "Sam's talkin' sense—you'd better listen."

Face still bright red, Zulowsky looked back and forth between Tom and the pistol. He had been hit with hard objects before; that was plain from the scars on his face. He knew what was coming, and his only immediate defense was retreat.

"They're heathens!" he snarled.

"You're the heathen. They ain't done nothin' to you. And neither has Sam. We ain't gonna let you start a blood bath here, and that's exactly what this would be. You can't tell me Baron would think it was a good idea."

The mention of Baron's name seemed to penetrate Viktor's brain at last. He stared at Tom for a few more seconds, then looked over at Sam, his resentment still simmering, but no longer fighting Sam's grip on the rifle. In spite of his precarious situation, the big man still had to save face. He dropped his fist.

"Get your hands off the rifle. I ain't gonna ask you again."

"You got shootin' out of your head?" asked Tom.

"I ain't gonna shoot nobody," grumbled the big man.

As the tension drained out of him, Tom holstered his pistol and looked at Sam. Sam's eyes, full of unfettered fury, blinked and stared back at him for a moment. Slowly, he released his hold on the rifle, flexing his salt and pepper-whiskered jaws.

Viktor lowered the rifle and let the hammer down, his eyes moving back and forth sullenly between the partners.

The rest of the camp gathered around, with Baron one of the last to arrive. By then the tension was already dissipating. The Professor and Baron moved up close to the trio. Baron looked back and forth at the three of them, his eyebrows arched.

"Would anyone care to tell me what this is all about?"

Sam and Tom looked at each other. Viktor tried to meet Baron's eyes as he polished the Ballard's barrel with his coat sleeve.

"It's done now," Tom replied.

"It's done?" repeated Baron impatiently. "I demand to know what went on here."

Tom took a deep breath and sighed, meeting Baron's eyes. "We were discussin' the shooting of folks who hadn't asked for it. It's not a good idea to rile people you ain't at war with."

"That makes sense to me." Baron nodded. He turned his eyes and looked closely at Viktor. "I assume you agree, Vik?"

Viktor stopped polishing the Ballard and met his boss's eyes uneasily. "Yes sir. Makes sense."

"Of course you weren't going to shoot any Indians, were you, Vik?"

"No sir," said Viktor, a bit sullen.

Baron turned to Sam. "What's the situation, Mr. Coffey?"

"Looks like we have a predicament that needs tendin'." He gestured down into the canyon and then walked over closer to the slope.

The others followed, and all could see the bunch of Apaches gathered below. They were much closer than the day before, and it was obvious that some of them were nervous and wanted to be on their way. Several had already moved toward the side canyon where they had spent the night. Others, most of them warriors, were standing in a tight group, with weapons at hand. They looked on with a ready stance. Two others had come forward from the group, and Tom said, "They want to palaver."

Baron, face puzzled, looked at Tom. "They want to what?"

"Talk."

"How do you know that?"

"The one has his hand raised, palm forward," chimed in the Professor. "I think that's what that means."

"Close enough," said Sam, watching the group through the binoculars he had retrieved from Tom. "Only it's not a 'he'. That's a woman."

"A woman?" echoed the Professor and Melissa.

"Yeah. There are some new arrivals, but I think most of them are a bunch we had a run-in with back on our ranch," said Sam.

Baron lowered his glasses. "You fought them?"

"Not exactly. It could have come to that, but we both backed off. They stole a couple of our cows, but you can see they're starvin'. We didn't think it was worth anyone gettin' killed over. They just wanted to get somethin' to eat and then get back to Mexico and hide."

Baron studied Sam. "Then... they aren't that dangerous."

"He didn't say that," Tom cut in. "It could just as easily have gone bad for us that day. It was only their leader that stopped them—that woman."

"The woman's their leader?" said Melissa.

Tom just nodded and gave her a little smile. "At least she was before all them warriors joined up."

Sam said, "Some of them wanted to kill us to keep us from turnin' them in to the Army."

"Well then," Baron pointed out, "won't they have the same fear now?"

"I hope not, but we have no way of knowin' what's on the newcomers' minds," replied Sam. "Still, that old woman's shown herself to be pretty smart once. We can only hope she's still got a lot of say in their affairs. One thing I think is in our favor, they can see we're headed into the backcountry and equipped to stay a while. By the time we come back they can be long gone, and they know it. Besides, if they wanted a fight they'd normally leave the women and children up that other canyon."

"Do you dare bank on that?" Ashcroft spoke up.

"I'd bank on it," cut in Tom.

Ashcroft rubbed his jaw. "Why do you suppose they would want to talk? Are they asking for more food?"

"That I don't know," replied Sam.

"What would you advise we do?" It was Baron once again asking for advice from Sam. It seemed he had come to accept that at least in knowledge of this savage world Sam was his superior.

"If you agree, I'll go down there and find out what they want."

"If you think that's necessary, you definitely have my permission," said Baron without pause. "If they're so scared of being turned in, I'm curious as to why they would come out in the open this way."

"I'll go down with you," Tom volunteered as Sam turned to face down the canyon.

"No, you best stay here. They already know me. I'll be all right." Sam reached down and picked up his rifle from the rock he had leaned it against earlier.

"Won't that be a sign of war, taking the rifle?" asked Delbert Moore, from off to the side.

Sam looked over at him. "It'd be a sign of ignorance if I didn't take it, son. Apaches look down on a fool." He turned to Viktor. "I hope you don't need it, but I'd be obliged if you keep an eye out with that Ballard. Just in case."

A look of pride welled up in Viktor's eyes, and for several seconds he met Sam's gaze. He shrugged his massive shoulders, somewhat straightening his coat with the movement. His glance slipped toward Tom without resting on him, then returned to Sam. He took the unlit cigar from his mouth and spat, patting the rifle butt. "I'll do what I can, but I sure won't be surprised when they decide to take off your hair."

"Apaches ain't a scalpin' tribe," Sam retorted quietly.

He turned and walked down the slope. At the last moment, thirty yards away, he cast a glance back at Tom, who raised his rifle and nodded. "Last chance, Coffey! I'll still go with you."

Sam started his descent again, hollering back over his shoulder, "If we forced them Apaches to look at your ugly mug there might be shootin' after all."

Tom grinned and spat. Old Sam. He hoped he knew what he was doing...

Walking over to a big boulder, he went and crouched down behind it, sliding his rifle barrel up over it for a rest. He looked over at Viktor, who stood poised with the big Ballard rifle. He hoped it didn't come to shooting. The big man could just as easily shoot Sam on *accident* as one of the Apaches.

The others gathered around Tom and Viktor. True to his word, the big ex-stevedore watched for a while, then found himself an advantageous position leaning up against a boulder, as Tom had done. He laid his derby hat on top of the rock and rested the heavy barrel of the rifle across it, then waited. No one spoke. They all seemed to be holding their breath.

Viktor Zulowsky's thoughts were on Sam Coffey. That was one brave man walking down that hill. He would gladly have driven Sam's face through the back of his skull with his fist, but he wasn't about to let some skulking heathen kill a man with guts like that. He would shoot every last one of them to keep that from happening.

Sam reached the group of Indians safely, and for several minutes Tom and the others watched them in conversation. Finally, Sam walked over to the travois with several of the Indians. One woman was waving wildly around, and finally fell down on her knees, throwing her arms over what Tom presumed was a body prone on the litter. After nine or ten more minutes Sam left the group and started the long climb back up to the archaeologists.

Five minutes later he stopped before them, breathing hard. He gave a grudging nod to Viktor. "You won't need the elephant gun." Then he turned to Baron.

"They've got a hurt man down there. He shot a javelina two days ago with his bow. When he went to gut it, it was playin' dead. It slashed his arm to the bone. He's in a bad way, and they don't have anything left to dress the wound with. They don't even have a medicine man with them. They're askin' for our help."

"Absolutely not," replied Baron without the slightest hesitation. "We can't delay this expedition for even one day without putting it in jeopardy. Besides, even if we waste our time and help him he could die. Then what happens when they decide to blame his death on us? No. If they had gone with the others then this would never have happened."

"No, they'd be starving to death in some white man's prison instead," Sam growled. "I told 'em I'd do what I could."

"As you are of course well aware, you were hired as a guide for this expedition, not as its authoritative voice. You should have asked me before making any foolhardy promises." Baron clipped off his sentence, and he seemed to derive deep sadistic pleasure out of the look that filled Sam's eyes.

"I gave my word," Sam said coolly.

"Yes, but you did not have authority to give mine." Baron folded his arms, indicating that the conversation had ended.

"Then I reckon you folks are going to have to go on without me," Sam said.

Trying hard not to look at Melissa, Tom spoke up. "I'll have to stay with Sam."

Melissa Ford had tried to step in before Tom could speak. Now she followed his statement. "I have acted as a nurse more than once, Mr. Baron. Upon Professor Ashcroft's request I brought a number of medical supplies with me. Please don't take this as a challenge, but I would feel of very low character if we did not stay and try to do something. That man might die without us."

"I concur, Mr. Baron," spoke up Ashcroft. "Dressing the man's wound is the least we can do."

Baron's eyes flashed about the group, seeking out support. At last, they fell upon his brawny right hand, Viktor Zulowsky. Vik's eyes were on Melissa, and when he caught Baron's gaze on him he cleared his throat. "I don't see that it would hurt to let the girl dress that Indian's wound and then send them on their way." He looked over in time to catch the look of pleased surprise on Melissa's face.

"Really, Mr. Baron," the Professor cut in again. "It is only Christian."

With a disgusted look on his face, Baron turned away, his glance sliding off of Melissa. In all probability, it was only the woman which kept him from cursing, as he was still obligated to play the eastern gentleman, even out here in the rough country. "Do what you please," he said, turning to Sam. "But I hope this doesn't cost us the entire expedition. And nothing had better happen to Melissa." With his shoulders tight and stiff, he tramped down the slope and disappeared amid a cluster of striped gneiss boulders.

Viktor watched him go, then turned to the others. "That's right—nothing better happen to Melissa."

                    *   *   *

Among themselves, they decided that Tom, Melissa and Viktor would stay at the Indian camp, rather than to make the wounded man be dragged all the way up the ridge to their own.

Sam went down with them to make introductions before returning up the ridge to the others.

Melissa spent the day cleaning, caring for and dressing the young Apache warrior's wound and then monitoring him to see that his condition remained stable.

The Apaches were fascinated with the white woman. It was probably the first time they had seen one practicing medicine on one of their own. Full of curiosity, they swarmed around the woman throughout the day, inspecting her medicines and other medical supplies and generally making her day one of frustration. Now and then, one of the children would become brave enough to take some of Melissa's hair in their hands and look at it admiringly. Tom stayed by her as often as he could, much to Viktor's obvious irritation, so he could ward away the Indian children when they became too annoying. Once, when Melissa pinched a flea that came out of the wounded Indian's hair and flung it away, Tom laughed and recited her an old ditty he had heard:

"The big fleas have little fleas upon their backs to bite 'em. The little fleas have other fleas, and so on ad finitum." He looked at her without smiling, only his eyes a-sparkle, which she seemed to think even more funny than the silly rhyme. In fact, the rhyme wasn't that funny at all, but because she had been so full of tension all day it was just the release she needed, and they both laughed for several seconds.

Tom stopped and looked fondly at Melissa. "That wasn't even all that funny, was it?"

"It wasn't funny at all!" she said with a shrug. "That's what made me laugh so hard!"

While Melissa, Tom, and Viktor spent the day with the Indians, the others killed their time exploring, particularly Sam, Alfredo and Juan Sanchez and Quiet Wind. The old woman, although she had grown up in these mountains, had forgotten much

about them. Somehow she, Sam and the Sanchezes got linked together, riding and walking many miles that day in exploration.

It was toward evening that they came to the head of a vast,
beautiful canyon, where a wide creek ran down and spilled off a
slab of rock, creating one of the most beautiful waterfalls Sam
had ever seen. All around the falls were granite boulders, their
sides matted with thick, silky moss, and in the shadows of the
rocks arced ferns and lilies. Along the north side of the canyon,
Douglas fir trees towered, and some even clustered sporadically
along the south. It was a miniature Eden—a sight to behold.

But it was Quiet Wind's rapt reaction to the scene that chilled
Sam to the bone. For a long ten seconds she simply stood staring,
and then this woman who was usually so quiet and reserved began
to jump up and down in elation and then burst out in excited song.
Sam and Alfredo understood none of her words, but Sam surmised one thing: Quiet Wind had come home.

CHAPTER NINE

Before nightfall, on their way back to camp, Sam, the Sanchezes and Quiet Wind rode by the Apache camp. The woman was very reluctant to go in with the other two, and the Sanchezes weren't particularly happy about it either. After all, Quiet Wind's tribe, the Pima, and the Mexicans, had long been bitter enemies of the Apache. But when it was plain that Sam was going into the camp whether they did or not, they followed, with wary eyes.

It was with a glad heart that Sam observed how far the Apache brave had come toward recovery. The old woman Sam had met during the cow thieving incident came to him with the twelve-year-old boy known as Sad-Boy-With-A-Stick—Dove, to the white man. Tom came over and stood beside Sam while Melissa stayed with the wounded brave.

The old woman, Weaving Cradles, looked him up and down with what seemed to him could only be considered softness. Dove stood there with that same proud defiance with which he had faced him the first time, but in his eyes was a memory of Sam's mercy. Sam had no doubt this band of Apaches, as numerous as they now were, could kill him and everyone involved in the expedition. But because of his and Tom's courage and mercy he knew their group would be spared.

Old Weaving Cradles looked at Sam. She spoke soft words, and he waited for Dove to translate. "You are a brave man. A wise man. A man of mercy. My mother says this. I tell you our people, the Tinne-ah, have not understood this mercy. It is a white man word. A white-eyes way. Between the Tinne-ah, this mercy is good. But for others it was not needed. For me, it creates a warm heart inside. I am hoping you understand."

Sam grinned, his teeth sparkling under his mustache. "Dove, I understand what you're saying." Knowing Apache customs, and the customs of some other Indian tribes, Sam knew it was not good to speak a person's name to them, but because Dove was a nickname given him by white men it was acceptable. "I hope that your brother will be well. The javelina can be a mighty foe, for such a small one."

Dove translated this to Weaving Cradles, who smiled again. Her words in return were as soft as before, but she spoke with authority, and the other Apaches within earshot stood and listened with grave, interested faces. Dove smiled as his grandmother finished. "My mother says you have a strong face—a face much like a Real Person." This was how Apaches and other Indian tribes referred to themselves, as most tribes generally believed themselves to be the only true people, which justified the killing or enslaving of other tribes. "My mother says you will always be thought of... not an enemy... a... In my tongue, a *schicho,* a..." He paused, searching his head for the word.

Sam finished his thought. "A friend?"

Dove's smile returned. "Yes. A friend. Schicho."

Now Weaving Cradles spoke again, and her eyes strayed a couple of times toward Melissa. Dove translated: "My mother, she says she would like to say some words to the healing woman."

Sam and Tom both grinned. Tom turned and spoke Melissa's name, and she looked over, surprised. "Come over here. These people want to talk to you."

With her nervousness showing in her eyes, but her chin up high, Melissa came to stand before the Apaches. The old woman studied her face for many seconds before beginning to speak. When she was done, Dove smiled.

"My mother, she says you are wise of medicine. A great healing woman." Weaving Cradles spoke again, and again Dove gave his uncertain smile. Melissa had been with them the entire day, but she still seemed to intimidate him. "She would like to give you a name, a name as the Tinne-ah would give to their own. She would call you White-Dove-Who-Heals-With-Her-Heart."

With a warm feeling rising in his chest, Tom looked over at Melissa. Tears were shining in her eyes. She nodded and looked up at him. Then she returned her eyes to Weaving Cradles. "Will you tell her that I am honored? I will never forget this day."

Dove translated, and Weaving Cradles turned her eyes from him to Melissa. The old woman smiled, shooting ragged canyons all across her face and lighting it up more warmly than the Arizona sun. Weaving Cradles walked over and held a down-turned fist out to Melissa, who understood and offered her open hand. The old woman let something roll into it, and Melissa looked down at it before quickly closing her hand on what appeared to be a very old Mexican coin of gold with a hole drilled through it. She had been wearing a silk scarf tied loosely around her neck, and on a whim she reached up and untied it, handing it to Weaving Cradles. The old woman smiled again and nodded. Then she turned once more and spoke to Sam.

Dove watched his grandmother and listened to her speak, then looked at Sam and Tom. "In the morning we will go from you to our home in the Cima-Silq. It is with our kind hearts that we must leave you."

Sam grinned once more, Dove's broken, courageous English warming his heart. "Our hearts go with you, too. I wish you luck in Mexico."

The Apaches would need more than luck, he thought with sadness. They would need a miracle to survive in a continent where everyone was an enemy.

*   *   *

True to Dove's word, the Apache band pulled out in the morning. Sam slept in, and he woke almost too late to see them go. Even as it was, he was sitting there in his disheveled blankets, his hat clamped awry on his head, as they departed. Neither Dove nor Weaving Cradles turned to look up the mountain toward them. The only person who looked back was a young child clutching a tattered corn shuck doll. Melissa Ford raised her hand in farewell, and a tear raced down her cheek.

Dowdy Ross made sourdough biscuits that morning to celebrate what the Professor termed as Quiet Wind's "coming home." Sam and Tom could see that this homecoming meant something very important to the expedition, but it was obvious that they were not to learn just what, at least not for a while longer. But knowing what the party sought would not help Sam and Tom do their job any better, Sam knew. On the contrary, the Professor advised them, their own feelings of wonder might drive them insane. Sam and Tom laughed about that comment once they were off by themselves. On the contrary, it was comments like that from Professor Ashcroft that were driving them insane!

Everyone glutted themselves on biscuits and gravy, and when the gravy was gone they topped the last of the biscuits with dried apples and pears that had been stewed and sweetened with molasses. Knowing about the waterfall from Sam and old Alfredo, they finished up the last of their water there in camp, then struck the tents, rolled up their bedding and made ready to move operations. According to what Quiet Wind told the Professor, they had only one more move ahead. Their next camp would be their last. It was from there that the goal of the expedition would be accomplished... or fail.

The excited apprehension of Professor Ashcroft and his entourage that morning was thick enough to grease axles with. Not having any clue what it was they were after didn't matter.

"You reckon they're lookin' for a fountain of youth or somethin'?" asked Tom while they were saddling their horses.

Sam grunted. "Too late for us, Curly. If that's all it is we might as well go home."

"Maybe it's the Seven Cities of Cibola."

"Maybe the Holy Grail," Sam countered.

Tom raised his eyebrows, turning with his arm draped over the saddle to eye Sam. "You know about the Holy Grail?"

"I'm not some Dark Ages pagan, Tom. You ain't the only one who ever listened to a preacher," said Sam in disgust.

"Yeah?" returned Tom. "All right then, what is it?"

"What's what?"

"The Holy Grail!"

"Well, for Pete's sake—I don't know. *Some*thing with holes in it, I reckon. I don't know as I ever ate one."

Tom frowned at the half-smile on Sam's lips. "There's no help for you, you know it? The devil's got his pitchfork up your rump a yard and a half."

"That's a relief," replied Sam. "I was startin' to think all that pain was hemorrhoids from too much time in the saddle."

Grunting in disgust, Tom reached down, grabbed his latigo, and pulled it up tight. Then, while throwing a cinch knot, he turned to look again at Sam. "I'm disappointed in you, you know it? You don't know anything about what you were told in Sunday School, and now you go spoutin' doctor terms that no self-respectin' man would ever mention. Hopeless. Plumb hopeless."

Sam grinned. "Don't you forget it."

With their own mounts standing saddled and ready, Tom and Sam went to help Alfredo and Juan Sanchez pack the mules. One of them tried to bite Sam on the rump, and he bumped it hard in the nose, as if on total accident.

"Don't you go gettin' rough, old man," Tom said, watching his partner. "He's just doin' his Christian duty, I figure, tryin' to nip some of that evil off your hide."

"Find another hide to flesh, Curly," said Sam. "You're startin' to sound like a preacher instead of a two-bit cowpuncher."

"You two sound like my grandparents." The voice speaking those words was delightful and soft, but just as playful as the two partners. Melissa Ford threw back her hair off one shoulder when Tom and Sam turned to look at her, grinning.

"Just don't say we look like 'em," pleaded Tom. "I was just startin' out to have a good day."

Melissa laughed. "Would you care to help a lady up?" Saying that, she clutched her reins in her left hand and took hold of the saddle horn, cocking an eyebrow at Tom.

"Don't let anybody say I ever turned down a lady," Tom said with a grin. With that, he locked his hands together for the woman to use as a stirrup and boosted her up. As he turned back to his own horse, he caught Viktor Zulowsky standing with his mount thirty feet away, giving him a hard stare. Sam noticed it too.

"You better watch your back, Curly." He tried to speak softly, but by Melissa's look she must have heard. "That feller is an interested suitor if I ever saw one, and he's a hell of a lot bigger and meaner than you—and younger, too. The only thing he might not be more than you is dumber."

Tom feigned shock. "Why, Sam! I can't believe you'd say such a thing." He threw a leg over his saddle and looked down, jerking Cocky's head away from the thorn bush he was about to take a bite of.

Sam had no reply this time. He just climbed aboard Bruiser, grinned, and reined over to where Professor Ashcroft was dusting off his coat, waiting for young Delbert Moore to finish saddling the Professor's horse. Sam wanted nothing more than to suggest that the Professor learn to saddle his own broncs, but as long as he was being well paid he guessed it didn't much matter what the Professor chose to do with his time. He just hoped there was always somebody around to change his diapers.

The last man in his saddle was Ross, after he had lashed back onto a pack the shovel used to bury the coals of his breakfast fire. The Professor looked around the group, his countenance full of muted excitement. He had that studied look of most professional scientists: nonchalance in the face of some great revelation. It was as if they did not want the rest of the world to know that they, well-educated men, could experience the thrill of new discovery. "Let's be off, Mr. Coffey. Take us to our canyon."

Sam simply dipped his head in reply and rode over to where Quiet Wind sat her rangy pinto. He nodded to her to lead the way, and the old woman set off at a ground-eating pace. She knew exactly where she was going now and why—which was a sight more than Sam and Tom knew.

"That's a good sign." Tom's voice broke Sam's concentration an hour into the ride. Sam looked over, then followed Tom's eyes skyward to see a golden eagle perched on a rock that overlooked the trail, fifty feet above their heads.

"Don't know if it's a good sign or a bad one," Sam said. "But it sure is pretty."

"Over the mountains of Muldaroon, into the land of Bambeegal—painting his shadow across the lake, flies the guardian of gods—Golden Eagle." Tom grinned at his own recitation, showing his renowned dimples.

"You got a poem for about everything, don't you?" Sam remarked. "Too bad you don't use some of that memory to remember to watch where you're goin'."

Tom jerked his eyes back to the trail as his horse was about to run into a boulder, and he jerked the animal aside. "Dumb horse," he said with a curse. "Watch where we're goin'."

"Cocky's just a dreamer like you, Tom," Sam said with a mischievous gleam in his eye. "Always dreamin'."

Tom stared at his partner. By the look in his eyes Sam could tell his mind was churning. Finally, he turned his gaze back to the front and leaned back casually in the saddle, spitting into the rocks beside his horse's feet. "They ran out of brains, so they had to use ham; they filled up his skull and named him Sam." Tom looked over smugly at his partner, wiggling his eyebrows.

"Well, at least I've got *somethin'* useful in there," Sam growled. "That's more'n I can say for you and your head full of horse biscuits."

Tom gave a hearty laugh and turned to look back at the long line of horses and mules stretched out behind them. "Well, you said I have a poem for just about everything."

*   *   *

It was an hour after their noon rest that they came to the canyon. The shrill of an eagle flying high above them seemed to herald their arrival. Sam looked up, wondering if it was the same bird they had seen earlier. If so, it had traveled far.

Quiet Wind had gone on ahead of the caravan, and she came jogging her pinto back now, riding right past Sam and Tom and up to the Professor. The whole procession ground to a halt as she spoke rapidly with him.

Melissa Ford, as excited as Sam and Tom had ever seen her, could not hide her desire to move on. She waited for half a minute, then gigged her horse with her heels and brought him up alongside Tom, gazing past him toward the verdant canyon. From where they sat they could see its yawning mouth, and raising their eyes they viewed its upper reaches, where gray rocks intermin-

gled with timber, and numerous precipices, draws and ridges created a tapestry. Even from where they sat, hundreds of yards away,
they could see the silver ribbon of a waterfall gleaming in the sun,
halfway up the highest rampart.

Wordless, Melissa pointed toward the silver stream, turning
to look at Tom, beaming. He had already moved his eyes to her,
thinking her every bit as breathtaking as the landscape painted
before them.

"Somethin', ain't it?"

The woman's teeth lit up her face, and her eyes sought out the
magic in Tom's. "It's something!"

After several more minutes, and a short meeting with Stuart
Baron and Viktor, the Professor and the other two rode up to the
head of the column. Not wanting to be left out, Delbert Moore
and Dowdy Ross quickly followed. The Professor studied the
group with his most affected wise gaze.

"There is excellent water ahead," he said, drawing his thumb
and forefinger along both sides of his jaw until they met at his
chin. "We shall take a rest there, perhaps two or three hours, and
enjoy the fruits of this place and the chance for our mounts to
recover from the journey. We will also fill all drinking vessels
and our barrels at the pool there, as there will be no water accessible from above. Then we will begin the climb up the south side
of the canyon. Quiet Wind tells us there is a wide, flat place halfway up that would be ideal for setting up our operations. There
are also grassy meadows there for the animals to graze."

Tom and Sam shot each other a glance. Sam frowned. He was
growing more irritated by the hour at guiding an expedition for
which his bosses hadn't enough trust in him and Tom to reveal
the real purpose. This secrecy was going to have to end soon or
he was going to quit and go home—just on principal.

"Operations," said Tom with a derogatory smirk. "I'd sure
like to know exactly what that means."

"You read my mind, pardner." Sam's voice was quiet enough that no one else could have heard what he said. But the truth was he would not have cared if they did. And the glance Professor Ashcroft threw toward him was enough to let him know the Professor must be aware of his and Tom's discontent.

But as they started on once more and soon came around the face of the mountain and into full view of the beautiful canyon and the waterfall, their aggravation was for the moment forgotten. This was too awe-inspiring a place for them not to be enthralled.

Melissa rode up beside Tom again, and without waiting for anyone to help her down, she almost fell, mesmerized, from her horse. She seemed to lose all consciousness of her surroundings, letting the horse's reins drop as she moved toward the waterfall. Everyone, even Viktor Zulowsky, stared about in rapt attention at the beauty of this secluded glen, the sparkling gray rocks of mica-shot granite, the cool, moist moss, the water cascading off the slab to splash with abandon into the roiling pool below, which looked mint green through the bubbling foam. There were two golden eagles in sight now, one soaring three hundred feet over the falls, the other perched on a dead pine branch that hung precariously into the steep corridor falling off into the creek bed. From the pool at the base of the waterfall, the creek, in full glory, bounded and thrashed among fallen boulders, marching on its ever-wending way toward the sea.

"My Lord," Sam heard Dowdy Ross say, just above a whisper. "Glory be."

Quiet Wind was sitting on a boulder, and tears stained her dark cheeks. Delbert Moore stood with his head thrown back, staring toward the mountains that towered like looming castles over the canyon. The two Mexicans stood with their mules, and Tom was beside Melissa, almost feeling her heartbeat.

After three hours' rest, the party started reluctantly on, following a well-worn trail up the left side of the creek. The path, steep and treacherous, ground sharply up through jagged bedrock and scree, with Douglas fir trees jutting out of the ground on either side, clutching onto life by tenacious roots. At times, the way would start to level out, then once again lurch upward. It was over this harsh, beautiful terrain that the cavalcade made their slow ascent.

Fortunately, it was only a half hour before the trail began to widen out, the tree roots became more firmly imbedded in the soil, and then the earth flattened into a park of long, rank grass, emerald green in color, littered with white boulders and seedlings of fir and pine. It was a lovely area, paling only in comparison to the scene at the waterfall below. To the left, the meadow faded into evergreen forest, with low-lying bushes guarding the roots of the larger trees. On the right, the landscape sank off sharp, plummeting two or three hundred feet to the creek bed below. Vegetation was sparse for the duration of that drop, for it was marked by nearly solid rock. Most of its greenery was represented by a heavy coat of moss fed by mists rising up from the brawling, cascading waters. Fortunately, the rock along the edge of the cliff was mostly solid granite, newer stone, by geologic time, not yet rotted by the ages. The boulders huddled there provided a number of royal thrones from which an adventurous soul might gaze out over the gorge and dream.

With a reverent sense of awe, they pitched camp. Sam and Tom, although habituated to sleeping on open ground, accepted the offer of one of the Professor's spare tents. It wasn't likely that they would sleep in it unless it rained; they could never see their way clear to missing the heavenly display of stars. But it was an apt place to store their belongings, and it seemed obvious to all that they would be camped here for some time to come.

There were five tents in all. The Professor, of course, had one to himself, as did both Melissa and Dowdy Ross. Delbert Moore had the dubious pleasure of sharing a large one with Baron and

Zulowsky, and Tom and Sam pitched theirs on the farthest edge of camp, near the scattered trees in the meadow. The Mexicans made preparations to sleep out in the open, like Tom and Sam would, and Quiet Wind set about building herself a shelter of stout poles laid over with saplings. She was an industrious woman, and she never ceased her labor until it was too dark to see.

As the sun began to set, and the camp itself faded into cool violet-gray shadows, the mountaintops turned gold by the flood of orange sunlight. The conifers growing mostly on the northern slopes above took on warm hues, and aspen leaves rattled, fresh green and silver, in the evening breeze, sharing hushed whispers, secrets of the mountains and the forest. Songbirds filled the woods, offering merry melodies, full of obvious content here in their own heaven.

As for Professor Ashcroft, he stood staring up the mountain. His calm façade had disappeared, and to Sam and Tom he seemed no different than any young child on the eve of his birthday, or the holiest of days, Christmas. When the gilded light lifted from the slopes, and only the last faint wisp of cloud above held a hint of the vanishing gold, the Professor began pacing, and even after everyone else had gathered around the campfire, and still an hour later when supper was served, his restlessness held him a slave. Sam watched him stride to and fro, looking up frequently at the purple mountain face. Once in a while he would stop, support one elbow in the other hand, and cradle his jaw with his fingers, staring up the slopes at who-knew-what. Well, apparently, *everyone* knew what, thought Sam with more than a little resentment.

Sam did not like to think of himself as an overly curious man. He definitely did not like his curiosity to get the better of him. But this time it was eating him up inside. What secrets did the Professor believe this mountain held? Why had he asked Quiet Wind to lead them up here, so far from their New York home? When, if ever, would the Professor reveal what he was after? And what was so important here that men would pay total strangers good money to guide them to it?

The mountain kept those secrets. While the crickets made their music in the dark, and distant wolves, in some far-off glade, wailed at the sky, calling each other together for the night's hunt, the breezes swirled in the trees and swept up from the canyon floor. The owl moaned, plaintive, in the trees, and Sam found himself lying warm in his bed, smelling fresh grass and pine tainted by the horse sweat on his blankets.

What, he wondered, did these mountains hold in store for him and Tom? And would they like the answer once they learned?

CHAPTER TEN

To sleep... To dream... Tom Vanse could only wish for either one that long, restless night. Words kept running through his mind, but for some time he couldn't place them. Images were rampant as well, mostly of Melissa. But some were darker, and fleeting— glimpses of something unknown, and very strange. Something for which he could find no explanation at all. Something his instincts told him did not want him here.

Tom was not a superstitious man. He never had been. But this night he could not swear that ghosts did not exist on the earth. *Something* was here with him. Some kind of dark presence. Sam never stirred, yet he wondered if he was awake too. How could something as powerful as what Tom felt not awaken others?

Then the words came to him:

> ". . . To die, to sleep;
> To sleep: perchance to dream: ay, there's the rub;
> For in that sleep of death what dreams may come
> When we have shuffled off this mortal coil,
> Must give us pause . . ."

Tom sat bolt upright in his blankets, with sweat standing cold on his face. He looked around disconcertedly as pieces of Hamlet's soliloquy kept running through his head... *in that sleep of death what dreams may come...*

Long ago, to impress Beverly's parents, Tom had committed those Shakespearean lines to memory. *To be, or not to be.* Every school child had heard those six words a hundred times. And Tom had heard them a thousand, or at least it seemed so. For ever since taking them into his mind, they had seeped into his soul. But at no time had they come to him as strong as they suddenly did tonight. *Conscience does make cowards of us all...*

The words ran over and over in his head, and he lay back down, his sweat beginning to dry, and stared up at the stars, transfixed. What exactly did all those Shakespearean words mean? Had he ever pondered them long enough to truly understand? And might they mean a dozen different things to a dozen different people, even a dozen different things to the same person, depending on the time and the current circumstances in their lives?

Tom was thinking too much. Disgusted with his inability to sleep, he got up and put on his pants and boots, treading off into the darkness to relieve himself. Once he could think clearly, he wrapped a blanket around his shoulders and sat on a fallen log at the forest's edge and looked around at the gray tents that hulked up like silent ships on a calm but brooding sea.

The moon was coming back, now a golden, hazy sliver. He could see the entire globe, but most of it was dark like the sky, all but the crescent and a thin silvery-blue outline on the opposite side. "Beautiful" could only weakly describe the image. A cricket chirped in the bushes, and now and then another one joined it for a brief duet. But most of them had gone quiet. The wind had also stilled, and there were no night birds. This night, indeed, was like the sleep of death.

Now that Tom was more awake, his wandering thoughts didn't bother him so much. But still he wondered... What was haunting him? And did he dare ask Sam about it in the morning? They were best of friends—closer than most brothers. But did a man share *everything?*

Without thinking, he began to whisper those now famous lines. "To be, or not to be: that is the question."

A soft voice broke from the shadows. "Whether 'tis nobler in the mind to suffer the slings and arrows of outrageous fortune, or to take arms against a sea of troubles, and by opposing end them? To die: to sleep; no more..."

Somehow the voice didn't startle Tom like it should have, although he jumped a little at the first sound. The truth was this person should have scared him more than any other. If he had a lick of sense she would have.

"Did I wake you up?" he asked Melissa.

The woman shook her head quickly. "No! I... I couldn't sleep." She seemed about to say more, but then her lips closed.

"Me neither," said he, and her reasons, like his own, gnawed at him. "What kept you awake?"

She laughed, a sound of embarrassment. "You would think I was a silly little girl if you knew."

Without knowing why, Tom felt the hair on the backs of his hands stir slightly. "I think you're wrong. Tell me."

"You know Hamlet?" It was as if she hadn't heard him.

"I learned that little bit a long time ago. Tell me what bothered you, Miss Ford."

She squared herself to him, searching him with eyes that to him were only dark pools under the thin light of the moon. "You told me it didn't bother you if I called you Tom. So you must call me Melissa."

Tom smiled, not his all-consuming smile, but an easy, thoughtful one. "Melissa, then. But only if you tell me what kept you awake."

"No dreams," she said abruptly.

"How's that?"

"No dreams. Oh, how I wanted to go to sleep, to dream peaceful dreams of mountain meadows and autumn lanes and spring schoolyards. But I couldn't sleep, and it was sad. I couldn't sleep, so I couldn't dream. I'm sorry," she said, dropping her head and suddenly folding her arms across her chest. "I told you you would think I was daft."

Tom stood stock-still for a long time. *Daft?* Not even close. "I don't, Melissa," he said. "It's not that different from what I was thinking myself."

She tightened her grip around herself and looked up at him. Neither of them was able to see the other's face clearly, but there was an electric energy moving back and forth between them. Her lips parted. That much he could see. "So... Did you also feel... It's as if there is something evil here, some kind of darkness beyond the fact that the moon is barely there. Tom, I swear I know how foolish this sounds, but—"

Tom reached out and took her shoulders in his big hands. "It doesn't sound foolish at all. I felt it too."

Tom suddenly felt a gush of air, and instinctively he ducked. Melissa ducked too, and let out a squeal. Then she whirled, and they both watched a huge owl sail out across the canyon as the moon gifted its outstretched feathers with vibrant silver. On its silent wings it had come down and floated right past them.

Before they knew it there was movement all around the camp, the men stepping out of their tents with rifles in hand.

"What is it?" said the Professor in a voice that was beyond concerned.

Melissa laughed. "I'm sorry, Professor Ashcroft. We were talking when an owl flew past and startled me."

"An... owl?" After a few moments, the Professor was able to force out a laugh of his own. All the others looked at her and Tom, and most of them shortly returned, with a little grumbling, to their beds. Soon, only Sam and Viktor remained with them.

Viktor took a step closer and reached boldly for Melissa's elbow. She moved her arm at the last moment, as if by accident, and his hand fell away empty. In a gruff voice, he spoke as if to cover embarrassment. "You scared us. You ought to go back to your tent. You can't ever tell what's lurking out here in the dark."

Tom sensed a restraint, and a forced politeness, to the woman's response. "Thank you, Mr. Zulowsky. I would like to enjoy the fresh air for a few more minutes. But I appreciate your concern."

Viktor stared at her, purposely avoiding looking over at Tom. Perhaps because no one could really visualize the expression on anyone else's face, a fight was avoided. If Viktor could have seen the ire building in Tom's eyes it might have been different.

"All right," Viktor finally said, with a quick sideways glance at Tom. "You have any problems, you give a yell, and I'll come running. G'night."

Tom could see the woman smile, and she replied with all calmness. "Good night." Once the big man returned to his tent, Sam stepped forward, scratching the back of his head under his hat. Like all men of the range, when he came out of bed the hat was the first thing donned. To any outdoorsman, it was almost as natural as opening one's eyes. Sam turned and watched until the movement in Viktor's tent died down. Then he eyed his partner.

"Tom, I know you're going to say you're not doing anything contrary on purpose to rile that big gent— But maybe tomorrow you can just walk up and spit in his breakfast. Or maybe you'd like to knock his hat off the cliff—or throw some sand in his eyes."

"Huh?" Tom looked at his partner.

"You heard me. There's a fight comin', and you might as well hurry it up."

Melissa laughed, a sound of embarrassment. Tom's neck warmed a little. His partner sure had a way with words.

"You sound like my mama," he said, in answer to which Sam nodded his head knowingly.

"Yeah, but I won't be holdin' your hand and wipin' your nose when you get whupped."

Tom grinned, in spite of himself. "Neither did she."

                    *   *   *

Somewhere in the night, sleep stole in to claim Tom, long after he had seen Melissa back to her tent. For the first time that trip, he awoke after the sun was already touching the mountain-tops. Rubbing the back of his neck, he stumbled out to the fire, where Dowdy Ross greeted him a bit coolly.

"You sleep in any longer you'll go without breakfast." The cook's cool blue eyes held Tom's as he was reaching for a biscuit.

Too annoyed to risk an answer, Tom simply nodded. He had intended to get himself a bowl of stew as well, but in light of that comment he took another biscuit and walked away from the fire. He could feel more than one set of eyes on his back, but he didn't look that way.

Sam was out grooming a horse at the picket line, and Tom realized with a grin it was Tom's palomino, Nicker. Good old Sam. "Your eyes goin', Sam? That's my horse."

Sam straightened up slowly, pushing a kink out of his back. His eyes narrowed. "Comb your own horse then."

Tom laughed. "Sorry. I'm the one that didn't get any sleep; what're you so ornery about?"

Cocking his head, Sam wiped at his mustache. "Sleep? You have trouble sleepin' too?"

For a moment, Tom was silent. "Sure did. You?"

Sam nodded, giving Tom a hard, narrow-eyed stare as if by that means he could deduce his thoughts.

"Somethin' strange in these mountains," Tom said. "Melissa had the same problem. I wonder how many others felt it."

With a shrug, Sam ran the brush deliberate and slow down Nicker's glistening golden hide. The animal's skin quivered, and he whickered quietly and cast an eye back toward his groomer, who gave him a couple of sound pats and left his hand resting on the broad back.

"Maybe we oughtta go have a palaver with the Professor," Sam suggested.

"I'm all for it."

Together, they walked back past the cluster of tents, but Professor Ashcroft was nowhere to be seen. When they found him, he was standing at the far edge of camp, where the terrain started its abrupt lift again, continuing on up the mountain ridge in a broad, twisting trail. The mire of bighorn sheep and deer tracks in one place that had been muddy but long since dried was enough proof who kept the steep trail trodden down.

Sam's eyes left the Professor and followed up the trail naturally, the way a tracker's eyes will. There was nothing much different about this trail to differentiate it from many another mountain pathway, except perhaps for its width, for it was wider than most. Other than that, it wound up through patches of rock, vegetation, and was still going without much change when it faded from sight. Sam's guess was that it would continue all the way up the ridge until it found a decent place to cross the top and drop over the back side. That was *if* it was only a sheep trail. If it was used by man as well, who knew where it would go? Possibly even all the way around the canyon face, although from where they stood it appeared to be very steep and hazardous.

Tom addressed the Professor before Sam could find the words. "Mornin', Professor."

The older man cleared his throat, dividing a glance between the two of them and swallowing. "Good morning, Mr. Vanse. Mr. Coffey. I trust you slept well?"

Tom gave him a wry half-smile. "I wonder if anybody did. I wanted to ask you about that."

"Pardon me?"

"I don't quite know how to say this without sounding the fool, Mr. Ashcroft, but it seems to me there was an awful lot of restlessness last night for no obvious reason. I'm not sayin' I believe in spooks, but I have to say there's somethin' up here that seems pretty disturbing. I'll speak for both me and Sam when I say it's gettin' a little old feelin' like we're the only two men up here besides the Sanchezes that don't know what we're lookin' for. Considerin' how poorly Sam and me—and Melissa—slept last night, I'm ready for some answers."

The Professor looked back and forth between them again and took a deep breath. "Mr. Vanse, please believe me when I say I understand exactly how you feel. I can tell you this: We are seeking a people—not an entire race, per se, but the remnants of a race we believe may have died out up here at least seventy-some years ago. If we find what we seek it will be extremely important to the scientific community, especially for this arca. It will add a whole new chapter to the archaeology of the American West.

"Archaeologists hesitate to talk too much about an excavation or an exploration until we turn up whatever it is that we seek. Please forgive me if I seem a touch superstitious. It's simply part of being a scientist, I suppose. I know that sounds like a contradiction—the marriage of science and superstition. But you might be surprised to learn what some scientists find plausible."

"That's all well and good, Professor," put in Sam, "but am I wrong in assuming that everyone knows what we're after but Tom and me? And the Sanchezes, of course."

The Professor met his eyes. "In point of fact, Mr. Coffey, yes. You are wrong. Quiet Wind, Melissa, Mr. Baron and I are the only ones who know exactly why we're up here. So you see, you are not alone. Give me two days, gentlemen. Just two days. I hope to have something tangible for you by then. If I have nothing, then I will tell you what it is that I seek—regardless of superstitions. But you must agree to be patient with me until then."

The determined look in the Professor's eyes told both Sam and Tom they had pried all they were likely to from the Professor. Sam grunted a half-hearted thanks for what he had told them and walked off, but Tom stayed behind. He and the Professor were searching each other's eyes when the Professor clasped his hands behind his back and turned to look back up that winding, rocky trail that seemed to lead into the sky. When Tom's eyes followed, a strange chill passed up his spine. From down in the canyon the cry of a red-tail hawk shrilled on the morning wind.

It was at that moment that the first tremor tickled the Santa Catalina Mountains.

CHAPTER ELEVEN

Something seemed to roll over beneath their feet—like some gigantic serpent or other-worldly demon. It was there one second then was gone. The Professor whirled back to Tom, who was staring at him, dumbstruck. Ashcroft's mouth opened. "What in the name of—" He clamped his jaw as suddenly as it opened, and the look of alarm that leaped into his eyes sent chills down Tom's spine. His voice rose loudly enough for everyone in the camp to hear. "Earthquake!"

Sam had hurried back to them with the whole camp in turmoil. "Earthquake?" Sam growled, echoing the Professor's word.

Ashcroft turned to him. "I'm sure of it," he said. "I've never experienced one, but I've read enough about them." Shooting one more glance up the winding trail, he looked at Sam and Tom. "You must excuse me, gentlemen." He walked briskly to the fire, where most of the others had gathered and were involved in confused conversation.

"People! People. Listen to me!" Ashcroft held up his hands, trying to silence the group. A helpful roar from Viktor Zulowsky did the trick, and Ashcroft looked them all over in one sweeping glance. "My friends, what you just experienced was an earthquake. I have read that they are quite common out here in the West, and most of them are very small, as the one you just experienced. There is no reason for alarm."

"Well, I *am* a bit alarmed, Professor." Stuart Baron's tone was flat. Ironically, he was probably the only one in the group brave enough to admit the fear that everyone felt. "I have also read a bit about earthquakes. There are times that they can continue—and worsen. What we just felt is often only a hint of what is to come."

The Professor sighed, practicing patient calm. Sam had read enough faces to know he was putting on a show. "Many times this is true, Mr. Baron. But there are more times when it is an isolated event. Chances are this is only a tremor and it will probably be the last of it. I couldn't help hearing some of you talking about leaving. We can't just go back down the mountain when we've come so far."

"I'm not suggesting any such thing," said Baron tightly. "This is as much my expedition as it is yours, in the sense of hoping it succeeds. But at the same time, if there are any steps we might take to prepare for the worst, I think it would be wise to do so."

The others seemed in agreement, though for a moment no one spoke up loudly enough to draw attention from the group. When someone did speak it was Quiet Wind, and although it was in her native tongue, her meaning was plain. She said her piece as if everyone there would understand her, and then she marched out to the picket line and started saddling her pinto. The Professor practically ran after her, and for several minutes they fell into a heated debate. Alfredo Sanchez and his son Juan kept staring in their direction, and it was plain to Sam where at least the older Mexican's thoughts were going.

Viktor Zulowsky's voice brawled over the chit-chat of the others. In spite of its volume, he came across with surprising calm. "Know what I think? We brought a few bottles of whisky—for medicinal purposes. I figure there's no time we'll need it more than right now."

Baron's eyes shot to the big ex-stevedore, and Sam followed his gaze. The businessman's response surprised him. "You know, Vik, I think that's a pretty fine idea. Why not have a little pull at the bottle? Mr. Ross?" He turned and snapped his fingers, motioning toward the packs.

Ross stared at him, lips drawn in a tight line. After a moment, he seemed to relax, and with a cautious glance toward Professor Ashcroft, he shrugged. "That may be just the ticket at that."

He walked over, knelt down, and untied a pack. Obviously knowing right where to reach, he came up with a long, dark brown bottle. With a conciliatory nod to Viktor, he took the cork in his teeth and yanked it free. He stared at the others thoughtfully for several seconds, looked back at the bottle, then spat the cork into the brush.

He looked a question at Melissa. "Are you interested, Melissa?"

Melissa quickly shook her head, glancing over at the Professor. "No, thank you, Dowdy. That's way too strong for me."

Ross gave a brisk nod of his head. "All right then. I hope you'll pardon me this." Tilting back his head, he took a long swallow. When he lowered the bottle and opened his eyes, they went directly to Baron. There seemed to be a challenge there. It might not have been the camp cook's place to take the first swig from the bottle, but in his subtle way he was letting the others know that he was as good as any of them. He didn't have to walk anywhere to pass off the bottle. Viktor was already in front of him taking it ungently out of his hand and commandeering his own swill of the amber liquid. He ended the show with a loud laugh, more to cover the twist of pain that crossed his features than because he found anything humorous.

Trying to seem nonchalant, Melissa hurried over to Sam and Tom, looking back over her shoulder at the others, Viktor in particular. She smiled at Sam, but her eyes lingered on Tom.

After Baron drank of the bottle, it went to Delbert Moore. The young man didn't appear to want his turn, but he took a sip to save face. Common politesse and custom would otherwise have

made him look like he was unappreciative of his company, and
that was one thing the young man could not afford.

Old Alfredo Sanchez took a long swallow as well, and he
didn't object when young Juan had his. By then, the Professor
had left Quiet Wind and started back over to the group. The wizened woman had stopped saddling her pinto and walked over to
sit on a dead tree several yards into the woods, at the edge of the
meadow.

The Professor watched while Viktor Zulowsky took his second pull at the bottle. When the big man finished, he smiled to
see Ashcroft standing there, and he thrust the bottle toward him.

The Professor paid the bottle a bored look, then scanned the
group, his eyes finally resting on Baron. This was the only man
of the group that he seemed to accept as his equal. "Are you certain we should be indulging in liquor at this moment, Mr. Baron?
Maybe we need to talk—alone."

Baron raised an eyebrow. No one spoke. It was Sam who left
Tom and Melissa and walked over to break the silence, his deep,
resonating voice drawing everyone's attention.

"Whatever you want to say, Mr. Ashcroft, you'd best say it
right here. What you decide means as much to the rest of us as it
does to you."

The Professor whirled on Sam. His glance did little to conceal
the flash of anger and disapproval at Sam's insolence.

"He's right." Baron's words surprised Sam. "This isn't the
time to go off making decisions without the group. We did, after
all, procure the services of Coffey and Vanse. And everyone
else's life is just as much at stake as our own."

The Professor drew a deep breath, then turned and squared
himself on Sam. "Mr. Baron is right. Mr. Coffey, I apologize if I
seemed short. This incident is a little... Shall we say *discon-
certing?* Unfortuitous, to coin a new word. We must sit—over
coffee—and decide what our course of action is to be. I do not like

the thought of being responsible for any loss of life in the event that another, more dangerous, tremor is forthcoming."

Tom walked over, with Melissa close beside him. "If you all will excuse the intrusion, I would say we're safer here than anywhere."

"And what would make you an expert on it?" asked Baron, offering no apology for his brusqueness.

Tom smiled slightly. "I've been in an earthquake before."

This statement caused the Professor to turn his attention fully on Tom. "Do tell? Then please, Mr. Vanse. Enlighten us with your opinion, since I am reasonably certain that no one else in the group can say the same."

"All right," said Tom. "I was caught in the middle of an earthquake in California, in country a lot like this. After it was over I had a good chance—and good reason—to look around and take notes on what saved my bacon. Look around us. We're at the edge of timber, but with the land slopin' like it does any trees that fall are most likely gonna fall the other way—except for that big one, maybe." He pointed at an ancient pine. "Those rocks up there aren't in line to come rolling down into camp. More likely, if a big enough shaker came along to make them move, they'd go down the canyon. But we start off this mountain and we're right where we don't want to be. If this trail starts to slough off, there's only gonna be one way to go—down. We'll go off into that canyon, and I'd reckon there's no defense against what would happen to us after that."

Baron listened quietly, and as Tom spoke, his eyes scanned their surroundings. By the end of Tom's soliloquy, Baron was nodding. "I think he's right, Professor. From what I can see of the country around us, and also going by my memory of the scenes we passed through, I can't imagine there is any place safer than right where we are—assuming another, larger, tremor were to occur before we could make it safely out of the mountains. I vote to wait it out here. After a day or so, if nothing further has happened, we might as well start what we came here to do. But as much as it might hurt to have to wait now, I don't think we should risk spending a great deal of time up in those rocks or setting up any of our equipment up there until we've waited to see if that tremor was just a precursor to something worse."

The Professor's eyes were locked on Baron's. Finally, a smile lit his face. "Hear, hear. That is how my vote is cast." Once more, he scanned the group, making a point of looking at each one there. "Anyone else?"

Everyone seemed to be in agreement. A few of them looked to Tom, and their glances seemed to thank him. Through no intentional act of his own, he had experienced an earthquake, and at least for the moment that made him someone of vast importance. Predictably, only Viktor's face looked grumpy when he looked at Tom, for he would not like knowing that the mere guide had taken on such status in the eyes of everyone else there.

With the decision made, the Professor, Melissa and Delbert Moore began making tentative preparations to explore. Conversation concerning the quake was conspicuous by its absence. No one seemed willing to risk offending the gods speaking of it.

The Professor jammed a pack with his necessities. He filled two heavy canteens with water and laid them beside the pack, then went to the woods, where Quiet Wind sat with her back to the camp. As he drew near, her back stiffened. He reached her and laid a hand on her shoulder, causing her to tense even more.

He spoke to her in Spanish, and after several soothing sentences she looked up at him. Then she glanced at the moun-tain. At last, she seemed to steel herself and stood up. Together, they walked over to the edge of camp that faced the winding trail. The Professor watched her expectantly. The old woman's arm came up, her finger pointing up that narrow trail. The fringes on her sleeve quivered in the breeze.

*   *   *

It struck Sam and Tom as odd that the Professor was willing not only to go up that trail himself, but to drag the others along with him. After all, it didn't seem they had waited a sufficient amount of time to be sure there would not be further tremors. But go they did. Whatever was up there was calling to the Professor like the mysterious sirens. In the end, Tom decided he had to go up the trail as well, to protect Melissa if he could. And Sam went—because Tom was his partner.

At least when it came to the horses the Professor was willing to listen to Sam's advice and leave most of them below. In the event of a worse tremor, it would be much easier for them to get into cover on foot without the horses. Either way, Sam and Tom would have left their animals below. As it was, they brought only one animal, and this was one of the mules, a dark bay with a tan nose they called Darkie. He was one of the more stoic of the long-eared pack-bearers, who had never given them any trouble. They loaded Darkie down with the Professor's tools and instruments, and then off up the trail they set. Not a soul remained in camp. Apparently their curiosity had overrun their fear. Quiet Wind made her way up the trail in front of them all, her head and eyes straightforward in a very unwary, un-Indian-like way.

Even though the trail up was fairly wide in many places, much of it was overgrown with brush and scattered with rocks. Yet much of it was level, and with very little clearing of debris it might have been a serviceable road for a vehicle as wide as three or four feet. In several places there were obvious depressions that went for some distance in particular flat stretches of rock. The Professor stopped at one such place about two hundred yards up the mountain.

Quiet Wind, twenty feet ahead of the nearest explorer, heard everyone stop. The Professor glanced up from the ruts toward her as if he wanted her to verify something. But because of the distance between them, he looked back down, then at the others. "See this mark here, where the rock seems to sink? This is the track of some type of conveyance—a cart. Probably drawn by oxen or mules."

Sam and Tom glanced at each other, and Sam lifted one shoulder in a little shrug, half-smiling. Maybe the Professor didn't need his services after all, he thought to himself. But this cart track, probably from many years before, was fairly obvious. Not all sign would be so clear.

The ancient track was, to Sam, proof of what he had believed, that this was a man-made trail. This wasn't a track that could be left by a single use, but a place where many wheels, over time, had worn down into stone. Further proof of the trail's man-made nature was the general flatness of it, even beyond the rock.

Professor Ashcroft hollered something ahead to Quiet Wind, then turned to the others after her brief reply and said, "The place we intend to reach is only perhaps three hundred more yards. She says she can see it from here." He motioned Sam and Tom on.

As they climbed, the beauty of this rugged canyon again struck Sam. From up here, they could see many of the falls along the course of the creek far below. The quickly descending waterway shone silver where the sun glanced across it, and the falls, one of them ten or fifteen feet tall, fell misty and sparkling white, giving birth to and sustaining life for the wealth of greenery around them. Large trees towered there, some of them sycamores over one hundred feet tall. There were also willow, walnut, and ash growing along the stream bed. And up along the rugged canyon slopes stood blue oak, slowly surrendering to pine and a few scattered cypress trees among the prominent junipers.

Sam looked over at Tom, knowing his attention would be rapt. His partner's poetic side could not deny the sheer rugged beauty of a paradise like this. And as Sam had also known—and somehow wanted—Tom was walking beside Melissa, sharing the scene in silent admiration. He couldn't help a glance toward big Viktor Zulowsky, and *his* attention was on Tom, where it seemed to be more often than not. The look in his eyes was predictably dark.

CHAPTER TWELVE

"The cry of a lobo drifts canyon-wide,
His eyes on his mate, and his young at his side.
Sweeping like a garden, the canyon descends,
And the sparkling stream wends and wends..."

Tom Vanse spoke from the brink of the wide canyon, staring out across the expanse and feeling as if he stood there alone. Beside him then, he heard a soft voice. "Tom! That was lovely."

Turning, Tom looked over at Melissa. "Thanks. Sometimes I wax a little poetic. Just tell me to shut up if I disturb your peace."

She frowned. "Disturb my peace! You don't know your own power. Your voice is soothing. And those words! I love poetry. Who wrote it, do you know?"

Tom rubbed his jaw, finding himself uncomfortable under the woman's scrutiny. "Well, yeah, I know. I did."

"You say that in jest! Did you really?"

"Sure, I did. All Westerners ain't total illiterate buffoons."

"I certainly didn't think they were, Tom," she said innocently, holding back a smile. "You're full of surprises, aren't you? Is that the only poem you can recite?"

Tom chuckled. "It gets pretty lonely out here in this country. You'd be surprised how long a man can spout off poetry and useless words when he spends too much time alone."

A wind whirred up the canyon and lifted the hair away from Melissa's face, and she took a deep breath and sighed. Without turning his head, Tom watched her from the corner of his eye. She was gazing down at one of the waterfalls. He too turned to look at the water, and without his thinking about it these words began to spill forth quietly:

"To serve thy generation, this thy fate:
'Written in water,' swiftly fades thy name;
But he who loves his kind does, first and late,
A work too late for fame."

Again the woman turned to him, and Tom noticed the moistness of her eyes as they searched his. "Surely you didn't write that too."

"You're testin' me, aren't you? You've heard that one."

She flushed, "Well, it does sound familiar."

"A woman named Mary Clemmer wrote it," he admitted. "I've been tryin' to figure out for years what it means."

For a few seconds, she searched his eyes, then giggled. "Oh yes! Mary Clemmer. You know what it means, Mr. Vanse! Don't you?"

"It seemed mighty perty," he said with a grin. "I never try to read too deep into anything. That makes the magic sort of fall out of it."

This time Melissa didn't speak. She just gazed out over the canyon again and swallowed hard.

*   *   *

As they continued on up the trail, Melissa Ford was silent. A little to her right and ahead of her climbed Tom Vanse—tracker, cowboy, rancher, horseman, naturalist, poet. What else was this man? She felt a flush to her neck and found herself glancing around as if expecting to catch someone watching her.

Melissa had come from New York because she loved arch-aeology. She loved the study of history, anthropology, ancient civilizations. She had also come because she was a loyal emp-loyee, admirer and friend of Professor Preston Ashcroft. Never would she have dreamed there roved a man in these vast spaces with the good looks, charm and gentle nature of Tom Vanse. He even had his own good measure of culture, even if he had never heard the word—and an *unrefined* sort of refinement.

She found herself forced to analyze her feelings. She needed to help the Professor, to be an active part of this expedition. To dig and sort and catalog, and to support her employer in whatever way he requested of her. She certainly didn't need to be twit-terpated—by Tom Vanse or anyone else. Yet this man stirred her as she had not been stirred in years.

There was something about every one of the men who had ever courted her in New York. She could never place a finger on it. They always seemed somehow either too feminine, too affect-edly masculine, too large, too small, too boring, too fawning. Melissa was thirty-five years old, and what many called an old maid, although she had been married once, a long time ago. But she refused to re-marry simply because it suited the mores of so-ciety. Melissa Ford was a woman who had to be in love to ever again agree to something as demanding as marriage. And she had never been in love in her life—including the first time she married. But she had never felt the feelings she had now—not about any-one. And here she was, in the vast West, where the men were said to be barbarians, killers, thieves, vagabonds—knaves. Tom

Vanse was none of these things. He was, outside of Pro-fessor Ashcroft, possibly the most decent and sincere man Melissa had ever known. It was not supposed to be this way. Melissa had come west to work, to dig, to discover. She had not come here to fall in love.

*   *   *

Professor Preston Ashcroft was, in most circumstances, a pragmatic man. He concerned himself with facts such as what epoch a particular tribe of Indians existed, when and why a giant circle of earth had been mounded up in some fertile valley, why one tribe of ancient American Indians was warlike while another was not. Where a leg bone or a jawbone in a grave in Ohio had come from that measured one and a half times the length of an average human being's. Other than the little bit of time he spent with his harmonica, he didn't concern himself with emotions, music or great works of fiction or poetry. He lived a practical exist-ence and did not get mixed up in the affairs of modern man.

But there had been a period of over a year now that he had not been his normal self. The past year, since first catching wind that a discovery of such magnitude as what they sought today might fall within his grasp, he had become like a child. This was, indeed, an expedition the likes of which, if it ended where he hoped it would, might not be equaled for many years—maybe ever. If the tales of this Arizona canyon were true—and he had been able to find no reason, in spite of all his attempts, to believe they were not—this expedition and its outcome were going to create a mag-nificent stir in the scientific communities of the world. And the name of Professor Preston Ashcroft would live on long after his death.

He watched his beautiful assistant now and then, and he could see the same light in her eyes that he was feeling. He was happy to know Melissa cared about this journey of discovery as deeply as he. There were times, on the train traveling out to New Mexico and Arizona Territories, when he had thought Melissa seemed bored. He had wondered if he had made a mistake dragging her out here, far from her books of poetry, her operatic concerts, her nights on the town. Yet in the last two or three days he had seen her blossom. The excitement of this quest was taking a hold of her as it had him, and that made him vastly content.

Ashcroft felt his breath coming in shallower gasps now, not because of the climb, but because... Oh, glory, they were so close! So close to something he had dreamed of, since... It seemed forever. The steps seemed to go by so slowly. His legs should have been aching with strain by now, yet his feet moved of their own accord. Quiet Wind was up ahead of them, her eyes scanning the terrain, alert. There was an excitement in her as well. An excitement in all of them. Even in those who didn't know the purpose of the expedition, although for them it was the excitement of the unknown—an excitement absorbed from the Professor, Melissa, and the others who knew what they were here to uncover.

Earthquake be cursed! He was not going to let some mere tickle in the earth keep him from the discovery he had sought for so long.

*   *   *

Sam knew when the ground began to level out, when the giant mound of apparently solid granite heaved up on their left, when Quiet Wind began to turn around and gaze back at them with her eyes full of more excitement and anticipation and... fear... than he had ever seen her show. He knew they were close. They were... Well, they were *here.* With a smile, he remembered his trip out west as a child, moving to a new land. He would ask his father if they were "there yet." His father's dry reply was always, "We'll never get 'there,' son. Even when we get to where you think is 'there,' we will always be 'here.'" It had taken him years to understand the subtle humor and the truth in that statement. One could never arrive "there." Upon arrival, "there" automatically transformed into "here".

No, they were not "there" yet. But he knew they most definitely were "here."

The trail went on past the giant wall of granite, which rose fifty feet above the trail on the left side. There were a few precarious places where one might scale that wall, in bad circumstances where getting up it was necessary. But it would not be for the weak of heart.

Then, fifty feet up, the rock began to slope off, and there some hardy, resourceful vegetation clung to it stubbornly, even some large bushes and a few stunted pines. Grass grew there in semi-abundance, and several colorful stalks of blue penstemon swayed in the wandering wind.

Quiet Wind stopped. She stared, seemingly entranced, at the wall, and her wrinkled old fingers touched it and caressed it. What Sam saw was a wall of salt and pepper granite sparkling with bits of mica, with a huge jumble of boulders and brush in profusion at its base, partially blocking the trail. Some of those boulders had to weigh five thousand pounds. He turned his eyes instinctively to Professor Ashcroft to find that most of the others were watching him as well.

The Professor and Quiet Wind were now staring at each other, and the look on the man's face Sam could only compare to that of a child on Christmas morning. He searched Quiet Wind's eyes, his hands curled into fists at his sides. He seemed to be holding his breath, as if afraid that by breathing he would break some magic spell. Sam had no idea what sort of artifacts they were after. He did not comprehend the significance of this particular place in the trail. He knew only one thing: Professor Ashcroft had undoubtedly reached one of the highest places in his life.

Like a man possessed, Professor Ashcroft came out of his trance, and with the until-this-moment hidden strength and agility of a mountain sheep he leaped up onto one of the huge boulders and stood scanning the rock wall. Suddenly, his eyes lit up, and he whirled toward the others and then pointed back at the wall, crying, "There! There it is, my friends! Glory be, there it is!"

The others, overcome with curiosity, scrambled up on the boulders beside him, all but Sam, Tom and the Mexicans. They all stood staring, and even Viktor Zulowsky, for all his tough acting, remained transfixed.

It wasn't long before Melissa turned, seeking out Tom with her eyes. She quietly, almost reverently, motioned him to join them, and he did. That was the cue for Alfredo and Juan to climb up as well, and then Sam, stoic Sam, stood alone. He had done his job—whatever that was. He had earned his keep. Now he wanted to go back home to Nadia.

Was he curious to see whatever the others were gazing at? More curious than he had been about much else, except perhaps to see what lay in the Yaqui cave—and he remembered too well where *that* curiosity had landed him.

But it was his own stubborn pride which kept him from climbing up onto the rocks with everyone else. It still rankled him that whatever artifacts the Professor sought up here were so important, so mysterious, that knowledge of them could not be trusted to everyone. For that reason, and that alone, he stayed down on the trail. Just Sam and Darkie, the brawny mule that only cared about stripping the branches from a nearby acacia tree. Darkie had long since proven that anything green to him could make a meal.

It seemed like twenty minutes, but in truth the others must only have stood up on the rocks for less than five before some of their excitement began to die. No one spoke for a time, but he could see the looks on some of their faces going from excitement and wonder to dread.

It was Viktor Zulowsky who finally spoke, with the customary unlit cigar hanging from one corner of his mouth. "Even with dynamite it's gonna take a week to blast this rock away. And what about the door, Professor? You plan on blasting it too?"

The word "door" made Sam almost curious enough to climb up and see what they were looking at, but now that he had waited this long he didn't want to seem weak by giving in. Instead, he pulled out the makings and rolled himself a cigarette, which he put between his lips and promptly forgot to light.

After a few more seconds, Tom turned around and looked at him. Tom wasn't the begging kind, but the look in his eyes said he really wanted Sam to see what they had found. "You really oughtta see this, Sam. I got a feelin' you're seein' the beginnings of history bein' made."

Sam sighed. If he was going to climb the rocks, the time had come. Tom's invitation would let him save face and still satisfy his curiosity. With one last glance at Darkie, the last holdout, he climbed up onto the flattest-topped boulder he could find. His eyes fell as if by magic on the wooden door.

It was in reality only one piece of a wooden door, a door whose top was rounded, reinforced by a hammered iron strap, of which he could see only a few inches. The door appeared to be of oak, and if he was any judge it was quite old—ancient, even. He didn't know how tall or how wide it was because it was almost completely hidden by the rocks that appeared to have either fallen from the cliff above or been carried or rolled here by many hands.

One by one, everyone began to jump down from the rocks, and most of them sat down in one place or another around the big rock face. Sam dropped down, too, and after a minute or so only the Professor and Quiet Wind were left standing on the rocks. Both of them stared in wonder at what showed of the wooden door. And oddly, neither of them seemed to have lost the slightest bit of their excitement, even in the face of the giant task that awaited them of moving all those tons of rock.

There must indeed be some marvelous secret behind that door, within that ungiving mountain. Sam wondered if the Professor would tell everyone about it now. He certainly didn't intend on lowering himself to ask again.

He looked back up at the Professor and Quiet Wind. Both of them stood there like lost children who had finally found their home. The Professor's eyes actually shone with wetness, and as for Quiet Wind, tears had made streams down her dusky cheeks.

*   *   *

Dowdy Ross made a little fire not far out from the rock wall and took off Darkie's pack to extract a coffee pot, grounds and some water. Before very long, the huge pot was spouting steam, and the ex-cavalryman looked around at the others, all slumped in various positions about his fire, some having found shade from the sun by sitting against the rocks. "Anybody for some java?"

With a quick look around, Alfredo Sanchez smiled and said, "Sí. Coffee for me, por favor, señor."

Ross gave one of his little smiles and poured the old Mex-ican a cup full, then one for his son, who only smiled shyly in thanks. Delbert Moore and Viktor also took a cup, but no one else seemed interested.

Baron's voice broke an extended silence. "Professor Ashcroft. How long do you think until we can get to the door?"

Professor Ashcroft looked up, then glanced over at Viktor. "How long, Viktor? You're the explosives man."

Viktor knitted his brow. "A few days, maybe. It depends on how easy this rock breaks up."

A look of sickness washed over the Professor's face. The smile that displaced it seemed to Sam to be forced there. "Well. That's it then. But we are here, at least. And with all of these hands we should be able to make fast work of it."

Baron chuckled. "That's the spirit, Professor. Let's see what your hands can do." In spite of the smile on his face, Sam read a certain amount of disdain in Baron's expression toward Professor Ashcroft. It didn't take much imagination to see those two hitting heads once or twice before this whole party was over. Baron just did not have the vision for this expedition that the Professor seemed to have, and his tendency to be intolerant was sure to make him explode at Ashcroft before they had dug in those rocks for very many days.

Growing bored, Sam finally went and got a cup of coffee from Ross, who was sipping on his own. He had started to sit back down on his rock when his eyes happened to fall on the trail, and he caught his breath. Standing up, he began to walk along the trail, from the pile of scree and boulders to a point fifteen or twenty feet away. After several moments, the Professor, Tom and some of the others began to notice his strange actions.

Sam looked over at the Professor and caught his eye. "You might want to look at this."

The Professor stood and walked over. He hadn't quite reached Sam before he saw what he was looking at. His eyes stabbed along the ground, and a look of dismay washed across his face. There was a long crack, from a quarter of an inch to sometimes a full inch wide, running slant-wise along the trail. It started several feet in from where the trail fell off and dropped steeply down into the canyon. They couldn't see its beginning, for it lay under the rubble pile, but it ran downhill some forty feet. It ended at the cliff's edge, becoming just another crack in the rock. Only when studied as a whole did it seem ominous.

Sam gazed at it, then finally looked up at the Professor. "I'd like to believe that's been there a while, but I can't. See there where that bush's roots are exposed? It wasn't like that this morning. That dirt there hasn't been in the sun very long."

"So what is the significance?" the Professor asked. By the look on his face, he already knew the answer.

"The quake opened up this crack."

The Professor's eyes roved over the group, resting longest on Baron. Then he looked back at Sam. "We'll just have to hope that was the only tremor," he said bravely. He turned and looked at the pile of boulders and rubble, and then made a slow study all the way up the cliff's face to where it disappeared beyond the curve, covered by grass and precarious timber.

Without another glance down at the crack, Ashcroft turned to Viktor Zulowsky. "Shall we prepare for blasting, then?"

CHAPTER THIRTEEN

Throughout the day they blasted, big Viktor Zulowsky directing the work. Every time Sam thought of it he was bemused to think of burly Viktor as a dynamiter. He certainly wouldn't have seen the finesse for that calling in a glance, nor even a long study of the big man.

Sam and Tom, in moving stumps and boulders, had done their share of blasting, always using mud to plaster the sticks of dynamite to the sides of boulders, or in the case of the stumps simply setting the charge in a hole dug underneath. But with Viktor it was a fine art. They had to move the boulders bit by bit to keep from disturbing anything too extensively, and the big man had a perfect grasp on just how much dynamite to use each time, and exactly where the holes should be drilled to use it most effectively.

Because they were blasting in loose material, boulders that had fallen or been pushed from the ridge above to roll down in front of the big wooden door, the blasting was less scientific, the Professor explained, than had they been drilling into and blasting rock from a solid rock face. Because of this, even Viktor would use the method of plastering mud to the back sides of boulders, from time to time. But mostly, he employed either Sam, Tom, Delbert, or one of the Mexicans to hold a long, battered hand drill, while he wielded the double jack to drive the metal cylinder deep down into the rock, the other man turning the drill a quarter turn after each blow.

After a number of precisely placed holes had been drilled, Viktor would compel everyone to move off to a safe distance while he placed the various charges in the holes and capped them off, and then he would detonate the dynamite.

After each detonation, several of them would move in with shovels and start clearing out the debris, or in many cases simply pick up the now manageable hunks of stone and carry them to the edge of the chasm, where they would be rolled or tossed over.

The operation began as close to the edge of the canyon as possible, and for a while, due to the slope dip, which fortunately ran in the direction they wished the rock to be moved, there was little work involved after the blast. Most of the rock would be carried over the precipice by the blast. As soon as the charges were set off, they would move in, barely giving the dust time to clear away, and the drilling would begin again, wherever Viktor had decided the next line of charges should be placed. Then, once more, the big man would move everyone away, go in and select his charges and set them into the drill holes, insert cap and fuse, move to his own safe place and rock the mountain once more.

It was a long, tedious process, entertaining to watch for only the first several blasts, after which time it just became tough, demanding manual labor.

Throughout blasting, Viktor had to monitor the condition of the crack in the trail. He was concerned that a blast too heavy might cause the earth to continue to split, and there was no controlling the mass of boulders once that happened. The entire shelf could go off into the canyon, either at the time of the blast, or, much more unfortunately, when the workers were laboring, and unable to escape the falling away of their working surface.

Only Melissa was able to dodge the dirty, brutal work of the blasting and then clearing of debris. She asked several times if she could help, but the Professor would have none of it. Instead, he assigned her the task of walking around making sketches of the country, scratching out maps, and noting flora, fauna and geology. Everyone else, even the Professor and Baron, took their turn with the shovel and bucket.

Much of the time the Professor sent Tom along as well, and sometimes Sam, to identify difficult plants. They searched the area immediately surrounding the cave for artifacts, fossils, whatever might be of note in the journals that would accompany the reports of this dig on its future pathway through the tunnels and byways of the scientific community.

At one point in the day, Melissa came to the Professor and spoke in low tones. There was some long discussion, and after a while the Professor nodded and said something to her that made her turn and slowly start making her way back down the trail.

The conversation had drawn the attention of Sam and Tom, who were in the middle of drilling a new hole in one particularly large boulder. Tom straightened up and stretched his back, holding onto the drill, as Melissa started down the trail. "I wonder what that was all about."

"Don't know," said Sam. "Looks like she's goin' back to camp."

Without comment, Tom hailed Professor Ashcroft. "You might want to send someone with Miss Ford to keep an eye on her. We have no idea know what-all is up here."

Ashcroft turned with a notebook in hand, preoccupied. He stared at Tom for a moment, then seemed to come out of a trance and glanced back down the trail at Melissa's receding form. "Umm... No, Mr. Vanse. She requested to go alone. She is going down to the creek to bathe."

Tom felt himself flush slightly, knowing he had drawn all eyes. "Oh." He glanced over at Sam, then looked back at Ashcroft. "Well, I hope she brought a gun with her."

The Professor again continued to gaze at Tom as if deep in thought. Suddenly, he frowned and looked after the woman again. "Uhh... No, I don't think she did. But I'm certain she'll be all right." The look on his face as he turned away was not convincing. Reinforcing that notion, several minutes later when Tom glanced at the Professor again, he was looking off down the trail after Melissa. Concern filled his eyes.

Tom and Sam picked up and tossed small boulders and rubble toward the brink of the cliff for several more minutes before one that Tom threw narrowly missed his partner's head. Sam straightened up in disgust. "All right, Curly. Your mind's nowhere near here. You wanna trade places?"

Straightening out of a crouch, Tom looked at his partner, letting his hands drop to his sides. He started to make a heated reply, then stopped and sighed. He kept his response low. "You're right, Sam. Sorry. I just can't stop worryin' about Melissa. I've tried not to, but I've got a naggin' feeling."

"Well, you're not going to relax until you go down there."

The Professor had overheard them, and his voice suddenly rose above the other voices and the clatter of rocks from a bucket Viktor was dumping at the canyon's edge. "Everyone stop what you're doing for a minute."

Work ceased, and all eyes turned to the Professor. Sam drew a grimy sleeve across his wet brow.

"Melissa went down below for some privacy. She wanted to take a bath. I'd like all of you to get a quick bite to eat, and then perhaps we should go back down to camp for an hour or so and recuperate. It's been a good solid four hours of work, and I'm proud of all of you."

Finished speaking, his eyes swung to Tom, who nodded his appreciation. Back in camp, they would be much closer to the creek in case Melissa needed them. It was foolishness for them all to be so far away.

Each man and Quiet Wind ate a quick sandwich of a biscuit and salt pork that Dowdy Ross had prepared them, and then they started back down the hill with Darkie, the mule. Tom felt a huge sense of relief to be headed down closer to where Melissa might need them, but what he didn't realize was that every man there had been thinking the same thing. Melissa was the sweet-heart of the camp. None of them could live with knowing they had allowed something to happen to her.

*   *   *

Melissa Ford stopped at her tent and picked up a little carpetbag she had stowed with some clothing, some towels, a brush, and anything else a woman bathing in the middle of the Arizona high country would have use of. She removed any extra clothing from the bag, then started down the trail.

Halfway down the main trail, there was a side trail, much steeper, that branched off to the left and dropped into the canyon. For some time she stood there holding her carpetbag and studied the trail's descent. There were some type of fresh animal tracks there in the dust; she presumed them to be deer—some type of hoofed animal, to be certain. So the trail was indeed being used. It looked precarious, but if a four-legged animal could do it with no hands to catch its balance then she could too.

With that assurance, she started down. One thing was certain: the trail was made specifically because it was the fastest way off the side of the canyon down to the stream. It certainly hadn't been planned with safety in mind.

The trail looped and jagged around this way and that, snaking through brush and rocks. There were places cluttered by broken stone, and some littered with loose debris and evergreen cones. But it was no more hazardous than thousands of other mountain trails across the country, many of which Melissa had hiked herself, back in New York.

Back home, for pleasure or in association with her work, she had roamed the Catskills, the Adirondacks, the Shickshocks, the Ramapos. Then of course the famous Berkshires and the Taconic Mountains.

The country she called home had more than its share of rough terrain, although admittedly nothing like the dry, inhospitable desert mountains of Arizona. But this trail had nothing over on New York's own Shawangunks—or the "Shong-gums," as many of the locals called them. So it was with complete confidence that Melissa made the climb down, and the only incident of any significance was a close encounter with a twin-spotted rattlesnake that was so shy it just crawled away from her without even plying its tiny, four-segmented rattle. It was a much different encounter from several she had had with the fearsome timber rattlers of New York, and it made her smile to think of the comparison. Arizona was supposed to be so fierce, but no one could have proved it to her by her meeting with the shy rattlesnake.

She made it down to the creek, and for several minutes she sat there enjoying the view. Oh, but it was beautiful! Before the start of that day, she had not imagined anything in Arizona could be so wonderfully green, so lush, so full of life and nature's music. The pool that had formed at the point that the trail reached the creek was ten or fifteen feet across, and to her untrained eye probably four feet deep. The falls that gave it life rumbled over seven or eight feet from a shelf above, leaving a hollow back behind them that was almost invisible to her, full of curling mist as it was. Farther along, on the downstream side, the pool spilled over into the streamway again and stepped off down the canyon by many short spillways. All along the descent, thick moss blanketed the closer rocks, covering the true silvery gray color that lay beneath.

Just outside the roiling mint-green foam caused by the waterfall, Melissa saw a trout dart out from the far bank, take a fly that struggled on the surface, and sink back down with waving tail into the shadowed depths.

A pair of chipmunks strayed out of their rocky abodes and frolicked for a while above the trout's hiding place, then stopped and watched her, mesmerized. Frozen on boulders, their eyes bulged out, their little sides heaved in and out with breath. At last, one of them scampered away, and the other charged after it without a sound but that of its tiny claws scratching against stone.

Down the stream a little ways, where it fell off two large steps into a shaded corridor, a water ouzel landed on a rock in midstream. The little gray bird stood and watched her, his legs folding and straightening intermittently, so that he bobbed up and down. This characteristic motion had given him the nickname "dipper." After half a minute, he flitted away. Melissa smiled. How incredibly serene it was here! How alive she felt.

With a sigh, she unlatched her carpetbag and reached into it, pulling out a large, luxurious white towel to lay it across the rocks and let it warm. As hot as it seemed here right now, and hiking up the steep trail, she had experienced enough baths in the waters of mountain streams that she knew she would welcome a sun-heated towel when she came shivering out of the water.

She laid out her brush and other necessities, then took one last cautious look around before starting to remove her vestments. Due to the constraints of the Victorian Age, she was forced to unfold quite an array. Even in the mountains, away from civilized society, she was with men here, some of whom she hardly knew,

and it simply was not proper to leave behind any of the necessities. So she had to peel off her outer jacket, her blouse, a riding
skirt, riding boots and stockings. Then she took off her corset,
which she had left loose enough not to constrict her lungs as she
made her way along these steep mountain trails—a lesson she had
learned years ago.

Melissa stood now in just a frilly, cream-colored, snug-fitting
camisole, and bloomers that ended just below her knees. Otherwise, she was bare to the natural world. It was for only a few
moments, and in this state of undress she felt strangely at ease
because of the remoteness of this place.

On the edge of the rocks she stood like some kind of heron,
serene, exquisite, and very white. Her face and hands were almost
always protected from the sun, so they had little tan either, but in
comparison to her arms, exposed at the shoulder, and her calves,
they looked almost dusky.

She looked down at herself. It seemed odd to be able to stand
here like this in the middle of nowhere, with no fear of being seen,
to feel God's breezes against her flesh and through the thin cotton
of the camisole, while the sun coursed down on her. Because it
didn't matter in her Victorian world, where a woman must go
covered from throat to ankle, she had never wondered what men
would think of how she looked unclothed. If she did think of it
she would only blush. But she thought she looked good.

Perhaps it was sinful to think such things, but she felt like her
skin was still tight, even at her age, that her muscles were taut and
strong. These thoughts were nothing that would ever go beyond
her own head, but Melissa felt good about herself and the image
she portrayed. She was sad to think her young womanhood might
go completely unfulfilled. But she seemed to be in danger of it.
Her single, failed marriage, had been but brief and unfortunate,
and she had never missed that man. She was hording what was

left of her virtue for that perfect man who would sweep her off her feet. And then her mind turned of its own accord to Tom...

Taking a deep, calming breath and forcing Tom from her mind, she stepped into the bone-chilling water.

*   *   *

His teeth in places were worn nearly to the gum line. In one eye clouds had started to close in over a year ago, where the cataract had come in and seemed to worsen by the week. Now that eye was nearly sightless. Things seen through it were viewed as if through a heavy mist.

His claws were broken from too many accidental scrapes on rock, fighting ferocious foes like deer, javelina and bighorn sheep that in the prime of his life had fallen to him like babes. His tawny hide was riddled with scars, and his belly skin hung slack from age, and from too many missed meals. Recently, he had more than once lowered himself to dining on carrion. And carrion was not meant for his kind.

The large cougar lay on his right side on the rocks, sunning himself. He licked his lips and ran a huge, battered paw over an ear that was split down its middle from years ago when a younger cat had challenged him and he had been forced to defend his territory. The younger cat had come close to death before he thought better of the battle and escaped. The large cat had sat on a cliff's edge afterward, licking his wounds, surveying the ter-ritory—*his* turf.

Today was warm. The lion was lazy. But his belly was four days empty but for water. His perch overlooked the creek, and he waited there, hoping some weak prey would come for water and blunder into his path. Otherwise, the hunt had become too hard for him.

Suddenly, he heard the approach of footsteps. Sitting upright, but still not coming up on his sore paws, he perked his ears toward the creek. This was an uncommon sound—not sheep, not deer, not javelina. Made by no hoofed animal. But it was not a noise he had never heard.

Slowly, with all of the predatory instinct he had developed over years, he scanned the creekway with his good eye. Soon, his sight zeroed in on the maker of the footsteps. A "two-legged"...

Down the trail it came, a slender one of its kind covered in the strange skins he had seen two-leggeds wear. Soon, it stood on the bank, and its offensive scent rose like rotted flesh. His instincts told him to run. But his belly growled and bade him stay.

He pulled himself forward with his paws until he lay right on the very edge of his rock. The two-legged was twenty feet away; in his younger days, an easy leap. He licked his lips again. He blinked and scanned around, moving only his eyes. Usually these two-leggeds came not alone, but in pairs, or threes or fours. Sometimes many more. But there were no others, at least none who were close. His heart pounded harder. The big cat had never tasted human flesh. But here it was, so close. It rested a while, then slowly peeled off its strange skins. The big cat waited, watching the two-legged slip into the large pool. Slowly, on legs that were still powerful and deadly, he raised up. The human was only twelve feet away now. That was a leap he could still make...

*   *   *

Crooked Foot was his name. As with all Maricopa Indians, and most other tribes, he had been called many different things. There was his name of childhood, which his family had told him, but by which he had no memory of anyone calling him: Gifted Boy. He had a name from young manhood, The Rock Gatherer. He used to bring home all sorts of fancy stones, anything of bright, bold color that he could try his hand at making into tools or weapons. He was a swift lad, a brave hunter.

And then one fateful day he had put a poorly judged arrow through the hip of the cougar. It was a young cat, but strong, as cougars are. Temporarily stunned, or angered by the pain, whatever the reason, the cougar did not try to escape. It turned on The Rock Gatherer. It mauled his face, tore up his arm and chest. He was able to get his knife out and slash at the cat, and somehow he managed to sever two of its front toes. But the knife was knocked loose in the struggle. Lost.

The only thing that saved The Rock Gatherer, ironically, was a plummet off a twenty-foot embankment to the rocks below, where he shattered his left ankle. The fall saved his life, but it brought about the death of his little brother, Arms of Pine Tree.

His brother was a handsome boy, only five years old, favored by the Maricopa Cold Water band. The Rock Gatherer, twenty years old, had taken him out that morning to school him in the ways of the hunt. He showed him how to stalk a cat as a cat would stalk its own prey, then how to put an arrow through its heart. Only the one time its arrow did not go through the heart...

When The Rock Gatherer fell from the embankment, he was set free, to live. But the young cougar, still up above, turned on his brother, Arms of Pine Tree. The young boy died screaming, and The Rock Gatherer, lying below, could only listen and cry out helplessly at the murdering cat, imagining the worst. And the worst was what he found when he gathered the strength to drag himself back to the scene. Arms of Pine Tree, his innocent five-year-old brother, was torn and bloody... lifeless.

Fifteen years passed. The Rock Gatherer was no longer a part of the Maricopa Cold Water clan. Neither was he any longer The Rock Gatherer. The last shameful ceremony he went through with the Cold Water clan was really no ceremony at all. Some of the older clan leaders renamed him—for his crippled foot.

Crippled, he was no further use to the tribe as a hunter, and he had disgraced himself by causing the death of his own brother, a boy everyone else had considered too young to go on the hunt. A boy he had snuck out of camp in the early morning hours against the wishes of the man his mother had taken to her bed to replace his father, who had died of the disease of the rotting flesh after being accidentally wounded by an arrow.

The tribal leaders had shamed him with the name "Crooked Foot" and banished him forever from living with the Cold Water people. He was a detriment to the People. He could no longer serve them, and he had to go away.

Now, except for a dog he had rescued as a pup from an abandoned Apache encampment, Crooked Foot lived alone. He had the dog, and he had one other human being he associated with, although he would not have considered that man a friend. That man was harsh to him, and he hated his dog. Crooked Foot existed for one thing, which had been the case since his finding the mangled body of his beloved brother. He lived to kill the cougar with two missing toes—the toes which, to that day, still dangled from a string around his neck.

So many times in fifteen years he had been on the track of that cat. So many times it had slipped him. It grew older and older, and for many years more and more wily. And then something happened to it, and it began to weaken. Over the last year he had seen the prey it took become more and more the dregs of the animal kingdom. The cougar was losing its ability to take its pick of the herd. It was then that Crooked Foot knew—his quest would soon be over.

Earlier that morning, fortune had smiled on Crooked Foot. He and his dog had jumped the cat from a cluster of boulders. He knew the cat on sight by now, the big cat he had named Satanas— Satan, in English. The slashed ear was a dead giveaway, even if the ancient hide and huge, scarred head were not. In his crippled way, he gave chase, keeping his scarred red hound, bawling like a banshee, on a leash. He had learned to move well, although to anyone watching it would seem ungainly and without grace.

The cat had made an unfortunate jump across a creek, landing partly in a patch of shin-dagger agave. The spiny tip of one thick leaf opened up a gash on its foot, so that even when he ran only on the rocks Crooked Foot was able to follow. Now, only an hour earlier, Crooked Foot had found blood that was very fresh, and he moved in with all his hunter's care.

For over an hour he belly-crawled his way through the unforgiving Arizona terrain, inflicting pain on his torso and legs and forearms, but going on. He had trained the red dog to do the same, and it crawled beside him, hardly even panting.

When they drew near the canyon he was afraid the cougar would have gone up the far side, perhaps made a desperate leap up into the rocks where he could not follow. But when he eased his head up over the lip of a rock, there to greet his eyes was the cougar... and more...

To his complete surprise, Crooked Foot looked past the lion—*el gato malo*, the bad cat—to see a white woman. She was standing in the middle of a bubbling pool of icy water, exposed to sight from just below her neck up. Crooked Foot was stunned. First, he had never expected another human being here, and second, he would have never expected a white person—a white *woman*, no less, and a beautiful one at that.

Crooked Foot had lain one time, with one woman. It was the only time he had ever felt as if he was fulfilling the destiny for which he had been created—the destiny for which *all* people had been made by their creator, Thoshipa. Crooked Foot would never forget the feeling.

So he was not untouched by the sight of the beautiful woman, vulnerable, exposed and helpless. But there was something more important to him, after fifteen years—bringing down the cat that had killed his brother and had crippled him, scarred his face horribly, and shamed him out of the tribe of his own people.

Crooked Foot realized suddenly that he had to move. The cat was poised. He was going to spring. He had sunk so low that he was now prepared to eat human flesh. Although he had not intended it to end this way, his final arrow would be a gift to the cat. And to this woman.

Crooked Foot raised up as slowly as he dared and nocked an arrow. He brought up his bow, and because the cougar was so intent on the white woman he didn't see him. The woman had turned and risen up partway out of the water from where she must have been sitting before, and her back was to them both, so she saw no movement either. It was the time Crooked Foot had awaited for fifteen years.

The cougar bunched its legs and made to leap. Fifteen years caught up to Crooked Foot, and he thought with fear of missing this shot, of watching another human being killed by Satanas, el gato malo. Crooked Foot froze. For some reason, the arrow would not fly...

Even as he watched, the big cat sprang from its rock, hurtling into the open air ten feet over the bathing woman.

CHAPTER FOURTEEN

Crooked Foot's bow, made of mock orange, hovered at full draw.

His fingers clung to the string and the arrow.

The cougar seemed poised in mid-air. Time froze.

Crooked Foot's eyes, and instinctively his aim, and the line of the arrow, moved with the falling cat. If he loosed his arrow now it would be the most dangerous shot of his life, at least to the woman. But if he didn't, the cat would land on her. And with his nearly two hundred pounds and a drop of ten feet, even without his claws and teeth he could easily kill her.

It took no conscious thought. The arrow was lined up, and he moved it down to give it lead. His fingers relaxed, ever so gently, and then stayed there, pointing the way. His bow arm remained straight out as well, following the cat's easy arc.

He heard a warning scream, not yet realizing it was his own voice. Beside him, the red dog bayed. Startled, the woman whirled, lost her balance, and fell backward in the water. The arrow disappeared almost at the exact moment that the feline struck the water.

In the back of his mind Crooked Foot heard the ear-piercing scream from the woman. Because his instincts had taken over, he found his strong foot planted firmly on the rock, the bad foot splayed to the side, his bow arm locked and the fletching of a second arrow drawn back near his mouth. He had no recollection of even pulling the arrow from his quiver.

With a cloud of blood around its shoulders, the cougar came struggling up out of the water, ears laid back. Disconcerted, it started to paddle back around to face Crooked Foot and the dog. The woman was splashing for shore. Crooked Foot saw this in his periphery, but he never lifted his eyes from the cat.

Its face distressed, the cougar swam wildly, as if realizing too late the mistake it had made in leaping over the water. Crooked Foot's eyes locked on the animal's throat, and he loosed the arrow. This time the arrow not only disappeared, but he saw the path it left—a red, ugly slash below the cat's chin and to the left. Blood began to spurt into the water, and the cat's one good eye went even wilder. He had severed one of the arteries in its neck. It struggled for a few more desperate moments, and then it dis-appeared under the surface of the now rusty-colored water.

Crooked Foot looked up in time to see the strange white woman scramble up to the clothing she had on the bank and frantically knock everything to the ground by jerking her towel out from under it and whipping it up about her.

*   *   *

Tom Vanse and the others were descending the main trail when they heard a man's warning yell, then Melissa's frantic scream. Throwing caution aside, Tom drew his pistol and charged past camp.

He took to the treacherous side trail. He scrambled around hairpin turns, and when he could see where the trail connected below he even vaulted across the untrodden space between to shorten his path. Three times he almost turned an ankle, but that didn't slow him. Finally, he saw the place below where Melissa stood on the bank, holding a towel around her, and at the same time he glimpsed an Indian and a red, lop-eared hound dog dis-appear into some bushes on the other side of the creek.

With Viktor, Sam, Baron and the Professor close behind, Tom slid and careened dangerously down the trail, ripping a hole in the seat of his pants, bloodying his hand as he caught himself on a sharp rock. Thirty more yards... Twenty...

His boot toe caught on a rock and almost sent him head-first down the last ten steep yards of trail. As it was, he ended up rolling to a stop a little to the side of the trail, as Viktor Zulowsky lumbered on by. Getting his bearings as he stood up, Tom saw Melissa just ahead and to the left, and he saw the Indian and his dog come teetering to a stop on the far bank of the creek. He watched Viktor draw a belt knife and wade into the creek.

Melissa screamed. "Viktor, no!" He didn't hear her. She screamed it again, and Tom heard her say in a frantic voice, "He saved my life!"

Tom didn't know what this meant. All he knew was that Viktor had a knife out, he was blundering across the creek, and when he reached the Indian over there he was a dead man if someone didn't stop Viktor first. The dog was barking angrily, baring its teeth between barks. But Viktor was not deterred.

Taking a run, Tom leaped headlong off the bank and landed with his hands on Viktor's shoulders, pulling him down in the water. This was on the downstream side of the pool, and the water here was only two feet deep, but it was plenty cold. Tom and Viktor landed in a sputtering heap, Tom on his side, water almost drenching him completely. Viktor got his feet under him first and whirled to face his new challenger. By now, on the far bank, the Indian had wised up enough to draw and nock another arrow.

But he would have died before he could let it fly. Sam Coffey and Stuart Baron each stood there with a gun trained on him, and up above them Ross had also come to a stop, his rifle ready. The Indian stood no chance.

"Viktor!" Melissa screamed again as the big ex-stevedore lunged at Tom. "Stop it! He saved my life!"

Perhaps it was the frantic repetition of his name, perhaps the horrified tone in the female voice. Something finally reached

Viktor's fevered brain, and he stopped and looked around him, resembling a big grizzly bear hovering over its kill.

Melissa, having no time to be ashamed about how she was covered, stumbled down through the rocks to where Tom and Viktor had gone into the creek. She said in a calmer voice, "Viktor. Please. Listen to me. Look." She pointed toward the pool, and every eye turned that way except those of Crooked Foot. The lifeless body of the cougar was now floating on top of the pool, the water pink around it.

Looking up from where he still sat in the creek, it was like Tom was looking at a monster. He had never given thought to how big of a man Viktor really was. But here, sitting beneath him with Viktor standing at full height it created an ominous picture. Tom had a moment to contemplate how easily he might have died. Sheathing the knife and not even favoring Tom with a glance, Viktor turned and lumbered back toward the others.

Struggling up out of the water, Tom turned toward Melissa. The others were coming down to surround her. But her eyes, once they left Viktor, were on Tom. She reached out her hand to him, exposing a beautiful white arm. She took his wrist and turned his hand over to see the bloody cut. "Are you all right?"

"I'm fine, ma'am," he grunted, embarrassed. "A little wet."

To the side, Sam chuckled with relief. Then his eyes turned back to the Indian, who stood on the far side of the creek, his eyes filled with fear. The bony red dog leaned up against him, a snarl fixed on its face.

Melissa put a hand on Sam's shoulder when she saw him looking at the Indian. "I think he's a friend. That animal was trying to kill me."

When the story came out, the group turned their attention to Crooked Foot, and Melissa bade him wade across the creek. Tom, already being wet, went and dragged the cougar out onto the shore. As it was soaked with water, that was something of a chore.

The animal, from nose to the tip of its tail, was over eight feet long, and in its prime Tom had no doubt it would have weighed in excess of two hundred twenty pounds. Now it was old, blind in one eye, and too feeble to fill its belly very well. When the last merciful arrow took it down, Tom figured the cat weighed no more than two hundred ten when soaking wet.

Crooked Foot stopped before them, and the Professor, who had arrived a little later—and more carefully—than the others, smiled at him. Melissa was still standing there covered in her towel. Everyone tried not to notice.

"Our friend tells us she would have died but for you," Professor Ashcroft said to Crooked Foot in English. He immediately repeated the sentence in Spanish.

Crooked Foot smiled at him. One side of his mouth didn't come up naturally because of the mass of scarring there, but the smile seemed genuine, all the same. His bare chest was also marred by long slash marks, long since gone to scar.

"I speak *ingles*—good ingles," Crooked Foot said, grinning. "Good mission ingles from *el padre*."

Sam and Tom were both amused by the Indian's transition back and forth from Spanish to English.

"I am Professor Ashcroft," Ashcroft introduced himself. Then he went around telling the Indian everyone else's names. He had learned enough of western manners not to ask the Indian's name, and he stopped and waited expectantly.

"I am name by *Ingles* Crooked Foot. No say what my name in tongue of the People. You no could speak."

The Professor smiled at that. "Are you alone?"

"Yes, alone. No live with the People. Cold Water people my people. All gone, live in other place. Me no have people."

"We have a camp up above," said the Professor. "Would you like to come and eat?"

Crooked Foot gave his lopsided smile. "Crooked Foot eat very much, very much like big horse I am. Like good food. Much good food."

Everyone but Viktor laughed. The big man seemed still to be nursing his anger. Watching him, Sam figured it stemmed from two things. He was angry because he had not had a defendable reason to kill the Indian (an object he seemed to have come to the *Wild West* with a huge desire to accomplish), and he was angry that Tom had tackled him into the creek. Viktor was not a reasonable man when it came to his pride.

*   *   *

The Professor asked everyone to turn their backs so Melissa could get dressed. As she pulled off her soaked, now mostly clean camisole and bloomers and then put on fresh underclothing, she watched their backs with some amusement. It was a strange feeling to stand there completely unclothed watching the backs of a crowd of men whom she knew found her attractive.

Once she was dressed, and had laced up her walking shoes, she gave them the go ahead to turn around. They all turned and smiled at her, and Baron started up the steep trail. Everyone else followed, and Crooked Foot, confused, grabbed Tom's arm as he went by. "You eating what?"

"Good food," Tom said. He motioned toward Dowdy Ross. "Good cook."

Crooked Foot adamantly shook his head. "Crooked Foot no can go now." He pointed toward the dead cougar. "Must take care. Many harvests me hunt 'em."

When he understood that Crooked Foot meant he had to skin the cat, Tom hailed the Professor. "I'll stay back here with Crooked Foot 'til he's done skinnin' this cat, and then I'll be up."

The Professor seemed momentarily confused, obviously not understanding why anyone would want to skin a dead cougar. "Oh... All right," he said at last. "Meet us in camp then."

Sam also fell out of the group and came back to Tom and the Indian. Crooked Foot looked at Sam, and their eyes held for a long moment. Without speaking words, a bond seemed to form between them. "I thought I'd come back and see if there really is more than one way to skin a cat."

Tom laughed, but of course the Indian didn't get the joke. He just looked at Sam searchingly, then said, "You Injun too."

Sam was surprised. "Most folks can't tell."

"Crooked Foot tell. You good Injun. Strong. But someone tell me one time, 'Only good Injun dead Injun.' No?" He stared at Sam, and when Sam began to understand that Crooked Foot had made a joke, and the corners of his lips started to bend upward, Crooked Foot backhanded him lightly on the chest. "Funny, no? Ha! Crooked Foot make a funny laugh."

Sam and Tom both laughed. "Funny joke," agreed Sam. "Pretty funny."

Crooked Foot went to where the water-logged cougar lay warming on the creek-side rocks. He crouched, his bad leg splaying out to the side, and placed a hand over the cougar's heart. There was a long moment of silence as Tom and Sam stood watching the Indian make peace with the spirit of the cat. He had taken a life, and although they didn't understand the significance of this particular animal at the time they both knew that one must make peace with the animals he kills. This was the Indian way.

Opening up the cougar's paunch, Crooked Foot reached inside and pulled out the innards. He felt his way farther in and hooked his scarred hand around the heart, yanking it free. For a moment he looked at it, then raised it to his mouth and took a big bite out of the rubbery muscle. He held it up to Sam and Tom, but both shook their heads. "Heart tastes like the leg of a jackrabbit," Tom said.

Crooked Foot laughed and swiped at the blood on his mouth. He shrugged, then proceeded with contentment and reverence to down the entire heart himself.

The look on the Indian's now-bloody face was one of almost utter serenity as he made fast work of skinning the cat with his razor sharp knife. Then he cut out the backstraps, severed the backbone and broke it in half. He also broke free the skull, still attached inside the hide. Rolling the skull and the backstraps inside the hide, he stood and hugged it under one arm, then motioned down to the two halves of the body lying there on the rock. "Good eat. Taste like leg of white man," Crooked Foot said, looking at Tom and letting out a hearty laugh.

Grinning, Sam and Tom each picked up a half of the cougar, slung it over a shoulder, and together the three of them started up the trail.

Judging by the sun, it was somewhere around one o'clock when the earth began once more to roll over in its blankets with another violent tremor.

And Sam, Tom and Crooked Foot were still on the treacherous canyon-side.

CHAPTER FIFTEEN

Like the time before, almost as quickly as the earth began to tremble, it was over. Tom had lost his balance and went to one knee, and with his hand outstretched he steadied himself.

When nothing more happened, he lunged to his feet, staring at Sam. "I've got a bad feeling, Sam."

"*You've* got a bad feeling?" With a sour look on his face Sam looked over at Crooked Foot, whose eyes were bulging. "What about our friend?"

"I should no kill the *gato*," Crooked Foot blurted. "I should no have kill."

"Hold on," Sam soothed in his gravelly voice, taking Crooked Foot by the shoulder. "This ain't your fault, pardner."

"Sure," intoned Tom. "It's the second one. You hadn't killed that cat before the first one."

"Yes, that is true. But I was thinking of it."

Sam was intimate enough with an Indian's way of thinking to understand how superstitious they were. He decided there was no point in trying to convince Crooked Foot otherwise. He had already made up his mind that the earth's shaking was because of him. "Come on, Crooked Foot. Let's get up to our camp. Things'll be all right." But he looked over at Tom after saying this, and Tom frowned.

They reached camp ten minutes later, and Dowdy Ross had coffee going. The camp was dead silent. Dowdy sat by the fire, with Melissa on a nearby folding chair, brushing her hair silently as she looked at the ground. Viktor and Baron sat together. Baron had a plate on his lap, full of untouched food. Viktor was eating bread and beans ravenously. Alfredo and Juan Sanchez stood alone over by the horses. Quiet Wind sat cross-legged at the edge of the woods. Her arms were wrapped around her, and she rocked back and forth. Delbert Moore picked at his own piece of bread. His face was unusually pale.

Sam and Tom set the two halves of the cougar down on a tarp, and Ross looked at them mildly. "Supposed to have been a pretty popular food among the trappers. I've never ate it, myself."

"Tastes like venison," said Sam.

"We're... eating that?" asked Moore.

"Why not?" asked Sam with a shrug.

"But... Won't it poison us?"

Sam chuckled. "Why? You eat ham, don't you? Cougar's no different than pork—you just have to cook it clean through. Actually, I'd bet it's healthier than pork. Like Dowdy said, the mountain men ate it when they had the chance."

Moore found himself looking over at Viktor in dismay. The big man, with his mouth full and chewing away, just shrugged with a smug grin and clucked his tongue.

Soon, the Professor walked out of his tent, and his eyes fell on Sam and Tom and held. For a long moment, no one spoke. Then Ashcroft said, "You felt it."

"How could we not?" replied Sam. "Yes, we felt it."

"We've got to get packed up and get off this mountain," Tom said suddenly. "The quake I was in before started this way. Real slow, a couple of little quakes each one bigger than the last. Then the big one. *Real* big, Professor. Real big. We're takin' our lives in our hands here. And for what? Sam and me don't even know."

"You promised me two days," the Professor reminded Tom. "It hasn't been two."

"Maybe I'm not too sure I care what you're after," replied Tom. "Curiosity killed the cat, remember? This ain't over, Professor. It's gonna get worse."

The Professor stared at him. "Do you *know* that, Mr. Vanse? Can you honestly swear that to me?"

"Sometimes a man's got to follow his gut instincts. Mine are tellin' me to get off this mountain before we all get killed."

There was a sudden, soft voice at Tom's left elbow. "I'm staying here, Mr. Vanse."

Tom could almost feel the words coming out before they did, and they were words he feared. Melissa was going to stay. Of course she would. Tom could not see the Professor abandoning his quest, and Melissa would not leave the Professor's side. That left Tom with no choice.

Tom turned to look at Melissa, and the Professor came over and stood beside her, his way of taking a stand. They both watched him. Without a word, Tom walked over to his and Sam's tent, picked up his rifle and trudged into the woods.

Sam stayed, meeting the gaze of the Professor and Melissa. Crooked Foot, who seemed to have adopted him, stood beside him.

Sam and Melissa looked at each other for a long time. Finally, Sam cleared his throat. "I'm askin' you to treat that man gentle, ma'am. His heart runs him a lot, and he makes some fast decisions in life. We ain't talked about it, but I know him good enough to say one decision he's made is he thinks an awful lot of you. Mark my words. You decidin' to stay up here could get him killed. It could get us all killed."

With that, Sam followed Tom, and so, without a word, did Crooked Foot.

The timbered saddle where Tom, Sam and Crooked Foot wandered was smooth and easy on the feet. It was mostly pine forest, its floor carpeted with three-inch-long needles and dotted with cones. It was a healthy forest, alive with vitality, the trunks of the big trees charred with black from some long-ago fire but undaunted in spite of it. Very little deadfall marred the way. The three of them wandered for well over half an hour before coming out to a sweeping vista on the other side. The timber fell away from them, dropping down into a huge, forested bowl with green meadows sparkling here and there, some of them even larger than the ones back by their camp. Thirty yards away, two mule deer does and a fawn rose like wisps of smoke from the sun-dappled shadows downslope, looked up at the men for a few seconds, and then glided away into the underbrush.

The trio sat down in the thick, aromatic duff and studied the landscape. It was a far-reaching, beautiful country, a country completely unlike the Sonoran Desert below. Afternoon haze painted the far ridges blue, and this blue paled and paled with the distance until the farthest slopes were a bare, ragged wisp almost the color of the sky.

After a long silence, Sam drew the makings out of his vest pocket and rolled a cigarette. Without giving it any thought, he handed it to Crooked Foot, who took it gladly. "You good Injun," the Indian said with a crooked grin. He waited for Sam to light a match, then puffed on the cigarette while Sam held the match to its tip. He blew a smoke ring that sailed toward Sam before disintegrating. "I send you smoke signal." He laughed raucously. The sound even made Tom join in. Crooked Foot's sharp-witted humor and heart-felt laugh were contagious.

Sam rolled two more cigarettes, and the three of them sat and smoked for a while in silence and enjoyed the serenity of the scene without talking. Finally, Sam took in a deep breath. "I ain't never been in an earthquake, Tom. I got no idea how bad they can be. But I reckon you know I'll stay on if you do. If you decide to go down the mountain back to the ranch, we'll do that too."

"Me too," enjoined Crooked Foot with a smile. "Back to the ranch!"

Tom laughed and looked at Crooked Foot. "Who is this rascal, anyway?" he asked Sam. "You save his damn hide and now he thinks you're his master."

Crooked Foot shook his head. "No his damn hide. His *good* hide." Again, he grinned.

"Well, if it's all the same to you two," said Tom, "we'll stay on."

*   *   *

It came to seem as if Crooked Foot had been with Sam and Tom for years. He trailed them wherever they went, ate when they ate, drank when they drank. Back in camp, whenever Tom or Sam would say something even remotely funny Crooked Foot would give out with a hilarious laugh. Then he would coun-ter with a joke of his own, or else he would stop laughing, wipe his eyes, and look at one or the other of them and say, "You not funny." This, of course, would make all three of them laugh again.

In spite of their earlier scare, the camp returned to a state of outward normalcy within a couple of hours. It was late afternoon when the Professor suggested that they go back up the mountain. Since everyone was bored hanging around in camp, they all trooped up the trail with him, except for Dowdy Ross, who stayed behind to tidy up camp and start supper.

Sam, Tom and Crooked Foot, along with a word of encour-agement from Alfredo, had convinced Ross to serve stewed cou-gar that evening. It was a treat most city folks would never expe-rience and one that the many trappers they had men-tioned earlier claimed was the best tasting meat in existence, or at least one of them. The danger lay in not cooking it long enough, for if jerked or cooked improperly it had been known to sicken, and even to kill. No different from pork, one of humankind's mainstays.

Up once more by the cave, Crooked Foot watched the exca-vation proceedings with great interest. Viktor had chewed his ci-gar down to a nub, and he went to pull out another one. When he caught Crooked Foot looking at him with longing, he stood there just for a moment, then held out the spit-moistened nub of cigar. Although not very many men would have appreciated the gesture, Crooked Foot accepted it as a friendly offering, and he took it from Viktor and put it in his mouth. He sucked air in through the wet tobacco fibers and smiled broadly. "Nice big fat man cee-gar," he said. Stuart Baron, who was standing nearby, got a good laugh out of that.

By the end of the day, they had caught the scent of a remote cook fire several times, and everyone's stomachs were growling. Over the western horizon the sky turned pale purple-gray, and a far-reaching wash of yellow gold fingered outward like splattered paint above it. The few thicker tufts of cloud that sailed in front of the palette looked like mighty orange galleons.

"Let's all go down and get something to eat," suggested the Professor. "Tomorrow we can move the rest of this rock."

There was little reply to the Professor's comment, but none against it. With aching backs, hands and knees, they picked up whatever they thought they might need of their tools and trooped back down the trail.

*   *   *

The next morning they were up early, but it was impossible to beat Dowdy Ross out of bed. He had biscuits and cougar gravy waiting, with stewed tomatoes and cougar backstrap steaks. Breakfasts didn't come much more delicious and filling. The cougar meat tasted much like venison, but milder, and paler in color, and even Melissa ate some of it, although the thought of eating cat didn't seem to set too well with her.

They returned to their exhausting job at the cave entrance, and Sam and Tom found themselves getting more and more intensely curious as to what they would find inside. The morning's first blast seemed to move a few hundred pounds of rock, more than any charge Viktor had set off yet, but it made more slide off from above the cave as well.

They were now working much closer to the cave, as their work the day before had cleared a wide swath from the edge of the canyon rim. So Viktor had to use much smaller charges to lessen the danger of damaging the door. It went that way for the first three blasts, with rock sliding down to replace what was blasted away, and then slowly they started to gain. But by noon they could see it was going to take at least another full day or two of work before they could even think of getting access behind the door. The hardest part, naturally, was clearing the rock and debris that had been blasted loose. Carrying buckets full of rock, gravel and dirt, and lugging boulders that sometimes weighed upwards of a hundred pounds was no easy chore, not even for men as work-hardened as Sam and Tom.

It was in the middle of the afternoon when one particularly effective blast opened up a bit more of the large oaken door to view, and everyone crowded up on the rocks to see if they could get a better look. The only one standing on the ground was Sam, who wanted nothing to do with the crowd on the rock and was still stubborn about showing his curiosity, since the Professor had not relented and told him and Tom anything. But even Crooked Foot clambered up on the rocks to try and see what could be viewed of the ancient door.

It started with a tiny bit of a rumble—softer and more subtle by far than the blasting that had assaulted them off and on all day. A few pebbles and some dust rolled off the mountain and filtered down around those standing on the rocks. Everyone turned to look at each other, unsure if they had really felt the rocks tremble beneath their feet as they thought they had.

Then, with a vengeance, the world seemed to come apart around them. The trail started shaking, and all up and down the canyon could be heard popping noises louder than cannon fire.

Dust swirled skyward, and trees shook and tore loose from their moorings. Rocks cracked and severed, huge boulders tumbling here and there, some right past them on the trail.

It seemed twenty seconds, although in truth it was probably no more than five, that everyone stood on the pile of rubble and stared around them, striving to keep their footing.

"Get off those rocks!" Sam roared. His voice could barely be heard over the tumult of the canyon. He had no more than spoken when Tom started grabbing the others and shoving them toward the trail. The Professor leaped off and made to run back downhill toward camp, but then he gathered his senses and whirled again.

"Melissa!" He raised his hands to the woman. She tried to jump to him, but the earth buckled and surged, and she fell to the side. Luckily, between the Professor and Sam they kept her from hitting the rocks. Crooked Foot came off the pile of rubble next as it shook like marbles in a jar. He landed on his knees and rolled over, coming up surprisingly fast and nearly being knocked over again as Viktor made the jump. Baron's feet went out from under him, and he slid down onto the trail as the rumble got louder and the earth shook harder.

Now sizeable boulders were crashing and rolling down the mountain from above. Delbert Moore, who had been on the far side of the rock pile, could not get to his feet. Several huge stones roared past him, then on down into the canyon into an ever-growing swirl of thick gray dust, like mist from a tremendous cascade of water.

Suddenly, there was a loud explosion immediate to them. The crack that had started forming in the trail after the first tremor gave way. The escarpment seemed to hover there just for a moment, one massive wall of stone, dust and shrubs, and then it tipped toward the canyon and broke into thousands of separate chunks, making a noise louder than thunder. The rubble pile, no longer supported by that section of the trail, shuddered, and then the bottom dropped out of it. Moore, caught in the middle of it, started to slide off into the canyon with it.

There were now large rocks hurtling and rolling down off the mountain in droves, bouncing here and there, and now and then a tree broke loose from the rocky mountainside and slid partway down before coming to a halt. Delbert Moore started to go over, but there was one man there to save him—Crooked Foot!

The Indian, although terrified himself, had clambered back up onto the rock pile, and he was leaning over a large boulder on the far side of the rocks, where the trail had broken free and completely tumbled into the canyon bottom in a hurricane of dust and sand. Hanging there precariously, he clung to Moore by his coat!

CHAPTER SIXTEEN

Tom and Sam saw the two men's dilemma and scrambled up onto the rock pile, clawing their way over to Crooked Foot and the hapless Moore. Sam reached him in time to grab one flailing arm, and Tom clutched Sam. Together they heaved. The moment Moore found a hold on the boulder, he took it, then rolled over onto the top of the heap. The earth was still shaking, and they heard a loud crack above and looked up to see a huge ponderosa fall and break right in half, sliding down the sheer rock.

With the renewed energy of madmen, the foursome made a scrambling dash for the trail and dove off onto the hardpan. The ground stopped shaking as suddenly as if someone had turned off a switch. But debris was still tumbling down the slopes from above. The two halves of the ponderosa finally slid all the way down, struck the debris pile, and then toppled over and continued with a roar over the brink of the canyon. The four men were left alone here. They had been deserted in the midst of the quake—except for one man. Viktor Zulowsky.

The big man roared at them to get moving, and as Delbert Moore ran and Crooked Foot limped by, Viktor motioned almost angrily at Sam and Tom. "Come on! Get down the trail!"

In spite of Viktor's tone of voice, there was no time or reason for anger, and Tom and Sam did exactly as Viktor ordered. Watching leerily up the slope, they had to dodge some dislodged tree or a rock now and then, but without further serious incident they made their way back down into camp.

The world had gone dark. Like plumes of volcanic ash, dust vomited tan, brown and purplish gray out of the canyon's depths. Beyond their own world, which was this very canyon, more dust and several dense black clouds rose everywhere. The darker clouds appeared to be smoke—the smoke of wildfires. Everyone huddled in the center of camp, and there were a few trees down, one ponderosa across Sam and Tom's tent. Its huge root system had torn a hole in the ground big enough to serve as a grave for the entire group.

The cracking and popping up and down the canyon continued, the sound of rocks and canyon walls adjusting themselves in the aftermath of the quake. No one spoke. Melissa's face was white, and on the cheeks of Moore there was a wash of tears. Crooked Foot's dog, which had been wandering aimlessly, exploring the forest, was now huddled, shaking, against its master, its tail firmly between its legs. Its eyes showed white and darted all around. Some of the eyes of the others showed white as well.

Viktor knelt there doubled over, looking around with his teeth clenched, his eyes wild, as if waiting for the next storm to hit.

But the storm—for now—was gone.

*   *   *

Dowdy Ross managed to gather up enough of his tumbled down camp to prepare supper for the others, and by late evening, in a most subdued voice, he called them to the fire. They went in just as subdued a manner as he had bade them. The red hound was still slinking, hanging as if glued there to the side of Crooked Foot's leg.

From their tent, Sam and Tom had been able to salvage most of their belongings. They had been lucky enough that the tree fell to one side. Unfortunately, that was the side where Tom's rifle had been. Over the next few days he planned to saw at the big tree, trying to break it down to manageable pieces, but he had no idea what would be left of his rifle when he was finally able to free it.

Sam and Tom squatted or sat cross-legged on the ground with Crooked Foot and the Mexicans. The rest of them sat in their camp chairs. No one spoke, at least not at length. They each sat nursing coffee—some laced with "medicinal" whisky—spooning beef or cougar and beans into their mouths, chewing without looking at each other.

Dust continued to loom all around them like a heavy, un-breaking mist. It settled in their hair, on their clothes, in their food, as bad as any cattle drive Tom and Sam had ever experienced.

Beyond the bottom of the canyon, they could see two or three fires burning in different places. The Professor conjectured that they must have been caused by rocks striking together and spark-ing into dry grass. Whatever the cause, the smoke rose in ugly black and brown columns into the evening sky, and if it was like most Mays in Arizona the fires would go on and on, burning all the fuel they could reach before being extinguished by the monsoons of summer. An eerie magenta sun struggled like a bloodshot eye to glare at them through the dust and smoke of their shattered, eerie world.

Everyone had finished their bowls and set them wordlessly aside when the Professor broke the stillness. "We'll go home now."

For a moment, his voice seemed so foreign after the long silence that it was hard for each person to convince himself that it was real. In surprise, they started looking around at each other. The Professor didn't try to meet any of their eyes. He stared into the fire with a lost, empty look on his face.

"You gonna turn tail, Professor?" It was Viktor's voice, normally booming, now somewhat quieter. "Now that we're this close?"

Ashcroft stared at Viktor, and he looked back as if no one else in the camp existed.

Then Baron chimed in. "That's a good question, Professor. Will you pull out now that we've done all this work and the objective is so close?"

As if in a trance, Ashcroft's eyes slid to Baron. Then slowly they began to track their way around all the faces in the circle, which were lit by firelight made brighter by the sun's being blocked by the dust and smoke.

"Gentlemen, I don't know if you understand. You told me it might get worse, and I didn't listen. I risked all of our lives for this, and nearly got us killed. Because we have suffered a de-vastating earthquake does not mean it is over. I have read that aftershocks can be even worse. This time I'm ready to listen." He looked over at Tom for backup.

Tom shrugged. "They sure can, Professor. They sure can. But here we are. And probably most of what's going to fall already fell. You don't want to leave when you're this close. Listen to them. You'll never forgive yourself. Besides, if I judge correctly, that quake did more than half our work for us. It dumped half that rubble into the canyon."

Quiet Wind suddenly piped up. "It *will* get worse." The Professor looked over at her. Like everyone else, there was nothing but shock on his face. Quiet Wind was speaking English! "It will get worse," the old woman repeated. "Very much worse. Some will die."

"How would you know?" Viktor asked when he finally grasped the sound of Quiet Wind speaking English and collected his wits.

"The bones. I read the bones. We should not be here. The spirits are angry."

Viktor glanced around, trying to hide the discomfiture in his face. "Hell, just like Vanse said, that earthquake shook this place up so bad there's nothing left to fall."

"Nothing but us," said Quiet Wind. "I do not speak of shakes of the earth. There are other dangers here. There are those who do not want us in this place. The bones tell."

Crooked Foot looked around uncomfortably, then caught himself and looked down. He knew of one who would not want these people here. One who would be very angry to have them in "his" canyon...

"I'll send you a letter tellin' you what we find up there in that cave," said Sam suddenly.

The Professor's eyes swiveled to him. "Pardon me?"

"We'll write you all about it."

"Write me?"

"Come on! I've come too far to leave now. I wanna know what made it so important for you to drag all these people and truck clear out here from New York City and up this godforsaken mountain. You can't just walk away. If you were going to do that you should have done it when Tom suggested."

A look of dismay on the Professor's face suddenly started to fade. It finally turned to an uncertain smile, and he looked around the camp. Last of all, his eyes settled on Melissa, and he looked at her sadly, regretting most of all the terror he had put her through. "All right," he said, slapping his knee. "All right. We'll stay. And you—" he looked sternly at Quiet Wind "—this whole thing could have been much easier if you had told me you speak English."

"Don't like your tongue. Too much rules."

*   *   *

The Professor left the fire for a long time, and through the duration they could see a light glowing from his tent. It was full dark when he finally came back out. No one, even as tired as they were from the day's work and excitement, could even think of going to bed.

Professor Ashcroft took a long, speculative look around the camp, studying every face. At last, he walked slowly to the fire. "My friends. I am going to need all of your attention. We have come to a crossroads."

All eyes turned to him as he walked between Sam and Tom and moved to the far side of the fire, where everyone could see him. "There are those among you who know why we are here. You are few. The rest of you are here on faith. Faith in me, faith in science, or faith in one another. Whatever faith you have inside of you, or whatever reason you have for being here, the time has come to address what I believe we will be seeing in the morning.

"I know little of blasting, but I believe I know enough that I can surmise Mr. Zulowsky's work will be complete by mid-morning tomorrow. Much of this I judge by the fact which was pointed out to me that half of the work we had ahead of us was dumped into the gorge by the earthquake. True, Mr. Zulowsky?"

Viktor nodded. "Probably so."

"Then I feel this is the time to talk. Please bear with me, as I have quite a lot to say. I have tried to keep out all but the most salient points in what I have prepared to tell you, but there is no way to make this short.

"There are mysteries in the world that we cannot understand. Things that are so rare as to be hidden from us by nature, or by man himself. Of course you understand there are many reasons for man—specifically the government—to hide things. Perhaps he does it to protect us, to keep us from fear, feeling as if he is some kind of 'big brother' to the rest of the population. Perhaps he does it because of greed. Perhaps because he wants to keep the truth from others because he believes that in so doing, in keeping more knowledge for himself, he holds more power in life's game. As they say, 'knowledge is power'.

"What we seek in this canyon, my friends, is one of those forgotten mysteries of this world. You have perhaps seen hints of stories in newspapers in the not-too-distant past. If you have delved into any large museums, maybe you have seen artifacts that hinted at these mysteries. But nowhere that I'm aware of is there any story laid out before you that deals with what lies in this canyon, according to the knowledge of our friend Quiet Wind.

"Please understand that I do not wish to go completely out on a limb and describe to you what we believe to be hidden in that cave. If it is there, and if it is intact, that is to be left for your eyes alone to discover. You would probably think I had bats in my belfry if I came right out and told you. But I will give you some history of what we seek, and tomorrow, if—*when*—we find what we seek, you will know that it is far from the first of its kind.

"To save you from further enigma, I will jump headfirst into my account." As the Professor spoke, he took a pipe and tobacco pouch from his coat pocket, and he scooped tobacco into the bowl of the pipe and tamped it down with his forefinger. Then, holding the pipe in his left hand, he went on. "Please remember that what

I am about to tell you is not simply what I believe, but is backed by research and historical fact, including much history found in the Bible itself.

"Through science, we know that in the distant past many forms of life were much larger than they are today. Fossilized remains of plants such as ferns show them to have been gargantuan. Fossils of dragonflies with a twenty-inch wingspan have been found, as well as fossilized snails standing almost two feet tall. On the shores of our oceans, we have located shark teeth that are two and three times bigger than anything we find in sharks caught today. Flying reptiles dominated the skies in those days, like the Pterodactyl, with a sixteen- to twenty-foot wingspan. We know all this from their fossilized remains.

"We have complete skeletons of crocodiles thirty-two feet in length and turtle shells twelve feet long. And of course we all know about the dinosaurs, the largest creatures of all. More recently, we have animals such as the elephant bird, which if memory serves me stood some ten feet tall, and only in the last few centuries has disappeared from this world."

He paused, remembering his pipe, and took a match from his pocket. He struck it on his pants leg and lifted the pipe to his lips, puffing it into life as he looked about the faces around the campfire. He shook out the match and let it fall to the ground, then took the pipe once more in his left hand and resumed speaking.

"But, I digress. So much for gigantic organisms. The giants I would like to discuss with you walked on two feet, and for the most part looked like you and I." He caught a couple of confused looks and headed them off. "Please hear me out before you pass judgment. I know what I am saying will sound far-fetched to you, but give me a chance. As I was saying... Of course these giants were much bigger and stronger than we are, and in some cases looked different because some of them had six toes on each foot and six fingers on each hand. Some had two rows of teeth instead of one."

Sam shot a glance over at Tom, and Tom felt it and looked back. Sam could see the doubt in his partner's eyes, but he himself was not yet ready to scoff. Living with the Tarahumaras, in one of the wildest parts of deep Mexico, he had heard plenty of strange things in his younger days. He would give the Professor time to back up all he was saying.

"Perhaps for a moment I should revert to more familiar ground. We have all heard the story of David and the giant he slew, named Goliath, who was over nine feet tall and had brothers who were also giants. There were, as a matter of fact, many others." The Professor took in a deep breath, and then, using a notebook now and then for reference, he began working his way through an impressive count of documented cases of known giants throughout the history of the world.

He spoke of King Og, of Bashan, who was reportedly twelve to fourteen feet tall, and was famous for a huge iron bed he slept in that was later on display for many years in a museum in the Middle East. King Og also had sons similar in size. He himself was not only great in stature, but was reportedly well-formed, quite handsome, and intelligent. He ruled over sixty highly fortified cities of giants, and a number of smaller ones. His people and his warriors were mostly Amorites.

He referred to scripture, specifically a King Sihon who was *not* therein referred to as a giant but claimed to be such in ancient rabbinical records, where it was told that he was King Og's brother.

The professor looked about the group. No one there seemed ready yet to speak, and he went on.

"It was said that their grandfather, Shamhazah, was a fallen angel. These angels took the daughters of men to wife, and their progeny were giants, thereafter referred to as Nephilim or 'Rephaim,' which means literally giants. King Sihon ruled over many vassal kingdoms, cities and towns in the land of Canaan. Between the two giant kings they ruled over a land of giants who were observed when Joshua, Caleb and ten men crossed over into the Promised Land to reconnoiter, see who lived there and how difficult they would be to defeat. When they returned they reported that the land was full of giants that made them feel like grasshoppers.

"I hope I'm not overwhelming any of you," said Professor Ashcroft, looking around. "I know some of you will have more patience for this type of diatribe than others, but the last part is what I really want you to hear, and I think if you'll hear me out the rest will be of interest to you as well."

Sam looked over and caught Stuart Baron yawning. He just smiled. Of course Baron would have to show everyone how "above the rest of them" he was. To Sam, it didn't get much more interesting than what he was hearing, whether it played out to be true or not.

The Professor smiled, his enthusiasm for this subject obviously strong. He told of a ruler named Chedorlaomer and his Babylonian cohorts who had raided some four hundred years before Moses's time, and slew many of the Emim, Anakim, Horim, Zamzumim, and other Rephaim, and wasted their cities. He recounted how descendants of Lot and Esau invaded and defeated other giants, which left the trans-Jordan countries' control by the giants forever broken. After this, they still had to defeat the well-known cities of the giants such as Edom, Moab, Gilied, and Basham, on their way to Jericho.

After speaking more at length of King Og and his associates, and their defeat, the Professor sipped deep of his pipe, then said, "There were European giants as well, and even to this day they exist, but in small numbers, whereas they were numerous in the past. They are not so great in stature, though still very impressive.

There is so much proof of the existence of giants in Europe's past. Historical facts, paintings depicting giants on the walls of ancient caves, writing, carvings and legends in stone. Graves with complete skeletons, some still in armor, and buried with their weapons."

Professor Ashcroft began to puff on his pipe again. Its aromatic smoke had drifted throughout the camp, permeating it with a mild, pleasant smell. He seemed lost in thought, as if sim-ply enjoying the taste of the pipe smoke. But of a sudden he plucked it from between his teeth, smiled and said. "Please for-give me if I get carried away. I'll try to get more specific.

"One thing that explorers and navigators like Cortez, Coronado, de Soto, de Gama, Magellan, and Captain Cook, to name a few, had in common was sightings and actual encounters such as battles and business dealings with giants throughout the world. Some of the South Pacific Islands and the Americas will be our main consideration at this point. In 1519, the Spaniards, led by Alvarez de Piheda, explored the Texas coastline. They found the heavily tattooed, painted, and pierced nomadic Indians called the Karankawa. They held the Barrier Islands of the Texas coast. Their territory ranged from Galveston to the mouth of the Rio Grande and some miles inland. The Karankawa were superb hunters and fishermen, fierce warriors with six-foot bows and three-foot arrows and they stood about seven feet tall on the average. They were cannibalistic and powerful enemies to anyone trying to take their land away. In later years, disease, wars with the Comanche and other Indians, and land acquisition by newcomers began to bring them close to extinction. They were almost totally killed off by ranchers and the army.

"Before that, around 1542, about the time of the de Soto and Coronado expeditions, a boy by the name of Diego Duran and his family moved to Mexico, where he grew up and became a missionary among the Indians. Duran is a recognized authority on the history, culture, and language of the Mexican people. He was be-friended by, taught and shown many things by the Aztec In-dians, especially concerning the giants. He learned how to read the picture writing, manuscripts and native hieroglyphics. And in these writings was endless proof of the existence of giants in our continent. In Duran's journals he mentioned several occasions where he made contact with giant Indians.

"Bernardino de Sahagun, and Joseph de Acosta, two other respected historians of about the same period, also knew about a tribe of giants who once occupied central Mexico. But Duran's writings offer the best, most complete information on the subject.

"Now back to the Aztecs. Members of this tribe tell that at one time giants and a bestial people of normal size inhabited Mexico. Then in 900 A. D. six tribes from Teogol-Huacan—or the northeast—came to Mexico and settled there. They found two kinds of people west of the snow-covered mountains: The Chichimemecs, meaning hunters, were of normal size and lived a harsh, brutal existence in the mountains. They were unorganized as a people and lived like savages, often going naked like the animals they hunted.

"To the east were the Puebla and the Cholula, and they were called the Quiname, or 'men of great stature.' These giants were found in Tlaxcala, Cholula, and Huexotzinco. They were enraged at having their lands invaded, and many battles were fought over territory. Incidentally, according to the Aztecs, these giants also lived a bestial lifestyle and had their own abominable customs, such as often eating their meat raw on hunts.

"You might find yourselves asking how the invaders defeated the giants. Often it was through the use of guile and deceit, not strength in battle. They would invite them to a banquet; steal their weapons and then ambush them.

"The giants were said to be brave and valiant fighters, and they would fight back with tree branches or whatever they could find, but inevitably they were killed. According to Duran, they were pursued relentlessly and when there was no other recourse they would fling themselves off of cliffs. At last, they were killed off or chased out of the country. Although his personal contacts with giants were few, he had been personally present a number of times when the remains of giants were dug up, and the bones were enormous.

"I can go on and on about this subject—perhaps you can tell." The Professor gave a sheepish grin and glanced down at his notes. "But briefly, in the year 1519, Alonzo de Pineda encountered some giants on the banks of the Mississippi River close to the Gulf of Mexico. In the year of 1800, in the state of Ohio, a man named Aaron Wright, a farmer, discovered the bones of a race of men far larger than our own. There were skulls among those he discovered into whose cavities the entire head of one of us could be placed. There were jawbones that could be situated over my entire face. And the arm and leg bones were correspondingly large. These giants are known now as the Conneaut Giants.

"Then, once more in Ohio, in Seneca Township, another mound was unearthed, revealing three skeletons around eight feet tall. In 1829, and yes, again in Ohio, they found a skull that was larger than any other and with more teeth in it than the white race of today. I could speak to you of Shoshone legends from Idaho Territory, or of true, or assumed-to-be-true legends from many other countries of the world. But from what I've told you I think you can already begin to see.

"One of the more remarkable pieces of research I've found is the giant unearthed in California in 1833. This skeleton was twelve feet tall, my friends. *Twelve feet tall!* And to add a strange note, as I mentioned earlier, he had a double row of teeth on both top and bottom. I myself have met men of monstrous stature on this continent. One such was an Indian at least three feet taller than his contemporaries.

"The most recent account of which I'm aware is of a man from Kentucky, a man by the name of Martin Van Buren Bates. This man stopped growing at the age of twenty-eight, when he stood seven feet eight inches tall and weighed four hundred seventy pounds. What's more remarkable is that in his travels he met a Scottish woman who stood seven feet *eleven* inches tall, and the two were eventually wed, in 1871.

"What I'm trying to point out in all my rambling, and I could go on with much more in-depth detail than I have, is that giants have existed, from the Old Testament, to Indian legend, to burial grounds in the east, and even today. Gentlemen, that brings me to the purpose of our expedition: to find evidence of the recent existence in the Territory of Arizona of a now-vanished race of giants."

*   *   *

Tom and Sam sat on the edge of the canyon trail and gazed out over the black maw. Above them, between the canyon walls, a dazzling smear of heavenly bodies lit the sky like moonlit dust. There was no moon tonight, at least not one in sight. The partners sat there and pondered the heavens and let the Professor's words sink in. They were amazed that any stars were in sight considering all the dust and smoke that still hung in the air down low.

After Ashcroft's speech had ended, they had sat for a long time around the fire. No one spoke. It was obvious that those who had known what they were up here for were watching the others to gage their reactions. Tom and Sam were old hands at poker, skilled enough that they didn't think their faces gave any of their thoughts away. Alfredo and Juan Sanchez and Viktor Zulowsky were another story. And no one could have blamed them for the astonished stares they gave the Professor.

Tom and Sam had excused themselves not too much later and made their way down the broken, rock-covered trail. The earthquake had damaged it, but not nearly to the extent that it could have—and not nearly as much as it had destroyed the trail leading up to the cave. Here, it had left more in the way of debris than actual damage. They found no major breaks along the five hundred yards they hiked.

Tom and Sam sat there on the trail for half an hour before either spoke. It was Tom who broke the stillness.

"I don't know whether to slap myself or the Professor."

Sam looked over. He couldn't see much detail of his partner's face by the starlight. "Don't get hasty, Tom."

"Hasty?"

"Yeah, hasty. Remember, I lived with the Tarahumaras in Mexico for a while. I've heard this kind of story for years—especially about the Karankawa Indians. Some of 'em are pretty far-fetched. But there are some others that have a ring of truth to 'em."

"So we're s'posed to *believe* him?"

Sam stared through the darkness at his lifelong partner. "Believe him? No, Tom, you don't have to believe nothin'. All you gotta do is wait 'til tomorrow."

*   *   *

No one slept very much that night, each for his own reasons. Excitement, fear, curiosity, uncertainty—some felt a mixture of all these emotions. Even Sam, the infamous late sleeper, was up well before daylight, and they all sat around a sputtering fire as they waited for Dowdy Ross to declare breakfast ready.

As for Ross, it wasn't much work. He simply made up a brown cornmeal gruel, his pan big enough to serve five of them at a time. To make the gruel, he heated bacon grease to the point of smoking, then stirred cornmeal into it. Last, when it turned brown, he poured in canned milk and molasses. Sam and Tom were among the last five to eat. They were old proponents of gruel, but this morning their thoughts were on things of much vaster consequence than breakfast.

As the Professor had so aptly put it around the campfire the night before, everyone was now waiting to see if he had bats in his belfry.

Gray light washed over the mountaintops as Tom stood beside Sam watching him throw a crossbuck saddle on Darkie, the bay mule. It was all Tom could do to keep his own hands still. His heart thudded ponderously. No one spoke. Other than the clink of a coffee cup or a tin plate now and then, or someone coughing or blowing their nose, or the sounds of the stock, it was a silent camp. Outside of camp there were the tentative songs of birds, coming out of hiding to survey by the light of the new day the damage the earthquake had done to their home. A pica chirped from the rocks down the canyon side, and a hawk whistled from the trees above them. Several times he stretched his wings as if to fly, then settled back, folded them in place, and continued nervously to survey his world, jerking his head back and forth.

The Maricopa, Crooked Foot, was still with them, and the red hound slunk around camp looking at these new people, sniffing them out, trying to figure each of them out by their scent. Once, he got too close to Baron, and the businessman kicked at him and narrowly missed. Watching, Viktor frowned. He had once had a dog like that himself. Why did a man have to kick at it? It was only doing what God—or whoever had made dogs—wanted it to do. As much as he looked up to and admired Baron, he dis-approved of a man being cruel to an innocent dog.

The Professor started directing Delbert Moore, Melissa, Viktor and the others as to what he would need in the mule's packs, and tied on top of them. As light grew, everyone in camp spent a lot of time looking up toward the cave. Tom knew they were all wondering the same thing he was: How much was left of the trail? Could they even reach the cave now? It was because of this that they had decided to take only mules up the trail. If it had been badly damaged, a mule could be trusted to use its head and cautiously pick its way. A horse, on the other hand, was more likely to panic and end up at the bottom of the canyon—along with whoever got in its way.

Sam sucked down the diamond hitch over Darkie's packs as tight as he could get it, then cinched it up and tied off. Turning, he met the Professor's eyes. "The pot's full, Professor. Let's go see the cards."

Professor Ashcroft drew in a deep breath. He held Sam's eyes for some time, both knowing everyone else was watching them. His eyes swung to the trail, then made the slow visual climb as far up it as he could. At last, he blew out his breath and swept the group with a nervous glance. His hands were starting to shake. "Let's go, people." His last glance fell on Melissa, and her smile was filled with hope.

Along the way, boulders and trees partially blocked the trail. Some of the trees the mules could leap, but with others they had to stop and use their crosscut and bow saws and then roll them out of the way. They kept them on the trail rather than throw them over the brink in case they needed them for firewood later.

But it was more than tree cutting which made this climb longer than any of the others. The suspense in all of them had reached fever pitch. Tom pictured the big cave door. What was on the other side? Nothing, maybe. But what if the Professor was right? He wondered if it would be some kind of big old artifacts. Some big spoons or knives or bowls. Maybe it would be a big pair of old sandals or a spear too long for a normal man to wield. Then again the thought came to him: What if it was nothing? Then how horrible it would be for the Professor. He had hidden his emotions for most of the trip, like a veteran card player lacking only one card to fill a royal flush. But today he couldn't hide his expect- ations, his anticipation—his worry. Today was the day he would either justify his trip from New York or go home an empty man. It must be a horrible burden.

It took forty-five minutes longer than before to reach the cave, for they made a point of clearing what debris they could on the way up. There were two sections of the trail where the earth and rocks had given way, leaving the trail sometimes less than a foot and a half wide—a width that would have been uncomfortable at best if they had been mounted. At least the earth that remained seemed intact. Their biggest chore was to saw through two gigantic trees and push a number of boulders weighing fifty to four or five hundred pounds over the side of the canyon.

In spite of the obstacles the earthquake had handed them, they reached the cave to remark once again how in a sense the earthquake had been their friend. In its radical shaking it had broken loose the bad section of the slope, sending it in fragments down into the canyon bottom. What it had left there was a sheer escarpment of solid rock that dropped for one hundred twenty feet or more before meeting a steep slope of scree and broken vegetation. The break had taken with it easily nine tenths of the rubble pile, the boulders and broken logs that had blocked the entrance to the cave. There was perhaps a ton of broken material yet to be moved, but little more. Then whatever was on the other side of the door would be the Professor's to discover.

They all stood in awe, staring up at the mountainside, which had been scoured by falling rocks and trees. It loomed above them, bold and magnificent, still clutching onto some of the pines whose seeds had fallen into cracks to plant themselves, and whose roots had year by year split the rock face farther apart. The cave entrance was revealed there, in part. Now that the rocks had been swept away down into the canyon it was plain that what had appeared to be soot stains on the top part of the oak door were caused by a fire that had burned against much of the lower part. The bottom two thirds of the door, or at least what could be seen, were charred deeply, and only the covering of rocks had most likely kept it from rotting away. There were two windows to the sides of the door, and these appeared to have been somehow drilled out by whoever had lived here. Ominously, now that much of the rock pile had been cleared, it appeared that the tops of the windows and door both stood roughly eight feet tall.

Sam and Tom looked at each other. Melissa reached up and squeezed the back of the Professor's arm. Everyone else just stared. No one had missed the significance of the door and window height.

It was almost with reverence that Viktor conducted his blasting that day. An explosion would sound, tearing boulders into moveable fragments and sending some of them over the sheer edge of the new cliff, which now was only a dangerous ten feet from the entrance to the cave. The blast would be followed by a torrent of dust in the air, and the rattle of gravel—nothing more. No one spoke.

As the last of the rock was cleared by hand, and the Professor stood back and watched Viktor Zulowsky standing up to hoist a hundred-pound boulder, he saw the top of the doorway three feet over Viktor's head. Now that the rock on the trail had been cleared, it was plain they had misjudged the height of the doorway, for in reality it was nine, not eight feet at its top. But it wasn't that which was most impressive. A cave opening would be just as high as it would be; whoever chose to live there would have no bearing on that and would have built the door to fit. What seemed portentous was the fact that both windows were just as tall, and the bottom of each was at least seven feet off the trail. The Professor swallowed hard. It was almost too much to contemplate. How tall had these people been?

Professor Ashcroft turned about, eyes wide, face pale. He looked at the others. His words came slow, almost breathlessly. "I would like to take two people inside with me. Mister Baron?" Then turning, he reached his hand out to Melissa. Her eyes alight with wonder and a touch of fear, she took that hand and turned to seek out Tom's glance. He smiled and gave her an approving nod.

"A lantern," said the Professor. Viktor was the first to react, and he picked up the big lantern they had set near the side of the cave earlier, in anticipation. Viktor plucked a match from his vest pocket, struck it on the mountain wall, and let its flame lick hungrily on the lantern's wick as he pulled off the chimney. Re-placing the chimney, he handed the lantern to Ashcroft, trying to look nonchalant. Tom noticed that his big hand was shaking. Deep inside, he wasn't much tougher than anyone else.

It took a little cranking on the door's big, rusted iron handle to budge it. Then, thanks to rock still on the trail, it would only open two or three feet. But for now that was enough.

Professor Ashcroft turned to Baron. He still held onto Melissa's hand. "Shall we?"

Holding the lantern out before him, the Professor stepped beyond the portal of his familiar existence into an age of the past...

CHAPTER SEVENTEEN

For those who waited outside the cave of mystery, time seemed to hang. They stood staring, once in a while casting each other anxious glances. Sam Coffey not only seemed to hear his own pulse, but that of everyone around him. It brought him back to another breathless time, to those moments outside the hidden cave of the Yaquis, deep in the Bacatete Mountains, just before he and Tom made the discovery of their lifetimes.

Maybe Tom was thinking the same thing, for he looked over at Sam, and their eyes held. Inside the cave, for the first time, they began to hear muffled voices, startled utterances, hushed oaths. Once, Sam even heard Melissa speak God's name, which he had never heard her say before. Then, for what seemed like a long, long time, there was silence. Sam could hear a distant ringing inside his head, but no voices, neither in nor out. His blood pounded against his temples so hard he thought his hat must appear to be pulsating. He took the hat off and swept his brow with his sleeve. No one dared break the breathless silence.

Then suddenly the door creaked back open, and Baron walked out into the dusty sunlight. He moved like he was in a trance. Melissa came behind him. It struck Sam as very odd that she didn't look at anyone, not even Tom. Last of all the Professor stepped out. He stood in the slightly open doorway, his hand on the edge of the door, staring dumbly about him, at everyone, but at no one at all. He seemed to have been holding his breath for quite a while, for it came out now in a gush, and he shuttled his eyes this way and that, as if trying to get his bearings.

Viktor Zulowsky stood closest to the door, gazing at the Professor as he waited for some kind of word. Ashcroft's hand came up and grasped Viktor's muscular arm, and he looked up and up until their eyes met. "My dear Lord, Viktor. My dear Lord," he said in a voice of awe. It struck Sam that he had never heard Ashcroft call Viktor by his given name.

Viktor cast a look around at the others who had not yet been in the cave, then dropped his eyes back to the Professor. "Can we go in?"

The Professor raised his eyes slowly. "Uhh... Why, yes, Mr. Zulowsky, I suppose you can. Yes... Yes!"

He looked around him at the others, just then seeming to begin gathering his faculties. "For heaven's sake!" he cried. "Everyone. Everyone! Gather here. Gather here, friends."

His eyes jumped about the group willy-nilly. He seemed about to fly away, in his excitement. "You all must see this. Oh, heaven, but you all must. You will never see the like of it again in this lifetime—maybe not in a dozen lifetimes! But I must ask you to come two at a time, and follow in my footsteps. Please step lightly. *Please.* And touch nothing. The time has not come for that. Viktor? Delbert? Come with me."

Tom felt his heart sink. He wanted to go in. He wanted to go now! But each must take his turn. That, he understood.

Turning with the lantern in his hand, Professor Ashcroft shoved at the door. It didn't open any farther than it had before, but he shouldered his way through. Viktor was the first in behind him, then Delbert Moore. After ten or twenty seconds Sam heard Viktor swear in disbelief. In a few more minutes, he heard Viktor's disquieted voice again. "I've seen a lot of things in my life, but I ain't never seen nothing like this."

It seemed a long progression, then, before Sam and Tom had their turn. Next, it was Dowdy Ross and Quiet Wind. Then it was the Mexicans, only because Sam and Tom decided to let them go first, partly out of courtesy, partly because their stubborn streak had taken over and they wanted to show the Professor that they weren't in any hurry.

Finally, the partners were the only two who hadn't been in. Melissa spoke quietly with Ashcroft when he came out with the Mexicans, and the Professor smiled and nodded. Melissa turned and walked over to take Tom's hand. She looked at him searchingly, as if trying to memorize his face as it was before his views about life would change forever. Then she tugged him with her.

Sam was last. He swallowed and took a deep breath, knowing he was about to see something that had shaken the others to the core—several people who must have already seen much of the bizarre in their scientific world, to say nothing of the day to day oddities of life in New York City itself.

Sam set a foot inside, then the other. He was in the cave, with the bouncing, glowing yellow light of the lantern, inside with the semi-darkness—inside with the remnants of another world.

Artifacts of all kinds, far more than he had imagined, filled the room, appearing as his eyes adjusted. Long-dead torches protruding from sconces lined the walls. Petroglyphs also adorned the walls, seeming to dance, alive in the lurking shadows from the lantern. But it wasn't all of this that drew his eyes. It was the dead men. Everywhere. Five, six, eight of them. More! Dead men? Not just dead *men*. Dead... *giants.* Giants! Giants that had been petrified, turned black and wizened by time, but who seemed complete in every body part.

The hand and arm of one protruded from under a bed that must have been ten feet long. Another was curled up in the fetal position, his head and upper body covered by a woven rug. But most of them were piled along the front wall, one with his hands clutched about his throat, where a few inches of an arrow shaft protruded. Weapons were also strewn there—spears thirteen feet or more long, bows that were taller than Sam. And the arrows! Some must have been four feet long! Two or three had swords, at least one of them made out of the finest Damascus steel. One man still had a broad ax clutched in his dehydrated fist.

Giants... *Giants!* Not one of the bodies could have been shorter than seven feet, and one that lay near the door must have stood a full eleven. He was the one with the ax still in his fist, and the ax alone would weigh easily thirty pounds. The head of it would have covered a large part of Sam's torso.

Sam moved about the cave in a daze. He spoke no words. No one did. Other than dazed mumbling, what could a man say to this? What could a man even think? They were walking about a once-sealed cave with at least one man who had stood almost twice as tall as Sam, and in this day Sam was considered to be a tall man! It was inconceivable.

Even thinking back on the Professor's speech Sam had been prepared for nothing like this. Nothing! How could a man ready himself for a scene such as this? He couldn't. He could only walk into it with the hope that his mind was strong enough for him to remain sane when he walked back out. The Professor had been right. Nothing any of them could ever see again would come anywhere near to what they were witnessing now.

A bare fraction of what was in the cave had registered on Sam before finally Melissa paused at the door. He followed her numbly when she and Tom left with the lantern. Outside, he found everyone slumped around the cave entrance on boulder seats, or on the ground itself. There was no talk, no excited conversation, no whooping and hollering about great discoveries. There were only numb faces, staring in silent shock.

Finally, Baron began to look around, and Sam knew he was trying to think of something intelligent to say. "We've got to do something." Apparently, that was the smartest thing he could come up with.

Sam heard Tom laughing, but he stopped abruptly when the Professor's eyes speared him. After a moment, the Professor looked at Baron.

"Yes, Mr. Baron. We have to do something. But I think... I'm sorry, but it's going to take me a while to recover from what we've seen... What we've seen... Good heaven! Do you people realize what we've seen?"

He leaped up off his boulder chair and spun around, throwing his eyes about like fiery darts. "Do you realize what we've *seen?*" He ran to Quiet Wind, his face seeming to tear open with a huge smile. Grasping her shoulders in his hands, he jerked her up off her seat and whirled her around. "Lady! Lady! You have given me the world. There has never been a discovery of this kind, of a giant people so well-preserved. Never in recorded history! Quiet Wind! Oh, you beautiful woman!" In his excitement, he leaned and planted a huge kiss on her forehead.

The woman couldn't help the smile that came to her face. Everyone was smiling, in fact. The Professor's excitement was contagious. Even if they hadn't been enthralled to have been a part of this discovery themselves, they had to feel it with Ashcroft. The man was going mad with elation.

The group finally got themselves together enough for Melissa, the Professor, Baron and Moore to sit down and give their first impressions of the discovery, which Melissa penned in expert shorthand. After that, Moore took out all of his fancy photographic equipment and began taking photographs of the cave entrance and the burned door, along with the Professor and Melissa standing proudly, arm in arm.

To release some of the pent-up emotion inside them, Sam and Tom went off to find camp meat, Tom carrying a rifle he borrowed from Alfredo Sanchez. As they were leaving, they heard

Alfredo and his son talking about going for a walk. Viktor seemed content to sit and watch the proceedings at the cave—or to watch Melissa. And Dowdy Ross left the cave and traipsed back down the mountain to lose himself in starting the evening's meal.

A lazy rain swept in on Sam and Tom not far into the woods. They had separated and were paralleling each other one or two hundred feet apart, creeping along in hunter fashion. Sam moved like an earth-bound cloud, smooth, wave-like, touching the earth searchingly with his toe before placing his heel down behind it.

The rain was not enough to dampen things and soften the sound. It was up to Sam. A gray jay saw him and cocked its head. But it didn't call. Perhaps it thought him part of the woods. More likely, it had never seen a man and did not see him as a threat. A hairy woodpecker crept up the side of a ponderosa, tapping exploringly. The clouds hung low in the tree tops. Here was heaven. Sam and Tom had made the easiest money, on the most fascinating job they had ever taken. What more could a man ask for?

Like a ghost, not unlike Sam, a buck appeared in the mist. He was brown and scrawny now, not the magnificent beast he would have become when gold swept the aspens and auburn the waving grass. His coat was scruffy and unkempt, and he was ewe-necked like a Navajo pony. His rack was only heavy six-inch nubs covered in velvet. He flicked an ear, and his big dark eyes scanned the woods. He turned his head, seeking enemies with his nose, his eyes, his ears. He died looking straight through Sam.

"Good shot," Tom offered when he came to find Sam sitting with the velvet-antlered mule deer in the gloom, his hand settled on and feeling the last flutterings of its heart. The animal had one hole, through its forehead an inch above its eyes.

Sam finished his prayer, thanking God for the sacrificed animal, telling the buck itself that he was sorry he had to take its life, and asking it to share its strength with those who partook of it.

Gutting the deer took Sam only minutes, and together they hung it up in a tree and skinned it, then rolled its heart, liver, kidney and backstraps into the supple hide. Using his long-bladed knife to cut and then pry, Sam severed the spine at the third rib from the bottom, and unceremoniously he shouldered the lower half and started back toward camp. Tom followed shortly with the hide and prime pieces. They had thought to come here in the silence to talk of the cave. Somehow they couldn't discuss it. They were still filled with too much awe.

Things weren't much different in camp. Very little talk broke the clearing's quiet. There would come a time when they could share their views of the cave. But it was going to take a while.

It was almost dark when Sam thought to return up to the cave, remembering that no one there would know how to throw the diamond hitch over Darkie's packs. He found no one outside. They were all inside, and a strong orange glow came from there, flickering with the changing moods of the lantern lights. Sam wasn't sure if he wanted to go back inside. He hadn't had time to sort out his feelings yet, but although it was a remarkable dis-covery it was very dark in there. Not just physically, but spir-itually as well. Anyone could see from the positions of the men, the weapons in their hands, and the arrows in some, that they had died horribly. But it was more than that. Some evil lurked here, something that only someone very in tune with the Spirit might feel. It made him shiver when he thought about it. Sometimes it made him shiver even when he didn't.

The rain had stopped, but the clouds still drooped across the canyon, dragging their soft gray feet. Those merciful clouds brought down all the dust and smoke from the fires spawned by the quake.

It was in looking across the canyon at some of those clouds that Sam first saw the flicker of firelight...

CHAPTER EIGHTEEN

Walking careful in the rain-moistened rocks and earthquake debris, Sam stepped closer to the crisp new precipice. He had no undue fear of heights, but he had a healthy respect for a sharp edge like this, so recently created and holding the real possibility, before discovering its own strength, of splitting off again. So he stopped four or five feet from the edge, wishing he had his field glasses as he stared across the canyon.

The fire wasn't large, and now and then it flickered and almost seemed to go out. Then it would grow larger, recede again, and then glow steadily.

Who was over there? Suddenly, he thought of Crooked Foot. Where was the Indian? He had disappeared. Sam hadn't seen him or his dog for some time, at least since they had all gone into the cave. Could that be him now, on the other side? It would be a long, difficult hike, first forcing him to go at least halfway down the trail before he could find any access to the canyon, and then to clamber up through dangerous rocks on the other side. Sam decided it wasn't very likely to be Crooked Foot's fire. Who then? Prospector? Outlaw? Indian? Hunter? Trapper? Whoever they were, they were a long ways from so-called civilization.

He heard footsteps behind him and turned to see Viktor coming toward him from the cave's entrance. "Somebody's keepin' us company."

The big man stopped beside him, reaching absently into his vest to withdraw a cigar and pop the tip into his mouth. More often than not, Viktor chewed his cigars down to a stub before discarding them. But this one he lit. Then, as if the thought had just come to him, he looked over at Sam. "Cigar?"

Sam hesitated. He didn't really appreciate cigars the way some men did. But then this might be an opportunity to make an ally. Turning it down might accomplish just the opposite. "Sure, I'll try one."

Viktor dug for a second cigar and another match. When Sam had the cigar situated, Viktor struck the match and held it for him, then flipped it a couple of times to put it out. He looked at the match, seemed about to throw it, then crushed it against his shoulder holster before dropping it at his feet. Sam wondered if that was because Viktor had seen him crushing out his own matches.

Side by side they stood smoking and watched the far campfire. It must have been six hundred yards away, but it was big enough to see it flicker. "There!" exclaimed Viktor at the same time Sam saw a shadow pass in front of it. "Don't know who it is, but he's this side of the fire now."

Sam simply nodded. He felt Viktor's glance on him for some time then before the big man spoke. "What do you think of the cave?"

Sam raised his eyebrows, looking over at him. "Never seen anything like it. Never dreamed of anything like it."

Viktor grunted. That about said it all.

*   *   *

When the others came out of the cave fifteen or twenty minutes later, the campfire across the canyon had died down nearly to nothing. The Professor stopped beside Sam, and Sam motioned toward it with the nub of his cigar.

The Professor stared for a moment. "What's that?"

"Somebody's fire. Been there a while."

"It wasn't there earlier, was it? A camp, I mean."

Sam shrugged. "Don't know, but it's there now."

Baron paid the fire little attention. "We need to get on down the trail while there's still some light to see by. That mule's going to break a leg."

With a laugh, Sam shook his head. "That mule could make it to Tucson from here blindfolded and not get a scratch. You'd be surprised what a mule can make his way through in the dark. Anyone breaks a leg it'll be one of us."

Baron only grunted. He didn't care for being spoken out against, but he didn't bother to say it. Sam felt it. They loaded the packs and balanced them over the battered cross-buck. Even in the light that was almost gone, Sam was able to throw his diamond hitch, and then they all tramped back down the hill. It had been some day.

Supper was a quiet affair. Sam and Tom had both naturally figured that when the cave was opened and they all got to see whatever was inside the talk that night would be lively. But they never figured on what was actually inside. Seeing any mum-mified remains had a sobering effect on most people. Seeing remains of men *that* size was going to take a while to digest. How did someone begin to discuss a discovery like that?

*   *   *

The next morning's meal was different. The camp was abuzz with conversation. Everyone had slept on the discovery, sorted through their own emotions, and it was almost as if they were in a race to see who could voice the most words in the shortest time.

Before everyone was half done eating, Professor Ashcroft, Melissa and Delbert Moore were already gathering their gear and the instruments, notebooks, and pencils they would need that day. With the sun not even touching the highest peaks, the troop set off up the trail, eager to be back to work.

Sam and Tom had decided before sunup to go for a walk in the forest, and without speaking to anyone they had disappeared into the timber. They returned to a mostly empty camp—empty except for Ross, who was cleaning up. Sam set off up the trail, with Tom not far behind.

Professor Ashcroft and Melissa saw them coming up the trail and met them partway. "I think someone went through the cave after we left!" Ashcroft exclaimed with an indignant frown.

Sam raised his eyebrows. "Do tell. They take anything?"

"I can't be sure," he said. "Possibly one of the swords."

"Leave any tracks?"

Ashcroft stood there for a moment looking perplexed, and then a light came into his eyes. "Ah! I hadn't thought of that. Maybe we should look."

Even as he spoke, Viktor came waltzing out of the cave with Moore not far behind him. Baron exited a few moments later. Sam gave the three of them a half-amused, half-disgusted look. "We'll look," he grunted. "But I wouldn't count on finding much. Any tracks that were around are probably pretty well ground out by now."

He started to scout around the area, and he could immediately tell the Professor was right. Not only had someone been there, but it appeared as if that someone had carefully covered their presence. He found where someone had taken dust and sifted it onto several places in the trail. The problem was that in trying to hide their tracks, and perhaps not wanting to leave obvious fingerprints where they had picked up the dust for sifting, they had taken the dust from elsewhere. It had a slightly different hue that set it apart from the dust already on the trail. It could have been dust that had filtered down during or after the quake, but there were fresh tracks—it looked like Moore's—in the under-layer of dust. At least they were fresh since the earthquake. Sam knew that

by the fact that they were made by Moore when he was in a relaxed, ambling mode, and headed uphill, not running hell-bent
back down.

The fact that the now-proven prowler had attempted to hide
his presence made it all the more intriguing to Sam, who continued to scout the area. At one point he found evidence that made
it look like the person had gone up over the rock face of the mountain in leaving, rather than pass the cave mouth and have to brave
the remnants of the trail on the other side, which were almost nonexistent and very hazardous. The face of the mountain wasn't exactly safe either, but at least it was solid.

At the base of the mountain where the prowler seemed to have
gone up was the only real sign he had left, and Sam stooped and
studied it for some time. It appeared to be a toe mark—not bare
toes, of course, but the toe of a moccasin, rather than a hard-soled
boot or shoe. The thing Sam couldn't reconcile was its size.
Something was very odd about it, and that was why he spent five
times longer analyzing it than he normally did on any other track.

Tom finally left his conversation with Melissa to wander over
to Sam and crouch down nearby, making sure not to step on any
sign Sam might need for whatever jigsaw puzzle he was solving.
"What do you see?" he asked. In spite of Tom's own tracking
abilities, which as a cowhand he was able to use to figure out such
things as how many cows were using a particular waterhole, and
how long ago, he was almost useless here. Cows didn't purposely
hide their trails. Sam was the only one on that mountain besides
Crooked Foot and perhaps Quiet Wind who could make these
small signs into a storybook.

"Somethin' strange," Sam replied to his partner. "I make out
what appears to be the track of a man's foot—in a moccasin."

"Crooked Foot?" Tom suggested.

"Naw, it's pretty straight," Sam said with half a grin.

"Funny," Tom said. "Seriously, he took off without a word to anybody. You think he liked what he saw in the cave and decided to loot it for himself?"

Although preoccupied, Sam immediately shook his head. "No-o. This toe track looks like it's six inches wide. That's what I can't quite figure."

"Six inches wide!" Tom exclaimed. "I'd say he was steppin' in the same track so he'd be less obvious."

Sam didn't seem to hear. He leaned and looked at the track closer, then raised up again. Slowly, he began to shake his head. "Good thinkin', pard. But that's not it. It just blends right to-gether—smoother than a man could do unless he turned around and did it on purpose. And what would be the point of that? Only thing I can figure is he's wearing some kind of big, strange moc-casin, like maybe a man would wear if he had to cross snow or quicksand or mud—somethin' that would give the bottom of his foot a lot of surface."

Tom nodded. "I guess that could be it. I never would have thought of it. But heck, if he really had a foot six inches wide that's as wide as one and a half of mine together."

Sam stood up and let his eyes climb the steep mountainside. It had always been mostly rock, but the quake had done a good job in shaking off most of the dirt that had settled on it over the years. Sam figured if he wanted to take the time to climb it he could learn more about the prowler, but if this one wanted a sword bad enough to scale that rock, then maybe he needed the sword more than the Professor did anyway.

Sam went back to Professor Ashcroft and explained what he had found and what he thought it meant. The Professor had been suspecting Crooked Foot, too, and he still didn't seem thoroughly convinced that it wasn't.

What made the Professor suspect Crooked Foot even more was Viktor's suspicion. Hearing the conversation between Sam and Ashcroft, the big man stopped across from Sam and threw in his thoughts. "The little thief stole my gloves, I know that. He was eyeballing them and asked if he could hold them. He even put them on. And then they disappeared. It's like they say—you can't trust a damn Injun."

One side of Sam's mouth raised sardonically. "That's right, Viktor. Hell, we're all cut from the same scrap of muskrat hide."

Viktor drew back his chin, a cynical look in his eyes. "Who's *we?*"

Sam just grunted, only half amused, and walked off. When he was gone, Viktor gave Tom a hard glance, and Tom nodded. "Yep. He's half Choctaw. And I've never known him to steal a thing. But come to think of it—he snores pretty loud, so I reckon he's stole a lot of sleep from me over the years."

"Funny," Viktor said sarcastically. "A damn Injun, huh?"

"No. A Choctaw." Without awaiting any crude reply, Tom turned and followed Sam away.

Viktor turned around to see the Professor standing there frowning at him. "I still lay my money on that stinkin' Crooked Foot."

*   *   *

Throughout the day the expeditioners trooped back and forth, cataloging every item located in the cave, carting some of them back down the mountain when they had enough built up.

Around three in the afternoon, the Professor had decided they should start bringing some of the more valuable items in closer to camp, and Melissa was coming down alone, carrying a par-ticu-larly precious cargo—a set of golden goblets. She was only thirty yards out of camp when she ran into big Viktor headed back up the trail. "Well, well, well," came Viktor's cocky voice. "How lucky can I get? The lovely Miss Melissa, and she's all alone."

"Hello, Viktor," she said civilly. It was as much as she could muster. In truth, it was more politeness than she felt the need for, but that was the way she had been raised.

Viktor took a deep breath. "Been wanting to talk with you—in private, that is." It was only so private, as Dowdy Ross, Sam, Tom and the Sanchezes were just out of sight and hearing, hunting in the woods for more firewood.

Melissa's voice was calm, but she did not smile. "Viktor, if you don't mind, I'd like to go past. I'm in a hurry."

Viktor laughed a bit harshly. "Guess that's part of what I wanted to talk to you about. Seems like you're always in a hurry these days when it comes to ol' Vik." He tried to keep his smile, but much of its genuineness had failed. He took the ever-present unlit cigar out of the corner of his mouth. "You used to talk to me now and then. Now you're always in a hurry. But you sure seem to have time for Indians—and *other* folks." With an exas-perated sigh, Melissa bent over and placed her cargo of goblets on the ground. Viktor, hardly missing a beat, went on. "Matter of fact, you sure seem to make plenty of time for that Vanse character."

It was at that moment that Tom walked out of the woods with an armload of sticks, and he heard Viktor before he saw him and guessed by his tone who he was talking to. He dropped his load and sauntered in that direction.

Melissa looked tiredly up at Viktor. "I'm sorry if you had other expectations, Viktor, but our relationship has never been an-ything more than a casual acquaintance. I certainly never meant to give you the impression that it was anything more than that."

Viktor seemed used to having women like him, or at least ad-mire him for his animal manhood. He grunted. "Well maybe you figure I'm not good enough for you, like some of them other up-pity folks back in New York. Maybe..." The big man stopped talking as he simultaneously heard a stick pop behind him and saw Melissa's eyes widen. His face hardened as he turned to see

Tom walk up and come to a stop. The big man thrust the cigar back in his mouth and stared at the intruder, his eyes narrowing.

Tom looked from Viktor to Melissa. "Ma'am. You all right?"

Viktor bristled up and growled, "Just what do you take me for? Butt out, cowboy. You got your nose where it don't belong. You got a short memory. I thought I told you..."

Tom turned fully to Viktor, his body going taut. Was this the big moment everyone had been fearing? He was ready. He might go down, but he would go down swinging.

Melissa's voice broke Tom's concentration. "Viktor! Let me handle this—please." She pivoted her eyes to Tom, and part of her expression was pleading, but it was a part he didn't catch. "Mr. Vanse, this is a private matter. If you'll excuse us I would appreciate it." Taken aback, Tom's eyes grew uncertain before he could cover it. Melissa continued to stare at him. "Please."

"Sorry, ma'am. My fault," Tom mumbled. With the little pride he had left he turned and beat a retreat back to camp.

Viktor's smile returned, and he looked at Melissa in a new light. He let out a laugh. "Well, now. Maybe I was wrong about you." He laughed again. "You sure told him where the hen lays its eggs. And here I thought you was going sweet on that... *turd* kicker. Maybe you'll come to see it my way after all. Woman like you needs a *real* man. You got spunk, Melissa. I like that in a woman. I surely do. I'm thinkin' our problem is we never really had a chance to get better acquainted. I figger you might decide you like having me around."

While Viktor said his piece, puffing out his chest and talking big, Melissa stared at him, her expression becoming more and more incredulous. Finally, she held up her hands and gave a little shake of her head. "Oh, no, Mr. Zulowsky. No, you don't. I thought I made myself clear before Mr. Vanse showed up. I am absolutely *not* interested in getting to know you better. I'm quite satisfied with our relationship as it is. Mr. Vanse may not meet with your definition of what a man is, but he meets with mine, and I enjoy his company. If this hurts your feelings I'm sorry. That is not my intent. But you simply cannot go on believing there is any chance for you and me.

"I have never purposely tried to make you believe that I wanted more from you than the casual acquaintance our job calls for. I am going back up the mountain now, and since you held me up I would appreciate it if you would take these goblets to camp for me. I have work to do." With those terse words hanging in the air, she spun and started her long hike back up the mountain.

Viktor's eyes followed her until she disappeared. His smile had vanished and his face was red. His jaw muscles worked in a fury, and his teeth clenched on his cigar. With no warning, it fell in two and thumped against his chin, held together only by a few strands of tobacco leaf. Face reddening even more, he ripped the collapsed cigar from between his teeth and dashed it to the ground, spitting out what was left of it. "The hell with you," he growled as he stomped away, viciously giving the boot to a clump of brush unfortunate enough to be in his way. His brogan tore it from the ground, making its pungent scent rise into the air as it gave up its life to his ire.

*   *   *

When Tom walked away from the confrontation between Melissa and Viktor, he strode into camp and jerked Alfredo Sanchez's rifle out of his bedroll, where he had stowed it earlier. He had not yet accomplished the major job of freeing his own weapon from under the tree that had fallen on their tent during the earthquake. Moving on to the horses at the picket line, he heaved his saddle blanket and saddle up and onto the back of Cocky without ceremony. He slammed the rifle into the scabbard.

Sam followed him to the horses. He stood by while Tom threw the saddle on and drew the latigo up tight and hard. "You're gonna make ol' Cocky spill his brisket," he jabbed lightly. Tom didn't comment. "What's the hurry?"

Again, Tom made no reply. He grabbed the reins and the saddle horn and swung his leg over the horse's back. Cocky seemed to know enough right then not to buck. It was obvious his rider wasn't in any mood for games, and Cocky had been around enough to sense it.

"I've seen more talkative hoot owls," Sam said. In spite of his joking words, concern filled his glance.

Tom turned and looked down. "I've already done too much talkin'. I think I'll do some ridin'."

"Interested in comp'ny?"

"'Fraid you wouldn't find it much company," Tom said. "I'll be down the trail." Without another word, he jerked Cocky around and kneed him out of camp.

Sam couldn't help but be concerned about his partner. Something was chewing on him. He thought about tailing him, but that would be as advisable right then as tracking a bear with a bellyache and an eyeball in its backside.

Sam met Dowdy Ross back at the fire, where he deposited an armload of punky wood. He stood by while Ross threw together a pot of coffee. After several minutes of silence broken only by the quiet rustling of the sack of beans, the crackling of the grinder, and the *clink* of the porcelain-coated pot and its hinged lid, Ross looked up, wiping at his longhorn mustache.

"Won't be long now, Coffey." He chuckled as he realized how that sounded. "Anybody ever mention you got a difficult name?" he joked gruffly. "Want some coffee, Coffey?"

The cavalryman let out a little laugh at his own humor. It struck Sam that it was one of the few times he had heard Ross laugh when it wasn't over something Melissa said. "Bein' serious, though—you want a cup?"

Sam grinned and said in his voice that he remembered a woman once describing as "honey flowing over boulders," "Don't mind if I do. Thanks, Ross."

Ross took up an enamel cup and spun it through the air. Sam caught it deftly.

"Your partner seemed to be in a bit of a hurry," Ross mused.

"You might say," Sam agreed. "Didn't say what was gnawing at him. Reckon he'll have to sort it out."

"I reckon. Seems like a pretty squared-around fellow. Sometimes a man just needs a little time to get his troops all in a line."

They stood there for a long time speculating over the fire and not talking. When the coffee pot started sputtering, Ross opened the lid to pour in the grounds, removing it from the flames. After it had sat brewing for five or six minutes, he poured his cup, then held out the pot and filled Sam's when he met him halfway. After holding onto it until it had a few minutes to cool, Sam took a sip. The simple feel of its warmth making its way down his throat calmed him.

They had seen Viktor stomp away some time ago, and twenty minutes later Melissa came into camp. It was evident by the way her eyes scanned the area that she was looking for something—or some*one.*

Ross jumped up, his eyes a-light. "Hello, Miss Melissa. I just brewed up some coffee—can I get you a cup?"

Melissa smiled. "No, thank you, Dowdy. It sounds inviting, but there's something I have to take care of." Taking one last sweeping glance around, she turned to Sam. "Do you know where I might find Tom?"

"Well..." He paused, and she pleaded with her eyes.

"I need to talk to him."

It struck Sam then how dense a man could be. The reason he seldom saw his partner so unfriendly was because he had never seen him when he was seriously taken with a woman. Up until the last few days, his long-lost Beverly was his only true love, and the rest were just for fun. He'd been having the nagging feeling that Melissa was becoming more than that.

"He rode out of here over half an hour ago. He didn't seem real taken with the idea of my comp'ny. But you, now—that might be a different story."

"Thank you, Sam," Melissa sighed. "I'm pretty sure I know what's bothering him. I might as well tell you—it was my fault."

Sam eyed the woman, a smile in his eyes that never quite reached his lips. "Don't you worry, ma'am. Tom's a tough nut, but I'm sure you'll sort it out. If you wanna go look for him, I'll saddle up your horse."

"Oh, thank you. I would very much appreciate that."

Sam nodded and walked out to the picket line. When he had saddled the sorrel, and Melissa came over with a jacket under her arm, Sam took it and began tying it behind the saddle.

"If you're goin' out alone, I wish you'd take my pistol with you. I can show you how to use it."

"No need," she said with a smile. She reached into the folds of her riding skirt and came up with a .32 caliber Smith and Wesson. "I can shoot."

Sam raised an eyebrow, then grinned. "I'll just bet you can, ma'am. You get in trouble, you fire a shot. We'd hear it echoing up this canyon."

"I can defend myself."

"I'm sure you can. But there's things a little pop gun like that just can't knock out."

Melissa eyed him for a long moment, then looked down at the gun in her hand. She looked at him again. "Thank you, Sam. I'll remember that."

CHAPTER NINETEEN

Melissa Ford rode easy down the canyon for ten minutes, skirting boulders and other debris in the trail here and there, and letting the horse step lightly over one place where a fissure four inches wide had split the hardpan during the quake.

She spotted Tom's horse tethered to a juniper about sixty feet up the hillside to the right of the trail. Farther up the slope was a scattering of stunted pinyon pines that grew tighter together until being halted by a sheer rock face that curved away out of sight.

Melissa walked her horse off the trail, through the lightly scattered brush and trees. It took her a bit, but in time she saw Tom, standing stock still up on a low rock ledge, rifle in hand, watching her. She climbed off her horse and tied him to a bush, then walked up to Tom.

"You sure looked lonely," teased Melissa, trying to make the situation light as she met his eyes.

"Not in particular."

Melissa sighed, and her smile disappeared. "Please forgive me for invading your privacy, Tom, but I needed to talk to you."

Their eyes held for a long moment until finally he reached his hand down to her. She took it, and he helped her up onto the ledge, the remains of numerous strata of rock that had weathered away intermittently, creating a series of jagged steps leading to a sort of bench big enough for two or three people. It was a perfect vantage point from which to survey the trail below, and the vista of canyons and mountains spilled out toward the horizon.

Melissa looked over the natural steps and bench, which seemed to beckon them. "Can we sit down, Tom?"

He stared at her as if he hadn't heard. "Uh, yes, ma'am! Of course." He lunged up the broken steps in several easy strides and jerked off his hat to brush away a spot on the rock bench. When she reached him, she looked at it and smiled her thanks, then sat down. He took his place a couple of feet away.

Melissa laughed. "You really don't have to sit way over there. I promise I won't rub off on you." He couldn't help but laugh, showing his dimples. That seemed to please her. "Really, Tom, I hope I'm not invading your privacy by coming here."

"The truth is, ma'am, you ain't invadin' my privacy. I'm here because of you anyway. I ain't sure why you're here, but I'm glad you are. I wanted to apologize to you. Viktor was right. I butted into somethin' that was none of my affair, and I should have known better." To get the apology out, he had to look away, concentrating on the canyon below them.

"There's no reason for you to be sorry. You thought I needed help. Why should you apologize for coming to my rescue? But even though it meant a lot to me, it could have ended badly." He gave the woman a puzzled glance. "Honestly, Tom. I'm very touched that you were concerned about me. But please understand that I had to send you away to avoid a fight."

Tom grunted. "I'm not afraid of Viktor."

Melissa shook her head adamantly. "Tom, you've got to listen to me—please. I admire you for not being afraid. But you *should* be afraid of Viktor. You're a tall man, and I can see you're very strong and able to take care of yourself. I would have little fear if I knew you were my guardian. So with that in mind, I hope this doesn't sound insulting: You would be no match for Viktor in a fist fight.

"I've seen him in fights. I once saw him fight with three local toughs when we were all walking through Central Park, planning the logistics of this trip. These men were insulting to me, and to all of us. I suppose they had it coming, but Tom—he almost killed them, all by himself. Viktor grew up in a poor neighborhood where you had to be tough to survive. What he didn't learn about street fighting there he picked up on the docks. That's how he got all those scars on his face and his hands. Don't ever fight him if you can avoid it. I promise you he will not fight fair. He will use every dirty trick known. He will hurt you. He'll kill you if he can, especially because he knows I like you."

Tom stared at her as she talked, and when she finished he shook his head in amazement.

"What is it?" she asked.

"Well... I guess I was mighty wrong. I was thinking a while ago that you were mad at me for buttin' in where I wasn't wanted. But the worst thing was... I guess I suddenly realized how much you mean to me. The thought of losing out on you left me with an empty feeling. Not that I got any claim to your feelings! Anyway, that's why I rode down here—to sort things out. To get my herd wrangled all into their rightful place."

She giggled at his words. "Well there's one thing you'd better 'wrangle' right now."

He waited for her to tell him what that one thing was, but it wasn't something she could say with words. Scooting over closer to him, she put her hand up against his cheek and leaned in. Softly, like the brush of warm velvet, her lips pressed against his. His heart quickened, beating hard against his chest. It had been years since any woman had stirred him the way Melissa did.

When their lips parted, Tom was speechless. Finally, he said, "Melissa, you make it pretty hard to breathe."

Melissa laughed and threw her arms around him, laying her head on his shoulder. He squeezed her to him, savoring her closeness and the fresh smell of her hair.

Her whisper brought him back to reality and made him release her. "I had better be getting back."

"I reckon so," Tom agreed. "It won't look too good for you to be down here alone with me."

She searched his eyes. "That's the last thing I'm worried about."

Tom stood up and helped her to her feet. He stepped around her and off the ledge, then took her hand to ease her way down the broken steps.

Melissa caught a serious look that had come into Tom's gaze, and she looked a question at him. Feeling caught, he forged on. "Could I ask one question?"

"Do I have to answer?"

He shrugged one shoulder. "Sure would help. You and Viktor... is—"

"Is there anything between us?"

He laughed, embarrassed. "Yes ma'am. Or was there ever?"

"No. Never. I have been very careful to keep our relationship a casual working one. Viktor, it seems, would like things to be different, and I had to be pretty blunt with him today. He mentioned that I always seemed to have time for you, and I told him I like you and enjoy your company." That revelation made Tom smile. "He's bitterly jealous of you, Tom."

"I figured that much out. Thanks for answering my question. I guess we better—" With his sentence only half complete, he froze.

Melissa's eyes widened, and she started to follow the line of his gaze up the slope behind them. "What is it? Tom, is something wrong?"

"Don't turn around," he warned, trying to keep his voice calm. "Let's walk to the horses—real easy-like. I want you to ride out slow, like you're just ambling your way home. Once you're out of sight, get back to camp as quick as you can without makin' a lot of noise and find Sam. Tell him to get down here fast and bring his rifle. Tell the rest of them to keep their eyes peeled for trouble—you hear?"

For the first time, he seemed to notice the revolver in her holster, nestled into the folds of her skirt. "Can you shoot that?"

"I can," she said, reaching up to rub the goose bumps off the back of her neck. Before she could say anything else, Tom took her elbow and steered her to the horses. Instinctively, he drew her sorrel's cinch up tighter and helped her aboard, then handed her the reins. "Don't look up the hill, Melissa. Act calm. There's somebody up there. I've gotta find out who—and how many. You see anybody on your way back to camp, don't you stop for a second. Don't hesitate to shoot them if they try to stop you."

"But what if they are planning to come and talk with us?" she asked, her eyes wide with concern.

"This is no place to be sneakin' around. If they had good intentions they'd have called out to us."

Melissa reached down and squeezed his hand, whispering, "Please be careful." With one last look, she turned her sorrel and let him pick his way down to the trail. Tom could see it was all she could do to keep him at a walk.

Turning, now ready to do battle if necessary, he melted into the shadows of the big juniper where Cocky was lashed. He turned his head and watched Melissa until she was out of sight, then looked back to scan the rocks and trees above. For several minutes he waited, watching. No movement anywhere. Hoping to seem nonchalant, but realizing how it would look to anyone watching, he eased the rifle out of his scabbard. With its hard metal and wood against his callused hands, he again sought out every shadow in the landscape, checking in a three hundred sixty degree radius. No one. Nothing. Not even a bird.

A minute passed. He waited. Who was up here? What were they after? How many enemies did he face? Would he see Melissa again?

His hands tightened on the rifle.

He stood utterly alone, but for his horse, and the seconds came crashing down around him. Time existed no more. Something lurked above him. He didn't hear or see it—he felt it. He had never been a man to fear the unknown, but at the moment he felt his skin crawl, and fear tackled him. What he sensed here in the emptiness was a dark evil like he had never known before, but akin to what he had felt just before he and Sam, hidden in the half-light, first heard the Yaquis riding down the canyon toward them in that Bacatete canyon one year ago. But that had been only eerie. Not evil. What he felt here was dark. Ominous... truly evil.

After another minute, he heard a faint noise again, and he keened his ears, his fingers set to work the lever of Alfredo's rifle. Rocks rattled faintly. He finally realized as it grew louder that it was someone coming horseback down the trail below him. In a few more minutes Sam appeared in the trail, riding Gringo. With the sharp eyes of the woodsman, his partner spotted Cocky, and then Tom stepped out to meet him.

Sam gave the terrain a sharp, intent scan, then left the trail and tied Gringo to the first juniper. He came on up the hill afoot, moving slow, his eyes always working—his eyes, ears, even his nose—and of course that other sense, the one that all wanderers of the wild country must hone to survive.

By the time Sam reached his partner, he had felt what Tom did, and it showed in the wild look of his eyes. "My hell. What's up here?"

Tom kept his voice low, one eye still on the rocks and trees above, the other on Sam. "What do you mean?"

"Can't you feel somethin'? Or is it just me?"

Tom couldn't help but laugh, nervously. "It ain't just you."

"So what the hell?" Sam said, reaching up under his hat brim to rub the short hairs that rose on the back of his neck.

"I don't know. I saw a shadow up there—there, on that rock. I'm half-tempted not to go up there, the way this place feels, but that's where I saw it."

"You an' me both, pardner. You an' me both." Sam's eyes picked apart the terrain, especially the sun-lit escarpment Tom had pointed out. "We'd feel perty foolish if we *didn't* go up there, though, wouldn't we?"

Tom simply nodded. He looked at Cocky, prompting Sam to glance down at Gringo. Both were thinking the same thing: Did they leave the horses and make the steep grade afoot, chancing someone's circling around and stealing them? The inhospitable slope above answered the question for them, and with the silent agreement that long-time partners share, they started up the slant.

Suddenly, Sam drew up. Whoever—*what*ever—they were stalking had been taking very deliberate steps from rock to rock, only now and then having to resort to stepping on a dead, earth-bound branch. Twice, he walked on clumps of grass, crushing them to earth. But there was a brief stretch, perhaps seven feet long, where it was dust and a little gravel, broken by a scattering of bunchgrass. Here, the person had made a leap, aimed for one of the clumps of grass, but had barely missed it. It was here that Sam pulled up and crouched.

Tom stopped and squatted beside him, rifle across his legs. Both of them stared at the remains of what appeared to be some kind of track there by the bush. "What in the name of..."

Sam squinted his eyes up, his brow knitted in obvious confusion. What he and Tom were looking at was no doubt a track, but... It was once again as if it were *two* tracks somehow meshed together. A chill went up Sam's spine as he thought of Indian legends he had heard. It was said that some kind of hair-covered, ape-like man wandered the wilderness, a creature fast enough to run down deer, strong enough to carry full-grown men away to be devoured. Some called him Sasquatch. Some Bigfoot. These were legends that Sam, growing up with a Choctaw mother, had heard and believed from his earliest memory. Similar stories had been passed to him around Tarahumara campfires. Yet believing these stories and actually thinking he would one day run into that legendary creature were sharply at odds...

He brushed the legends away. This was no "Bigfoot." This track was made by a moccasin. He couldn't see lace markings, for any good moccasin maker would have put them up along the sides of the foot so they wouldn't wear out from walking on them. But he knew it was a moccasin track from the lack of toe marks. What in the world would leave a track the size of—

Without warning, Sam felt the crushing grip of Tom's fingers on his shoulder, and he winced. Tom said, "There! Look!"

Sam followed Tom's pointing finger. Far away from them across the valley and above the timber on the far side, stood a man on the very top of the silver-rocked cliff. He was next to a dead, gnarled tree, one hand resting on a branch that swept out away from the rest of the tree alone, curving dreadful and lonesome like a gallows arm.

At first glance Sam would have said it was an Indian. He had long, flowing hair that lifted out to one side with the afternoon breeze, a breeze that would blow stronger up there at the point of the cliff. He wore no shirt, and what appeared from the distance to be a broad torso was tanned a deep brown. At that range he seemed to be wearing leggings of lighter colored buckskin, although legs that hadn't been as often exposed to the sun might look that way, too. He had on a navy blue or black breech cloth that waved in the wind, like his hair. The other hand, the one not resting on the tree branch, appeared to be clutching a long bow, holding it like a walking stick, with one end resting against the earth. The only thing that seemed out of place was one fact: His hair, rather than black, appeared almost blond in this light.

A shiver ran up Tom's spine, and he cast a sideways glance at his partner. "That can't be the man that made the shadow I saw. He couldn't have got all the way over there and up on that cliff that fast. So there's more than one."

Sam didn't argue. The man appeared to be six hundred yards away, and the cliff on which he stood must have been two hundred feet high. "It's a cinch he don't live up here all alone," Sam agreed.

"Well, he gives me the shivers," Tom said. "I don't plan on goin' all the way over there to palaver with him, so if it's all the same to you I say we get back to the horses. If there's even one other up here besides him, there's probably more. What we *don't* need is some bunch of jaspers circlin' around behind us and relievin' us of our ride home."

Sam grunted agreement. "I reckon if he wants to talk to us we'll see him again. Let's go back. We found your bugaboo."

The partners made their way back to the horses, both of which stood tethered where they had left them. There was little talk along the way. Both men were concerned with their own thoughts. Neither spoke of it, but they each pondered the dark presence still hanging in the air.

Whoever that man was who had watched them, he was no ordinary man.

CHAPTER TWENTY

They sat around the campfire in the late dusk, and from across the canyon a wolf hurled his chilling croon into the night sky. His voice sounded deep, resonating, like that of a pack leader. But there was no answer.

"Got too old," said Sam quietly.

Dowdy Ross was sitting there puffing on an ivory-bowled pipe, and he paused and studied Sam for a long moment, then finally said, "How's that?"

"The wolf," Sam clarified. "Musta lost his mate. Then got too old to hold his pack, and some young buck beat 'im out. Now he's on his own."

Dowdy sucked long and deep of his pipe, squinted through the campfire smoke at Sam, and finally whispered out his own sweet-smelling cloud to brace the woodsmoke. "I guess I have to ask—how do you know this?"

A short chuckle escaped Sam. "Sorry. Just thinkin' out loud. How do I know? Nobody answered him. That bottom-of-the-well voice could only be a big old wolf—a boss lobo. Or at least he was. No pack would have wandered that far off from their leader unless he'd got kicked out and replaced—or else some hunter or trapper killed his pack."

"Kind of like somebody our age, you might say," Dowdy mused.

One side of Sam's mouthed ticked up in a wry smile. "Kind of like. And just as wily, too."

Dowdy nodded his appreciation of that comment, sucked his pipe stem, and stared across the lost space.

Sam and Tom had shared their story with the others. Because they had to maintain the armor of tough, valorous men, they omitted mention of how whoever had been watching them had made them feel. Otherwise, they told it all. Everyone contem-plated in silence, imagining who might be sharing these moun-tains with them. As the evening shadows grew ever deeper, the question be-came more and more ominous. It was in this eerie, uncertain at-mosphere that Sam heard the first sound.

It began as a rattling of rocks, one particularly large stone bounding into the canyon below and flinging back a hollow echo as it careered away into the abyss. There followed a grating of metal on stone, and then a long silence.

By the end of that hush, Sam was sequestered along the edge of the trail, and Tom, rifle in hand, lurked on the opposite side of the camp.

Dowdy took it upon himself to break the silence. "You, out there in the dark! You don't sing out pretty soon you'll be fuller of holes than a flannel cake. This place is bristling with rifles."

A few seconds of silence, then a voice quavered down from up the trail. "Sorry, neighbors. Didn't mean to rile you. Seen your light and smelt your fixin's, and I thought mebbe you'd be kindly enough to invite a harmless old hoot owl in for a cup o' tar."

Ross scanned toward Tom, then Sam. He looked last of all toward Baron, for assurance. His eyes never even lit on the Pro-fessor.

Before Ross could speak, Baron rose. "If you're friendly, come on in. If you're unfriendly, you'd better keep moving down the mountain."

"I'm friendly," intoned the voice from the dark. It was the voice of a man who had smoked many a cigarette and spent nights in the cold, days in the heat, and months choking on the dust of the Arizona desert. The metal clicking against stones began again, getting louder and louder, until finally a man and two burros, one gray and one brown, both with shaggy mops of hair between their ears, materialized fifteen feet away in the hazy firelight. "You folks sure I'm welcome?" he asked politely.

"Come on, old timer," Sam replied, only a few feet away. "Light 'n' set. We been listenin' to our own palaver for too long anyway."

A big grin parted the man's grass-thick whiskers, and he came on in, the burros following him without visible means of control. He was a tall man, but stooped like a willow bent in the wind, and gaunt as a jackrabbit. His face, slat-narrow, held two forlorn-looking, cavernous eyes, and his full lips sported the remains of a bad sore beneath the scruffy black whiskers. In spite of his gaunt appearance and wrinkled skin, he appeared to be less than fifty years old—really no "old timer" at all. He was dressed in a blue plaid shirt and multi-patched tan canvas britches.

"Howdy, all," the newcomer said, stopping in the firelight and hooking a thumb in his belt. "I orter interduce my two pards, Biscuit and Java." He pointed first to the gray burro, then patted the brown. "Oh, an' folks down Tucson 'bouts calls me Skillet. Skillet LaChance. I answer to most anything, however—mostly to meal call." He gawked about in expectation of garnering a laugh.

"Come on and sit down, Skillet," said Tom, stepping forward from across the camp and taking charge while the others were still trying to collect themselves and take in the strange appearance of the man, an obvious prospector by the pick and shovel protruding from Java's pack, and the gold pan snugged down on top. "The coffee's just gettin' about right, friend, and—" He laughed as the burro named Biscuit stretched his neck out and tried to lip one of the biscuits from the pan. "Looks like your burro's beatin' you to it, but I was about to say there's a couple biscuits left."

"Dang yuh, Biscuit Eater!" The prospector swatted his burro's rump, making it flinch and move away warily, turning its ears back at him to see if he was still on the attack. "Durned ol' feller," LaChance said, stanching a grin. "We bin fightin' ever since I give him his first taste o' flour."

"I suppose the other one drinks coffee," quipped Sam, recalling that LaChance had introduced the brown burro as Java. This brought a hearty laugh from the prospector, who promptly leaned down to snatch one of the biscuits while Dowdy Ross was pouring him a cup of coffee that had started to look more like thin mud.

"Is that how you named your pets?" followed Melissa innocently.

LaChance stood there dumbfounded for a moment, then suddenly seemed to realize what the woman was talking about and guffawed. "Pets! Missus, them is just walkin' foodstuffs. Them ain't no pets." He playfully scratched Java's forelock and patted his shoulder. "Ain't that right, old boy? But no, seriously, you got it half right. Ol' Biscuit—he ain't truly so old—he's on'y four—he's been stealin' biscuits since I give him a spoonful of flour one night, just like I said. Java got his name on'y because of his color. Thankee," he said as Ross handed an over-sized tin cup of coffee over to him.

LaChance squatted near the fire and looked about at the others, studying each in turn. His jaw hung unhinged, allowing the others to glimpse a disarray of broken and discolored teeth. Now and then he would take a bite of biscuit or sip from his cup, and those were the only times he seemed to shut his mouth.

Sam broke the temporary silence. "I'm curious about somethin'. Tell me just how in tarnation you got down that trail!"

LaChance looked up, raising his eyebrows. "Huh? Weren't much to it."

"Did you see the cave?" asked the Professor.

"I didn't see no cave. But then I didn't come all the way down the trail. I come over the saddle through the pine forest. And it's dark in there, folks. Almighty dark. A different kind of dark than just no light, if you know what I mean."

This brought an eerie silence down on the camp until Ashcroft cleared his throat. The Professor asked LaChance a few general questions about the country, but otherwise the group as a whole seemed to have been stilled by his comment about darkness—particularly Tom and Sam.

When LaChance admitted he had been in the high reaches of the Catalinas for the better part of four months, Melissa was aghast. "You don't get lonely up here?"

"Never rightly said that, missus." He ducked his head. "But truth be known Biscuit an' Java been the best comp'ny a man could hope for—meanin' no offense."

Melissa just smiled, and no one else filled the empty space with words, except for the Professor and Baron, who had moved on to some conversation of their own.

LaChance went on, seeming glad of the chance to exercise his voice box. "I like it out here—that's God's own honest truth. Take ol' Tucson, that's a bloody hole for a feller like me. I ain't old enough for the scum of that town to feel merciful t'ard me, an' I'm just differ'nt enough as to make 'em notice me. I go for supplies, and then I get. If I stay I'm liable to get hit over the head or even get my throat cut, or maybe some dang rascal—pardon my language—will pistol-whip me just to rip a giggle. I feel a bunch safer out here with the critters. If I hit it rich ever again I won't make the same mistake o' goin' to Tucson. I'll be lightin' out for the east, for some place civilized."

Melissa Ford's guarded smile said she appreciated that comment, and she looked over at Tom. Since it was hard for him to take *all* of his attention off her, he happened to glance her way at the same time. He just smiled back at her.

The Professor broke in on the conversation once again. "So you must be very familiar with this country, Mr. LaChance."

"Dang, sir! I ain't no *real* 'mister,' if you don't mind. Druther you just called me Skillet. Friends o' mine give me that name, back around sixty-nine. I was cookin' for us all. Fact is, I was cookin' when they all was out prospectin'. That's when the Apaches—Cochise, it was—killed 'em all. Not a one left. Just ol' Skillet. That's what happens when I try to camp with friends."

A long silence followed as LaChance sipped his coffee. Finally he looked back up. "But yer question was do I know this country. Good as anybody alive, I reckon. High and low, dry and snow. Knowed folks who come up in here and never come down. I always watch to see. They've found folks up here without heads. Found one my own self. Swear to heaven. Sorry, miss," he blurted, seeing the sick look that washed over Melissa's face. "No call for that kind o' talk. Shame on me."

Melissa shuddered, but she didn't allow the comment to scare her away from the conversation. "Aren't you frightened to stay up here without other people?"

"Other people? Shucks, missus. Biscuit and Java ain't just good comp'ny. They're also perty good alarm bells. An' they c'd shore kick the mustard out of any ol' prowler who gets fresh."

After the comment about finding people up there without heads, the entire camp had pinned their attention on Skillet, and he seemed to take a great feeling of importance therefrom. "There's strange things up in this country, things no man can rightly explain. But you wouldn't know it 'less you been up here long as I have, and seen what I seen. I've haunted these mountains pert' near five years now. But I been feelin' somethin' real eerie up here of late. Somethin' my guts tells me even Biscuit and Java cain't kick off the mountain. Time to spend a little spell down in town, I reckon, till I mebbe get shed of the jitters."

Munching on his second biscuit, with the camp good and properly spooked, Skillet LaChance started toying with a loose flap of leather sole on one boot. He asked for some rawhide to tie it up until he could find pitch to glue it "good and proper." Once Dowdy Ross accommodated him, he set to his task, all the while telling stories of things he had seen. In the beginning, all of them centered around eating.

"I've ate many a armadillo when I was scourin' around down Texas way," he offered, going on to tell about digging them out of their burrows and chasing them on hot desert evenings down narrow cattle trails, grabbing them by their stout-as-rope tails to avoid their being able to dig into his flesh with their fearsome claws.

"I ate a rattler a couple weeks ago," he said next. "Durn thing. Tried to strike on ol' Biscuit, it did. 'Course you can see Biscuit made short work o' that snake. Good eatin'. Mighty good." He scratched at his jaw, leaning back his head a bit to admire his handiwork on the boot.

"Had me a partner tried to bed down with a snake one evenin'. Bit him where no self-respectin' friend could help him." Here he let out a long chuckle, blushing when he looked up and caught Melissa watching him, enthralled.

Trying to shunt the crude story, he said just the wrong words. "I make my strike, I'm goin' into town and buy me a night at Sally's—er, uh—I mean, I'm gonna go into town an' whoop it up, shore enough."

To cover the prospector's embarrassment, Tom asked, "I assume you'll spend the night here with us, Skillet."

LaChance's eyes darted shamefully to Melissa, and he coughed. "Well, no, I didn't rightly figure to. I told you, there's real strange things up here, folks. I been feelin' haunted, like I should get off this hill, and tonight the feelin' is strongest of all. I'd surely rather not stay up here and have to find out why."

He looked around the fire, catching every eye intent upon him. "Reckon I've done most the talkin' and not rightly heard: You all got big plans up here?"

"That's private, mister," Viktor spoke for the first time, a little roughly.

LaChance studied him closely, his eyes unafraid. Proving to be more shrewd and gutsy than most would suspect, he let his eyes slope away. "Anybody got chewin' material?"

Sam gave a soft, good-natured laugh, hauling out a sack of tobacco which he passed to the prospector. "Keep it," said Sam when he tried to hand it back.

"Thank yuh kindly, friend." The prospector scanned the group again, holding every eye except Viktor's, whom he ignored. "Well, you plan on goin' up farther, 'course that's up to you. But I was you, I'd give a second thought to it. A second an' maybe even a third and a fourth one. There's things not right in these mountains. Ain't been for some time. Even Biscuit and Java will tell you that, if you watch 'em long enough."

It was pitch black around camp, and a slice of moon knifed through the eastern mountain ridge. Like wandering cattle, the stars hung in droves, and Pleiades crackled with brilliance. There was an aura about camp that the entertaining appearance of Skillet LaChance had not been able to overcome. In fact, some of his portentous words only made it stronger. Sam and Tom, who were the only two who had actually seen the strange man who tonight held this camp in his grip of fear, were also the only two who made any attempt to keep conversation going with Skillet. But even they could not shake the feeling in their bones.

LaChance bit off a big chaw of tobacco, and then he chuckled to himself. "I never got a chance to tell nobody 'bout this, but since you folks're so lively—" his eyes cut back and forth mischievously "—mebbe you'd 'preciate it. There was this young feller down to Tucson walks into the Shoofly restaurant. He's been out prospectin', much like myself, an' luck ain't been good—much like myself." He looked around to catch a smile or two from his captive audience. "Anyway, this here gent is gettin' nigh scrawny enough to slide through a picket fence, and he bellies up at a big long bench table, like they has in some o' them boom towns. He don't really have enough coin except mebbe enough for some Arbuckle's, but he sees this ol' man there next to him starin' at a bowl of stew that's just a steamin' up in front of him an' smellin' real good. The old man, he's a-starin' an' a starin', an' after a while the young prospector, why he gets to thinkin' this old man's got no intention whatever of eatin' that there stew. So he ups an' says, 'Hey, old timer. You gonna eat that there stew?' The old timer looks at him kinda sleepy-like an' says, 'Naw.' The prospector says, 'Then you mind if I do? I'm powerful hungry.' Old man says, 'He'p yourself.' He slides the bowl down to the prospector, and that young feller, why, he goes to eatin' that stew like there's no tomorrow. Gits down t'ard the bottom, and all a sudden he sees a slimy dead rat in there. What does he do but heaves up that whole mess o' stew right back into the bowl. The ol' timer looks at him, kinda sleepy-like, an' says, 'Yep. That's about as fur as I got, too.' "

Of course LaChance knew what was coming and had himself ready to laugh before anyone else even caught the joke. His guffaw filled the fire-lit camp, and it was soon followed by a hearty roar from some of the others. Even the Professor and Melissa laughed at the tasteless humor. Skillet slapped his knee in self-congratulation, as if he had accomplished some important mission.

"Well. Guess I best be movin'."

No one replied.

"Really gotta be headin' on down the hill."

Again, no one had a response for him.

"It's pretty dark, and I swore I wouldn't spend one more night up here, so I'll be on my lonesome way."

Several eyes turned to him, and a few heads nodded.

"Well, I guess mebbe I don't have to leave so soon," Skillet said with an uncertain smile. "Not while you folks are bein' so friendly an' all."

Sam grinned. "Grab your bedroll, pardner. There's more than enough room—for you and your burros too."

"Naw," said Skillet, standing up abruptly. "Thanks for the invite, but I orta get movin'."

Sam and Tom caught each other's eyes, and Tom winked. He stood up, stretching his back. "Well, old timer, if you gotta be movin' just make sure you watch out down the trail about ten minutes. There's a stranger down there prowlin' around that we don't know the intentions of. Maybe more than one. So you just look sharp."

Skillet looked down the trail and rubbed his chin whiskers. "You know, I plumb forgot Java was pickin' up somewhat of a limp earlier. It might not hurt to rest him up for the night."

Sam was standing now, and he pointed off into the darkness. "There's a good flat spot here, pard. Make the most of it."

Suddenly, they heard branches popping back in the trees. Every hand reached for whatever weapon they had near, and again Sam and Tom faded into the dark. Another branch snapped, and someone cursed in Spanish. Skillet LaChance chuckled. "It's just a couple o' greasers I saw earlier," he said confidently.

"They are Mexicans," the Professor corrected.

"Oh, uh, pardon me, mister," Skillet said, flushing. "Gits to where a man don't hardly recognize what he sees anymore. I plumb thought they was greasers." He looked around the camp, embarrassed, but no one was watching him.

"*Hola* to the camp!" a rattly voice came from the dark. When Baron told them to come on in, two men and their horses, with a packhorse in tow, appeared from the shadowy woods.

One of the Mexicans had gray-streaked hair, and his face was a wadded up brown bag. Shabby, patched clothes and tattered brogans attested to his poverty, and his hat resembled a wet blanket. His partner, in sharp contrast, wore a flat-brimmed, flat-crowned brown hat with conchos stacked side by side all the way around its band. His jaw was whiskered, and he had a slit of mustache on his lip and a deep cleft to his chin. He dressed in the short jacket of a charro, with the fancy, embroidered pants to go with it, and expensive boots with big-roweled spurs. On both hips rode pearl-gripped Remington Frontier revolvers, their nickel-plate gleaming in the firelight. The partnership could not have looked more unlikely.

The pair came in, the old man introducing himself as Guillermo de Madrid, and the younger one as Portento Gutierrez. Most who knew him, according to the older man, called him Pistolito.

As they introduced themselves, sat to a cup of coffee, and spoke of their time prospecting in the Catalinas, the disparities between the newly arrived partners only became more obvious. De Madrid was a used-up old man, his family all lost to bubonic plague passed on by a nest of ground squirrels they had trapped and eaten on the bluffs above Mexico City. He seemed cordial enough, but unable or unwilling to look anyone in the eyes as he spoke, and his handshake was without substance. Sam didn't think much about this last, as he had known few Mexicans who had shown any strength of grip in their hand shake. But beyond that there was something about the old man that Sam didn't trust. He didn't know for sure why.

Then there was Pistolito. He seemed no more trustworthy than his old partner—maybe even less—but that was where any resemblance died. The young man was full of himself, a braggart, and seemed to fancy himself a ladies' man. He made a point of flirting with Melissa Ford every chance he could, and both Tom and Viktor noticed it, Tom with amusement, and Viktor with smoldering eyes.

The camp was still adjusting to all the new company when suddenly Viktor looked up toward the mountain and the trail and let out a loud, startled curse. All eyes whipped toward the mountain. Their gazes focused on a large object coming through the air, an object that appeared to be a boulder.

With speed they could not counteract, it hurtled straight at them.

CHAPTER TWENTY-ONE

Almost everyone was on their feet by the time the fast-falling object struck the ground, but no one had time to run. It lit with a thud, and the wind from it made dust whirl up, and the fire fan wildly, sending ash and sparks dust-deviling off into the dark.

Among a good deal of cursing, a new noise reached everyone's ears. The sound made their blood run cold...

The once-round object, which now glowed orange in the firelight and appeared to be the full hide of a bighorn sheep, had flopped open. Its outside edges lay unmoving, but its center appeared to be a huge, roiling mass, and from somewhere in its midst one or another rope-like shape would dart out randomly every second or so. The din coming from this pile of objects had reached a crescendo, and even those who had spent little time out in the wilds knew what it was.

There before them writhed dozens of rattlesnakes, some of them as lively as they could be... and very angry. This sight—and the noise—in a matter of mere seconds emptied the camp.

Perhaps too stunned or disoriented, or simply too irate to flee, the snakes gathered themselves on the hide, or in the dust near its edges, wherever they had landed. Some of them writhed violently, and to Sam and Tom, who had dealt with snakes before, it was plain these several were in their death throes. Several others were quiet, and just lay there staring, likely paralyzed. But many of them, limber and tough as rattlers can be, were full of life, and they had coiled up and raised their upper lengths, willing to strike anything that came near their fangs.

Other than cursing, there was no talk in camp, at least nothing intelligible. Dowdy Ross was the first to react rationally, and he did so at about the same time several of the snakes were gathering their wits enough to start looking for an escape. Dowdy grabbed his shovel and collected an unwilling snake on it, then quickly tossed it down the slope toward the canyon. Seeing this, Alfredo and Juan Sanchez followed suit, and then Tom, and Pistolito Gutierrez. No one else made any move to help.

Sam had enough dislike of snakes that he would just as soon have started shooting them, but he respected what Ross was doing. For one thing, his practical side told him until they found out why the snakes had been thrown into their camp—and per-haps more importantly *how*—it was a good idea to conserve ammunition. It was obvious they had more dangerous enemies out there in the dark than a pile of rattlesnakes.

Growing bolder with familiarity, Ross picked one of the snakes up by its tail when it refused to stay on the shovel, and before it could react he flung it over the edge into the abyss. It was obvious that at least seven or eight of the serpents would not make it past the point where they landed. Wherever they had been thrown from, it was far up the slope, and inevitably several of their backs had been broken, or they had some other internal damage. Dowdy prudently collected those, chopped of their heads to be on the safe side, and threw them over by the campfire, where later they would serve as a meal for the more adventurous mem-bers of the group.

The work of ridding the camp of snakes was done in grim silence. Those who were brave enough to undertake it seemed strong in their common purpose, and they knew what needed to be done. For those who didn't take part, there were fifteen min-utes to contemplate the significance of this event. While they did so, they stood armed and ready, gazing into the darkness around them for any other hostile move.

When Ross picked up the last writhing snake and threw it— this time far over the rim of the canyon, Sam watched it go and then turned and gave Ross a long, hard look. Everyone cast their eyes uncomfortably about, no one wanting to be the first to speak. As was often the case, it was Viktor who broke the silence. He was holding a pistol in his fist.

"What in the *hell* was that?"

Every eye turned to him, but there was another long silence. "It's pretty obvious *what* it was," said Baron at last, with a touch of disdain in his voice. "The question is, why?"

"And more importantly," said Professor Ashcroft, glancing with dread-filled eyes up the mountain, "by whom? How much do you suppose those snakes must have weighed altogether?"

Tom turned to Sam. "What would you figure?"

"How should I know?" retorted Sam. "I left my snake scales home."

Tom laughed. "A little pun, huh? Maybe one or two pounds apiece, on the average," he mused. "And there must've been thirty of 'em." He turned and looked upslope. Even in the dark, they all had a good picture in their memories of the country's lay-out. There was no place within fifty yards that the thrower of the snakes could have been to lob the snakes down into camp at the angle from which they had come. It was ominous to think how far away whoever had thrown the snakes must have been.

"A minimum of thirty pounds," mused Stuart Baron aloud. "Possibly sixty. Plus the hide, which has to weigh at least five or ten. That's a possible sixty-five, maybe seventy pounds." Now he, too, let his eyes trail up into the dark.

"The closest place they could have stood for the bag to drop at that angle must be two hundred feet away," said Delbert Moore. "Several men must've heaved it together."

Sam scoffed. "You know how hard that would be to do? That hide had to've been originally tied for it to hold together like it did. If there was more than one man tossin' it, where would they get a handhold?"

"Maybe they used some kind of catapult," Melissa suggested. The comment made everyone turn to her in surprise. There were a few nods of respect for the suggestion.

"Is this so important?" barged in Pistolito suddenly, and turned his eyes to Baron. "It is as you said. The question we should ask is *why* it was done!"

The Professor looked at the Mexican, blinking—a dumb-founded steer. His eyes scanned the group.

"Whoever it was knows his trick could've killed some of us," Sam growled. "That's what we'd better keep in mind. He means business." He had his rifle in his hands, and at least half of his attention, even as he spoke, was devoted to the darkness around the camp.

"You talk as if you're convinced it was one man. That's impossible," Baron followed bluntly. "What you said seems common sense on the surface, about it being hard for more than one man to grip that skin if it only had one handhold where it was tied together in the middle. But no single man has the strength to throw a bag that heavy for any distance. And I agree with Del. From the layout of the slope, that must have flown at least seventy yards! You ever seen a man who could throw even thirty-five pounds a distance of *fifty* yards?"

Tom spoke up. "What about Melissa's suggestion? I wouldn't think it's that far-fetched. It could have been some type of catapult."

There were a few conciliatory nods, but the group didn't seem to buy into that idea. Finally, Sam spoke. "We're not going to find out anything until mornin'—that's all we know for sure. I'm takin' a lantern out there and make sure there ain't any of them snakes left, and then we'd best post a couple of guards through the night—and from now on. This could get serious next time."

"Oh, yes—*next* time. Heaven forbid," snapped Baron.

After Sam, Tom, and a handful of the others went to the canyon's edge and made sure there were no lingering serpents, they came back to camp and threw on a few hunks of wood. On Sam's suggestion, he and Tom took up their rifles and stationed themselves at opposite sides of camp. Starting with them, each guard would take two hours. In the stygian darkness it might be two of the longest hours of their lives...

*　　*　　*

The night passed without event. The following morning Sam and Tom were up not long after Ross, and they noticed that the two Mexicans, de Madrid and Gutierrez, had already gone, probably scared away by the night's events.

With a pot of coffee under their belts, the partners ascended the ridge that paralleled the trail and did a little scouting. In spite of the gray of the coming day, what they found was nearly as disturbing as the night's events. There was sign, although someone had attempted to obliterate it—and done so fairly well. But the closest the sign approached to camp was farther than either Ross or Baron had guessed—a total of ninety yards. The implications were unnerving.

Melissa's idea must be the closest to the truth. Whoever it was must have used some sort of catapult to launch the snakes. It was the only explanation that made sense. But that still left the question, why? The answer seemed simple: Someone didn't want them exploring the cave...

They returned to camp to witness an angry tirade by Viktor. He raged about camp, throwing things here and there and cursing. "You take someone in, treat 'em good, and look what comes of it! I knew we shouldn't have done that. Damnation, I knew it!"

When Tom stopped near Melissa and looked a question at her she said quietly. "It seems someone stole Viktor's box of cigars. He gave one to the Indian, Crooked Foot, for saving me. Now he's blaming him for taking the whole box."

Tom sighed. As much as he hated to admit it, Viktor could be right. It was more than passing strange how suddenly Crooked Foot had disappeared, and Viktor was positive that his gloves had disappeared at the same time. Crooked Foot could easily have left so suddenly because he didn't want to get caught with the gloves. And he could just as easily have returned in the night to steal the cigars. If Crooked Foot had enjoyed the flavor of the first one Viktor gave him the theft was entirely plausible—although how he snuck past the sentries was certainly a mystery.

Viktor finally ceased his rant and sat down grumbling over a breakfast of biscuits and gravy. No one went near him. He resembled nothing more than a sulking bear, defying anyone to come too near his meal.

It was only after breakfast, when everyone was preparing to go back to the cave, that anyone approached Viktor, and that was

Sam. The big man had come from his tent, and he was pulling gloves on his hands. Sam looked at him musingly for a moment, and Tom, who had also noticed the gloves, realized before his partner spoke what was coming. "You're pretty positive Crooked Foot took your cigars, aren't you?"

"Damn right I am."

"It wasn't too long ago you were pretty sure he took your gloves, too. What happened? He bring 'em back in trade? A packrat will do that, too."

Viktor's eyes flashed to his gloved hands. His face reddened, and he looked quickly around. "Who knows? They just showed up." He turned and trudged away without a word of his normal growling, and Sam grunted and looked his victory at Tom.

Everyone made the climb up to the cave to help in carrying artifacts down to camp. Everyone, that is, except for the prospector, Skillet LaChance, who had had more than enough of this place after the rattlesnake incident. He loaded his burros and made his way off the mountain following the vanished Mexicans.

Many hours had been spent in taking measurements of triangulation for each object in and around the cave, putting down descriptions and making sketches of the exact positions in which every object had lain upon first discovery. Now it was time to bring them safely down and prepare them for their long journey back to the museum in New York.

Everyone would have preferred to package and haul the artifacts using pack animals, but considering the shape of the trail, Sam and Tom had convinced them it wasn't safe taking a mule up there and risking caving the sides of the trail off even more. This was one time when Viktor, the dynamiter, agreed. Horses were never even considered, since they never seemed as cautious, nor as interested in preserving their own skins as the average mule did—the trait probably most responsible for their reputation as being "stubborn as a mule."

Because Professor Ashcroft had assumed jealous guardianship of the cave, he went in first with only two people, Melissa and Baron. Within half a minute, he came raging back out, his eyes flashing. "Someone has been in here!"

"How do you know?" asked Sam.

"The earth has been disturbed. And I'm fairly certain there is a lance missing."

"It's that damn Injun," Viktor said angrily as Baron stormed out of the cave, leaving only Melissa inside. "I told you he couldn't be trusted!"

No one said anything. The notion seemed believable to everyone, even Sam and Tom, considering Crooked Foot's sudden unexplained disappearance. As far as Sam was concerned, it didn't appear to be a large loss, though, and he figured Crooked Foot had as much right to anything in the cave as the Professor did—maybe more. But of course he wouldn't voice the thought.

Sam spent some time scouring the cave floor for sign that would confirm or allay Viktor's suspicions. Whoever had gone through the cave had blotted out their tracks. They hadn't done a good enough job to hide the sign of their passage, but all they had needed was enough to hide their identity, and they had accomplished that. One thing they did manage to do with a fair amount of expertise was to hide the direction from which they had approached the cave. Sam was able to finally ascertain that they had gone downhill, and he followed their departing trail partway, but somewhere the sign became lost among the tracks of everyone else who had hiked up that morning. One thing was clear: They had either come down the mountain face itself—or they had come up from the camp...

*   *   *

The Professor, although seeming more irritable than normal, was able to go on about his work with little ill effect. Viktor, however, groused throughout the day about his stolen cigars, and time and again he swore revenge on Crooked Foot.

Toward mid-afternoon, Dowdy Ross came up the trail to tell them noon dinner had been ready for some time and that if they wanted it palatable at all they had better come back to camp. Everyone headed down. Everyone, that is, except for Sam and Tom. They had decided among themselves on two things: one, they wanted to look around in solitude for any sign they might have missed earlier as to the identity of their thief. Two, they had not had a very good chance to look the contents of the cave over themselves, and both of them brimmed with curiosity.

Because they knew the Professor wouldn't want them meddling in the cave, and because he was likely to return at any time after he had eaten, they decided the first order was exploration. With light, nervous steps, they made their way into the cave, lanterns held over their heads. A number of items had been carried down the hill, but of course the most impressive objects still remained—the giants.

In awe, Sam and Tom studied the mummified figures, at least one of whom must have stood four and a half feet taller than Tom's six-foot-four. It was a daunting realization which left them both in silence for some time.

Tom was kneeling by the door, near that largest warrior, mesmerized by the sunken eyes and hollow cheeks, the skin that had shriveled and sunken in as moisture receded and now hung like draperies against his arm and leg bones and his ribs. But unlike draperies the skin had gone taut and hard.

"Watch it, Tom," he heard Sam say, and he looked up at his partner. "Someone's comin'." Tom stood up quickly, and Sam leaned toward the door and looked out. Soon, Melissa appeared. "It's the girl."

His alarm turning to a feeling of pleasure, yet worried what Melissa might say when she found them there against the Professor's wishes, Tom dusted off his knees and stepped outside. Sam followed.

Melissa smiled at them. "It's hard to keep your curiosity inside, isn't it?"

Tom grinned. "Nigh impossible."

Melissa seemed slightly out of breath, and her cheeks were flushed. "Did the Professor ever tell you the story about this cave?" she asked, looking from one to the other.

Sam looked at Tom, whose eyes went back to Melissa. He shook his head. "The story?"

"Well, I know he told you about the history of giants around the country and the rest of the world—things like that. But I don't think he ever told you about this cave—*these* giants. Would you... Are you interested?"

"Interested! Very much," Tom rushed out.

Smiling, Melissa waved her arm toward the few boulders that were left on the trail. "Sit down. I'll tell you about it."

Melissa gazed out over the canyon and drew in a deep breath. She leaned up against one of the larger of the rocks and looked at Sam and Tom, who watched her expectantly.

"What I know of this place is what Quiet Wind has told us, and what she knows was passed down through her family. Many years ago these giants came here from no one seems to know where and enslaved the local Indians—the Pima tribe in par-ticu-lar—Quiet Wind's people. But I will tell you more of that in a minute.

"In the meantime, the story that Quiet Wind told to us goes something like this: Her people a generation before her time were taken captive and forced to work in silver mines for these giants. As you might know, gold is normally also found where there is silver, but the largest veins in these mountains were silver, and these giants exploited them heavily. At one time there were even what Professor Ashcroft refers to as 'giantesses' who lived among them—their females. It is said that there are rich mines along this canyon that the Indian people worked in as slaves. Many of them died there due to the cruelty of the giants, either because they worked them too hard, with little rest and little food, or because... Well, frankly, Quiet Wind makes the claim that the giants cannibalized many of them. According to Professor Ashcroft's research, and the work of others, this seems to be normal among gigantic peoples.

"The cruelty and murder of course resulted in a deep hatred of the giants, and the Indians eventually revolted, as enslaved people often do. The legend is told that some of the Indian women were being kept here in the cave for the entertainment of the giants. These women were involved in a plan to provide casks of wine for the giants one particular evening, and the giants indulged in a long-lasting drinking session.

"That night, the Indian men came up here. The doors were always kept barred shut, but the Indian women removed the bars from inside while the giants were drunk—Quiet Wind believes her people might have put something extra in their drinks to make them sleep more deeply. Then the men outside built a large pyre filled with green wood and leaves and lit it.

"The women came out, leaving the door open so the smoke could enter. It took a while, but the giants finally woke up and tried to close the door, and by then the cave was filled with smoke. The door wouldn't close all the way by that time because of burning branches, and the fire outside was very hot. The giants tried to get air by putting their faces up to the windows, and the Indians threw rocks at them to keep them back.

"Others had managed to make spears and bows and arrows, and they used these to great advantage in discouraging the giants from escaping the cave. By the time the giants were desperate,

Quiet Wind tells that it was too late, as they had breathed too much smoke. They died as you can see them, in horrible positions of terror, hiding like rabbits."

Sam and Tom watched Melissa, mesmerized. Finally, Tom let out a long sigh, as if by Melissa's finishing her story she had released a hold on him. "So why didn't the Indians take all the gold and the weapons and things in there?"

"Well, as you can imagine they were much smaller than these people and couldn't use their weapons. But it would have mattered little, because of the natives' superstitions. It was be-lieved that the giants were evil, and that taking their belongings would only bring evil upon Quiet Wind's tribe. So they all agreed to seal up the cave, rolling rocks and other debris down in front of the door from the mountain above until it was hidden, as we found it.

"Her tribe went next, and with dried mud and broken grass they sealed up all of the mine entrances in the canyon as well. They wanted only to wash their hands of this period in their lives, and the story is that they gathered all they owned and traveled many miles away from these mountains, far to the west, possibly as far as California. It was only when Quiet Wind was a young child that her people returned to this canyon once more, perhaps to come full circle, in a sense."

"That's quite a story," Sam said. "It ties in with everything we found, too. The charred wood inside the door, those men lying there against the front wall. Quite a story, all right. And all that wheat and corn survived because they sealed up the cave so good the packrats and mice never could get in."

Tom nodded. "Knowing what happened here sure makes it come real, doesn't it?"

Melissa nodded and rubbed at her arms. "Goose bumps!" she said with a laugh. "So would you like to go back inside with me?"

Tom shrugged. "I would."

"You bet," Sam agreed. "Nothin' like havin' our own personal guide."

So the three of them went in. To add to the light from his lanterns, the Professor had been using the series of torches set into sconces along the walls. Out of the ten sconces, they were only able to wrench four of the remaining torches free. The other torch handles seemed to be somehow swollen, so that only with a great amount of force could they be freed. Sam and Tom lit a couple of the torches and one lantern and followed Melissa slowly about the cave as she explained what she knew of each artifact.

One item that greatly intrigued Tom was a huge bow, as tall as he was. To one end of it was still attached a long strip of braided, hardened sinew, and in a quiver that must have measured four feet long were seven or eight arrows. Most of them had iron points, but two of them had tips made of what appeared to be silver. Tom looked at Sam and Melissa, hoisting the bow and arrows up. "Now *there's* a weapon!" he said admiringly. "I read once in Harper's Weekly about a tribe of Indians in South America who had long bows like this and would lie down on the ground and shoot them by holding the bow with their feet and drawing back the string with both hands. The writer said they were pretty accurate and could shoot three or four hundred yards with them if they wanted."

Sam whistled. "There's a shot I'd like to see!"

Melissa laughed, and when Tom looked at her in surprise she said, "You're not serious, are you? Four hundred yards? That's farther than I would shoot my rifle."

Tom shrugged and grinned. "Well, I don't know. I only read it, I didn't write it." Hefting the bow again, he looked at it admiringly. "That's some stout wood."

"It gets harder and harder over time," Sam offered. "It'd take some man to shoot that now."

Melissa and Tom laughed, then Tom stopped and studied the bow for a second. "All right, pard, I'll take that as a challenge. Help me string this up."

Sam let out a chuckle of his own. "Tarnation, Tom. You're some man, but you ain't *that* much man!"

"Just help me string it," Tom insisted.

"No, you mustn't," said Melissa. "What if something were to happen?"

"Don't worry about that," Sam gruffed. "He doesn't have what it takes to break a piece of wood like that!"

Tom gave him a sarcastic smile. Together, they leaned their weight into the bow, and after struggling with it for a minute they were able to slip the knot in the loose end of sinew over the bow tip. With a studiedly haughty look, Tom then picked it up and placed an arrow in it. The arrow itself was at least four feet long. Turning to face down the long corridor that led to the back wall, he raised the bow and went to draw it back. The wood hardly even showed a sign that he had pulled against it. He tried again, and Sam chuckled dryly.

"Put it away, Curly. You're makin' yourself look bad in front of the woman."

One side of Tom's mouth raised in a self-deprecating smile. "I just wanted to see."

"Well, you saw. Guess you won't be out huntin' us up any deer with that, will you, big boy?"

"Go suck a button," rejoined Tom.

*   *   *

They had been in the cave exploring its treasures for over half an hour before Melissa decided they had been there long enough and talked them both into leaving with her and going back down to camp. With the fatigue of explorers who have been long in the presence of a find too incredible to contemplate, they traipsed down the mountain. They had no idea they were walking into a hornets' nest.

CHAPTER TWENTY-TWO

They could hear the commotion before they reached camp. As usual, the loudest voice was that of Viktor. As they drew near to camp they could see a cluster of people near the fire pit, and there was angry shouting and gesturing. Big Viktor stood out from the crowd, not only in size but in position. He faced them, his voice booming. In one hand he held his pistol.

Sam, Tom and Melissa hurried into camp. It was the Pro-fessor's words they made out first. "You don't know that it was him, Viktor! Be sensible, man!"

"Who the hell stole them then—Melissa?" thundered Viktor. "Those cigars have been around this whole trip. The first time they come up missing is when that stinking thief isn't around for anybody to see him smoking them. Explain that!"

"Well you can't simply shoot a man on your suspicions. And even if you caught him red-handed, theft isn't a killing offense!"

Sam looked over to see Crooked Foot at the back of the group, sheltered by Dowdy Ross. The rest of them were in a loose knot between him and Viktor as well.

Baron's voice rose for the first time, his bark drawing Viktor's crazed eyes. "What are you going to do, Viktor? Shoot them all? I'll buy you a new box of cigars when we get out of these mountains. I'll even make them Cubans! Come on, man—you've got to calm down."

Viktor's eyes seemed glazed over as he stared at his employer and friend—the man he looked up to most. Everyone waited, frozen in place. Finally, Baron walked close to Viktor and slapped him on the arm. "Come on, Vik. Let's go for a walk. You can smoke one of my cigars—or chew on it, as you please."

Blinking away a little of the glaze in his eyes, Viktor scanned the group slowly. He had embarrassed himself, and that made it hard to back down. Whatever the cause, the whole camp had placed themselves at odds with him. It was not something he would soon forget. Finally, he turned and jammed his pistol into the shoulder holster, following Baron into the forest. They were lighting cigars as they disappeared out of sight.

For some time the camp was as silent as night. Tom and Sam walked over to the ever-present coffee pot and poured themselves a cup. Melissa went to the Professor, but she only searched his eyes. For a long time no one could speak. Even though Sam, Tom and Melissa had come in last, the pall of deadly danger still hung in the camp and told them it was no time for words. Crooked Foot had gone to a big log and sat down in a daze, staring at his feet with his elbows on his knees and his hands hanging down in front.

After Tom had finished his first cup of coffee, he poured another and went over to sit beside the Indian. Crooked Foot looked up at him in surprise. For a moment he stared at him as if he had never seen him in his life. Then, after many seconds, the words of Crooked Foot were the first to break the silence.

"No take cigars," he said quietly. "Crooked Foot no take."

Tom studied his eyes for a long time, trying to read behind them. Finally, he nodded at him, giving him a wink. "Don't you worry, friend. I believe you. Have you eaten anything?"

"Bread. A small fish."

"Hungry?" Tom asked.

Crooked Foot nodded hesitantly, then looked beyond the fire pit. There lay the dressed carcass of a young javelina. He motioned toward it with his hand. "Good eat."

"You brought that here?" Sam asked as he walked over.

"Yes, Crooked Foot kill. Good eat."

Sam looked over at Ross, who was stirring sugar cubes into a cup of coffee. "Hey, Dowdy. You want help cuttin' up that hog? This feller's hungry."

Ross blinked his eyes as if shaking himself out of a trance and looked over. Then his eyes swung to the carcass. "Oh yeah. Thanks, Sam, I plumb forgot. Don't worry about it—I'll get it." He stood up, easing himself slowly to stretch out his right hip, which always gave him trouble. As if on an afterthought, he limped over and handed the cup of coffee to Crooked Foot. "Here you go, my friend. There's plenty of sugar in it. That'll be a good and tender pig. Thanks for bringing it in," he said as he drew his belt knife and walked over to the carcass, which smelled badly of musk, but which at this moment no one seemed to notice.

The exchange seemed to break the spell of doom that was over the camp. It was still daylight, and while daylight remained so did a sense of temporary respite from whatever the cold, dark night would bring. Conversations began to spring up all around, as if the camp were taking its first breath in many minutes. To a stranger listening it might have seemed false—a way to blot out the scare all of them had had on Crooked Foot's behalf.

A distant sound reached the camp, and everyone stopped talking until they could tell it was coming from down-canyon. It was the sound of horses making the climb up. Soon, it was a steady clopping, coming from more than one horse, and after another minute the two Mexicans, de Madrid and Gutierrez, showed up on the trail. Looking a little sheepish, they rode into camp and climbed down. Tom stood up to greet them.

"Hola, amigos! We figgered we'd seen the last of you two. What brings you back here?"

The older man laughed, glancing around nervously. "Ahh... We just decided we had to see if silver was discovered. You know—curious."

"Why don't you just tell them, Guillermo? Tell them about the ghosts?"

Again de Madrid let out a laugh. "It was nothing. Nothing!"

"Is there any whisky here?" Gutierrez asked, turning away in disgust.

Tom looked over at Baron. "Well, you'd have to ask him. But I'm curious about those ghosts."

Gutierrez squared himself to Tom and lifted his chin. "There is something in the air in these mountains, señor. Very strange. Guillermo, he decided he would rather leave here with all of you than just with ourselves alone. Old man!"

Tom chuckled. "Well, I've felt it too, Pistolito. I can't say as I blame him."

The two men walked off to tie up their horses, and the camp returned to normal.

Twenty minutes later, Baron came walking back into camp and sat down on a log end he had padded with a blanket. He set his rifle before him, then started breaking it down and cleaning the parts with an oil can and a couple of rags. He had donned a pair of oil-stained cloth gloves for this task so the sweat from his fingers would not taint his precious rifle.

Sam saw that Ross had finished skinning the javelina, and he walked over and said something quietly, then took his own knife and sliced off a half-pound chunk of thigh. He grabbed one of the metal skewers they had for this purpose, ran the meat through with it, and placed it over a couple of supports that hung over the smoking fire.

It wasn't long before the odor penetrated the camp, and everyone's mouths began to water. Viktor pussy-footed in just as Sam was pulling the spit off the fire. He was standing there quietly looking around the camp to gage their willingness to let him back in their circle when Sam walked over and handed the skewer to Crooked Foot.

"There you go, partner."

Viktor couldn't seem to contain himself. Baron's cigar hadn't been quite big enough to calm him down all the way, and seeing this was all it took to bring his anger back. He remarked sullenly, "So the thief gets the first spoils, huh?"

Tom had gotten up to stretch, and he was standing closer to Viktor than Sam. He gave him a mild glance. "He brought the pig in. Seems only fitting."

"Yeah, he brought it in. Just like he brought my cigars *out.*"

"You'd worry at a dead fly," Tom said. There was half-friendly humor in his eyes, but Viktor didn't see it or didn't care.

"What did you say?"

"The cigar issue's over. They're probably somewhere around camp, anyway. You'd better let it lie."

Viktor's voice continued to grow louder. "I ain't lettin' nothing lie. Damn thief will get what's coming to him." Tom shook his head. Whatever he started to say was cut short by Viktor. "What are you shaking your head at, Injun lover?"

Tom did the wrong thing then. He laughed. Viktor must have thought he was being mocked.

"Well, that's it." The fist came through the air with no warning. Tom thought Viktor was calmed down enough, or at least intimidated enough by Baron, that his brashness was brushed over for a time. His guard was completely down, and he took the blow on the cheek and stumbled backward, going down.

Suddenly, the camp was on its feet.

"Viktor!" Melissa's voice was almost a scream.

The big ex-stevedore didn't hear it. He advanced on Tom with obvious intentions of keeping him down.

Besides Melissa, no one spoke. This was a man's camp, a man's fight. These men, with the possible exceptions of Delbert Moore and the Professor, had all spent time around tough men, where tempers could explode violently, with or without drink. Sam and Ross had definitely seen their share, and mostly likely the Mexicans had too. It wasn't the place of other men to jump into a man's disagreement unless one man was pursuing an unfair advantage. The protocol was honored in this case only because Tom was able to roll and lunge to his feet before Viktor reached him. Otherwise, Sam would have stepped in.

Tom met Viktor's rush head-on. Even Viktor, the hardened street fighter, stumbled backward when Tom's head hit him in the chest like a battering ram and his legs pistoned forward.

Viktor was busy trying to keep his feet as Tom drove him back a couple of yards, but Tom had no such worry. He was able to plunge several hard blows to Viktor's left side with a fist that had seen more than one barroom brawl.

It was only a matter of a second or two before Viktor's feet found an obstruction, and down they both went, Tom landing hard on Viktor and knocking the breath from him. Judging by Viktor's appearance and by what Melissa had said of him, he would not be accustomed to being the underdog, even briefly. If Tom had been the vicious street fighter Viktor was he would have followed up his temporary victory by getting up and landing a few well-aimed kicks at Viktor's guts or his head. But Tom couldn't fight that way. He stood and backed away from Viktor while the heavier man struggled for his breath.

Finally, with a gasp, Viktor rolled over and shoved himself to one knee, watching for Tom to come raging back in. Tom should have known better. He should have done just that—taken Viktor down again in his moment of vulnerability. He didn't—he allowed him to get back up.

Now the heavier man came in more wary, more like a big cat than like the rhinoceros that had first rolled this ball. Like a pugilist, he held his fists before him, ready to block or to dish out blows. He had no pugilist's grace, however. He was bent far over at the middle, with his chin tucked. But his heels were flat on the ground. For a man who was supposed to have won so many fights, he did not appear to know the first thing about stance.

Tom could see Viktor had hardly been shaken, and he knew this fight had just begun. Yet he waited for his foe to bring the fight to him. This had been a long time building, and Viktor's hatred, jealousy, and fury would make him dangerous—but also careless.

Tom met Viktor's rush when it came, but he was only able to block the first blow. Like a bull, Viktor came on through Tom's defenses, tearing and hammering with his fists, oblivious to anything Tom could hand him. Tom's best defense was to stay out of the bigger man's way, but there were too many obstacles around the camp. He stumbled over a bedroll, and a well-placed blow from Viktor almost sent him to his back.

Somehow, he kept his footing and sidestepped Viktor's next rush. He sent a sledge hammer fist into the side of Viktor's rib cage before the man could whirl again.

That one hurt Viktor, but not enough. His body had taken worse blows than that, and it was hardened by time, experience— and hatred. Somehow, Viktor managed to get a hold of Tom's shirt with his left hand, and while holding onto it he began pummeling him over and over again in the body while Tom tried to block the blows. A half dozen of them landed before Tom drove down in desperation onto Viktor's instep with the heel of his boot. With a growl, Viktor turned loose and stumbled back, grimacing.

Tom swung with all his might, his fist catching Viktor on the edge of the jaw. Tom was no lightweight, and the blow drove Viktor back. But it didn't send him to the ground as it had many another man. It only seemed to make Viktor more determined to fight through the pain. He came in with a snarl, and the two men stood almost toe to toe, trading blows to the body.

Without warning, Viktor grabbed Tom's sleeves and dropped hard to the left, throwing Tom off balance and to the ground. Viktor followed up his advantage, kicking Tom in the chest before he could rise and knocking him flat to his back. Viktor's next move was a gamble; if it worked it might win the fight. By Tom's good chance it didn't.

Viktor leaped in the air with intentions of landing both feet in the middle of Tom. Tom rolled just in time, and Viktor landed on his opponent's side and lost his balance, hitting the ground hard.

Groaning with the effort, Tom rolled and came up. There was one opportunity, and although he hated dirty fighting he could see this was not a test of manly skill. It was a battle of anger, and that meant no holds barred.

As Viktor started to rise, Tom kicked him in the side of the face, knocking the heavier man down again. Sputtering curses, Viktor came up bloodied, with a handful of sand to Tom's face. Tom had reacted in time to close his eyes, but still he had to brush at his face to keep the sand from going into them.

Viktor pressed his advantage. As he gasped for breath he lunged up off the ground and grabbed Tom by the shirt, flinging him around. They were getting dangerously close to the canyon's rim now, where the ground sloped off sharp and gravelly, and slick with shale, for ten yards or so, then dropped over the sheer rock face for twenty feet.

Tom landed on his side, and as disoriented as he was he was unable to check his momentum. He teetered on the edge of the slope for a second before Viktor brutally shoved him in the chest with the bottom of his boot, sending him sliding down. Tom managed to grab onto a bush part way down and stopped himself.

Swearing, Viktor grabbed up a broken branch that lay nearby, and digging his heels against the shale and gravel, he started down toward Tom. A couple of expert swings with the branch at Tom's hands could easily send him back into a slide, and then it was only a matter of yards before the cliff's edge.

The sudden explosion of a pistol shot was daunting in the mountain air. Sam's booming voice was even more threatening.

"I wouldn't, Viktor. He goes over that edge, you go too—with a bullet in you."

Viktor had frozen at the sound of the shot. He stood pre-cariously on the slope, the sides of his boots dug into the gravel, and stared down at his foe. One good kick would send Tom over the cliff, and everyone knew it.

Without taking the chance of losing his balance, Viktor couldn't quite turn and look at Sam, so he spoke out the side of his mouth, while still looking down at Tom.

"Coffey! You cut me to the quick. You think I'd do a man like that when he's helpless?" Before Sam could answer, Viktor held the stick down to Tom.

For a moment, Tom hung onto the bush with both hands. Then slowly he relinquished his hold with one hand and grabbed the stick. He was, for the moment, completely at Viktor's mercy. All Viktor would have to do now was shove forward with the stick, and Tom would be driven backward, fall head-first down the slope, and it was very unlikely he could catch himself before going over. But then Viktor would die. If he thought Sam was making an idle threat, he was wrong. Could Viktor sense that?

The look in Viktor's eyes was still full of ire, but he forced a smile as he pulled back and helped Tom rise to his feet. The two of them turned and scrambled back up the slope, sending gravel and some of the smaller pieces of shale down the slide and making them career off into the canyon below.

They met Sam on top, his gun still drawn and cocked. With a smirk on his face, Viktor turned and started to dust off the tattered remains of Tom's shirt, but Tom slapped his hand away and stared at him hard. He had come too close to dying to want Viktor's hands on him, even in the unlikely event that he really was trying to be conciliatory.

Both men had blood running from the corners of their mouths, and Tom's lower lip was split down the middle. Their cheeks were bruised, and the skin to the side of Tom's left eye was torn. A trickle of blood ran down Viktor's upper lip from his nostril, and his cheek had been gashed by Tom's boot. Their hands had also taken a battering, and Tom was nearly shirtless, since Viktor had chosen several times to use his shirt for handholds. Both were a sight to behold, and the vicious fight had left the camp breathless and still.

Tom walked up to where they had a large steel pot with water in it for washing up. By the look in Melissa's eyes it was obvious she wanted to walk over and ask him if he was all right, but she didn't. She remained with the Professor, throwing worried glances at him now and then.

It was Ross who met Tom at the trough with a washcloth and dunked it into the water, then handed it, dripping wet, to Tom. Tom started sponging off his face with it, but he paused when he heard boots crunching in the gravel.

The rest of the camp was watching, their attention rapt. Tom was surprised to turn and see Viktor standing there, dusting off his shirtsleeves. Tom offered only his side to Viktor, his legs braced and slightly bent. He didn't know what to expect.

"You throw a mean punch, Vanse." Viktor dabbed gently at his cheek.

Tom stared at him, trying to read behind his eyes. He was surprised to find no look of malice. "You're no mama's boy yourself. You put on quite a contest."

Viktor started to smile, stopped, then let out a little chuckle. Tom was shocked when the heavier man's hand came out between them. After two or three seconds, he reached down and shook it.

"I think next time I'd rather have us fighting back to back than face to face," Viktor said with a nod. With that, he turned, not looking at anyone else, and disappeared into his tent.

CHAPTER TWENTY-THREE

The rest of the day was spent in further excavation and in taking steps to preserve the mummies. Melissa continued cataloguing each item that was removed from the cave and spent no small amount of time making exact notes of where it was taken from.

Each step was covered in minute detail, for the Professor knew this would be their only chance to have it documented properly. Once something was moved, they could never again be sure where it had come from, and to the Professor that seemed of vast importance. Melissa had told them he intended to recreate the scene in the cave in some manner once they had everything back at the museum.

Melissa's notes were so specific as to detail how many inches down in the dust and sand an item had been found, and they used triangulation to pinpoint the precise location. For Professor Preston Ashcroft, this expedition would probably mark the crown-ing achievement of his scientific life. He could not afford to leave any T uncrossed.

Toward mid-afternoon, Ross went back down to camp to check on supper. He had Dutch ovens buried in the ground that were stuffed with javelina, rattlesnake, deer or cougar meat, potatoes and other vegetables, stewing amid the heat of coals that had been buried with them. By the way Crooked Foot watched Ross as he walked down the trail, it was obvious that he would have liked to go with him and fill his belly some more, but he didn't seem brave enough yet to leave Sam and Tom and take a chance of running into Viktor by himself.

Shadows had lengthened, and the brightness of the lanterns inside the cave began to rival the brightness of the western sky before the Professor decided to call it a day. By then the air was thick with dust raised by their walking back and forth between the cave and the trail. It hung in the still air, smelling not unpleasant even while it tickled their nostrils. They were all dirty, tired and hungry, but the day had been well worth their efforts.

As they trekked down the trail, Sam and Tom walked side by side at the rear of the group, and Crooked Foot stayed as close to them as he could. Viktor had taken the lead, with the Professor and Melissa behind him. The two newly arrived Mexicans, Guillermo and Pistolito, stayed to the middle of the group. Neither of them had truly been much help in the day's work, but their curiosity made them stay. Besides, they knew they would get to eat with everyone else at the end of the day.

They sat around the fire later and ate their stew. Each different meat tasted good, but something had gone out of the camping experience since the bout with the rattlesnakes. No one felt the comfort they should have sensed here. Even the original feeling of accomplishment had diminished, since they spent the evening in fear of whatever more was to come. It was difficult to believe that whoever had thrown the rattlesnakes into camp was finished with them. It had been a deadly trick to play, and no one with that much animosity was simply going to give up and go away.

Throughout the evening either Sam or Tom, sometimes Dowdy or Viktor, would disappear into the dark, listening to the night, peering into the shadows, waiting.

It was at one of those times when camp was quietest, and when it was brightest—when every member of the expedition, including Guillermo, Pistolito and Crooked Foot, was sitting around camp starting to feel almost comfortable—that it began.

There came a *thump* out in the forest, twenty yards back from the nearest tent. Everyone jumped up from wherever they were seated, looking in the direction from which the sound had come. All they had heard was a thud, as if from the stamping of a horse's foot. But it sounded out of place. Something was not right.

Another bump sounded in the night, this one off to the left. By now, Sam, Tom and Ross were standing out in the dark, their rifles in hand. Sam peered carefully around him at the darkness. So far there was no clue what was making the noises, but he guessed something was being thrown. He waited, straining his eyes into the black.

Before anyone could say or do anything about it, the wrinkled old Mexican, Guillermo, threw a pile of dead fir boughs onto the fire, and the flames raged up, lighting the camp wonderfully. Sam swore and yelled for everyone to get out of the light.

Within seconds something came smashing into the fire, sending sparks and burning brands all about the area. Several seconds later it happened again, only this time the object missed the fire and landed in the well-lit area between it and the canyon. It was a rock! A rock that must weigh half a pound or so—and it had come from the direction of the canyon!

Sam's first thought was that someone had come to the edge of the canyon, less than forty yards away, and was tossing the rocks at them. If they were, they were fools, but how else could the rocks have come from that way? The other side of the canyon had to be four hundred yards across at its closest point...

"Tom!" Sam hissed. When his partner answered and he could make him out, he motioned him toward the cliff's edge. They made their way just out of the fire's glow, to the slope where Tom had fallen and nearly gone over. They scanned the rocky edge.

Nothing...

But Sam had already decided he didn't expect to find anything. Any man standing in that loose gravel and shale would have had to make a noise of some kind. Besides, any man throwing rocks at their camp would probably have lost his balance and gone sliding down toward the brink of the cliff. With the hair prickling up on the back of his neck, Sam raised his eyes to gaze across the canyon in the pitch black. Even the sky, dark as it was, was not as black as that stygian universe in this chasm and on the other side.

Then, even as he watched, he saw the orange flicker of a flame as it sprang up over there. It must have been three, maybe four hundred yards away. Could it be farther? He didn't have much time to contemplate that, for suddenly a rock cut the air over his head, and then one of the horses screamed.

Raising his rifle, Sam aimed at the firelight across the canyon and levered three shots at it. The fire kept flickering—a distant star. Sam hadn't believed he would hit anything, but it did him good to think he might have made whoever was lobbing rocks at them uncomfortable. He sensed another object move through the air, and everyone heard it hit one of the tents. Someone all of a sudden tossed a huge pile of dead wood on the distant fire, and it blazed up on the canyon-side, its center showing white. Together, Sam and Tom threw several shots that way, hoping whoever had fueled the fire was still nearby.

Another rock came flying and landed near where Sam stood, rolling away ponderously toward the fire. That one looked to weigh a pound.

Sam and Tom waited in the darkness as their own fire died down. No one was about to add any more fuel to it. The camp had been emptied, and no one stood in the light now. The night was alive with the scared breathing of the expeditioners...

*   *   *

Later, everyone but Sam and Tom lay in their tents, or in their blankets out on the ground. Sam didn't imagine there was much sleeping going on. Not after that night's events. After the last rock rolled toward the fire, there had been nothing more. Two or three hours had passed since then, with no sign of further danger.

Their tent still lying beneath the tree that had fallen on it, along with Tom's rifle, Sam and Tom lay on the ground beneath the stars. It was where, in the absence of rain, they would rather have spent their nights anyway.

Judging by the lay of the Big Dipper, it must have been around three in the morning when the horses started to nicker nervously. Sam woke from dozing to hear the hush of Tom's feet moving that direction, and he got up and circled around from the opposite side of the picket line. He could hear three or four of the horses fighting their ties, so he quickened his steps while still trying to be as quiet as possible. Besides the horses and a chorus of crickets, there was no sound in the night. It was probably some prowling bear, bobcat or cougar stirring the horses up, but that was enough.

Sam arrived at one end of the picket line at almost the same time Tom arrived at the other. Sam tried to calm the horses down by touch. He peered into the darkness, but there was nothing to be seen. There was no moon, and the woods were black.

After a long moment, when the horses had mostly settled down, he thought he heard rustling off in the bushes. It was a brief rush of noise, as if someone had lost their balance and thrown aside caution trying to catch themselves. Then once more the night was still...

Sam worked his way down the line of horses to Tom. They stood together in the dark, afraid to speak and draw anyone's attention to them.

They heard a branch pop up high in the forest, toward the dome of rock out of whose bottom Nature had carved the cavern. Both of them sharpened their eyes that direction, although of course nothing could be picked out of the dark.

Twenty minutes of silence had gone by, with the occasional creaking of two trees against each other and the chirp of the crickets, when they heard the sound. It was a muffled crunching in the bushes, and with a series of ponderous thumps it started to grow louder and louder. Pretty soon they could make out the bounding noises of a large rock rolling down the slope.

Since the earthquake had failed to send any rocks this far down the hill they were not worried, yet the sound was ominous out there in the dark. They at last heard the rock as it slowly came to a stop thirty yards or so away. After that, there were several more of them, perhaps five or ten minutes apart, but none came any closer than the first. Still, it was enough to keep them on edge. There would be no sleep that night...

*   *   *

The morning wasn't filled with the excited talk it should have been. Everyone huddled around the fire in their heaviest clothing long before the sun came up, nursing cups of coffee. Gray shadows made of the world a hushed, gloomy scene, and the sounds about camp were just as subdued. When they were stoking up the fire they saw the rock that had landed in it—a good-sized one perhaps a pound in weight. This made everyone turn and glance across the canyon to where the fire had been the night before.

Finally, Baron's voice broke the silence. "Well, that ought to be proof enough of that catapult theory. There's no other way a rock could have been lobbed that far."

Tom glanced over at Sam, trying to read the look behind his eyes. As much as Tom wanted to believe that, he had an eerie feeling there was no catapult. It was too obvious a statement to say there was something wrong on this mountain. But Tom had a feeling it was much farther reaching than he or anyone else realized. He had little to base that feeling on, just a gut instinct that was turning his stomach over inside. He looked back down, staring into his black coffee as he nursed his own thoughts.

Finally, he got up and wandered out to the brink of the gravel slope, holding his coffee, nuzzling his cheeks against his upturned sheepskin collar, and staring across the gloomy blue-gray shadows at the far side of the canyon.

He heard the yelp of the Mexican as plain where he was as anyone in the camp.

"Mi madre!" came the startled voice of Pistolito Gutierrez.

Tom whirled toward the voice just as everyone else was leaping up off their seats. The Mexican continued to spout epithets, and, moving cautiously, the group migrated to the horse picket line. Following close behind, Tom picked up Sam's rifle as he went. Taller than anyone else there, he could easily see over the tops of their heads. In this case it didn't matter, however, for the object of their attention was suspended high above the ground, pinned to the side of a big pine with one of the long spears they had taken from the cave of the giants.

Skewered there and dangling in death like a grotesque Christmas tree ornament was the carcass of a deer.

CHAPTER TWENTY-FOUR

It was one of those moments that seems to hang in time, where each person numbly searches his mind for anything that might make sense. But no one thought of any such thing.

The first words uttered came out of Viktor Zulowsky, when he shattered the third Commandment. Sam looked over at him and replied, almost without thinking, "God didn't have anything to do with this."

Viktor shot him an angry look, but for once he didn't reply.

Hardly another person caught the exchange, as the rest of them were still staring up at the deer. This wasn't some little Coues whitetail, but a good-sized mule deer doe, probably one hundred-fifty pounds of her. The top of her head was at least nine feet up the tree, and her hooves came nowhere near touching the ground.

From out of the deer's throat, in front of her spine, stuck the eight-foot spear. The fact that so much weight rested upon it, yet it did not move, proved that its point must be buried deep into the bark of the tree. But there was no explanation for it—none of it.

Sam gathered his wits enough to begin looking for tracks, but he saw none. It wasn't only that the expeditioners had trampled them out, either. That was true directly around the base of the tree, but farther out from it the ground had been disturbed by none of them, and still Sam could find no sign of who had come here in the night. There were a few indentations, the forest duff there was too thick and coarse to leave any distinct sign.

When he turned and looked back at the doe hanging there, Tom was watching him. Their eyes met, and held. Sam jerked his chin, indicating for Tom to follow him. Together, they walked off to the far side of their tent, and finally Sam turned to his partner.

"Big enough sign for you, pard?"

Tom studied his eyes for a moment, then glanced over in awe at the hanging doe. "That's big sign, all right. You have any idea what to make of it?"

"I don't want to even guess, my friend. Not yet. Let's walk."

Wordlessly, Tom followed Sam out beyond the horse picket line and on to where the mountain started to climb. Here, Sam suddenly stopped and crouched, fingering the earth in front of his feet. He looked over at Tom, and although he didn't speak, Tom followed his glance downward. There was a fresh depression there in the earth. It appeared to be about eight inches wide and half an inch deep in the forest duff. It was the second time Tom had seen such a mark.

"Bet we find more of these going up the mountain," Sam said.

"It can't be what it looks like," was Tom's reply.

"Can't it? Who put that deer nine feet up the tree?"

Tom swallowed hard and looked back at the deer again. "I was trying not to think about it."

"I'd like to forget it, too, but I've known for days there's somethin' strange on this mountain. We can't just forget it."

Sam turned and moved up the mountain, threading his way through the rocks and bushes along the path taken by whoever had rolled the rocks the night before. Tom followed in silence, and within thirty yards they had found three more of the depressions, and a few that might have been the same but were too faint to be sure.

The sign was something Sam wouldn't soon show anyone but Tom: the indentation made by toes and the ball of a foot through the rawhide sole of a moccasin...

Tom stood thirty yards up the mountain, looking down the slope toward the trail that led to the cave. Chills raced suddenly up his spine and raised the hair on the back of his neck. Somewhere out there awaited something like he had never seen. Something he knew could destroy everyone in their camp.

He turned to Sam. "Want to go for a ride?"

"Where to?"

"I don't want to say just yet. But load for bear."

They trod down the hill and saddled their horses. They stowed their rifles in the scabbards—Tom still using Alfredo's—filled their vest pockets with shells, and mounted up. They rode by a silent camp. The others were eating breakfast, and now and then they would look up at the doe that still hung ominously where they had first seen it. Their eyes turned to follow Sam and Tom as they rode out, but no one spoke. The clattering of their horses' hooves on the rocky trail added to the eerie stillness.

*   *   *

Leading the way down the trail to the place where Tom and Melissa had sat, Tom turned Nicker and rode him straight up toward the junipers. His first stop was at the big juniper where he had thought he saw movement. Here, he dismounted. "How about lettin' me borrow Gringo for a minute?" he asked Sam as he too climbed down. Sam gave him a queer look, then handed him the reins. "No, you hang onto those for me."

Saying that, Tom put a foot in the stirrup, then hoisted himself up so he was kneeling in the saddle. Perched thus, he peered into the branches of the juniper. There, as he had suspected, was a perfect window, between eight and nine feet off the ground. It wasn't a natural window. Branches had been broken off to create it, and at least one of them was an inch in diameter. It would have taken a person of some strength to break off that branch, alive and healthy as it had been.

Tom slid back out of the saddle and took control of Nicker once more. Without saying anything to Sam, he turned the horse. They had to ride downhill to get where they were going, for as they had learned before, the way up through here was steep and rocky, treacherous for anything but a mountain goat. So they rode downhill, then circled around the bottom of the slope and into the valley where they had seen the man watching them from the distance. Here, Tom drew Nicker in.

"What's your plan, Curly?" said Sam dryly.

Tom ran a sleeve across his mustache. "I figure if we don't ride over there we'll both regret it."

Sam only nodded. He had already known the answer.

They rode down into the valley. At the bottom, the way was level and grassy, studded with low-lying brush and a few outcroppings of rock and yucca. The grass this high up was still dark green, and waved in the breeze, and from the green patches across the canyon it was plain that more than one spring was close to the surface there. It was beautiful country, in spite of the feeling of foreboding here.

They pointed their horses toward the tan cliffs that soared upward and blocked in the opposite side of the valley. As they approached them they could see that they were taller than they had first guessed. In fact, instead of one hundred feet, as they drew near it appeared more like two hundred.

The partners pulled in a hundred feet out from the jumble of rocks and scree at the bottom of the cliff. They scanned both ways along the broken rock face, and it was obvious there was no way up for horses, at least not from this approach. The only place they thought might be accessible was far down the valley, maybe eight or nine hundred yards. It looked as if the cliffs fell off there and maybe came to an end.

Instinctively understanding each other, they split up, Tom riding to the left, and Sam to the right. A minute later Sam yelled out, and Tom rode back to him. There, in the side of the cliff, a series of hand and footholds had been hammered out of the rock. It only took a quick glance to see they were too far apart to be of much use to Sam and Tom.

Once again on that silent agreement shared by long-time partners, they rode farther along the cliff until Sam spotted a place that was accessible to a man with strong hands and an adventurous spirit.

Tom turned and looked at Sam. "Looks like a man could make it up here. Or do you wanna ride down the valley and see if there's an access there?"

"We're this close," said Sam. "We don't know how it looks down at the bottom of the valley, but I know I can make this climb."

"Well, I've gotta know about that tree, Sam. But I can't climb up here."

"I know," Sam nodded. "You never could take the steep places. I'll go up, but I'll want you to go out there far enough that you can see the tree—and watch close."

"I will, pard. Sing out if there's trouble."

Sam grunted. "You can bet on that."

Without any further comment, Sam hopped off Gringo and stood looking up the cliff. He didn't look back at Tom. He just started to climb.

As he had hoped, Sam found several wide places along the ascent where he could pause and stand with both feet, catching his breath. He didn't bother looking down at his partner, who he knew would be way too small to give him any comfort now. The cliff didn't seem any shorter now than it had when he started.

It took twenty minutes for him to reach the top, and he pulled himself over its lip with a grunt. Instinctively, he drew his pistol and came to his knees, looking around. The scenery he and Tom had not been able to see because of the high rock face was a lovely panorama of cliffs and canyon walls, splashed with spring wild-flowers and tall, waving grass. Another ridge of mountains hunched up some two miles in the distance, but between it and Sam were no less than four narrow canyons, patched with dark timber, brown clusters of granite and lush grass. The granite, ac-tually gray, only looked brown because of being covered with li-chen and a wash of minerals known as desert varnish.

Turning, he scanned the cliff's edge, and there, not fifty feet from him, was the dead tree they had seen from below. Only the tree, like the cliff, was much larger than he had believed. He walked to it with his heart pounding in his throat and his hand turning sweaty on the butt of his revolver. All too well he remem-bered the branch upon which the long-haired man had rested his hand while watching him and Tom. Even now he could see the picture of him standing here. Any tracks he might have left had long since been made nearly impossible to read by the mountain wind, but nothing could hide the tale that the out-curved branch seemed to cry out loud.

He turned around and looked down into the valley at his part-ner, and by the way Tom stared at him Sam could tell that he knew, too. The branch where the man's hand had rested, so totally at ease, was eight feet above the ground...

Sam had known. Somehow he had known the truth he had been trying to hide from for days. Too many signs had led to the conclusion that now could not be ignored. There was a man—at least one—up here in these wild mountains that stood an easy nine feet, perhaps ten feet tall!

To use the word that had brought terror through many a child-hood bedtime tale—a *giant*.

And that giant did not want them here...

Almost numb, Sam scouted the area for sign. Other than a broken branch here and there, or some disturbed lichen or bent grass, there was none. The winds had done their job well. He walked to the cliff's edge and looked down at Tom. At last he waved. There was no reason to speak—and every reason not to.

He wanted to avoid going down the cliff face, so he turned to his right, where the country sloped downward gently. He waved Tom that way and watched as he led Gringo in that direction, hopefully to meet him where there was an easier descent.

As it turned out, the only way down was a steep talus slide. But it was better than crawling down mountainsides that were little better than cliffs.

Breaking a stout limb where it hung half dead from a nearby tree, he used it like a ski pole to keep his balance as he slid down amid the rocks and dust. Twenty feet from the bottom the rocks stopped sliding abruptly, and he was forced to run the rest of the way down to keep from pitching forward. He came to a stop at the bottom, in a cloud of dust and rattling rocks.

Tom was waiting for him there. Once more, they stared each other down. Finally, Tom said, "We gotta get out of this country—now."

Taking his reins out of Tom's hand, Sam sat down on a big boulder that had toppled from the escarpment above. After a few moments, Tom climbed down and stood there beside him. Finally, Sam looked up at him. "We can go, but I'll wager the Professor won't. And what about Melissa?"

"If the Professor stays, so will she," Tom replied woodenly.

"That's the way I figure. And I know you too well to think you'll leave her up here."

Tom attempted a smile and slapped his leg with the reins, heaving a big sigh. "We'll have to talk to them. Somebody's going to get killed if we stay here."

The ride back to camp was mostly a wordless one. To the tune of plodding hoofs and creaking saddle leather, accentuated by the occasional jingle of a spur, the two men had plenty of time to think about what they had gotten themselves into. They also had time to contemplate the ramifications of what they had learned. Somehow, by some miraculous means known only to God and these mountains, a monster—a relic—from straight out of the pages of mythology had survived here in this boulder-strewn country for who-knew-how-long without being discovered.

Judging by the stature of the man they had seen standing up at the tree, this man would have to weigh five, maybe six or seven hundred pounds, and very little of it was fat. This was not the kind of a man who sometimes showed up in freak shows or circuses, with long, gangly legs and a misshapen body. This one was a beautifully proportioned, muscular man who just happened to stand three or more feet taller than the tallest men Sam and Tom had ever laid eyes on.

The partners rode back into camp two hours after leaving. Ross was the only one in sight now, but Crooked Foot soon came from the trees beyond the picket line. He had obviously been waiting for their return so he could once again feel protected. Even so, he looked at them with a vague sign of worry in his eyes as they climbed down and picketed their horses.

It was plain that something was strong on Crooked Foot's mind, but he didn't say a word as he stood by and watched Sam and Tom. They didn't feel much like talking either, so when they turned back toward camp, and a cold breakfast, none of them had uttered a word.

Ross stood up from stirring the fire as they approached. His eyes went from one to the other. Of course he wouldn't be able to read what they had found—no one would. But he was astute enough to know they had found something.

"I kept the coffee hot," he said by way of offering. He bent to his left and retrieved two tin cups from the top of a stump, handing them over wordlessly. He poured each cup full as they held them out. Crooked Foot stood there staring, only now, in all the uncomfortable silence, he was starting to fidget and look toward the trail that led back down the canyon.

The silence of the camp finally weighed too heavily on Dowdy Ross. He had waited for them to drink their cups halfway down, but he could wait no longer.

"You found something down there, boys. I can see that a mile off. I need to know."

Sam and Tom studied the retired cavalryman for a moment, and then Sam looked over at Crooked Foot and gestured toward him with his cup. "Maybe you oughtta be askin' him. Maybe we all should." The color of Crooked Foot's face deepened. He tried to meet Sam's eyes, but couldn't. "You got somebody runnin' these mountains that's half man and half bear, my friend. Don't try to tell me you didn't know about him."

The Indian looked as if someone had kicked him in the stomach. All three of the bigger men were staring him down, and there wasn't a hole big enough to crawl into. He ran a hand over his face, as if to scrape some of his distress away.

"Who is he?" asked Tom. "Don't be afraid of Sam."

Crooked Foot tried to smile. He looked behind him again, but there was no escape. "Big tall Injun. He call by Mexican name, *'Sombra del Muerte'.*" He scanned their faces, trying to make sure they understood his broken English.

"As white eyes talk—Death-Shadow."

The trio studied his face and the sound of his halting speech. Finally, Tom's voice broke the silence. "His name is... *Death-Shadow?*"

"Sí," replied the Indian with a vigorous nod. "Death... Shadow. *Death-Shadow.*" He looked around at the others. Then he turned back to Tom, who was the tallest by a couple of inches. He pushed his fingers lightly against Tom's chest, then gestured up and down to indicate the height of him. Next, he stretched his hands about three feet apart and held them up toward Tom's head, nodding and looking at the others to see if they understood. "*Muy... grande.* MUY!" he repeated. "Much very big."

To drive his point home, he brazenly grabbed Tom's big hand in both of his and held it up. Enthralled, Tom didn't fight him. Crooked Foot let go with one hand and held it palm down several inches higher than the ends of Tom's fingertips. "Mucho hand—this way!"

Stunned, Ross's eyes jumped to Sam and Tom's faces, hoping to see the same disbelief in theirs that he felt. When it wasn't there, he looked back at Crooked Foot. Sam and Tom hadn't relinquished any of the small, eerie clues they had picked up during the past few days, so Ross had no way of preparing for this moment. At last, his eyes returned to Tom and then rose three feet above his head. His face had turned very pale.

"There isn't any truth to this... is there?" His eyes shot back and forth between Sam and Tom.

Sam's eyes held only a steady stare. It was Tom who finally nodded, slowly. "It's true, Dowdy."

"So the rocks, the deer, the bag of snakes... It was all... *him? One man?*"

Again, Tom nodded. "One big hombre."

With a wild look in his eyes, perhaps the first time Sam had ever seen real fear there, Ross turned and scanned the canyon and the mountains around. "Melissa!" he gasped suddenly, looking up the hill.

Sam held up his hands. "He must know about guns, Dowdy. I think in the daylight we're safe."

Ross's breath caught, and he swore. "What if there are more of them? By the name of the Saints, we've gotta get out of these mountains!"

Sam threw down the rest of his coffee and set his mug on one of the fire pit rocks. "The Professor won't go."

"By damn he won't!" Ross exclaimed. "When he finds out about this... this *monster?* He'll leave—for Melissa."

Tom shrugged. "Well, you know him better than we do, Ross. Reckon it's time we go find out."

Five minutes later, with the hot coals doused and leading two pack mules up the precarious trail, the four of them marched toward the cave of the giants. Tom couldn't help but picture those gargantuan men lying up there, cold and shriveled, and still... And he could not help but contemplate the knowledge that one of them still ran these mountains... very much alive.

CHAPTER TWENTY-FIVE

Carefully negotiating the bad spots where the trail had sluffed off into the canyon, the four of them, Sam, Tom, Ross and Crooked Foot, arrived at the cave of the giants fifteen minutes later.

They could hear laughter for a while before their arrival, and it wasn't hard to recognize the boisterous voice of Viktor Zulowsky. But there was a false ring to that laughter, and his appearance bore that impression out. There was no feeling of levity on this mountainside. There was only the picture of a group of people striving to appear jovial while fervently involved in a work they wanted to be done with.

Stuart Baron made no pretense of being in a good mood. He was sucking furiously on a black pipe, sitting by himself on a boulder and staring up the canyon. His Ballard rifle rested across his knees. Sam knew Baron was aware of their presence, for he had looked over once at them as they first topped out near the cave. But he hadn't acknowledged them with so much as a nod.

Viktor stopped laughing and gave Crooked Foot a malevolent stare, and Quiet Wind only nodded gravely as she came toting a basket full of gold and silver jewelry and trinkets past them, setting it down in what appeared to be a communal spot for depositing anything that came out of the cave, in preparation for packing it back to camp.

Melissa was one of the next ones out of the cave. As her eyes met Tom's she caught her breath, and a huge smile lit her face. She was holding a crusted, time-hardened bear hide.

Tom smiled back, but it wasn't the light smile he would have liked it to be. Melissa caught the gravity in him, and her eyes swung to Sam, then Ross. "What is it?" she asked finally, her eyes tracking across the three of them in search of an answer.

"Better bring the Professor out here, honey," said Ross with the special gentleness he only used on her. "Everyone else, too."

For a moment longer, she searched his eyes. Then she whirled and hurried back into the cave. In a moment, the Professor, the four Mexicans, and Delbert Moore emerged, blinking against the sunlight. Melissa was behind them.

The Professor was wiping his hands off on a dusty white rag, a nervous motion. He looked back and forth between Sam, Tom and Ross. Last, his eyes fell on the mules. "Good morning, gentlemen," he said at last. "Did you forget we decided not to risk bringing any animals up that broken trail?"

Sam nodded. "It's important for us to get back to camp as fast as we can. We decided to risk it."

The Professor nodded, eyeing them carefully. "You have something to tell me?"

For a long moment the gathering was breathless. Everyone, even Baron, had stopped before them. The ominous feeling that had descended was like a sickness in the air, a pall that no one could help but sense. Baron seemed to cease breathing as the look about the three men came home to him. He plucked his pipe from his lips and lowered it to his side, staring at them. Even Viktor had nothing to say.

Tom turned and glanced at Sam, and by this Sam knew he had been elected as the spokesman. He pulled in a long breath, and let his eyes scan the group. He didn't relish what he had to share. He was going to look like a bearer of fairy tales—a fear monger, bringing to them a story not so unlike "Jack and the Beanstalk."

His eyes had locked on Professor Ashcroft's. "There's no easy way to say this, because it's going to make me and Tom look like fools. I'll just say it plain. As you've already figured out, there's someone up here who wants us out of this country. This man is..." He stopped as he tried to find a way out of uttering the word 'giant'. Just before looking back at the Professor, he shot a glance toward the cave, the final resting place of men who would have towered over Sam, Tom and Viktor. He drew himself up. "To put it bluntly, he stands at least nine feet tall."

Long seconds ticked by. All eyes were pinned to Sam. Not so much as a breath could be heard. The silence was broken by the loud guffaw of Viktor. It burst like thunder from his throat and shook them all. Finally, he slapped his knee.

"You're a real funny man, Coffey. Did one of the mummies come back to life, or what?"

Sam stared Viktor down, then swung his eyes back to the Professor. "He goes by the Mexican name of Sombra del Muerte—

Death-Shadow. And you might as well know now that he lays claim to these mountains."

Now even Viktor grew quiet. It was as if putting a name to the... *monster* brought life to him. A strange, pinched look of fear surrounded Viktor's eyes. He licked his lips and looked at Baron. The businessman stood stock-still, his pipe clutched in his fist.

"How... Have you *met* this man?" faltered the Professor finally.

Tom shook his head. "We've seen him. But Crooked Foot *knows* him."

The crippled Indian suddenly took on a much larger measure of importance, and everyone's eyes honed in on him. After a moment of silence, the Professor, Baron and Viktor started firing questions at him. Startled, the Indian stepped back.

"One at a time!" Sam growled, his well-deep voice rising above the rest. When they had quieted, he said in a softer voice, "Give 'im some room to breathe."

"Who is this man?" Professor Ashcroft blurted. "What does he look like? What does he want with us?"

"*Muy grande... hombre*," said Crooked Foot haltingly. Again he held his hands about three feet apart and pushed them toward Tom, who stood at his side. "Like Tom, but more big, like this." He elevated his hands toward Tom's head.

Baron stared in amazement, then finally growled, "So what does he want? What's he after?"

"His... gold. Silver." He motioned toward the cave. "His fathers'. He wants the white eyes... gone. This place—his." To punctuate his words, he waved an encompassing hand over the cave and the entire canyon. "He say this—all his."

The Professor's face was pale. "Will he take it by force? These things he feels are his?"

Crooked Foot stared at the Professor, seeking comprehension. Finally, he turned to look at Tom.

"Will he kill us to get what's here?" Tom asked.

The Indian's head began to move, slowly at first, then ended in a vigorous nod. "He kill," he averred. "He kill all to take back... *this."* He pointed at the cave. "And the eye of the hawk."

"What is the 'eye of the hawk'?" asked the Professor.

"This."

The single word came from the lips of Quiet Wind, and everyone turned their eyes to her, surprised to hear her break her usual silence. She held up a long cylinder of what appeared to be tarnished bronze, which mimicked the color of her hand. It was about two inches around, and toward its top was an intricate statue of the head of a hawk with its beak sharply forward, open slightly, and its feathers swept back fiercely at the back of its head.

Baron leaped forward, practically jerking the piece out of the old woman's hand. "The Hawk's Eye!" he uttered with a look of triumph. The others looked at one another in wonder as he held it up so that the back of the hawk's head was aligned with his eye. Then he lowered it and looked back at Quiet Wind.

"Where was this?" She turned and pointed, speaking in Spanish.

The Professor cocked his head as she talked, then looked at Baron. "She said it was wrapped inside the bear hide. So... are you planning to tell us what this is?"

"Certainly I'll tell you," replied Baron. "This is the real reason I am here—the reason *all* of us are here, in effect. The reason our backers were willing to fund this expedition from the beginning."

Puzzled, the Professor looked back and forth from Quiet Wind to Baron. Baron chuckled. Even with the revelation about the man named Death-Shadow, his entire mood had changed. "We have reason to believe this canyon holds veins of silver that could open this country up wide to mining ventures. This"—he held up the Hawk's Eye—"is the key."

For seconds, the Professor, along with everyone else, simply stared at Baron. Finally, Ashcroft said, "You mean to tell me... The scientific importance of this expedition meant nothing to them? The only reason you came here was for the promise of silver mines?"

Baron brushed that off. "Don't be silly, Professor. Of course they're interested in the giants and the cave. Who wouldn't be? It's intriguing. But old artifacts and mummies don't make this world go around. Silver and gold do."

Trying to push this new revelation aside, the Professor finally sighed, then took another breath. "Don't you think there's a more important question at hand than mineral wealth?"

Baron gazed back at him, then finally laughed. "You mean this... *giant?*" He said the last word in a derisive tone, looking over at Crooked Foot and those who stood with him. "Listen, Professor, I don't know what we're being taken for, but I for one am not the imbecile I have obviously been mistaken as. There is no mysterious Goliath living in these mountains." He shot a hard, challenging look at Sam.

Sam let one corner of his mouth raise in a smile. "What are you afraid of, Mr. Baron? You think I'm trying to scare you off so I can steal your silver mine?"

The businessman's gaze grew even harder. "I won't be spoken to in that tone of voice. Not by some backwoods redneck. Don't forget who's paying for you to be here, Coffey."

Sensing the ire that was building in his partner, Sam calmly reached out and laid a steadying hand on Tom's forearm. "Mister, I'll stand for a lot of things when I'm ridin' for a brand. But bein' called a liar and thief isn't one of 'em. You're a proud man, and I won't ask you to take back what you said, but I wouldn't push it."

A sharp retort formed on Baron's lips, but after a brief search of Sam's eyes it died away. "I guess you must really believe what you've told us, Coffey, but you're obviously mistaken. Someone is up here, certainly. And that someone is playing tricks on us to try to drive us off. It's as simple as that. Men as large as you speak of no longer exist—at least not unless they're some kind of misshapen freak."

"The man I'm talking about is built like an athlete," countered Sam. "I'd venture to say Tom is built as well as most men I've met, and the man we saw was even more athletic looking than he is—from what we could see at the distance we saw him from."

He sensed, more than saw, the jealousy this statement brought to Viktor's eyes, and on an afterthought he said, "And he had the powerful muscles of a man like Viktor in his chest and arms as well." This brought a look of pride to the big man's eyes. "He was no misshapen freak. No more than the ones in the cave."

Melissa was staring at Tom, her face a few shades paler than normal. Delbert Moore was the same. Pistolito licked his lips, glancing about at the surrounding country. His hand came up to rest on the pearl butt of his right pistol.

Viktor, like Melissa, stared at Tom, then let his eyes pass over Sam, and last of all, Crooked Foot. Finally, he uttered Baron's name and motioned him away from the others. They spoke quietly for a few minutes, and finally they walked back over to the group.

Baron spoke in a quieter, less cocky voice. "All right. If this... *giant* is out there... what do we do? He's one man. And surely he has no firearms. Do we simply give in to him?"

"What if there's more of them?" inserted Delbert Moore. "What if there's a whole tribe?"

A few eyes turned to Crooked Foot with the obvious question, and he understood and quickly shook his head. "No others. Only Death-Shadow."

Sam looked at the Professor and repeated what Baron had put into words. "So do we give in and leave? Or do we stay and risk somebody gettin' killed?"

A lifetime of dreams was wrapped up in the scientist's face, dreams of the expedition-of-a-lifetime that would make his name remembered in the scientific world perhaps forever. Melissa might not have the same dreams, but she had a strong professional and personal attachment to the Professor. She would stay here because she knew it was what he wanted. Most likely Del Moore would too. And if Melissa stayed, Ross would never leave. Baron was here for the money, and Viktor was like his shadow. The only ones in question became the four Mexicans, Quiet Wind, Sam and Tom. But it hit home to Sam that he couldn't count on Tom being rational either—not while Melissa was still on this mountain.

Sam wiped at his mustache. "This Death-Shadow lives up here, and he's bound to know this country like you know your own parlors. He'll know every hidin' place within fifty miles of here, every spring, every cave, every stinkin' hole in the ground. He may not have the same weapons we do, but he's got one just as powerful, and maybe more powerful—darkness. He can hide up here where we'll never find him and come in to kill us when the sun goes down, and there won't be one thing to stop him. Not one damn thing.

"He's playing with us. Or warning us. He prob'ly could've killed us all by now if he'd meant to. But I'm bettin' if trying to scare us don't work—he'll go farther. There's gonna be some serious consequences if we decide to stay here. We'd best be ready to face 'em."

Baron had the Hawk's Eye clutched almost fiercely in his hand. He looked down at it, then let his eyes sweep upward through the canyon. "I've come too far to turn back now."

The Professor was watching Baron as he spoke, and then he turned and ran his eyes over Sam, Tom, Ross, and last of all the Indian. "You know I have to finish what I came to do, gentlemen. There may never be another find of this caliber on the American continent. Sometimes the risks of science are high, but for the sake of mankind we take them."

"All right." Sam looked over the group. "Your decision. Then we'd better move fast. You'll need to get all this stuff down off the mountain as quick as you can. And as for the silver" —he looked at Baron— "I would come back for it with more guns than we have here. If it's as rich as you say it shouldn't be any trouble paying for a bunch of boys who won't mind fightin' this Death-Shadow for it."

Before Baron could voice his reply, Viktor cut in with a brisk nod. "I'm for getting all this stuff out of the cave and getting down out of these mountains. When Melissa's safe we can come back."

Giving his protegé a sharp look, Baron clamped his jaw shut. Viktor had played the "Melissa card." Finally, he looked back at Sam. "If you're agreeing to stay here and offer your help, then I'll go with what Viktor suggests. I agree that Melissa should be taken safely down the mountain back to Tucson. But while we're here I am going to conduct a search for the silver mines that were closed over by the Indians after the revolt. It will pose no deterrent to the Professor's plans to discover their exact location before we go."

Sam shrugged, and Tom said, "Suit yourself. As long as we all agree on getting Melissa some place safe."

*   *   *

The work in the cave went on apace, even without Baron and Viktor there to help. Earlier, with the Hawk's Eye in hand, they had explored around the front of the cave and moved a twenty-pound boulder to discover an oval-shaped hole in a large shelf of rock that jutted out from the cave entrance. This, so the tale had come down to Quiet Wind, was the socket meant to allow entry of the Hawk's Eye.

The Hawk's Eye was a simple sight, much like a peep sight on a rifle. Through the back of the brass hawk's head was drilled a pin-sized hole, and it exited out the front—straight through one of the hawk's eyes. When seated solidly in the bottom of its socket, one had only to lean down and peer through it to pinpoint the exact location at the head of the canyon where the sealed mine was supposed to be.

Viktor and Baron had found a way up to the head of the canyon after returning to camp, then going out beyond where the horses were picketed and riding up around the monolith where the cave of the giants had formed. After a time, those working at the cave could see the two tiny forms, and their horses, far up the canyon exploring. Three hours later they came walking back up the precarious trail. There was no satisfaction on Baron's face as he stopped in front of Sam.

Without any ado, he said, "I need you and your partner to go up there. We'll stay down here with the Hawk's Eye and point the way for you if you need it."

Tom walked over and stopped with a big grin on his face, chewing on a toothpick. "Country changed a little once you got up there, huh?"

Baron ignored him and continued talking to Sam. "It should take you under an hour to get up in the general area. Take a look through the sight from here so you can get an idea of where you'll need to go. When you get up there we'll direct you by hand signals. You have field glasses, correct?"

Sam nodded but didn't speak. He wasn't particularly happy to go up the canyon and do Baron's bidding. But as he and Tom had agreed, it was after all Baron who was paying their wages, and they had signed on to ride for the brand, in cowboy lingo.

Sam crouched down and wiggled the Hawk's Eye cylinder around in its socket, making sure it was seated well. Then he peered through the eye, getting a bearing on the area of the upper mountain where they had to go. Tom followed suit. Without a word, they turned together and trudged back down the trail.

It took them over an hour to get up to the top of the canyon, not because they couldn't move as fast as Baron and Viktor, but because they purposely dallied down in camp and had a cup of coffee and made themselves a sandwich before even going to saddle their mounts.

Once they had saddled Bruiser and Cocky, it was easy work for Sam and even Tom to follow the trail left by Baron and Viktor. The trail led them around the rear of the mountain. There the timber sometimes grew like dog hair, and numerous deep, fern-filled pockets back in some glen surprised them. They had to jump several fallen logs and skirt huge holes left by fallen trees, and twice they had to ride around large wet areas where springs surfaced and made the footing mossy and full of muck.

They finally came out of the woods back up on the ridge and rode its razorback until they could almost see down the canyon, not far from where the silver mine should be. Here, the trail started across the canyon at a place where it was growing shallow—almost at its head—and they had only to fight some low scrub brush and skirt a few pinyons and cypress trees to make their way to the area where Sam believed the Hawk's Eye had directed them.

Around the area, they found a profusion of tracks left by Baron and Viktor. They had ridden around and around through the trees and loose talus and boulders, but obviously they had no idea where they were going. Sam took out his binoculars and peered down the canyon. Baron must have been waiting anxiously, for the moment Sam picked him out in the lens he could see the man's hands waving exaggeratedly to his left.

Sam grinned, watching through the glasses. As he handed them to Tom to have a look he said, "Looks like the old boy's gettin' himself worked into a lather."

Tom chuckled. "Good for him to sweat a bit." Putting down the binoculars, he took Cocky's reins up once more from where he had dropped them on the ground and started in the direction Baron was guiding them. After fifty yards or so they completely left behind the area cluttered by horse tracks. They crossed a steep section that made them scramble to keep their balance, an area from which Tom wasn't particularly keen on looking down. Had they slid for ten or fifteen feet, they would have reached a tall escarpment that fell sharply off to end in an uncomfortable look-ing patch of boulders below.

Coming off the slide and around a tight corner, they found themselves in a wide, flat area where both men and their horses could stand without danger. To their left was a vertical, pock-marked face that appeared to be made of sand and clay, with bits of straw sticking out of it—simple adobe. The wall ended at a height of ten feet, where it ran into a solid rock shelf of crumbly granite hanging out over the adobe like a natural awning.

Sam looked at Tom. "What do you think, pard? I'd lay odds we found Baron's mine."

Without comment, Tom took a pick off his saddle. Making sure Sam wasn't behind him, he swung it, and its sharp head rang off the hard adobe.

"Been there a while," he remarked, then swung again. It took several of his hardest swings before he made much of a dent. The point of the pick sank about halfway up to the head, and Tom grunted with satisfaction. "It's adobe, but leave it another fifty years and it's likely to be hard as the granite."

The partners took turns at the pick for ten minutes or so until finally it broke through. After that, the work didn't become any easier, but at least they knew for a fact they had found what they sought. Behind the foot-thick wall of adobe was a black hole that glowered back at them like a vindictive eye, angry for this dis-ruption after all its years in hiding.

Ten minutes later, they had carved a hole the size of Tom's chest. Enough sunlight spilled through that he could lean his head inside and at least see how far back the hole went. He wasn't sure, but in the dim light he thought he might have seen some digging tools of a much older style than his and Sam's. The hole went back until it disappeared in an unfathomable depth of darkness.

Tom pulled his head out and looked at Sam. "If there's a mine up here, I'd say it's a ninety-nine percent sure bet this is it."

Sam nodded. "Well, that's good enough for me. Let's go back."

*   *   *

They met Baron back at the cave in the late afternoon and told him what they had found, and for the first time in a day or two the businessman smiled. "Good work. Tomorrow we'll go up there and dig it out a little more and get some ore specimens."

The Professor had just stepped out of the cave, and as he heard the last words from Baron a little frown creased his face. But the moment Baron looked over, he turned with his latest armload of treasure and deposited it with all the rest that waited for its trip down the trail. By that time, the Mexicans, Melissa, Ross, Moore and Crooked Foot had all gone down the mountain. Remaining were only Baron, the Professor and Viktor.

When they returned to camp, Tom was shocked to go to their tent and find that it was now uncovered. The big log that had lain across it had been sawn through in several places, and the pieces rolled away. He immediately dropped down to go through the tent looking for his Marlin rifle, but all he found was some clothing and a few other belongings. At that moment Crooked Foot came limping up, smiling. Tom looked down to see the Indian holding his rifle out to him. He was glad to see it, but the gladness turned to disappointment when he saw a large crack across the stock. It would be a debilitating injury.

Crooked Foot shrugged apologetically, then held up several fairly long strips of rawhide. "Use... these." Tom looked down at them, and suddenly what Crooked Foot was suggesting came to him like the ringing of a bell.

"You're right, Crooked Foot!" he said happily. "That'll work like a charm!"

Although it was disappointing to think of the damage to his rifle, only one year old to him now, it was exciting to know he could easily put it back into service, and even though it would never be as pretty, when he was finished with it it would be stronger than when it was brand-new.

He walked to Ross' tent and got a big black pot from beside it, then went and poured some water into it, dropping all the strips of rawhide down in. Setting these aside to soak, he looked over at the Indian, who had been following his movements. Crooked Foot smiled with satisfaction and gave a big nod of his head.

Later, when supper was over, Tom and Crooked Foot sat side by side, and Tom pulled the rawhide strips from the water one by one. The water had turned a faint milky white now, and the strips were completely soaked through, as limp as dead night crawlers. Melissa finished drying the dishes for Ross, and then she came over and sat on the other side of Tom.

"What are you doing?"

He looked over and smiled. "Crooked Foot sawed that big log off our tent while we were gone today, and he dug out my rifle. Unfortunately, the stock's busted. I'm going to put the old Injun fix on it, though. Watch this."

While she watched, mesmerized, Tom roughed up the broken stock with a hunk of granite, which would give the rawhide a solid place to grab onto. Then he took the strips of rawhide one at a time and wrapped them tightly around the broken part. From Dowdy Ross' well-managed tool kit, Tom took a hammer and several tacks, and he drove the tacks through the exposed ends of the rawhide. Then he held it up in front of him and nodded with satisfaction.

"That will hold it?" asked Melissa dubiously.

"Sure." Tom reached over to his warbag and pulled out a strip of rawhide that was much like the ones he had soaked. He held it out to Melissa, who took it. "That's what the rawhide started out like. When you put it in water it becomes like what you saw me wrappin' the stock with—almost like a wet noodle. But when it dries it'll be back like that again—hard as a rock. This stock will be even stronger than it was before."

Melissa looked at the hard rawhide, then reached into the soupy water to draw one of the wet ones out. She set the dried piece on one of her legs and took the wet piece in both hands, stretching it out. She smiled at Tom. "That's a pretty nice tool."

Tom laughed. "We use it for just about everything, from hanging doors to fixing broken fence to resoling a moccasin."

*   *   *

That night, the camp, for the most part, slept peacefully. Tom and Delbert stood first watch. When dawn came, Sam and Viktor, the last guards, met it with open eyes, and fingers stiff from the cold. Sam was on the side of camp nearest to the cave. He picked up his Marlin and moved down the slope to where Viktor sat nestled between two fallen logs.

Standing over him, he surveyed the misty blue ridges and the depths of the canyon below. Nothing moved but an armload of songbirds that were scattered like ornaments in the trees up and down the slope. They bounced here and there between branches, flashing their bright red, yellow and blue flags of color and twittering their freshest songs. A yellow warbler stopped only ten feet from Sam, perched like an autumn leaf on a frail black branch of a dead aspen. When he raised his hand to wipe at his mustache it sailed away down the slope.

Sam rolled a smoke and lit it. When he saw Viktor glowering up at him, he remembered his cigars. He held the bag of tobacco and cigarette papers down to the bigger man, but Viktor waved them off. With a grunt, he shoved himself up to one knee, resting that way for a moment.

"Quiet on that end," said Sam.

Viktor nodded. "Same."

"Too quiet for that big bruiser," Sam observed. "Wonder what he's cookin' up."

"Aiming to get himself blasted off this mountain is what. No man is so big that Baron's rifle can't take him down enough notches to bury him."

Sam looked blandly away. He sensed the kind of man Death-Shadow was. Viktor had no idea what it took to survive in these mountains. The man could be watching right now. He might be laughing at the cocky way Viktor moved around camp, laughing because next to him Viktor would look like a child. Laughing because he had spent a lifetime learning to fade away shadow-less into the rocks and trees, leaving little sign of his passing.

The expedition was a camp full of dead men if they stayed here much longer. All the big man had to do was want it. Unless sheer good fortune intervened, there was little defense against such a juggernaut as Death-Shadow.

Death-Shadow... It seemed so strange to think the name. *Death-Shadow...* What sort of a man was he, inside? What were his needs? Did he desire anything that other men desired? Did the treasures of this mountain truly mean anything to him? Did he simply wish them gone so he could live in peace, or did he want them gone so he could retake what he felt belonged to him?

The yipping wail of a coyote floated out across the canyon, eerie for its suddenness and because at that distance and in that gray light the owner of the voice could never be seen. It cried out three times before Sam heard the ever-so-faint reply from over the far ridge.

Viktor struggled the rest of the way to his feet. Sam glanced at him, and Viktor was studying the tobacco in Sam's vest pocket. Finally, he said in a brusque voice, "Maybe I'll try some of that."

With a half-smile Sam tugged out the sack and handed it to him. Viktor had been in the West long enough to see cigarettes rolled, but his own big fingers went about it clumsily, spilling many bits on the ground before his wrinkled, half-torn specimen of a quirley was ready for the match. He made a sour face and moved as if to throw it away, then cleared his throat and stuck it grudgingly between his lips. Before he could take a match from his own pocket, Sam had one out, and its brief glory flared against his thumbnail. Sam held it out to Viktor, who sucked on the smoke until its tip glowed. The first draw made him cough, and he looked quickly away from Sam and scrubbed at his chin.

When the coyote called again, they turned their eyes that way together. "Lonely dog," mused Sam. Viktor grunted.

A moment later they saw a lantern come to life inside Ross's cook tent, which also served as his sleep tent. He politely kept the clatter to a minimum, and they had always thanked Melissa for that. He certainly wasn't being quiet to appease the men.

With the unsettling knowledge of what was living out there, probably not very far away, sleep had not come easy that night for Tom. Now he came stooping out of his tent and stood to his full six-four to stretch his back. He already had his rifle in his hand. The rawhide had mostly dried during the night, and by noon it would be solid. It was already tighter than anything Tom could have applied short of a vise.

Sam heard the voice of Professor Preston Ashcroft. "It's a crying shame we have to go around here like some armed encampment. I knew there would be ghosts on this mountain. But I certainly never counted on what we've found."

Viktor and Sam exchanged glances, and Tom turned and looked over at the Professor. No one seemed to know to whom he was speaking, so no one replied.

While the Professor was at his preparatory work, Sam went over and crouched down to start a fire. Seeing a duty, Viktor wandered off to their woodpile and gathered an armload of wood of varying sizes. Tom watched him and nodded grudgingly. Then he got up and went over to the trash pile that had been collecting since their arrival. From among it, he began to collect tin cans that had held tomatoes, peaches, and the like. He took Ross's hammer and an awl and started punching holes into the cans.

As the camp continued to come to life, everyone emerged wearing jackets, or if they didn't they soon corrected the oversight. The air was perfectly clear, thin, and cold. The morn-ing star hung shivering over the eastern horizon—shivering and quivering and practically bursting with its will to hold out. But the sun conquered it as always, and before long the first golden rays struck the farthest line of hills. Here in camp they continued to shiver around the fire while Ross brewed coffee and set his sourdough biscuits to bake in two massive Dutch ovens. He cut off hunks of bacon and let them fall sizzling into a skillet whose outer surface was crusted with years' worth of grease and ashes. Then, in a third Dutch oven, this one about eight quarts, he dumped cans of pinto beans until it was within two inches of the top. The fire was still burning too brightly for a good cook fire, but Ross, like everyone else in camp, knew the urgency of every minute on this mountain. They must get done with what they had come for and get out—before someone was killed.

Ross was watching Tom curiously, and finally he walked over to him, before throwing the bean cans on top of the trash heap. "What are you cooking up there?"

"A warning bell," replied Tom. "That is if I can borrow your ball of string."

Ross shrugged. "You got my curiosity boiling. How could I turn you down?"

Tom grinned. "Tonight when we go to sleep I'll run a string the whole way around camp, and out by the horses too. I'll hang a bunch of these cans together in a few places along it. Then if anybody who doesn't know about it comes sneakin' around—*bam!*—it'll be like the school bell."

Ross grunted. "I'll be. Pretty smart thinking." He slapped Tom's shoulder. "There's eight more. Put them to good use."

About then, Melissa stepped out of her tent and disappeared beyond the horses. Several minutes later she returned, the last one to come up to the fire. "Look!" she exclaimed, pointing.

Out across the canyon, a puff of smoke rose, then another and another. It finally solidified into one long column, too big for a cook fire. It drifted up into the windless sky like a pointing finger.

Baron hurried into his tent and came back out with his telescope, setting its cold brass tube against his eye. Underneath his dark mustache he puckered up his mouth, as if somehow that might help him to see better. "Unbelievable," he whispered after several moments.

"What is it?" barked the Professor. Baron handed over the telescope wordlessly. In a second or two after it came to a steady position, he let out a whoosh of air. "Ye gods. He's tremendous."

CHAPTER TWENTY-SIX

No one could see the man across the canyon clearly with the naked eye, so one by one they gazed through the glass. There, seated on the far side of the fire, the big man called Death-Shadow sat with his arms crossed, watching his flickering flames. Tom wondered if by the greater size of his eyes he could see them even when they could not see him.

Without uttering a word, Baron left again and came back with two sticks tied together with a strip of wound leather, and his big Ballard rifle in the other hand. As everyone watched in suspense, he went out to the edge of the canyon and sat down, then set the ends of the sticks on the ground, spreading them out to form a bipod that he held with one hand. Next, he set his rifle barrel in the center of the sticks and leaned into its butt plate, adjusting the sticks to the proper height for his eye.

Suddenly, Ross, who had the telescope at the moment, swore and said, "There he goes!"

The man called Death-Shadow had turned and slipped from sight. Only the smoke of his fire could be seen now, rising slow into the air.

Baron lurched to his feet and let out a string of curses, and when finally the Professor said sharply, "Mr. Baron!" he just glanced over at Melissa and turned away without comment or apology. He went back into camp and poured himself a cup of coffee, then stalked off into the timber beyond the horses, his rifle dangling from his hand.

The chill was still on the hills when the lot of them trooped up the trail. The breeze coming down-canyon would have been welcome had the early morning air not been so cold. While the Professor and his contingent worked their cave, Baron pressed Sam and Tom into service, and with Viktor, they all went far up the canyon once more and dug into the newly discovered mine.

From their first meeting, Sam and Tom hadn't been all that impressed by either Baron or Viktor. They had seen some good points in Viktor since then, along with the very bad. However, today at the mine was the first time they gained much respect for Baron. He took off his coat, vest and shirt and went right to work alongside them, taking his turn with a pick. His was the lithe, muscular torso of a pugilist, his stomach flat and cut deeply, his arms finely sculpted, his back smoothly v'd. He had a fine dusting of dark hair on his belly and a coarser patch in the center of a flat, square chest.

With precise, calculated swings, Baron sent the point of his pick deep into the hard adobe clay, and until the sweat ran down his white torso in the ever-warming day, he did not show any sign of needing a rest. His only obvious weakness in this chore was his need for leather gloves, while Sam and Tom, although they also used them, could have done the same work without them. This sort of labor had filled many of their days.

The vigor with which Viktor performed his task was no sur-prise to either Sam or Tom. But seeing him with his shirt off upped both of their eyebrows. It was common knowledge that Viktor had honed his fighting skills on the docks, and it was as-sumed that the bulk which could be seen even through his coat and vest had been gained through the lifting and loading of heavy barrels, crates and bales of whatever came his way.

But the belly fat that might have been presumed to mar the beltline of a man of Viktor's build was nonexistent, and the chiseled muscle that rippled along his arms, back and chest made Tom and Sam eye the man with new respect.

Unlike Sam, Tom and Baron, Viktor had very little hair on his chest, and that allowed a view, especially after his muscles were pumped with blood from ten or fifteen minutes of hard labor, of a heavily striated chest, and a muscle groove down his belly that looked as if it might have been slashed there by a buzz saw. Tom suddenly realized how lucky he had been to hold his own so long in a fight with a man of this physical prominence.

With all four men as physically fit as they were, it seemed like no time before they had the adobe mixture cleared from the opening of the mine, and the deep maw in the face of the canyon-head lay revealed. It was only ten feet tall at the middle, sloping down to perhaps six before the walls turned completely vertical. At the threshold line, it was fifteen feet wide. It went back only about thirty feet, however, and this fact seemed to bother Baron. He was the only one among them who could be considered expert in the identification of mineral values, so the other three stood back while he explored the guts of the mine with a one-handed rock pick, a lantern and a magnifying glass.

Once the initial curiosity had worn away, Sam, Tom and Viktor began to get more and more relaxed until finally all three of them were lounging about the opening looking at Baron now and then, and the rest of the time letting their eyes explore the sides of the canyon.

Sam leaned against one side of the mine entry, while Tom sat on a large boulder just outside, and Viktor lazed with his feet splayed out in front of him, his heels pressed against the steep slope, elbows rested on his bent knees.

The sounds of metal chipping away at rock seemed to become ever more frantic over the hour and a half that Baron explored the walls of the mine. His muttering also grew in intensity and frequency, until finally, at the end of the session, they all heard the hammer go flinging hard against the back wall of the cave, and Baron plied the most versatile string of blasphemies he had shown off on the whole trip. It was a verbal display of such magnitude that it would most likely hang in a blue cloud over the Santa Catalinas for generations to come.

By the time the tirade was over, he was standing facing out from the mine, and Viktor, whose perch was several feet farther down the slope of the mountain, had turned around to look up at him. Sam and Tom were both watching him, and Sam glanced over at his partner and hoped he would have the couth not to voice the half-humored musings that were evident in his green eyes.

"Well... damnit all to hell," said Baron, a fairly mild epithet to round out the collection of colorful phrases and profanities he had put into play moments ago. He didn't even offer a glance at Sam or Tom, who to him it was obvious were mere peons whose only worth was in being exploited for hard labor. Looking at Viktor, he growled, "This mine is worthless. I wouldn't waste a convicted felon digging on these walls."

Viktor swore too, out of deference to his boss—a sort of verbal salute. He rubbed the palm of his right hand with his left. "That was a nice lot of work for nothing."

Baron grunted. "Well, don't forget—there are supposed to be *two* of those hawk's eyes."

Viktor rolled one shoulder in a lazy shrug. "That's true, but we only have Quiet Wind's word to go on for that, and it's just hearsay to her. Who knows how many people that story came down through? We've just about scoured the cave, and I'm starting to think the Indians took the other one, if there ever was a second one. Where else could it be?"

Baron's reply, in its flat, lonely ugliness, was one word, which hung in the air sounding more vulgar and evil than all the others combined.

With little more spoken, the four of them collected their horses and meandered back up over the mountain and down to camp, where they smelled cooking but saw no sign of Ross. They picketed their horses and returned to the cave of the giants.

By the time they arrived it was around one o'clock, and the Professor, in kindness for Melissa, was talking about taking dinner. The four newcomers didn't argue the point. They had worked up enough appetite for two men each. Tom walked over near Melissa and made big Viktor scowl.

Baron said, "Is Ross in camp? We didn't see him." That made everyone look at each other, and the worry that statement brought to their eyes was impossible to hide. Having made the comment, Baron turned and walked down the hill, striding tall and straight-backed in spite of his weariness and deep disap-pointment at what he had found in the mine.

Viktor stood for a few moments more, chewing the insides of his cheeks while he stared at Melissa and Tom and tried to look like he wasn't. Finally, he followed Baron down the canyon.

It was openly difficult for Preston Ashcroft to tear himself away from his work, but one more look at his patient helper and he succumbed. "All right, dear. I suppose we should go find you something to eat. I'm sure you're famished, and you've done more than your share of work this morning. I can't thank you enough." He looked around at the others. "Let's go have a feast!" he declared, and with relief they all formed a column, heading down the mountain. No one mentioned Ross again, but he was strong in all of their minds.

Tom had noticed partway down the trail that Crooked Foot wasn't around, and he mentioned him to Melissa. "I don't suppose he stayed with Ross, did he?" He was mildly alarmed at the thought, since Viktor must have long since reached camp and was still hostile toward the Indian.

"I haven't seen him since we ate," Melissa replied. "Maybe he did."

That answer made the trip down the trail seem all the more urgent to Tom, but when they arrived Viktor was lounging by the fire, and Crooked Foot was nowhere to be seen. However, to the relief of all, there was Ross, bent over his Dutch ovens like always. Tom asked him about Crooked Foot, but before the cook could answer, Viktor growled, "The little thief's making himself scarce so I won't kill him."

Tom ignored Viktor, and Ross poured Tom a cup of coffee. "He and the dog drifted out of here not long after breakfast. Haven't seen 'em since."

Taking the coffee, Tom sipped it and gave the surroundings a speculative look. "Huntin', maybe."

"Yeah," said Viktor in rejoinder. "Huntin' a hole."

"Or maybe he is going to find the big Indian, this Death-Shadow, and tell him everything we do," suggested Pistolito.

That made Viktor's eyes turn harder, and everyone looked at each other. "It wouldn't surprise me one bit if he's right," Viktor growled. No one argued the point. How could they know, one way or the other?

An hour later the whole group was hard at work napping, a chore which seemed much more pleasing today with the cooling breeze that had increased during the morning and still whirled down-canyon. Leathery old Guillermo de Madrid had gone off into the forest, and after several minutes Sam heard him cackling with apparent glee. Pistolito squinted up at him, coming out of sleep. "What's so funny?"

"Look at this!" the old man said, shoving a little box toward him. "The gods, they are smiling!"

The younger man sat up, situating his hat on his head. He rubbed at his eyes, then took the box obligingly out of his partner's hand. He opened it up to reveal a dozen or more cigars. "Ah! Bravo, mi amigo! We will smoke good tonight!" Then his voice got much quieter. "But... what about..."

Hearing the talk, Sam sauntered over to the two of them and hunkered down. "What you got there, amigos?"

Guillermo snatched the cigar box away from his younger friend and showed it proudly to Sam. "I went out to, you know, lighten my belly. An' there I fin' it, this treasure from the gods."

Sam looked musingly at the cigars. "I wouldn't be too hasty, boys. I think it belongs to one man, and he's... Ha! Well, he ain't no god. I'll go you one farther an' wager he's pretty angry about losin' them things."

The two Mexicans were frowning now. Guillermo opened his mouth. "You mean..."

Sam nodded and gave a half grin. "It belongs to Viktor. And he'll want them back, I guarantee you. I think you two had gone on down the mountain when the big stir about this box came up." He turned and sighted along his finger at Viktor, who lay dozing against a log. "There he is. Maybe we ought to go show *him* what you found."

"Ahh..." The older man looked speculatively at the sleeping Viktor. The big man had made no pretense of liking him and Pistolito—or the Sanchezes either, for that matter. "Perhaps you would do the honor of returning his cee-garos to him."

Sam grinned and gave a nod. "Let's see what he has to say."

He took the cigars and walked out to his tent to rouse Tom before going to Viktor. Tom was dozing under the wind-whipped canopy of the tent. "Tom, you might want to see this." With that, he turned and strode away, assuming that Tom would think he had some earth-shattering sight to show him and would come straight away—which he did.

Sam went right up to Viktor and nudged him with his toe. Viktor rolled over and shot an angry look up, blinking. "What the—"

Grinning, Sam said, "Hey, Viktor. I got somethin' you might be interested in."

Viktor managed to sit up, pushing his hat back on his head. He stared straight up at Sam's face and didn't notice what he held at his side. Finally, he struggled up, wiping the sleep out of his eyes. He didn't need to speak, for the hard look in his face said it all: *You'd better be sure you have something awful important.*

With a mocking look of humor, Sam raised the box, and for the first time Viktor saw it. His jaw couldn't help but fall open. "Where in the name of the devil did that come from? You find that Indian?" He snapped his eyes about; they were suddenly full of malice.

"Didn't have to," said Sam. "Guillermo and Pistolito ran into this. Maybe they can show you where."

The old Mexican didn't seem altogether pleased that Sam had fingered him, but when Viktor, Sam, Tom, Baron and the Professor came over to him he obligingly took them out into the woods where there was a fresh pile of dirt, and a pile a little bit older not far away. Between the two fresh mounds where Guillermo and someone else had evidently answered nature's call and then covered their work with a shovel was a large patch of grass and one lone shrub about two feet tall and fairly bushy. "There," said the old Mexican, and he pointed at the base of the shrub.

"Why the little—"

It was probably a good guess, if anyone had been guessing, that had Viktor been able to think faster on his feet he would have hidden his reaction. As it was, a sudden look of recognition leaped to his face as he looked down at the mound of dirt and the bush, and after a moment his face reddened, from his neck up.

"Huh." That was all he could utter. He stared at the ground, then looked up at Sam. It was a cinch he could feel the eyes of everyone else on him, and he didn't like it, not one bit. He snatched the box out of Sam's hand and turned on his heel, tromping back to his tent.

"So... Let me get this straight before I say anything that will make me look like a buffoon," said Baron. "Viktor's cigars were not taken by the Indian at all—he put them out here himself and forgot them when he was...?"

"That would seem to be the case," said Tom. "Good thing we didn't let him kill that poor cripple."

Baron nodded and then laughed heartily. "Good thing, all right."

They all returned to camp, and of course Tom had to relate the new discovery to Melissa, though he tactfully made sure Viktor was nowhere around to hear. The big brawler had to know he was going to be the talk of the camp for a while, though.

Viktor didn't remain in his tent for long before coming out and making himself another biscuit and bacon sandwich and sitting on a log near the fire's ashes. He would look at no one.

The wind was still blowing, and anyone downwind from the fire pit had it rough. It was no longer a breeze, but a stout wind with occasional gusts up to thirty miles an hour. Sam looked up-canyon at the sky. It was still blue, but he wondered what was blowing in.

"Ross, why don't you draw out one of those whisky bottles again?" suggested Baron suddenly. "It's been a long day, and I think we could all use a little refreshment."

Pistolito looked up happily as Ross complied, passing coffee cups around and pouring a little whisky in each. Melissa was the only one who turned it down.

"A toast!" said Baron. They all paused, and he looked carefully around at the ring of faces. "A toast to a good group of people and a job well done—almost."

They all drank, the Professor a bit hesitantly. He seemed unsure what Baron had meant by his use of that last word.

After a moment of silence, Baron looked over at Ashcroft. "Mr. Ashcroft, what exactly is left in that cave?"

The Professor knitted his brow. "Well, let me think... In the way of artifacts there is very little that has not been catalogued. A few shards of pottery, perhaps. We need to do a little more digging in the floor. Then I would like to make a few detailed copies of their drawings on the wall, and some measurements. After that, we can start bringing items down here that we have felt until now would be safer in the shelter of the cave."

Baron grunted. "You know we are basically here because your backers would like to see these silver mines exploited." The Professor nodded. "And you have of course seen the... *instrument* known as the Hawk's Eye. Have you seen another like it? There are purported to be two."

The Professor stared at him blankly. Finally, he shook himself and replied, "I have not. I didn't feel it that important to look for it, to be truthful. I came here to perform an archaeological dig."

"Well, Professor, the stories that came down to Quiet Wind were very certain about a second Hawk's Eye, and I must find it before we go down this mountain. So either you allow me to scrounge through all of those items you have stored in that cave or you offer me some suggestion of where else I might look."

"What if the Indians took it with them when they left?" asked the Professor.

"The Indians didn't take it," Baron said derisively. "They were deathly afraid of anything that belonged to those giants. They wanted only to kill them and get as far away as they could. That second Hawk's Eye is there, Professor. We *will* find it before we leave here. Tonight I will go through all of the items we have carried down the hill. Viktor will go through the piles up in the cave. We will find the Hawk's Eye—or we all stay."

The Professor stood up abruptly. "But, Mr. Baron, we all agreed that Melissa should be taken to safety as soon as possible. And what of Del? And the Mexican boy? They have no reason to stay in danger's path up here. We should take them down below."

"Not until you help me find that damn piece of bronze," Baron snapped.

"You don't have to be rude," Melissa cut in suddenly.

Before the Professor could shush her, Baron growled, "You keep your mouth shut, young lady. If I want your opinion I'll ask for it."

The whole camp was silent for a moment. Surprisingly, it was Viktor who spoke. "Aw, listen, Mr. Baron. She was just trying to stand up for her employer. Just how I think you'd want me to do." Uncharacteristically, Viktor looked around the circle as if asking for support. The implied plea surprised Sam.

Baron stood up, his eyes burning into the Professor and ignoring Viktor entirely. "We *will* find that Hawk's Eye, Professor. You will see to it."

With that, he turned to Viktor. "Instead of sticking your nose in where it doesn't belong, Viktor, go up to the cave and start going through those piles. Find that thing."

He looked over at Melissa. "If you want to make yourself useful, rather than opening your mouth when it isn't asked for, come and keep track of what I'm moving around. And you can do the same with Viktor," he told the Professor. "Otherwise, I take no responsibility for what shape this stuff ends up in."

He turned to the canvas shelter where they had been stowing items brought down from the cave. Viktor, Professor Ashcroft and Delbert Moore trudged together up the trail to the cave.

*   *   *

The work in camp and in the cave became tedious. Viktor seemed to have taken on a whole new edge, and he made no pretense of caring how he treated the Professor's artifacts. He ignored his pleas repeatedly, and shuffled things back and forth, dropping some of them to the floor.

Tom and Sam hiked up to the cave as evening came on, and as it grew dark they went inside. They didn't like the way Viktor blatantly ignored the Professor's requests, but he didn't ask for their help, so they stayed out of it.

Along the walls of the cave were the ten torches, five on either side, where the giants had drilled holes obliquely into the stone and inserted the torch ends to hold them erect. Although these, like everything else in the cave, were of historical significance, the Professor had allowed some of them to be lit to aid in illuminating the cave, whose dingy walls excelled at absorbing light. Sam and Tom took it upon themselves to explore back into the cavern a little more, since Professor Ashcroft had declared his work there complete. Without asking permission, they took down a torch, lit it, and wandered back into the dark passage.

They had gone only a ways before they heard angry voices back up at the front of the cave. When they returned, they found Baron, Quiet Wind and Melissa there, along with Delbert Moore, the Professor and Viktor. Viktor had accomplished moving three quarters of the pile of catalogued items to one side, and Baron was now in the middle of going through the others and throwing them on top of the discarded pile even more roughly than Viktor had been.

"Please!" Professor Ashcroft protested. "You can't treat something of this age carelessly. Why have we come so far, gentlemen, if you're so bent on destroying it now?"

"Shut up!" barked Baron. "If you don't want damage done then get in here and help. It's getting dark, and we have only so much time. That... *thing* out there is not going to hold off forever.

And I'm not leaving here until we've exhausted every possible means of finding that so-called Hawk's Eye. I'm not joking."

Turning away, he went back to his calculated work. His only bow to the Professor was to start handing things to Melissa, if she was ready, as he picked them up and made sure none of them held the Hawk's Eye. "Light some more of those torches," he muttered to Viktor as he worked.

The big man went to comply, and Tom decided since they were almost done, and since Sam had his own torch, that he might as well have one too. He was immensely curious about what lay farther back in the shadows of this rock abode. Reaching up, standing on his tiptoes, he grabbed one of the torches. It was one of those that seemed stuck soundly in the hole, and he had to wrench on it and jerk it back and forth before it finally came free. Then he slid it out of its niche.

As he did so, something made a slicing sound, and he looked down in time to see an object drop from the stem of the torch and catch the light of other torches as it landed with a soft *tink* in the sand.

CHAPTER TWENTY-SEVEN

For a moment, Tom stood and stared at the object that had fallen from his torch handle. He knew he should recognize it, but it was such a surprise to see it suddenly lying there that it took a while to register on his mind.

It was about one and a half feet long, bronze in color—a cylinder of metal apparently. On one end of it was the three-dimensional depiction of the fierce head of a hawk with swept-back feathers.

After a moment, Tom sensed that Sam had turned his attention to him. He glanced up to see that his partner's eyes had locked on the object in the sand. Sam looked up, and their eyes met. It was at that moment that it came home to Tom what he had found.

The second Hawk's Eye.

The sounds of things being moved around continued behind them as Sam and Tom stared each other down. Baron was muttering, the Professor was voicing a complaint, and Viktor was cursing something. Tom reached down at last and picked up the Hawk's Eye. He was reluctant to turn to Baron, but at least his revelation would save the Professor the pain of watching the way Baron and Viktor were treating his beloved artifacts.

Tom walked over to Baron, who was crouched on the ground. "Is this what you're looking for?"

Baron looked up, irritation in his eyes. The look faded instantly when he recognized what Tom was holding. He leaped up. "Where'd you find that?"

"It fell out of one of the torch handles."

Baron snatched the object out of Tom's hand. "That's it! That's the other Hawk's Eye." Laughing, he held it up triumphantly to the Professor, then to Viktor. "We've got it, Viktor. We've got it! This will be the one."

They all sensed that Baron was right. For some reason this second Hawk's Eye had been carefully concealed in the torch handle while the first one was discarded loose among the other objects in the cave. It stood to reason that this extra care was because the other mine, the one pointed out by the first Hawk's Eye, had played out. The location of the real working mine was something the giants had foreseen a need to keep hidden from public view, and if not for a fluke it might never have been located again.

Baron now turned to Sam. "Well, Coffey. I guess you know what I need you and Tom to do, don't you? This is one time where I'll have to concede defeat in advance. I tried this once, and I guess I'm not cut out for looking at a spot from way down here and then recognizing it again when I'm way up the canyon. This time I'll send Vik with you."

Tom sighed wearily and handed his torch over to the Professor. Sam followed suit, saying nothing in reply to Baron. He figured his silence was answer enough. All of them walked outside, and it was plain the Professor, who had put the torches down in the cave before coming outside, was greatly relieved to know his museum pieces would suffer no more abuse at the hands of Viktor and Baron.

Baron walked over to the bracket cut into the rock where the Hawk's Eye would go and with a smug smile on his face started to slip it inside. Everyone watched him, expecting it to drop easily down in. To their surprise it wouldn't even start. Frowning, Baron

tipped up the Hawk's Eye to look at the bottom of it as if something were amiss. Then he tried it again, and still it would not fit.
Clenching his jaw and starting to redden around the collar, he
straightened up. "Where's that other piece?" he asked angrily.

Consternated, the Professor went into the cave and came back
out with the first Hawk's Eye. Baron took it and laid it over the
new one, then swore with great depth of feeling. The cylindrical
base of the new piece was at least half an inch bigger in circum-
ference than the older one.

To say Baron looked frantic would not do him justice. He
was too proud a man to let so weak an emotion show. But there
was definitely a heated play of emotions on his face as he
searched the area all around for anything else that resembled the
first bracket. Not simply out of curiosity to see what this eye
pointed out, but armed with the desire to deter another of Baron's
tirades, Sam and Tom began to search with him, and so did the
others. There were still piles of rock and debris around the cave's
entrance which had slid down off the mountain during the earthquake. Those that could be moved or swept away with any ease
quickly were. When it came down to a handful of larger boulders,
they put their muscles together and rolled them off out of the way.
There were only two left when they found it—the proverbial hidden door.

Sam, Tom and Viktor were required to upend the four hundred pound behemoth of rock that had landed closest to the cave's
entrance, with gravel and dust settling all around it. As it rolled
away, there beneath it, the second hole winked like the Hawk's
Eye itself, deep and black... and waiting to point the way to a silver mine that could be worth hundreds of thousands of dollars.

Baron shouted with triumph and spun around, looking at the
others and slapping Viktor on the back. "Now *that* is our keyhole!"

With renewed confidence and a smug look, he bent and slid
the Hawk's Eye into the hole. Then, crouching, he sighted toward

the top of the canyon through the pinhole that was the actual "eye" of the hawk statue. This time, because of the angle of the hole in the rock, the sight led to the far side of the canyon and farther up, almost to the top. Sam noted with a touch of uneasiness that this was not far from where they had last spotted the man the Professor in his campfire conversations had started referring to not as Death-Shadow but as the "Santa Catalina Giant."

"Well, men, you know what to do," said Baron. He waved a hand at the Hawk's Eye and looked in turn at Sam, Tom and Viktor. Since Sam was closest, he got down and peered through the pinhole. Of course nothing much could be discerned from this distance of over half a mile, but a minute's study through the sight gave him a good idea of where the mine entrance should lie. Next, Tom and Viktor took their turns.

When Viktor stood up, Baron was smiling. He had walked to his pack and pulled out a book—a journal, from its looks. Holding it in one hand, he slapped the open palm of his other hand with it. "I'll be here writing when you need me," he said. "I'll set up the telescope."

Sam looked up the canyon, then raised his eyes to catch the location of the sun. "I know we hired out to work for you, Baron, and we'll live by the bargain. But part of my job is keepin' people safe. I ain't goin' up there tonight."

"You're not *what?*"

"Not tonight," repeated Sam. "The way I figure it, that's at least an hour and fifteen minute climb up there, not counting the time it'll take to find the exact location. After that, it'll be an hour and fifteen or more back down. And then throw in the time to use the picks and see if it's even the right place. We have three hours left of daylight. I'll be damned if we'll be caught up there after dark with our... *friend.*"

His eyes hard as chert, Baron stared at Sam. Finally, he nodded. "I don't personally think it will take that long to ride up there.

But if something were to happen I don't want to take all the blame. We can wait until tomorrow."

Sam nodded and started to turn away, and as his eyes crossed Viktor's he thought he saw a vast look of relief on his face. Viktor wasn't stupid. He had guessed what fate might await them if they made that exploration this late in the day.

"We have three hours," Baron stated, turning to the Professor. "We can move the rest of these artifacts down the hill to camp and be that much closer to riding out of here if you'd like."

The Professor looked to the west. The wind that had begun to blow had never stopped. In fact, it had worsened. And the sky, although still cloudless, had a strange brown cast to it. "No," he said, "I think we should wait. The things that are still in there, the mummies included, will not take bad weather very well. They are safe where they are. We must leave them until we're ready to depart."

"Your choice." Baron turned to Viktor. "We might as well go down and celebrate then."

Viktor grinned, but for once he had no reply. Sam believed part of his grin was from relief.

*   *   *

Supper was waiting when they made it back to camp. In spite of Ross's best efforts, they had to eat it with a measure of grit in each bite. Cast iron lids could only protect the food up until the moment when they were lifted, and plenty of dust had blown into the pots at that point. Afterward, in the fading light and under cover of the buffeting wind, Sam and Tom went into the timber to look for game. A young buck with cautious, wet eyes reflecting the sky entered a glade, and Tom killed it with one bullet.

Sam heard the shot, and they met together in the falling light, cleaned the buck, and started off with Tom dragging the carcass behind him. In the timber, the wind whistled like mysterious flutes, and like voices of the long-dead it moaned. In such a remote canyon land, with the mummies of unknown, ancient giants lying ominous and cold not far away, it couldn't help but bring an eerie feeling down onto the forest.

Big pines creaked together, and now and then dead, rusty needles pattered like rain on the forest floor. Even down here in the shelter of the stately trees, the dust smell grew stronger, and beyond its veil, light was quickly vanishing. Most foreboding of all, the noises of the deep wood were absent. Tonight no nighthawk swooped the sky with its high-pitched squeak, no owl made its lonely, questing call from the lofty boughs of the Douglas fir. No wolf or coyote cried, and the crickets—silent as death. The violin-wind and the creaking of the majestic, furrowed trunks sang the only discordant harmonies in the forest that night, and behind every deadfall lurked an awful, leering giant with arms the size of a strong man's thighs...

They reached camp just before the darkness would have made their movements hazardous, and Melissa spotted them with a look of relief. Tom smiled at her and said, "Spooky out there tonight," as he dragged the buck on past and to the fire.

He returned to where she was trying to drive the stakes of her tent deeper into the ground, and taking a big rock he went to the other side. They worked against the buffeting of the canvas, flapping and slapping and mocking their work. A long shroud of clouds had scudded over the moon and stars, and as it made it three-fourths of the way over the camp a few scattered raindrops tapped against the tent, once again mimicking the sounds of falling pine needles.

Melissa stood up from the last tent stake and hugged her arms about her. Tom came to stand beside her. He wanted to hold her, but he wouldn't do it, not here in camp. He didn't want to embarrass her, and he didn't want to cause more trouble with Viktor not until they were out of these mountains. The woman looked up at him, her eyes shining in the flickering light from the campfire, which was ten yards distant.

"It's been a long time since we could talk, Tom. How have you been?"

Tom grinned. "Good. Good as can be expected, since I don't sleep much at night anymore."

Melissa agreed with a nervous laugh. "You aren't teasing there. How could anyone sleep knowing... *he* is out there?"

In spite of his better judgment, Tom reached out and squeezed her elbow. "We'll be off this mountain soon. This'll all be just 'fond' memories."

She laughed again. "That's true. And what about..." She stopped there, and for a long time he studied her, waiting.

"What about what?"

Another laugh. "Oh, nothing. Just thinking out loud."

"Can I buy you a drink?" Tom asked suddenly. When she smiled and nodded, he walked with her over to the four barrels they had lined up beyond Ross's tent. Taking a community ladle, he opened the nearest spigot and filled it to the brim. Then he held it out to her. She drank slowly.

"Best champagne ever!" she said with a giggle. "My, how you treat your women."

He chuckled. "Best that money can buy, Miss Ford. Nothin' but the best will do for you."

"And how you talk." She reached up suddenly and touched his cheek. Just as quickly, her hand fell away, and she gave a little, meaningless shrug and laughed away her whimsical gesture. "I'm a fool." Her voice was wistful.

"You ain't a fool, Melissa. Just a woman who dreams small."

"Small?" she echoed him, unsure of what he meant. "If you said that to Professor Ashcroft he might take it as an insult."

For a long time he held his voice in check, trying to pick out the details of her face in light that was now about as dark as it would get. That made it harder to see, but much easier to speak. The wind helped too, because it almost made his own voice seem like it was coming from someone else.

"I'm a small fry, Melissa, in the scheme of things. I don't have much in the way of looks or smarts, and not much of a way to make a living. I don't have much of a bankroll, either."

She reached out in the dark, and almost as if by magic her hand found his on the first try and closed over it. "Wrong on all counts, my big man. I've never seen a more handsome man, nor a more intelligent one. And the way you make a living... Well, Tom, you ought to hear how some people speak of the American cowboy in the East. There are those who talk them down, but even to them, down deep in their hearts it is a magical way of life, one I have always dreamed of taking part in. As far as the bankroll, I don't care. My parents didn't exactly leave me poor."

He laughed to cover his embarrassment. "Reckon we're gettin' the cart ahead of the burro, little lady."

She didn't answer him with words. She simply stepped up on her tiptoes, and there in the shelter of the dark and the howling wind she found his lips with hers.

*   *   *

That night the wind brought its reinforcements, called into action every banshee, every ghoul, every shrieking vampire that the nighttime mountains might conjure and threw them all full-force at the little camp on the canyon-side. The tents flapped and creaked and tried to take wing. Many times in the night someone could be found outside one of them pounding a stake back into the ground, and the punishing gale tried as it might to rip loose the very threads that held the tents together.

Gravel pelted the tent-sides, maddening, horrible. Sand beat on canvas, hurled by goblins and witches and fiends of the night. Cold wind. Hard wind. Wind shrieked among the boughs of pine and fir and aspen. Called out its words of vengeance and destruction and bloody red hell. Sent tiny flocks of needles flying like missiles. The sound of demons moaning—the devil's children. Hateful wind that even owners of windmills would despise. Worst of all, it shook and rattled the cans that Tom had strung around the camp's perimeter, and the clanking sound of tin against tin was horrendous. Tom finally crawled out of his blankets and went to cut it all down.

Ross was also up, shortly after he went to bed, to douse his fire completely, turning its ashes into a gooey pot of tar. Then, in the night, sometimes they could hear tin plates rolling, cups hitting the ground, and above the moaning wind the sound of Ross's curses. Viktor's voice came battering once, swearing at the wind, hating another force that he couldn't fight—like Death-Shadow, the Santa Catalina Giant...

Then, somewhere in the blackest depths of the night, while Tom and Sam lay in their tent with the Sanchezes, holding it down and feeling it try to carry them all away, the vile storm began to fail. It was as if the hand of Zeus came and swept it away, down off the mountain, toward the far, dust-filled valleys below. Then there was the silence, and it seemed deeper and darker and more ominous than the wind itself. They all lay there in shocked quiet, listening for the next rush of cold wind, the next onslaught of giants' roaring breath that was not to come.

The storm was gone...

Weary and beaten, one by one each man and Melissa climbed from their tents, even though it was still full dark. Over the following hour, everyone found themselves shivering around a feeble fire that Ross, in all his wizardry, was trying to coax atop the wetted ashes into warming life. The canyon was strangely still. No conversation, no storm, no nature—nothing. The only sound was that of Ross trying to blow his traitorous fire to life.

Suddenly, old Alfredo Sanchez lurched to his feet, pointing. "Mi madre," he said quietly. "Look at that."

They had all turned to watch as, on the far brink of the canyon's black maw, a prick of flame violated the night. Soon, like it had done before, the fire grew and grew—up to obscene heights the flame leaped.

All of them were standing now, watching with fascination as the far away monster taunted them. They were all in this process of standing on the edge of camp staring when they saw one faint flicker of light that left the main fire. It seemed to hover by itself, and then, as they watched it, it went up and up, then began to arc downward, but grew larger and larger and larger until with a nerve-shattering *thwack* it crashed into the slope below them.

More than a few startled epithets cut the night on the tail of that surprise, and Sam ran down the slope a ways for a closer look. They heard him swear, a sound of awe, and soon he came back up to them. He was holding in his hand what at first glance appeared to be a short, slender spear. It was a piece of straight, hardened wood, bigger around than one of Viktor's thumbs and a foot longer than his outstretched arm. On one end of it were feather fletchings, and on the other was the stone head of a primitive arrow, the point alone weighing as much as four ounces. There were a few smoldering threads still stuck to the point with blackened, smoking pitch, and their tiny orange tendrils died even as the others looked on.

"There's another one!" Tom said, and as he spoke they turned to see a second flaming arrow slice through the air, making a long, high rainbow and landing dangerously close to them. This one managed to catch some of the trodden grass around it on fire, and Viktor stomped out the flames as he swore.

Three more missiles flamed across at them, all striking about camp, and two of them lighting vegetation. Sam had noticed Pistolito, who fancied himself as a gunman, getting extremely agitated as the display went on. Soon, the Mexican disappeared, and just as the sixth arrow come sailing across the canyon Sam saw him reemerge from the shadows carrying a seventy-six Winchester rifle.

The Mexican stomped down the slope with the rifle in hand, then stood there waiting as the glances of those in camp traded places between him and that far away orange glow.

But this time, when the little pin-prick of fire left the main body and came to the place from where it would be launched at them, Pistolito raised his rifle and aimed it at the far away flamethrower. As he jacked the lever and pulled the trigger, over and over and over, a shocking volley of rifle fire filled the night.

He poised on the brink of the canyon, his rifle belching smoke that writhed around him, and his laugh floated out across the canyon. Ross's fire had finally come to life, and Pistolito was perfectly back-lit now.

An eerie picture he made down there on the edge of their world.

He faced a giant serpent.

The strike of that serpent promised death...

CHAPTER TWENTY-EIGHT

Every eye was pinned to Pistolito Gutierrez when the snake's fang struck.

Not two fangs—only one. One single arrow, half again as long as any arrow an average man might wield, and almost twice as big around.

Pistolito was standing there staring across the canyon, holding his big rifle poised, wondering if any of his bullets had scored. They heard him mutter something that sounded like a profanity in Spanish.

Then came a whooshing sound and a dull *thwack.* The Mexican made a noise as if growling in pain, and they saw his head drop. The rifle fell from his hand and went skidding down the slope through the gravel. The very fact that he didn't seem to notice its descent was all the bad omen they needed.

Pistolito staggered around, both hands clutching something that protruded from just below his breastbone. Even at the distance all could see the look of shock and horror in his eyes, which shone against the firelight. He started to take a step upward, then folded and fell to the side.

Sam and Tom both rushed at the same time as he landed and started to slide. They scrambled down the dangerous slope and caught him just before he would have plummeted, but there was no saving the Winchester. It teetered on the brink for a fraction of a second, and then over it went. As its hammer struck the rocks below, a chambered round went off with one horrendous explosion that echoed across the canyon, startling everyone in camp.

The partners looked down at the Mexican, who was still struggling to breathe. Sticking from his chest was an arrow the likes of which they had never seen before opening the cave of the giants.

As gently as possible, they dragged the dying man up the slope and off beyond the firelight, where Ross brought a lantern to look at him. Before they found a pillow to put under his head, Portento, alias Pistolito, Guttierrez was dead.

Swearing as tears broke free and streamed down his face, old Guillermo stumbled off into the forest. The others watched him in surprise. Although he had been Pistolito's partner, no one had guessed they were close.

As for Delbert Moore, he took one look at the arrow, branching out from Pistolito like part of a tree, and went off from camp to void his paunch. Melissa stood white-faced, but she stood, all the same, until Tom took her by the elbow and led her back behind her tent.

Sam, turning away from the dead man, took his partner's cue. "The rest of you get behind those tents or inside until it gets light. There's nothin' we can do here."

Whether it sounded like an order or not, it made too much sense for even obstinate Viktor to ignore. He and Baron both went inside their tents and vanished, along with everyone else. The storm had kept them awake all night, but now, even if they had tried to sleep they could not have done so. The Santa Catalina Giant was carrying on the restless havoc of the storm...

*　　*　　*

In their blankets or out, most of those in camp spent the last hour and a half until dawn shivering. Only part of it was from the cold. Even Viktor was filled with apprehension. The big man would never have admitted to being afraid, but damn! There was only so much of this kind of warfare a man could take before he went insane.

The big man, knowing their enemy was clear across the canyon, had donned his warm coat and gone off into the woods to be by himself. He could hear the comforting sound of the horses nickering now and then, and he relied on them to warn him if danger lurked nearby.

What was going to come of this expedition? Until an hour earlier, there had only been threats and acts of violence that had taken no casualty. Now a man had died. Sure, it happened to be a stranger, and in fact a stranger Viktor didn't much care for. But it was a man who had slept and eaten among them, nevertheless, and that man across the canyon had had no idea who it was he was slaying. To him the Mexican was just as much a member of this party as the Professor or Baron. It was a sobering realization.

Yes, Pistolito had fired on the giant and thus brought down his ire. But any of the flaming arrows the man had flung before that could have killed someone in camp. The fact that he hadn't killed sooner, between his thrown rocks, flaming arrows, or the bag of snakes, was only a matter of good fortune.

Now the path of their fortunes had changed course...

Viktor rubbed his hands together, and when that didn't thoroughly warm them he cupped them and raised them to his mouth, blowing hot air into them. He laughed quietly to himself—hot air; that was something some people claimed he was full of!

How he hoped Baron would be satisfied by what the second Hawk's Eye led them to! Would they hold out another deathless day on the mountain? Or would the Reaper come to visit them once more?

*   *   *

Slowly, the fire across the canyon died, and predictably, by the time the sun struck the far side of the canyon and gave enough light for Baron to use his big rifle, there was no movement over there near the occasional wisps of smoke that continued to rise.

A pall of cloud hung over the mountain at the head of the canyon, and along its top it clung like fog. The wind would rise, rending the fog into ropy tendrils that snaked along the canyon top, and then a scattered flight of raindrops would rush the expeditioners, leaving dark splotches on the tent canvas and on their hats and clothing.

Melissa Ford sat at the fire, staring across the canyon where a puff of smoke had risen minutes before. In her gloved hands, she nursed a cup of coffee, but it wasn't enough to warm them. She was cold clear through—from the inside out.

She hunched her shoulders together under the heavy sheepskin coat Tom had loaned her. She felt the warmth of Ross's fire as it began to crackle and emit its searching fingers of heat. But still she shivered. It could have been eighty degrees and she would have shivered. She was going to for a long time to come.

*   *   *

Brave—or perhaps foolish—Professor Ashcroft stood on the brink of the canyon not far from where Pistolito's blood smeared the gravelly slope. He held a cup of coffee in one hand while his other was thrust deep into the pocket of his coat. He felt old.

By all the saints, he felt like he had aged ten years in the past week. So he had discovered one of his dreams here in this Santa Catalina wilderness. What of it? It had been done, as he learned, at great risk to himself and others, and the guilt of keeping Melissa here in the face of this mortal danger was almost more than he could take. What if something happened to the girl? He would not want to live.

Professor Ashcroft would be a long-remembered name in the scientific community. In one sad, worldly sense that seemed important. But in another way, the important thing was knowing for himself what he had accomplished here. It wasn't so much a *discovery* he had made. Quiet Wind might have chosen to show anyone else this place. He had simply been the lucky one that it fell to. But he had been the man to catalog it, to put it down for all the ages coming behind him to learn from. That would count for something... wouldn't it? Maybe not.

Maybe his name would be heard and read about in the annals of science only as the man who led the fateful expedition that perished in the Santa Catalinas. After Pistolito's death, the notion seemed frighteningly plausible.

*   *   *

Breakfast was a solemn occasion. It came late, since Ross had not been able to keep a fire going while it was dark for fear of flying arrows. In fact, it came so late that by the time it was served Baron was up at the cave sitting hunched over the Hawk's Eye, and Tom, Sam, Viktor and Delbert Moore, Alfredo and Juan Sanchez were weaving their way horseback through the mist-shrouded forest on the back side of the mountain.

Sam rode in the lead, his rifle across his saddle fork. His sharp eyes pierced the undergrowth, the deep pockets where spread the delicate umbrellas of ferns, the places where in silent nooks the moss grew thick and green on tree trunks, rocks and fallen logs. He was looking not only for living beings but for sign of snares or traps of any kind.

He stopped Gringo to let him blow, and the long line behind him slowly came to a halt. It was cold enough today that now and then a wisp of steam could be seen puffing out of a horse's nostrils. They hunched in their coats and eyed their surroundings wearily, ruing the loss of their night's sleep but knowing they could not rest now even if they had the chance.

Tom pushed Cocky through the bushes and spreading ferns until he was side by side with his partner. He took out the makings, slipped off a paper and handed one to Sam. Sitting with his rifle balanced on his legs, he licked the thin paper and sprinkled specks of tobacco across it before rolling it carefully over. He smoked very seldom, so this wasn't a task he could do one-handed, a talent many cowboys were proud to have perfected.

He gave Sam the tobacco, and Sam, a little more adept at such things, rolled his a little quicker, albeit more sloppy. Then the two of them sat polluting the achingly fresh mountain air and listening to the subdued sounds of warblers and a pair of whiskey jacks that dodged here and there in the timber.

"You ain't said much this mornin'," Tom noted.

Sam shot him a slanted look. "Much."

Not in the mood for any dry humor, Tom couldn't even fake a smile. "It's come down to the dyin'. Is this still worth it to us?"

Squinting against an errant cloud of smoke that got in his eyes, Sam took out the cigarette and spat against the gray, bare trunk of a dead fir. "Worth it? I don't know. But we hired out, Tom. I reckon we ride for the brand 'til it's done."

Tom nodded quickly, absently. He hadn't expected anything else, and he felt the same. But he was worried about someone besides himself now, and the idea that he and his partners were so far away from Melissa today did not sit well with him. "You think if we find this mine he's after Baron will call it good and let us get out of here?"

"I give up tryin' to figure Baron out," Sam rejoined. "Mostly, he's all about money, and that's the one thing we're gonna have to base all our figurin' on. He ain't like you and me, Tom. I ain't real sure he would give a thought to Juan or Moore or even Melissa dyin', not as long as he came out of here knowin' where this mine is."

Tom sat there a moment longer, pondering sullenly. Finally, he pointed forward with his chin. "Let's ride. You been without a bath too long for me to sit here downwind from you any longer."

Sam grinned dryly. "Problem is your coat ain't buttoned up tight enough at the collar, Curly. That aroma ain't risin' off me."

They wove on through the trees until at last the trail took them once again up on the rocky, windswept ridge. Here they picked their way carefully over the deadfall and past the bony, clawing, grasping arms of several pines that several hundred years of weather had twisted into bizarre, gnarled shapes. Their horses' shoes scraped on the exposed rocks, and they faded into the fog bank as its cool, caressing fingers reached out and wove around them. It was a lonely ridge, barren and cold and hard as ice statues, and the day promised to grow no warmer.

On the edge of the canyon, Sam chose to blaze a different trail from the day before. Rather than brave the canyon's steep head, he turned Gringo left, and they kept on until canyon and ridge became one. Up here the universe should have been all around them, but the rest of the world as far as they could see was enveloped in the same oppressive fog that surrounded them.

Up here in the emptiness the wind gusts were strong, and they buttoned their coats tighter and rode light in the stirrups, ready to kick free if their mounts should go out from under them. The shattered granite spine of this mountaintop made for hard travel. It was wet from the fog and rain, and the horses' hooves continually slipped and slid across the treacherous surfaces.

Even as he guided Gringo along the safest route, Sam's keen eyes had already picked the place in the canyon below where he thought the mine would lie. At least it was the vicinity that the Hawk's Eye had seemed to pinpoint. From up above, it didn't look like much work had ever been done there, but he had to concede that the alleged work had been close to a century back. Who knew what forces might have shaken this canyon since then?

At last it was time to descend into the canyon. Sam climbed down from Gringo and set his glass on the trail far below. He picked up the tiny form of Baron, which this time was so far away he wasn't sure he would see any of his hand signals if he needed to. He could see the canvas of the tents beyond, and the faint flicker of fire against the drab gray of the rocks, but he could see no movement there, not even the horses. It was too distant.

There was no argument from anyone about leading the horses down the steep canyon side. There were places where a slide might not stop for a hundred feet or more, and other places where if one fell it could end in a hundred foot drop off into some rock chute. So they led their horses and walked lightly, always uphill from each mount, always with a refuge in mind that they would make for in the instant that they felt their animals begin to lose ground. How easy it would be for a ten or twelve hundred pound animal to drag its rider down this mountain with it!

Sam stopped and surveyed the broken canyon. They were down out of the clouds now, and here it was just the drab loneliness of stunted pines and fir, and clumps of lifeless rock, stained by iron, dirt and lichen.

Sam glanced around at the others before he spoke. "This is the general area that Hawk's Eye points to, but I don't see any spot that promises anything. Better split up and scour it. One of us should find it—*if* it ain't gone down the mountain years ago in some earthquake."

Tom nodded agreement but said nothing. He wasn't keen about the steep terrain here and the prospects one would face if they faltered and started to slide. He looked back down the canyon to where the man called Death-Shadow must have had his fire that early morning, and from where he had flung his arrows. It was an awful long way across the canyon—a long shot even for a big caliber rifle—to say nothing of an arrow.

It was Tom who first decided to tie his horse and explore on foot. Taking his cue, the others did the same, and soon they were like a troop of ants scouring a hillock for bounty. And in fact they *found* bounty. Tom stumbled upon one hole in the canyon side that had been sealed over with adobe like the first mine opening, and once he dug inside he discovered a cache of dried corn. Even after however many decades it had been left here it appeared to be still good! He filled his pockets so he could offer Cocky a reward later for keeping him safe in this country straight out of hell.

Between the bunch of them, they uncovered several similar caches containing corn or wheat. But even once Baron got smart enough to create a big flag out of his coat to use for signaling they never located the second mine. It took them three hours to finally give up, and then it was Viktor who called a halt to it.

Sucking for air, he came huffing up to where Sam had sat down on a flat rock to survey the canyon below. When he reached him, he gave up after one attempt to speak and spent a couple of minutes just catching his breath. Finally, he said, "Looking at my watch, that's three hours we've dug through this canyon. Mr. Baron can't ask any more of us than that. This was one of those wild goose chases you talk about."

Sam nodded, his eyes narrowing as he continued to scan the canyon bottom and both sides of it. He ran a hand over his mustache, then tugged off his hat and scratched his head.

"He won't like it. That I'm sure of. But I agree. We're wasting our time up here. I don't know what used to be here, but it's buried now—unless that Hawk's Eye was only designating all these grain caches the whole time."

Viktor looked at him dumbly for several seconds, then let out a chuckle. Silence, then another chuckle. He went through that sequence three times, with each chuckle growing louder than the last. Finally, he burst into a long laugh. "Wouldn't that be the damnedest thing?" he said. "We come looking for treasure, and the only treasure they were trying to pinpoint was grain."

"Not much treasure greater than that, to a man starvin'," Sam mused. "You can't eat silver."

The big man gave a nod and let his eyes scan down the canyon until he could make out camp. "Two hours back to camp," he said. "I say we start now. And don't you worry about Mr. Baron. We've been together a long time, him and me, and we're real tight. He'll understand."

*   *   *

Baron took Viktor's news of their failure about as everyone except Viktor had expected. He flew into the worst tirade since the trip began. Any pretense he had put on in the beginning of being a man of some control had been lost with the realization that he might go back home to New York with no silver lode to show. His mood became so foul, in fact, that when they headed back down to camp Sam and Tom opted to stay at the cave.

Sam had killed a blue grouse with a hard-flung pine branch on the way down the mountain. It seemed small to a couple of men who had built their appetites weaving back and forth across the face of a canyon that threatened at any time to drop them off into oblivion, but a small meal was preferable to having to put up with Baron's ire around the fire down below. Anyway, this was one case where they both knew their eyes would be bigger than their stomachs, for the grouse was a good-sized bird.

Sam built up a fire in front of the cave, while Tom irreverently borrowed a big steel sword from inside and skewered the grouse with it, setting the sword handle across a big rock and angling the point up high so the meat wouldn't sit close enough to the fire to burn. Then he and Sam both lay down right there on the trail for a much-deserved nap.

*   *   *

Many of the world's best ideas are born of accidents and of the dreams of the weary. That day's best insight came from a combination of the two.

Tom had been in a state of half-sleep for twenty minutes or so when he woke up to turn the meat over. He poked his finger into the side of the grouse, and watery-looking blood oozed out of it. It was going to be good. He went to wipe the grease off on his coat, and his hand ran across a sticky spot, eliciting a curse from him.

Sam opened one eye and looked over at him, catching him trying to pick a hunk of pitch off the right side of his coat. Sam chuckled and worked himself up to a sitting position. "Might as well give up, old pard. I've tried gettin' that stuff off before."

He told a story of a man he had met who had been up in the wilderness so long and was so covered with grease, dirt and pitch that a variety of insects had been effectively entombed within his buckskin clothing. Both men laughed.

"How's the food comin'?"

Tom shrugged. "Maybe another ten minutes." He pulled a hunk of jerked beef out of his left coat pocket and tossed it to Sam. "See if this'll hold you."

Sam caught the meat out of the air and thanked him, then struggled up and stretched. On a whim, he looked over, and there was the Hawk's Eye, still jutting out of the rock where Baron had left it. He walked over and crouched down to look through it again, then checked the area it pointed out with his field glasses. Sure enough, he could make out a familiar little patch of junipers on the side of the canyon that told him they had hunted in precisely the spot the peep site pointed out. He sighed.

"What's the matter?" Tom queried.

"Nothin' much. Well, I reckon I was interested to see if that little stick actually led us somewhere valuable. It was a nice idea."

Again, he leaned down and looked through the hole. Suddenly a thought struck him. He reached out and grasped the top of the Hawk's Eye, exerting downward pressure on it. There was a soft grating sound, but from all he could tell the piece of brass had reached the bottom of the hole. It didn't seem to have given way at all, but still he leaned down and checked. The difference was minimal, but there was a difference. The sight seemed to point perhaps five or ten feet farther down the slope than where they had hunted.

Drawing part of his mustache into his mouth, Sam chewed on it for a moment, then tugged the Hawk's Eye up out of its slot. He squinted down into the hole, trying to see what lay at the bottom. It was too dark. Running his tongue along the inside of his lower lip, he sat there in thought. Suddenly, he looked over at Tom's coat, at the pitch spot he had given up on. That was it!

He startled Tom when he lurched to his feet so abruptly, and when his partner asked what he was up to he was too intent even to reply. He strode down the trail until he found the first place where he could make his way up the rock face. It took a few minutes to make the treacherous climb, but it proved worthwhile, for the first little Douglas fir tree he came to had a suitably large spot of pitch oozing out of its trunk. He pinched off a big hunk of the freshest, stickiest part he could find, then turned and picked his way back down the steep mountain face.

Tom was cutting into the grouse breast when he arrived back at the cave, and he looked up briefly but then returned his attention to the coming feast. Knowing Tom, he was curious, but since Sam had ignored him earlier he was returning the favor.

Without a word, Sam walked past his partner and picked up the Hawk's Eye. Glancing at the hole, he liberally smeared sap onto the end of the bronze cylinder, then slid it down into its hole. He made sure it was settled good and hard, then drew it back out. "Well, look at that!" he exclaimed.

Tom glanced over, feigning a lack of interest. What Sam was showing him was a bunch of gravel and debris clinging to the bottom of the cylinder. He picked it off as best he could, then wiped more of the sticky substance on the end and pushed it back down into place. It took him four times of doing this before the end of the Hawk's Eye emerged relatively free of debris.

With a gleaming eye, Sam turned and stared hard at Tom. His heart was pounding. He leaned slightly forward and let the Hawk's Eye slide once more down into its notch, and he wiggled it to be sure it was settled as deeply as it would go. With a big breath, he leaned forward and peered through the sight. By now, Tom was crouching right beside him, his meal forgotten.

"I'll be tarred," Sam said softly.

He eased himself back up and looked over at Tom. His partner's eyes were full of hope, and they searched his face. Sam just grinned and waved an inviting hand toward the Hawk's Eye. The look on his face said it all.

Taking a grip on the middle of the bronze stick, Tom leaned down into it and let his eye find the hole. Where it pointed was a full hundred yards farther down into the canyon than the lowest place they had searched that morning. And the area was noticeably flat and free of rocks and large trees. It was a place that had been cleared by man, a place someone had wanted to make free of anything that would prevent a large troop of men from moving freely around. And faint there to its side was a light-colored strip winding up to the ridge above the canyon—the kind of area that might see use by men climbing up and down the side of a canyon carrying heavy loads.

Sitting fully upright and giving Sam his craftiest grin, Tom reached out and slid the Hawk's Eye from its hole, then picked up a handful of gravel and dust and let it sift down into the hole. When he was finished, he slid the Hawk's Eye down in once more and leaned over to check his work. He kept adding dust and gravel until the Hawk's Eye aimed to precisely the same place it had when entrepreneur Stuart Baron had sat here directing his peons to find him a silver mine.

Then, as a last thought, he slid the Hawk's Eye down into a narrow crevice between two big boulders.

"How you plan to get that out of there?" Sam asked sharply.

Tom looked over at him with a blank stare.
"Get what out of where?"

CHAPTER TWENTY-NINE

Back at camp, Melissa woke up from her nap lying partway off her blanket, her hair in the dust. She sat up and leaned over, trying to flip her hair around enough to shake the dust out of it. Frustrated, she tugged at a little stick, then sighed and leaned forward with her elbows on her knees. She looked around the camp, and to her surprise she was the first one stirring. That pleased her immensely, for it opened up a window she hadn't seen for a while—a window to go down and wash some of the dust and the stink from her body. She enjoyed the life of an archaeologist, but a woman was not intended to smell this way. She had to feel clean again. It had been too long.

She stood up, wiping a hand wearily across the back of her neck to free some more of the dust and residue. Letting her eyes sweep the camp, she assured herself that no one was moving around. In the cool gray day, most of them were inside their tents making up for the sleep they had lost during the night.

Going into her tent, she picked up a small drawstring bag, a reticule, she carried her toiletries in. She stuffed her pistol in the bag too, then stepped lightly onto the trail.

Then she stopped. What was she thinking? Melissa liked to consider herself a courageous woman, one who could watch out for herself. Indeed, she had the pistol, and she knew how to use it. Her father had spent many hours in her childhood going against her mother's wishes to teach her how to shoot both a pistol and a rifle—even a shotgun. But this Death-Shadow was something like she had never dealt with. Would her little thirty-two caliber pistol hurt him enough to stop him if he found her alone on the trail—or at the spring? She knew the answer: a flat no. Looking longingly down the trail, she sighed and turned back to camp.

*   *   *

Tom and Sam, on their way back down the mountain, had begun debating whether to give in and show Baron their discovery. Did he deserve it? After all, his pompous attitude was putting them all in danger, and it wasn't as if he had ever shown a streak of politeness to either of them which would ingratiate them to him. It was going to take some consideration. Tom's first inclination was to leave the Hawk's Eye where he had laid it to rest and to never tell anyone they had discovered its secret.

They reached camp, and it was to Melissa's great relief. She had decided she was not going to get clean, but now, with Sam and Tom there to guard over her, she devised a way. Although slightly uncomfortable for all of them, she asked Tom and Sam to hold up a blanket for her while she performed her impromptu ablutions behind it with a basin and pitcher. Thus, she was able to feel clean without the danger of going down to the pool.

Not long after she had dressed again, and the three of them were huddled around the guttering fire, the others began to come awake. The Professor was among the first, and when the last of them had come to the fire and filled up on sandwiches of roast venison and biscuits, he put his hands on his knees and took in a deep breath.

"My friends, I would like to say you have all been wonderful on this trip. I am very happy with how it has gone, for the most part. You have been all a man could ask for, and I intend to make sure you are publicly thanked, as well as rewarded handsomely. Now, if you would accompany me, I believe we can begin to carry the last of the artifacts down to camp, and in the morning we can bring those mummies that will make this trip out with us. Then we can leave this fearsome land behind."

Sam chuckled, amused to think of this country as fearsome. He guessed it was, thanks to the presence of the Santa Catalina Giant, but it was not terrible. This was his kind of country, a country in which he felt very much at home. It was no wonder Death-Shadow wanted to protect his piece of it from outsiders.

They all trooped on up to the cave and began moving the last of the museum specimens, staying in groups of at least two. One or two people would carry a few items while another one, carrying a rifle, would guard them.

*   *   *

When the others marched up the trail to the cave, Baron had gone back to his tent to lie down and fume over his failure to find the lost silver mine. Even in his anger, sleep claimed him, and an hour passed before he came groggily awake. For several minutes, he lay staring at the ceiling of his tent. He wanted to let out a string of profanities. Better yet, he wanted to shoot something. Instead, he lay like a dead man. He had failed. By some twist of fate, his "Hawk's Eye" had been blind; it had led him only to a "treasure trove" of grain stores. There was no workable mine, at least not one that had been clearly marked for rediscovery. The revelation had shaken him to the core. This entire trip had been built with that mother lode of silver ore the foremost objective. He was going to return to New York with nothing but artifacts. It was the bitterest pill he had ever swallowed.

He guessed he should at least go up and try to act interested in the last of the scientific side of the expedition. Stuart Baron had never before been beaten—by anything. He was not going to let this setback numb him to the rest of life.

Rolling over, he sat up and leaned forward on his knees for a while. At last, he stood and stooped out of the tent. The day outside was as gray as his mood, but at least it had warmed up, and the wind had ceased.

He had the sudden thought that it was time he cleaned himself up. His hair was full of dust, and he could feel the grit of sand that had made its way down inside his shirt, clinging to his back and between the muscles of his chest. It was not a sensation he was used to, living in luxury in his New York apartment. He was used to the feel of clean silk underwear against his skin, of silky linen around him as he slept—or the soft skin of a woman bending to his desires. Oh, it had been a long time since he had seen a real woman, a woman he was interested in and who was interested in him in turn.

Too long...

He did what he could with a washcloth and a bucket of water, but it was a far cry from the fancy bathhouses in New York. He would have liked to go down to the pool in the creek, but considering what lurked out there beyond their knowledge, that would have to wait. Feeling somewhat better, he started up the trail, the Ballard rifle in his hand.

He had gone only a hundred yards or so when he saw the old Mexican, Guillermo de Madrid, coming down the trail toward him with a worried look on his face. The old man carried a .44-40 Winchester, battered with use and abuse. An expression of relief washed over him when he saw Baron.

"What's the matter?" asked Baron. "Why are you alone?"

"The woman!" shot out Guillermo. "She goes into the forest."

"She *what!*" shot out Baron. "By herself?"

"Yes. She see some strange pecking bird and wanted to go closer. She said she would be right back, but I don't know."

"Where did she go up?"

The Mexican turned and hurried back up the trail ahead of him. Baron wasn't in the same hurry the Mexican seemed to be, so he lagged fifty yards behind him. They had made it only eighty or so yards when they saw Melissa coming back down onto the trail. An irritating feeling of relief ran through Baron. It was irritating because he didn't like feeling protective of this woman who treated him so coolly. After all, he was a man of some means, very fit, and attractive in a manly sort of way, and it wasn't often that he didn't at least draw some favorable notice from someone of the female persuasion. But if he ever had from Melissa it was something he hadn't noticed; and he had looked.

Still, in spite of the feeling of not being "good enough" for her, he was happy to see she was safe, his worst thoughts unfounded. One death on this trip, even that of a bare acquaintance like Pistolito, was enough. He certainly didn't want to return to his backers with the demise of Melissa Ford on his conscience. Not finding the silver mine was shameful enough.

One thing Baron had to admit as he walked on uphill toward where Guillermo and the woman had stopped: Melissa was certainly lovely in the gray mountain light. He had always thought she was a very attractive woman, which made her indifference toward him all the more cutting. Even as he thought this, a smile lit her face shortly after seeing him. She had never looked prettier.

He started to say something complimentary.

Then the blur of motion caught his eye.

A huge, copper-colored form burst from the trees to Melissa's right. The Mexican turned with his rifle, and for an old man he was surprisingly fast.

But the Santa Catalina Giant was faster.

A hand lashed out, and gnarled knuckles took the Mexican in the side of the head, sending him sprawling down the trail. The Winchester clattered away.

The huge hand grabbed Melissa.

She screamed.

Baron's shocked eyes settled on the form of the man. The word "man" did not seem to fit. As Sam had sworn, he stood no less than nine feet tall. His forearm must be the size of Baron's thigh! He scooped Melissa up in one arm as if she were a toy.

Baron was an able man. A tough man with good wits and steady nerves. He collected both on the moment. He yelled out. The giant whirled toward the noise. Baron started to bring up his rifle. Melissa was right in his line of sight. With shocking speed, the giant dropped her.

She landed on the trail.

Up came an enormous, muscular right arm.

It bore what appeared to be a bow, and just about the size of the one they had found in the cave.

Everything in Baron's vision was blurred. Thumb touched rifle hammer. Rifle reared toward shoulder. Somehow the other man was faster than Baron. Impossible! Time stalled... The rifle was moving through tar. The mighty bow switched hands and rose into action like a falcon. An arrow came level. Rifle butt still rising to his shoulder... But now the huge copper fingers released.

Time, standing still... Something knifing through the air. No time to react. No chance to duck, dodge—even to fall. Against his rifle something heavy slammed. Something heavier hammered him between the eyes. No warning, no chance to recover, to rally. Everything going dark.

A sensation of falling... falling...

In the back of Baron's mind, screams. Melissa's screams. He couldn't move. Couldn't... *breathe*. He felt his body hit the earth.

Far away the sound of something heavy clattering on the rocks.

His beautiful rifle. Made of all the best materials that man could harvest or manufacture. Engraved by the masters. Embellished with precious silver. Yet it couldn't save his life, or the life of Melissa...

*   *   *

On the way down the trail with old Guillermo, Melissa saw what she thought might be an ivory-billed woodpecker. Excitedly, she told her escort what it was and how special it was, and then she laid her armload of treasure down on the ground and headed up into the trees, telling him she wanted one good look.

She found the bird, and she had been right. It was an ivory-billed woodpecker, and as beautiful as she had imagined. Making her way back down through the forest, she thought of Tom. It had been some time since she was so taken with a man. Her feelings for this one couldn't be completely explained.

She had been courted by handsome men before. By men who enjoyed the theater, fine dining, and dancing. Men who could converse on topics from religion to opera to architecture. Tom was like none of those. And perhaps in that very fact lay her fascination with him. He was tall, handsome, yet cut out of the same scarred brown leather as his chaps. Hands rough, deeply tan, brown hair curled over his ears. Mustache with its ends ever so slightly curled, and the "imperial" tuft that looked so dashing on his manly chin. Few men she knew in New York could claim the broad shoulders that filled out his shirts. Yet in spite of all that masculinity he could be very soft and gentle.

And fast to make her smile...

These were the thoughts in Melissa's head as she wound back down to the trail to see the old Mexican waiting there, and Baron coming up toward her. She smiled at Guillermo, then at Baron, and she meant to say hello.

But as if from nowhere a blur loomed in the corner of her eye. It came on the path she had followed down out of the woods. Before she could turn, there was someone beside her. A huge arm came out, and its owner backhanded Guillermo and sent him flying. Then he clutched her. She let out an involuntary scream. The stench of body odor, overpowering. She looked down at the largest foot she had ever beheld—by far the largest. And the thigh must have been thirty-five inches in girth, and all muscle.

As suddenly as she had been snatched, the huge man dropped her to the trail. Faintly, she heard the sound of Baron yelling. Like the sound of a faraway train, she heard a *twang* and looked to see that the huge man towering over her had loosed an arrow. It was so fast that its path could not be followed. But she knew where it was aimed, and that was where her glance sped. She was in time to see the arrow slam into the barrel of Baron's rifle, and the big gun swept upward and exploded with flame and smoke. It struck Baron a solid blow between the eyes, and then he was falling. He hit the trail, and his rifle banged onto the rocks.

In despair, Melissa tried to scramble to her feet. She let out another scream without intending to, made a leap up the trail— toward Tom and Sam and Viktor. Something caught her out of mid-air, a rabbit in a snare. The gargantuan arm dragged her back against the sweaty, copper-tan body.

He whirled. Melissa fought at the forearm of the giant claw that held her in its grasp. The man let out an amused laugh, and he lunged off the trail and up through the trees. He ascended the slope with astonishing speed. It was almost like being tied belly-first over a horse. With his left hand, he used his bow as a walking stick, thrusting it into the earth. His mighty legs propelled him upward through the timber.

Again, she screamed, this time deliberately. The bold giant of a man roared with laughter. Then she felt a blow to the side of her skull, and her head rang. She felt it loll downward, and they continued on, her feet touching the ground only now and then.

They stopped, and she could feel him wrapping something hard and sinewy about her. Then she felt herself hoisted up, and before she knew it she was far above the ground, with her back against her abductor's. He had her in some kind of a backpack. She was secure. There was no escaping this snare.

He sped on uphill. Her feet dangled beneath her, childlike. She almost could no longer feel them...

*   *   *

Sam and Tom were coming down the trail, their arms laden with future museum pieces, when the first scream made their hearts freeze. Viktor was behind them with a rifle. Their eyes spun to each other.

Seconds later, they heard the thunder of Baron's rifle. Tom's heart vaulted into his throat. He dropped his armload and started stumblingly down the debris-cluttered trail. He couldn't catch his breath. His vision was blurred. All he could think of was Melissa. He didn't even hear the others coming behind him.

A line of men with weapons a-bristle streamed down the mountain trail behind them. Tom slipped and almost fell. He caught himself against a boulder, pushed back erect. The near accident didn't slow his descent—especially when they heard two more spaced screams from the woman. He careened downhill at ankle-breaking speed, eyes scanning the terrain as he went. As he came around the last turn before camp, he saw the form lying still. Baron! He lay on his back, his rifle near his head on the trail.

Tom skidded to a halt with several of the others close behind him. Under the threat to Melissa, even Professor Ashcroft had shown himself no physical slouch. He had no weapon visible on him, but there was fight in his eyes as he looked down at his colleague, then swept the mountainside with his eyes.

There was a cry from the timber, and then they saw Guillermo come sliding and almost falling through the trees, headed like a cyclone toward them. He hardly had time to catch his breath before everyone was firing questions at him and he was trying to stutter out his replies.

Sam slid past Tom where he had stopped at Baron's head. A quick look about showed him huge tracks in the trail. They made a profusion of marks in the dust, and when they left it was not downhill. They turned and made their way up the steep hill and disappeared the way the Mexican had just come from. Sam cursed under his breath. Why had they let that woman go down the trail with only Guillermo as her protector!

As soon as he understood where the kidnapper had run with Melissa, Tom started up the hill. Sam scrambled after him and grabbed a shoulder, jerking him around.

"Hold it, Tom!" he growled. "Hold it. I know what you want to do, but look at you. You don't even have a rifle. He'll kill you without blinking an eye." His last words were softer. "Let's get down the trail and get the horses. We can track this man. Come on. Use your head. Don't let me down."

Tom sucked a deep breath and put a hand on Sam's shoulder, more to calm himself than his partner. "You're right. All right, come on."

"Better idea," said Sam. "I'll start up through here with my pistol, just to keep an eye on this trail and maybe see if I can spot them. You go get the horses and come back up here."

They didn't bother to tell anyone else what they were doing. Tom just dropped off the mountainside in leaping strides and made his way down the trail, and Viktor, catching on to their scheme, followed him. The others stayed with Baron.

Running down to camp, Tom felt like he had been punched in the stomach. He tried to force himself to calm as he saddled Nicker and Gringo, while beside him Viktor grimly saddled his own horse. Neither man spoke. When they had readied their gear, Tom finally turned and eyed Viktor.

"You going with us?"

"With you or without, I'm goin'," said the big man.

Tom nodded, and before he could check his words he said, "It'll be good to have you."

For several seconds, they looked at each other, and suddenly Viktor's big paw came up and clapped Tom once on the shoulder. He gave a sharp nod. "She means a lot to both of us," said Viktor, and neither of them spoke again as they climbed into leather.

They turned and trotted back up the trail. As they approached their group, Tom saw to his surprise Baron sitting up, the others crouched around him. Before reaching them, Tom reined Nicker and headed up the steep slope, and Viktor followed.

They caught up to Sam, and he informed them that he had seen plenty of sign, but had not seen Death-Shadow or the woman. Viktor swore. Other than that visceral response, Sam was first to speak, after a long silence. "We better move. That man's good enough at hiding his sign he could easy lose us and hide her away—if he leaves her alive."

Tom winced, glancing from Sam to Viktor and back. His words held no sign of doubt. "He'll leave her alive." And he started his horse through the trees.

Sam caught up. "Hold on. Let me ride in front, pard. I know you want to be Melissa's hero, but I can't afford to lose this trail."

Tom drew a deep, calming breath. "All right, lead the way."

Off they started again. When Sam glanced back the way they had come there was only dark timber. He guessed the others would go back to camp—at least he prayed they would. If they got Melissa back she was going to be in serious need of nurturing friends and a comfortable camp. And *if* they got Melissa back that would mean...

A meeting with Death-Shadow.

For a long time the trio worked a gentle sidehill. The vegetation varied from deep black patches of fir shading shrubs and pockets of ferns to more open areas of aspen and pine, dried grass and wildflowers. The terrain was inclined, with large gray boulders here and there. It sloped off into a forested bowl below them, and to the right, when they looked far enough, they could see where the mountain bled up into the gloomy sky.

As they traveled, picking up occasional sign, they could see that the slope to their right continued on, but it started to curve around before them. The forest in front and to the left fell off more and more steeply until, from what they could see through the trees, it emptied into a large, grassy valley. The forest growth changed gradually until the firs were the exception, as were the pines. Here, juniper and scattered oaks began to hold sway.

Far across the grassy valley swept the cliffs where they had first seen Death-Shadow standing at the dead tree. That plateau rose at an easy angle until it crested out in a heavy shock of juniper and oak that clustered about a single crown of broken rimrock. The plateau, the rimrock, and the mountainside they were following made one large hook-shaped border at the top of the valley, and because the mountain led them straight into the rimrock and junipers, they kept to it and let the terrain fall away to their left and disappear down into grass and tumbled boulders.

As the trail went on, it became more and more difficult to follow. The big Indian was using rocks more and more to his advantage, stepping from one to the other. And up here on the plateau there were plenty of them to utilize. There were, in fact, more rocks than anything else. Once in a while, Sam would locate a broken blade of grass, and one time he found a crushed ant on a rock in its death throws. Death-Shadow had come this way, and probably not more than half an hour hence.

Death-Shadow moved on cat feet, like a powerful jaguar, and never in a predictable line. At times Sam had to get down on his hands and knees and lower his face toward the ground to catch the light just right so it highlighted the mark of a toe or a heel in the dust collected on a rock. With this method, he was able on several occasions to sight on a trail and follow it for a ways. But this big man was canny, and he would abruptly change directions again, throwing off Sam's ability to follow him with any amount of speed. Here they found a twig snapped, here a pebble turned over with its darker belly now facing the sun. Here there was only a bent blade of grass to lead the way. They made their way across this plateau, and in time they reached the other side.

At that point, the cliffs dropped sharply off, too steep to think of a descent, and this time the drop seemed forever. The valley floor was no less than three hundred feet below them, tangled with brush, trees and broken boulders that had toppled off the cliff over centuries. With a sinking feeling in his chest, Sam got down on his hands and knees again and peered from where he had seen the last track. He almost immediately saw the trail leading away, paralleling the cliff's edge.

He practically leaped up. "Sneaky big beggar tried to make us think he went over the cliff. Come on!"

The three of them started off, sighting on a grove of trees a few hundred yards distant. Every now and then Sam would get down to catch the light in the tracks, and every time the sign he sought was there. Every time, that is, except when he had almost reached the trees.

Here, in the middle of shrubs and dry bunchgrass the trail petered out. Gone. Nothing left.

Sam continued crawling around, going back now and then to where he had last seen the tracks and making sure to keep Tom and Viktor out of his work so they wouldn't scuff up whatever tracks were there. It was twenty-five minutes of increasingly worrisome work before he grew desperate.

It was forty-five before he was forced to give up.

Sam sank bank on his lower legs and sat still. He didn't move, didn't look up at Tom and Viktor, hardly seemed to breathe. He simply stared off along the plateau toward the grove of trees and felt the energy drain out of him.

At last, he stood up and looked at the other two. "Lost the trail." He wondered if he looked as sick as he felt inside. Tom's looks matched exactly how he felt.

"Let's head for those trees," Viktor growled, drawing his pistol from its holster. "We've gotta move before he decides..." He looked over sharply at Sam and Tom, and then his face seemed to take on a haggard look. He swallowed hard and swept the plateau with his eyes. Everyone knew he had stopped himself from saying something about Death-Shadow killing Melissa—or raping her. This thought was in all their minds. But no one dared to speak it.

Sam jacked the lever of his rifle, then let the hammer down carefully on the live cartridge. Not daring to look at the other two, he started toward the trees...

CHAPTER THIRTY

The wind-swept plateau stood empty, and the vast expanse of the sky hung over them like a funeral shroud. A breeze had commenced to blow, and the dry grass shook and rattled around their feet. Sam, Tom and Viktor stood and stared around them, and the barrenness and the loneliness of this place struck out at them like a living thing.

Melissa was gone...

With guns drawn, they approached the trees, but there was no warning ring in Sam like he had expected. Long before he reached the grove of junipers he knew there would be no one there. The high-mountain wind kept the rocks scoured nearly free of dust. Their quarry had been able to use that to his advantage, and in spite of his gargantuan size he had moved across here with very little sign.

Sam knew, as any good tracker knew, that there was always sign. But when a man of Death-Shadow's caliber was the one being hunted, a man who knew every minute detail a tracker would be seeking, he could be expected to take great pains to cover those signs, or to make them as miniscule as possible. Even Sam, who Tom had bragged could track a grain of sand through a dust storm, had so far had no luck in finding anything he could positively identify as a mark left by Death-Shadow.

Like a hungry animal, Sam crawled over much of the ground on his hands and knees. Sometimes he lay for five, ten, fifteen minutes on his belly, studying what lay around him, first gazing far ahead, then peering at the smallest tufts of grass that lay before him and to the sides. He tried to put himself in the mind of the kidnapper. He tried to force himself to believe he would find him, to believe his own feet would somehow intuitively fall where Death-Shadow's had come down.

Then at last he just lay there on the ground, his rifle at his side, and stared—but at nothing. The giant had done what no man his size could do—he had shaken Sam Coffey from his trail. And Sam could almost have wept for the helplessness that knowledge left in his soul.

When at length it became obvious to Tom that his partner had given up, he slumped down on his rump beside him, his rifle across his thighs. He scanned all around them, his mind numb. Viktor was standing beside them, his pistol dangling from his fist. Tom pretended he wasn't there. He tried not to think of him, of Sam, of Death-Shadow... even of Melissa.

Thinking of her would drive him insane.

Sam finally pushed up to his knees, pulling his rifle up and resting its butt on the ground. He didn't look over at Tom. "We'll keep on along this flat. They had to go this way—there's no other place to go. He's a big man. He'll leave a sign, sooner or later. This ain't done—not by a sight."

Tom nodded, wordless. The encouraging words made him push to his feet. Sam got up too, and together they started out again, Viktor trailing them.

For several minutes the scenery didn't change. The junipers grew in stretches, and now and then they were interspersed with the curving red branches of madroño or the leafy oaks. The grass waved in wide patches between the trees, broken only by the shattered granite. Then for a long while it was only the rocks and the dust and here and there a clump of bunchgrass. A time or two

Sam thought he had found a smudge where a moccasin had passed. But it led nowhere, in the end.

To their left was a tall crown of rock that stood out like an ancient castle above the rest of the plateau. It was surrounded by a heavy forest made up almost exclusively of juniper. Not finding any sign leading into it, and a little leery as well, they skirted these trees. They climbed up over the head of the canyon, where the land flattened out, then fell off into a basin of tan, wind-scoured rocks. This ran along, painted with a smattering of stunted oaks, then disappeared in the timber that would lead them eventually back to camp. They followed this basin down to their left, but in the end it sheered off into a canyon filled with juniper, the red-branched Arizona madrone, often mistaken for manzanita, and more rock. Like all of the other terrain they had seen on this side of the plateau, it looked too steep for a man carrying a woman to go, and even if it hadn't there was no sign to be found.

Sam turned at last to Tom, and the look on his face seemed wearier than any Tom had ever seen. The heavy rifle drooped from his fingertips, and his face was drawn down with deep lines etched along it. Sam didn't speak, and Tom couldn't wait.

"I won't go back, Sam. They passed here. We know that much. I won't leave Melissa in his hands."

Sam listlessly moved his shoulders, attempting a shrug. "What will it get you? What if he just wants you out here alone? Or even both of us? In the dark, away from the group—he'd have us just where he wanted."

"There'll be three of us here."

They turned to Viktor, who had plodded slowly up to them and stood there eyeing them, his pistol dangling from his hand.

Sam looked from Viktor back to Tom. At last, he lifted a hand and drew the dust off his mustache. "We need to go back. Make sure the camp's settled. Then get a couple or three more of the

boys and come back tomorrow. We'll scour this place from top
to bottom. Somebody's bound to stumble on something."

Tom kept staring at him. He would have liked to believe what
Sam was telling him. In his own heart he would have also loved
to believe his own stance that the mere act of staying here would
bring some positive result. But deep down he knew—this hunt
was going to end with the same result as they had seen back in
Texas, with Trina Sward, in the clearing with the yellow bull and
the one-eyed cow. Tom knew it, and he knew Sam did too. Back
then, Trina had died, and there was not one thing they could do
to stop it.

They would never see Melissa Ford alive again.

*   *   *

The three men could talk all day about what they needed to
do, how they must leave, get back to the others. But when it came
down to actually doing it none of them seemed capable. It was
too difficult to abandon this plateau. To do so seemed like a death
sentence for Melissa.

So, keeping within sight of each other, they wandered the flat,
windswept bench for another hour or so. There were a few signs,
but most of them turned out to be made by bighorn sheep or deer,
except for one area they ended up learning had been disturbed by
a mountain lion. Any signs that might have been made by Death-
Shadow could never be proven.

It was with heavy hearts that they turned and plodded back
through the heavy timber. Each man knew the others had the same
thought in mind: What were they going to tell those back at camp?

Forty-minutes later, they reached the main trail. Like blood,
the western sky ran red as the three of them trooped down into
camp. A lonesome wind soughed through the treetops, and dust
skittered around the ground. The coyotes that seemed appointed
to serenade them came to the far edge of the canyon once more

and began to yap as the Professor, Ross, the Mexicans, and Delbert Moore turned hopefully to meet them.

Glum in appearance, and more glum in their hearts, the threesome could barely meet the expectant gazes. Baron came out of his tent and straightened up, looking toward them. His face seemed gray, and there was a purple swelling along his nose and around one eye, which was swollen almost shut. He stared at them for a few seconds, read their discouraged faces, then turned and stepped back inside his tent.

The Professor's voice sounded distant, lost. He gazed at Sam, slowly shaking his head. "Nothing?"

Sam shook his head in his turn and heaved a sigh.

Ross, standing at the Professor's right shoulder, bunched his jaws. He clicked his tongue involuntarily and blinked back hot tears. "Have some supper, boys. I imagine we'll want to be heading out there again early."

Without a word, Sam and Viktor walked to the flickering fire, watching it dive and waver back and forth against the shuffle of the wind. Tom, as if in a daze, went on alone and disappeared into the forest. This time Sam let him go.

*   *   *

No one slept much. The fire was deliberately put out early so as not to shed light on the camp. Bundles of supplies and artifacts, dyed blue-black in the starlight, piled up against the south side of the camp. Hunkered into the pile, Sam held his rifle. He wanted to smoke, but to be pinpointed by the orange tip of a cigarette was not a wise idea. Instead, he packed tobacco against his gums and sat still as a tree.

On the far side of camp, perhaps a hundred feet away, Delbert Moore kept watch. The young man had never balked about this chore, although fear was always strong on his face, particularly tonight. Sam had come to respect the city boy. He was of no great shakes as a mountain man, nor even any specimen of rugged manhood as a New Yorker, if compared to a man like Viktor. He looked soft, and he spoke soft, and he thought the weak thoughts of a man who was bred and lived his life fully in the confines of so-called civilization, and high society. Yet when called to duty he went, and he went with his jaw set, unwavering. Sam had seen Moore bow his head once, just at the edge of the firelight, and he raised a comforting hand to his eyes, hiding tears from the others. He guessed Moore must know Melissa pretty well. For Moore, for the Professor, for Tom... there was a lot of pain in the expeditioners' camp this night.

Without any reason, the hair suddenly began to prickle up on the back of Sam's neck. Involuntarily, he ducked his head and whirled around, but there was no movement in the night other than the soft sighing of the pine and fir boughs and the rattling of aspen leaves. He had already jacked a cartridge into the rifle's chamber. Now he carefully, soundlessly eased back the hammer.

He was on his knees among the pile of canvas packages. His eyes picked through the night shadows. His ears keened. The hollow echo of an owl's call carried from up the canyon. The breeze tugged at his hat. Somewhere close by, an animal scurried in the grass—something larger than a mouse, probably a woodrat. Packrats, they called them in the West.

A meteorite flashed brilliant across the night sky, leaving a long, glowing trail in its wake. The owl called again. Goose bumps rose on Sam's skin. It wasn't because of the owl, the rat, the wind. Something else was moving close by. Something big. Something untamed.

There was an almost inaudible *twang* somewhere in the night, and just for a second Sam cocked his head. The wind sang again and scattered loose pine needles against someone's tent. Suddenly, a horrible cry split the night. It was a man, a man nearby. A cry of pain, of desperation. One eerie word wailed against the night wind: "No-o-o." A strangled, choking sound followed. Something heavy fell. A man.

Standing half up now behind the canvas packages, Sam's eyes dug into the shadows. His entire body coursed with energy, with cold waves. He could hear the camp coming to life, tent doors being thrown back.

"*NO!*" He heard the word, and it was his own voice. "Get back inside!"

Even as he spoke, he moved, and something struck the ground where he had been. He glanced down to see the quivering end of what appeared to be a heavy stick there in the ground. Going by its angle, he raised the rifle and levered five shots against the rise of the ridge. Then he dodged to his left, and in that moment something cut the air by his coat. He fired again. This time he felt something hit him hard in the middle. Choking and coughing, he doubled over.

He had been struck! Was this how it ended? He went to his knees, dropping his rifle. He clutched for the arrow he knew he would find in his midriff. There was nothing. He sucked for air that for a couple of seconds wouldn't come. The sound of more firing split the night. As he looked up he could see the orange spears that accompanied each shot, and lead was spanging off the rocks not far away.

Then, from a hundred yards up the ridge, it rose again—that eerie, taunting laugh. The laugh that came from a deep chest, from a man who seemed not even human. Gathering himself, forgetting his pain, Sam fired toward it. The laugh came again, but from another point. He fired there, and it rose again three seconds later from ten yards away. Several of them fired at once.

The wind kept playing a devil's violin in the trees, quickening, calling out the ghosts of the Santa Catalinas. Then, from far back in the forest, Sam heard a deep, booming voice yell something he could not understand. Again, that laugh erupted, and his stomach hardened up like a ball of cold wax.

His breath came in a huge gasp. He felt around on his stomach again, finding only a dull ache. Looking down, he could see the form of a fairly large rock gleaming in the dark, the rock that must have struck him in the midriff. That devil had an arm!

The wind moaned and seemed to rise more insistently, as if for now it had taken their side and was sweeping the giant away from them. Sam thought he heard the distant laugh again, but it was quickly drowned by the wind.

He moved carefully through the dark, and even as a lantern flickered to life over by the tent of Dowdy Ross he found young Delbert Moore lying there by the log he had chosen as his shield. Even in the starlight Sam thought he saw the shine of tears down the sides of the young man's face. But they were the tears of death. He had dropped his rifle and was clutching the shaft of a huge arrow that angled out sideways from his coat.

Sam looked over at Ross as he came up. "Blow the lantern," he said, without his usual gruffness. He felt too bad to be gruff. "He may come back."

Tomorrow, the Sonoran Desert would seethe with May heat, and not all of it would stay down on the flats below. Some of it inevitably would climb the slopes, and they had to bury Delbert Moore as soon as possible, there on that lonely mountain...

*   *   *

The Professor knew Moore best. After breakfast the next morning he stood over the rough cross on his grave holding his hat in both hands. Tears gleamed in his eyes, but he stood and fought them for a long time, keeping them sealed off. His lips worked for several seconds before sound at last came from them.

"He was a good boy. Loyal is not a good enough word to describe him. Lord, keep Delbert Moore in your fold. He will be missed by his mother, by us at the museum and in the halls of the university. Somewhere I know he is flying to you. Please greet him there. He will make a good photographer, servant and friend for you, too."

For all his gathered strength, that last comment made the Professor's tears spill over, and he bowed his head desperately and clenched his jaws. Finally, he ended his eulogy with a hard nod. Then he turned away and walked down to sit at the edge of the canyon.

The others stood for a minute more, and finally Sam clamped his hat back on and reached down to pick up his rifle. Tom followed him a few minutes later over to the line of horses, where they fed on oats that half-filled their nosebags. It was time they started taking in some high-energy feed. They might be called on to take a rough road, and fast.

The decision had been made to try and get as much as they could down from the cave now, to be ready to leave as soon as they found Melissa. No one had any desire to remain on this mountain any longer than absolutely necessary. Sam and Tom were hitching packs on mules when the Professor stepped up to them to look over the operation.

After a few moments of quiet observation, he said, "I am forced to make a decision, I believe. A decision I'm sure you both foresaw. We cannot carry everything out of the mountains in one trip, not with the limited number of animals we brought. You see, I really couldn't have expected a find so monumental as this. We will have to take only two or three of the giants now and leave the others and some of the artifacts up in the cave. We'll come back for those later. That's my fault, gentlemen. I don't expect you to come back with us, although you're most welcome—and I would pay you more than enough for your trouble." They didn't respond for a moment, so he went on. "I couldn't expect anyone to come back up here after this."

Sam and Tom looked at each other, suddenly thinking the same thing. "You're not plannin' to head out now," Tom said by way of a question.

The Professor looked startled. "Certainly not! I hope you aren't. We must search for Melissa." He struggled to control his emotions as he looked back and forth between them. "Without you she is lost. I could not bear that."

Tom simply nodded. His throat was too tight to speak.

CHAPTER THIRTY-ONE

Standing away from the rest, Sam looked around the campsite. All was still.

The others sat or stood around, waiting for someone to decide when the time was right to go after Melissa in force. One way or another, this day, or the next at the latest, they would be leaving this mountain. The camp had been good to them in some ways, but Sam wouldn't miss it. There were too many bad memories. And like lonely sentinels, two crosses stood here that hadn't been before: Pistolito and Delbert Moore.

Sam looked up the ridge, wondering how he was going to pick up the trail he had lost previously. Suddenly, he heard a sharp bark. He looked over to see Crooked Foot's dog, the lame Indian behind him with a grim look on his face. The dog loped up the trail and started sniffing around.

Crooked Foot came to a stop in front of Sam, trying to catch his breath. He pointed down at the dog. "My friend, he can find Death-Shadow for you. He no like." Sam narrowed his eyes, looking down at Crooked Foot. The Indian gave a brisk nod as if to confirm what he had said and waved toward his dog. "Good. Trail. We find you a woman."

Sam laughed at the Indian's choice of words. "All right, friend. You find me a woman. Find her and I'll pay you good."

Crooked Foot smiled big. "You... maybe give me rifle?"

Sam gave his Marlin a look. "Well, maybe. Find her first."

The Indian nodded and said, "Death-Shadow, he try to kill you, yes? You keep... arrow?"

Realizing what he meant, Sam walked over to where the pile of packs still clustered. There, the arrow that had barely missed him stuck out of the ground. Sam nodded at it.

Crooked Foot spoke some words in his own tongue and made a clicking noise at the back of his mouth, calling the dog to him. He crouched down by the arrow as the dog came up to him. Again, he spoke in his language and made the dog understand that he wanted him to pay special heed to the arrow shaft. The animal's demeanor changed instantly. As he sniffed the wood he let out a low, deep-throated growl. He backed off a little, took a look around the camp, and whined. Standing up, Crooked Foot cocked his leg and snapped the arrow off with his foot. He picked up the shaft and held it out to the dog, who growled again.

"Where from he shoot you?"

Sam chuckled. "Luckily, he *didn't* shoot me. But where he *tried* from was up there." He pointed out the general area from which the arrow had come.

Saying no more, Crooked Foot turned with the arrow and started up the ridge, the dog following. Thirty yards up, the dog let out a shrill bark, then another. Crooked Foot turned and made a huge gesture for them to follow.

Without hesitation, they started up the slope. But a ways farther on, Tom grabbed Sam's shoulder and made him stop and turn.
"I don't want to be the one to sound like a wet blanket, but...
Could be he's leadin' us into a trap. We've been wrong about
folks before."

Sam shrugged. "Could be, Curly. I reckon we don't have
much choice but to find out."

Clenching his jaws, Tom looked down at his rifle. "All right
then. Head on. I'll go back down and bring up the horses."

The dog worked in silence. Only right close to him could his
snuffling for scent be heard. Sam and the Indian stayed close
enough to keep sight of the animal while letting him have the
room he needed to work.

They didn't see Tom again for some time, and when they did
hear him coming through the timber it was obvious he was not
alone. Sam paused and waited while Crooked Foot and the dog
continued on ahead. Soon he could see Tom riding along, leading
Gringo, and big Viktor was with him, his face set in determined
lines. He carried a Spencer rifle across his saddle horn. Tom and
Viktor stopped back out of the way with the horses, their eyes
scanning the dark timber.

They started to side-hill, and there were stretches where the
giant footprints were plain in the loam as the big renegade dug in,
trying to keep from sliding down the steep slope. The timber here
was deep and cool, and only now and then did they see any bird
life. A couple of times they crossed paths with red squirrels, and
once saw one with large, tufted ears, who barked and chattered in
the trees, yelling at the foursome and the dog in his own language
to get off of his mountain.

In the mottled shadows of the timber, a woodpecker hung
from the side of a ponderosa, its crest bobbing as it tapped with
its sharp beak, exploring for weak, beetle-killed spots in the bark.

The woods grew darker. The horses had a difficult time keeping their footing on the sidehill, and even the men occasionally had to grab onto bushes to hold them upright. There had been no attempt to hide the trail here. The dog continued on in a steady march, leaping downfall and going under those trees whose heavy branches had kept them suspended off the ground when they fell.

Sam could feel the living forest around him. He had grown used to the skittering of the squirrels as they raced through pine needles and up the sides of tree trunks. He was accustomed to the chirping of the occasional warbler or the falling, rising cadence of the brown creeper's whistle. But something dark and dangerous lurked here. It was not just his knowledge of who they followed, but an aura in the air itself. Now and then he looked back to make sure Tom and Viktor were still with them. They went on. He scanned the trees. The dog... The crippled Indian... His grip on the Marlin tightened.

They wove among the broken forest. A long-ago fire had swept through here, killing trees that stood and rotted, then finally fell. The musty, rotting duff on the ground gave rise to smaller vegetation, and in the shade of some of the gargantuan trunks there grew those gentle, wispy ferns that Sam would never get used to seeing. They seemed so far out of place on this mountainside of danger and death.

The dog began to act squirrelly. He fidgeted around and kept raising his nose to sniff at the forest air. Sam looked back at Tom. The horses were also dancing around, their eyes showing white as they flashed about, their ears pivoting this way and that. The dog ran a little ways upslope, stared that way with his ears shot forward and his hair standing up along his spine. He let out a low-voiced growl, then whipped his nose toward his master to make sure he had not deserted him. He took another step up the hill, then whined quietly. Slowly, he started to lower his head, stretching his nose forward and up the mountain...

Without warning, branches splintered and crackled above them. Sam dropped to a knee, bringing the Marlin up. There was the thumping sound of running on the soft mountain soil. The trees were too thick to see. Then he glimpsed the retreating rear end of a huge black bear as it bounded through the woods.

Sam knew bears. This one had been well aware they were there, for its senses, especially its nose, were keen. It had not run from being surprised, but had just let itself get scared. It had probably been stalking them for some time. The very thought made Sam's skin crawl. Someone else could be keeping them in his sights as well—someone who would not scare so easily. Taking a calming breath, he looked back at Tom, where he was busy trying to settle the horses down.

With a heightened sense of the danger here, Sam moved forward. He looked at the dog with a little distrust. If the animal was so intent on its trail that it hadn't spotted the bear for them before it got within twenty yards, how easy would it be for their quarry to double back and waylay them?

They stepped along with the dog now acting nervous and unsure of the trail. It was plain he was almost more concerned with his recent scare than he was with finding the quarry they had followed now for a good mile. A branch snapped up in the woods. Something big... Crooked Foot held up his hand, and Tom and Viktor, who couldn't have heard the noise, stopped the horses. They all waited. Another branch popped a minute later. A soft thump followed, and something brushed by a branch... The darkness seemed to close in... Sam felt a trickle of sweat crawl down between his shoulder blades.

His hands were moist against the metal and wood of his rifle. He involuntarily began to raise it to his shoulder several times, then relaxed it back down. His eyes scanned the timber. This time the dog's eyes, ears and nose were glued to one place up the slope, yet he didn't move. His tail was straight out behind him and one foreleg was poised half-bent. Sam dared a glance back at the horses. Cocky was fighting Tom's hold on him, shaking his head as he tried to work loose. Gringo stared uphill in the direction the dog was looking and rolled his eyes. He stamped a forefoot and made loose soil trickle down the hill. Viktor stood beside his big dark horse with his hand on its neck.

An errant breeze passed, squeaking a dependent tree against its supporter. Dead needles cascaded down. Far down the slope a beetle buzzed. Sam felt the sweat build on his forehead, against his hatband. He realized he was holding his breath.

Something in the timber caught his eye as he scanned past it. It was almost more sixth sense than any other that warned him. Raising the rifle halfway to his shoulder, he slowly scanned back over the area. Something was not right there, but he could not make out what it was. There was a patch of deep woods, a stand of low firs interspersed with branching bushes. In front of that place shone a sunny patch, making the darkness that much harder to penetrate. Then Sam realized what he was looking at.

Eyes...

When he found the two little reddish brown orbs that stared toward him, the rest of the puzzle materialized. It was the bear... As intent as any hunting eagle, it was watching them, its ears straight forward, its lip curled up above its top teeth. Even as he got the full picture, the bear moved its mouth, making a popping sound. The dog started to sidle away downhill, then looked at its master for reassurance. Slowly, it started back up.

Realizing the big bear had gotten its courage back, along with its curiosity, Sam's nervous edge grew. The bear would be foolish to attack, but if it had never before seen humans perhaps it had no fear. Or perhaps it had only dealt with humans not armed as well as they were. Either way, the animal was too close for comfort, and he was not going to just go away. This was a good-sized bear, almost certainly the old boar of the mountain. He was used to being king.

Lowering his eyes, Sam gave the soil near his feet a scan. Not far away lay a rock half the size of his fist. He stepped over to it and picked it up. He couldn't risk a shot right now, not when the man they hunted might be around the next tree. But they had to rid themselves of this nuisance. At a glance, Sam would guess the beast to weigh five hundred pounds—a gigantic black bear, and far too big to risk the chance of an attack.

Taking careful note of the distance, he reared back his arm. Without a sound, he flung the rock as hard as he could. It had only to travel fifteen yards, a distance any rampaging bear could have cleared in two seconds. The rock took less. With a sickening *thwack!* the stone struck home dead-center. It took the bear right between the eyes, and Sam would have sworn they bugged out of the skull half an inch. He swapped his right hand back to the action of the rifle, bringing it up to line its sights on this foe, and cocked the hammer.

But the bear, startled as could be, fell straight over backwards as if pole-axed and disappeared among the pine saplings. A second later, it bounded back up and gave out with a snort and a deep-voiced bark.

Sam was just squeezing the trigger when the big black ball of hair turned and fled up through the forest, letting out a little *whoof* now and then that got quieter and quieter as the sound of popping branches faded away.

This time the bear would not be back.

Sam heard the sound of laughter and looked over to see Crooked Foot. He had seen the man smile before, and he liked to crack a joke, too. But this time his whole body began to shake. Surprised, Sam looked back at Tom and Viktor, and they were laughing too, probably more at the Indian than at what Sam had done to the bear. Before long, all of them were laughing so hard it was hard to stop. Such is the high mirth that follows those moments of being scared out of one's wits.

Finally, they got hold of themselves and urged the bewildered dog on up the trail. Toward the end of the bout of laughter, he had been wagging his tail and panting openly, looking around at the others as if perhaps he was laughing too. But now, with one huge enemy chased away, he went back to being all business. He started back on the trace, and his spine bristled with rising hair almost from the beginning. For whatever reason, the dog did not care for the giant Indian they followed.

The very idea that Sam had just thought of Death-Shadow as an Indian startled him. He knew he had thought of the big man that way before, but what was Death-Shadow, really? He wore a breech clout of buckskin, and moccasins of the same. He carried and used a bow with dexterity and skill. And his hair streamed down below his shoulders. But what was Death-Shadow? Was he truly an Indian? Just a freak of nature? Or, more likely, was he descended from the mummies in the cave? Where had he come from? What did he truly want? Had he only wanted a female companion all along? Were his motives so base and instinctive? Would he be satisfied now that he had Melissa? Or was he driven by something more insidious?

If Death-Shadow was descended from the giants who had once worked the mines, would he not have a taste for riches as well? Could he be a Spaniard? And if so, how had he come down through the generations without others of his kind still living here? There were many questions. Many questions, and most likely no answers. Like the mummified giants in the cave, Death-Shadow would forever be a mystery...

On wore the day. The forest began to fall behind them, the pines growing sparser and sparser. They crossed over the head of the canyon, where the land began to level out. The pine and fir mixed with aspen, then with juniper and oak. At last, the country began to open up. They stood at the head of the canyon once more, with the wide, grassy valley below them, the cliffs beyond it, and the head of the canyon to their right and before them. Even from where they stood they could see the lone crest of rock jutting up through the junipers, five hundred yards distant.

As they moved toward that crest, the dog grew more and more excited, his ears twitching back and forth as he trotted forward at greater speed.

At one point, Crooked Foot had to call him back and hold onto him while he took a rest. With his game leg, this trek had taken a heavy toll on him. Sam had seen him wince several times as he set his weight down on his bad leg. The little Indian was making a huge sacrifice. Sam could not believe Crooked Foot was doing all of this simply to lead them into an ambush. God help him if he could not read a man any better than that...

They rested here, and even in the heat of the day Sam noticed the dog was shaking. He kept sniffing the breeze and then looking off to the north. Something was there. The dog knew it even if they did not.

The four of them crouched there together, the horses free to munch on the plateau's bunchgrass. No one spoke as Crooked Foot stretched his bad leg out in front of him and pretended not to be in pain. Finally, Sam could hold his curiosity no more.

"You don't know where Death-Shadow stays?" he asked.

Startled at the sudden sound of a voice after more than an hour with no one sharing words, Crooked Foot looked up. For several seconds, he simply stared, and then he shrugged and let his eyes sweep the plateau. "Big man, he no trust. No one. Death—Shadow—he live alone. No woman. No man. No... animal. Death-Shadow..." Here he paused, trying to think of the right words, the regret in his face showing how much he wished he was able to converse freely in their tongue. "No trust to me," he said. "Death-Shadow hide where no one knows."

A feeling of utter desperation swept over Sam, and he looked over at Tom because he sensed the same in him. Both of them looked at the dog at the same time, and when their eyes met again there was something of hopefulness between them.

"Can you keep movin'?" Sam said, standing up. Crooked Foot gave a big nod, but when he tried to stand he fell back. Sam gave him a hand up, and the Indian started to move on. But before he turned away Sam caught the devastating pain written across his features. He grabbed the man by the shoulder, making him turn. Then he indicated his horse. "Friend, you ride."

The little Indian searched Sam's eyes until at last a huge smile broke over his face. Sam had one of those intuitive feelings that the smile was owing not so much to the thought of riding the horse as it was to the fact that Sam had called him his friend.

After setting Crooked Foot up on Gringo's back, they started out again following the dog. They were forced to tie a tether of rope around its neck at that point just to keep it in sight. It ran from one flat rock to another, obviously rocks the big man had used as stepping stones. Because he was avoiding open stretches of sand and grass, the trail did not lead in a straight line. But looked at from the viewpoint of a big picture, one thing was obvious: Death-Shadow was heading straight for the cliff where they had lost him before.

And that cliff was where their trail ended again.

The familiar feeling of desperation swept over Sam as the dog tugged him right up to the cliff's edge. Obviously bewildered, the dog started sniffing back and forth around the rocks where the plateau dropped over and fell off into the next valley. Sam bent and removed the rope from around the dog's neck, hoping that would encourage him to branch out wider and pick up where he had lost the trail.

It didn't help. The dog kept sniffing right there at the edge of the rock.

Sam got as close as he could and peered over. His belief was driven home with force: No one could descend that cliff and live. At least no one human...

Sam turned and threw a glance at Tom, then moved his weary eyes upward to Crooked Foot. The Indian made a sad face.

At last, in frustration, the dog dropped onto its haunches and let out a series of barks and then a long, low, plaintive howl that swept over the rocky plateau like a cold wind.

Sam wanted nothing more than to do the same.

CHAPTER THIRTY-TWO

They hadn't stopped for long before they heard a sound, and they all turned with surprise to see Stuart Baron riding their way, leading a horse. For all his tough exterior, the businessman must care for Melissa. His coming here by himself proved that he thought enough of her—or was simply arrogant enough—to take the chance of a confrontation with Death-Shadow in exchange for the possibility of finding the woman.

A couple of minutes later, he drew his horse in beside Tom, saying nothing. Tom only nodded to acknowledge his arrival as the horses nickered back and forth in greeting.

Finally, Baron stepped down from his horse and cleared his throat. "I brought Melissa's horse—for when we find her."

The partners simply nodded. They were too weary to voice their thanks.

Baron grunted, apparently peeved at having his gesture taken for granted. "Well? I thought this dog was supposed to be so wonderful. Where's the woman?"

Tom didn't feel like responding. After a long moment of silence, Sam looked up from where he sat. "Lost the trail here."

Baron's eyes scanned the plateau, and he growled, "So much for the dog."

No one answered him for a moment. Crooked Foot squirmed in the saddle and looked away.

In the end, it was Viktor who spoke. "They're doing their best, Mr. Baron. Give 'em time."

Baron looked at his employee, raising an eyebrow. After a few moments, he nodded. He seemed humbled.

To still the thud of his aching heart, Tom pulled his tobacco out of his pocket and bit off a chaw. Sam was on the ground, looking out across the canyon, and he was too preoccupied to think of offering any to Viktor or Baron, who stood beside him. After a while he sensed the heavy man's eyes on him and turned to meet them. Viktor just gave him a sullen look and turned away, walking over to stand at the canyon's edge, ten feet away from Sam and the dog.

Tom sighed inaudibly. It seemed with Viktor he was always doing the wrong thing—or neglecting to do the right one. But did it matter? It wasn't as if he and Viktor would ever be friends. They were two big, proud, tough men interested in the same woman. It was not a combination destined to bring peace.

At last, Sam stood up and dusted off the seat of his pants. He had picked up a little stick, and he stuck it absently in the corner of his mouth. "Well. We'd better get to camp an' figure out what we're gonna do, I reckon. Sitting around here all day won't accomplish anything."

Tom sighed and looked out over the canyon. Where was Melissa? Was she still alive? She had to be. He couldn't contemplate anything else. But the situation seemed hopeless. How could they possibly find her when her kidnapper was able to vanish like a phantom?

They decided to descend off the south end of the plateau rather than pass back over the forested mountainside. Sam started to walk, then swore. Looking down, he gave the dog a hard tug, but the dog stayed seated. He dragged him several inches and swore again. "Get up, you mangy cur!" He tugged on the rope, but the dog fought to get back to the canyon's edge.

With a wry look, Sam grabbed the animal around the middle. It turned and nipped his forearm lightly, but he managed to hold onto it, and he took it over and hoisted it up to Crooked Foot, who latched onto it desperately, as if afraid he might drop his only friend. The dog turned and yapped at Sam, and he just grinned, then followed Viktor along the plateau.

Deep in thought, Tom took up the rear. He wanted to think of a mountain springtime, flowers in bloom, or a bubbling spring winding down through a patch of shaded, mossy rocks. He tried to think of that kind of thing, but his mind wouldn't stay with it. Inevitably the face of Melissa kept coming back into his thoughts.

The thought struck Tom suddenly how deeply he had fallen for Melissa. There had never been any doubt that he was attracted to her, although he was more than a decade older. But sometimes it took tragedy to make a man discover the true depths of his feelings. He knew now that he would do anything he had to to save Melissa's life. And if he could bring her back alive, he meant to marry that woman.

Several times as they trod on, the dog turned again and let out an almost desperate bark. The first couple of times everyone turned to look, half expecting to see Death-Shadow bearing down on them. Then only Sam and Tom looked. The last time, only

Tom, after giving the dog a hard, doubtful stare, turned to look across the empty plateau.

While Crooked Foot rode Sam's horse and Sam walked, still searching the ground for sign he might have missed, Tom decided to ride ahead. He left the others and went on down the plateau. At one point the rock began to drop steeply off, and finally it broke up and got brushier, but several game trails crisscrossed back and forth, and he found a tiny seep in the rocks where water had collected. He got down and drank and let the horse drink too. Then he stood and waited for the others to make their way to him. By now, Sam was horseback, riding Melissa's sorrel.

They came down to him, and when the others saw the mesh of trails, Sam nodded with satisfaction. "Good job, Tom. This oughtta lead to an easier way off this rock at least."

And so it did. It took them only ten more minutes to wind along the trail, through stunted, scattered pines and juniper, and come out on the wide valley floor. They rode across it silently, hit the mountain trail at last, and wended their way back up to camp. The hopeful glances that greeted them quickly vanished. They don't see Melissa, thought Tom. He couldn't blame them for being disappointed to see their mugs instead of the woman's.

While everyone else climbed down wearily and helped themselves to some cold beans, Tom tied Cocky, shucked his rifle and plodded a ways up the trail. He found himself overlooking the canyon. He fell onto his backside and crossed his hands in front of his knees, staring out over the expanses that reached, canyon upon ever receding, ever mistier canyon, to the hazy horizon.

How he needed a chance at this Death-Shadow! How he wanted him in his sights. If he had hurt that woman... If he had so much as put a single bruise on her...

But his thoughts were desperate. Tom had spent time around brutal, lustful men. In spite of all the good folks who had come to inhabit the West, it also harbored its trash. Out here away from white man's civilization, people became savage. They took to the ways of the land, and the land was harsh. The animals had no mercy for each other, not even the grass eaters. They would kill for the right to territory or the right to mate. Why would Death-Shadow be any different? Surely he had taken Melissa because he was a man... and she was a woman. It didn't have to be any more complicated than that. Yes, he was much larger than Melissa, but what difference did that make? Tom had once seen a man in a circus who they claimed stood seven feet tall, and his wife was only four feet. A three-foot difference. The difference between Death-Shadow and Melissa was greater than that, but not terribly. And besides, a man who had been alone for a long time would not stop to contemplate such trivial differences. To him, she would be just a woman... Tom shuddered and turned his thoughts away to the beauty of the land.

It was a beauty he could hardly perceive anymore.

*   *   *

After more than an hour, Tom headed back down to camp. He wasn't hungry, but he had to eat something to keep up his strength if he was going to keep scouring this country looking for Melissa. And that was something he had no choice but to do.

He had almost reached camp when he happened to glance up through the trees and let out an involuntary yell. There, standing on the tallest upturned boulder was the giant!

He whirled and levered his Marlin. He fired, but when the smoke cleared Death-Shadow was standing in a different place. Then he dropped from sight.

Turning, Tom ran the rest of the way into camp, where everyone stood watching up the mountain. Baron and even Sam had both stood to take shots at their nemesis, but neither of them had a chance to fire; he had moved too fast.

The giant appeared again, laughing loudly. All three of them fired, too hurriedly. It didn't matter, for he had already changed places. Now, from where he stood, he raised a fist high in the air and then shook it. He lowered his hand and made the throat-cutting sign, then turned and leaped out of sight.

With grim purpose, Sam, Tom, Viktor and Baron ran to start saddling up again. They chose rested horses, and saddled Melissa's horse for Crooked Foot to ride. Whatever his reason was for coming down again, Death-Shadow had offered them a new trail. They had to take it—even if it was a trap.

Using as much caution as they could afford, they headed up through the trees, leaving Ross and the Mexicans to guard the camp. Sam kept thinking of the possibility that Death-Shadow was trying to lure them away so he could circle around to camp, but it was a chance they had to take. Ross was a tough man. So was Alfredo Sanchez. Neither of them would be taken by surprise. And they had the ever-wary eyes of Quiet Wind as well.

The trip up through the forest to the head of the canyon did not seem so slow this time. The dog ran, at times, and once in a while they found themselves loping the horses once they reached open country. There was no sign of movement, but in Death-Shadow's headlong flight he had left plenty of sign. It hadn't taken long to see that he had no intention of circling around on the camp, or if he did their immediate pursuit had foiled his plans. Maybe he hadn't been counting on the dog.

Atop the plateau, studded with its brush and layered with its rock, nothing moved. The trees on the far side were unstirred by breeze, and only the grasshoppers hidden in the grass made any noise. Tom wanted to yell out. His anger and desperation screamed at him to yank his rifle and pepper the scenery with lead, but he held that urge at bay. He stood on the edge of eternity, it seemed, while Nicker blew and sweated beneath him, grunting and whickering and coughing as they climbed.

Even as exhausted as he was, Tom felt the danger of this wind-swept mountaintop. His skin had goose bumps on it, and a sense of foreboding curled around him like a living force. They scanned everywhere, expecting the giant to move out from behind the smallest clump of dirt, the tiniest rock. Somehow, Death-Shadow was vanishing. Was he even real?

Tom shook his head and rubbed at the ticklish back of his neck. He looked over to see that Sam was watching him, his face grim. They could see the dog was heading out on exactly the same trail he had taken before. There was something to it that they couldn't see.

They would have to trust the dog...

The animal tore along with its nose to the ground. It raced across the ever-flattening terrain, and to no surprise it ran right back to the edge of the cliff. Here there was a gnarled, twisted pine they had stood near before. The dog jumped up against its trunk with his forefeet and barked. First, the men looked up high into it, but it was obviously empty. Then they realized the dog was barking not up the tree, but at a branch a few feet off the ground, hanging out over the cliff wall.

With rising suspicion, Sam gave Tom a meaningful glance, then crouched at the branch and looked carefully over the cliff. He stared down into those shadows, searching for a hint, a sign of someone's passing.

At first glance, the cliff seemed sheer. But as Sam began to study it he made out a broken lip that, to someone who knew it intimately and had no fear of heights, might be used as a passage-way. The lip would go for a ways, five, ten, even fifteen feet, then break off temporarily. It would take up again, sometimes as far as five feet away, then scratch its way along the rock face. It finally led to a wider ledge supporting a half dozen good-sized pines that clustered around a jumble of rocks and brush and disappeared from sight around a broken corner.

Tom had come to lie beside Sam and look over the cliff wall. To Sam, it was a sign of the big man's fondness for Melissa, because Tom was not one to put himself over the edge of *any* precarious spot if he could help it. Tom turned and looked at him, and for several seconds their eyes held. At last, Sam came up onto his knees, and Tom did likewise beside him. Both of them let their glances travel along the edge of the cliff until they were lost in the crowded forest of juniper a couple of hundred feet higher up.

It was almost as if each man felt the heart rate of the other begin to quicken...

CHAPTER THIRTY-THREE

Melissa Ford lay still. Her heart was a bass drum. Only moments before, her captor had returned to this cave high up in the side of the cliff—in the canyon that paralleled the canyon of the giants. He had entered the same way they had come together, with her hanging from the harness attached to his back, climbing down by use of a couple of stout iron pegs that he inserted into holes drilled into the wall. He brought the pegs with him when he swung back down into the cave, leaving only the holes in the wall, inconspicuous to anyone who did not know what to look for.

The cave itself, dimly lit only by indirect sunlight, actually sat back a ways from the rim of the cliff, so that no one could see it looking over from above.

On the lower side of the cave, there was the very rough resemblance of a ladder that descended down through the steep rocks. She had had a brief glance at it as Death-Shadow was bringing her into the cave, and it would be of little use to a person with normal-sized legs. It appeared that a large column of the cliff had broken out there, leaving a rough chimney with solid rock running up both sides of it. Utilizing this natural feature, someone had at one time long ago carved notches into the rock on either side of the space, then whittled the ends of slender logs and set them into those notches. This created a very primitive ladder whose rungs were the logs and whose beams were the solid rock. In its current state, every other rung appeared to be missing—no doubt removed by the giant. He would be the only one with the length of limb to make good use of it. Death-Shadow's stronghold would not easily be found nor breached.

She tried not to look at her captor, afraid it would draw his attention. But she noticed he was short of breath, and when he had entered he was running with sweat, his deeply copper body gleaming. There had been trouble up above, she sensed. She could hear him behind her now, sharpening his huge knife against a stone. With awe, she had studied the knife earlier. Its handle appeared to be made from some type of antler, too big to be deer—probably elk. The blade was shaped like a butcher knife, too large for any normal man to wear as a belt knife.

But not this man...

Melissa's face ached where the Indian had slapped her earlier, knocking her temporarily senseless. In fact, her whole head ached. Her body hurt, too, from the strain of being carried in the strange, primitive backpack.

This giant man called Death-Shadow had run tirelessly with her, through the forest, over fallen logs, under grasping branches. It was as if she had no weight at all, a father with his child. The man's strength was incredible. His endurance was the makings of legend. She had no doubt that he could outrun any horse in a fifty-yard dash. She had seen lesser men do it in exhibitions in New York. She also had little doubt that given a race of two days he could walk most horses into the ground. There was no other way to express herself than to say she was in awe of the man named Death-Shadow. And she knew he could, with little effort, kill her and every man in the expedition...

The giant had not harmed her, had not... *taken* her. But he had stared at her with lust in his eyes. Melissa had no idea why the big man was waiting. But one thing she did know: He would not wait forever. And there would be nothing she could do to resist...

No matter what the future held, it would do her no good to ponder it. Melissa let her head drop over to the side. She lay on her back on a pallet of musky smelling furs, her hands bound behind her, and her feet as well. At her throat hung a heavy rawhide thong which had been threaded through a wad of cloth, something which it was plain the big Indian intended to use as a gag later on.

From where she lay, on the floor close to one wall of the cave, she had a view of the incredible vista that stretched out before her. It was as if she were in another world, where looking toward the bright outside world her eyes fell upon a vast expanse of sky and shredded, thready cloud, with majestic walls of rock and timber that stretched into the distance, bleeding away in ever-fading shades of blue until the last of them nearly matched the color of the sky. It seemed, to her, as if there were no ground, only these high, unbreachable cliffs and brassy skies.

Hearing footsteps, she saw Death-Shadow come past her, padding almost silently in a way she would never have believed something so huge could do. He stepped to the very edge of the dim-lit cave and stopped. He still held his huge knife and the sharpening stone, and for a long time he cocked his head, listening. The sweat on his massive body had mostly dried, and now there were just a few scattered droplets that clung to him, stubborn, like tiny diamonds.

The giant's long pause gave Melissa a chance to study him thoroughly. In fact, she felt compelled to stare, and if she had wanted to drop her eyes away she didn't know if she would have been able. It must have been something akin to the awe-struck way a person will stare at a well-muscled draft horse—a sight not to be taken lightly.

In spite of the giant's height, he looked every bit as muscular and graceful as any professional athlete she had laid eyes on in all her years in New York, a city that boasted the best of everything (whether it was true or not!). His shoulders were so large she could only guess at their width, but they must surpass Viktor's by over a foot, and Viktor's were likely the largest she had ever seen on an athletic person. If Death-Shadow's were very much less than a yard wide she would have been surprised.

His back, knotted with balls of muscle when he moved, sloped sharply down to narrow hips, from which his legs erupted like tree trunks. His muscular, striated calves were the size of a powerful man's thighs. Maybe Melissa was no judge of such things, but she couldn't pick out a physical flaw in the man, other than a jagged nest of scar that marred the back of his right thigh— and that was only aesthetics.

She could not help her thoughts straying to Tom, Sam and the others. She was sure of one thing: They would come looking for her. There wasn't a shred of doubt in her there, at least about Tom and Sam. And she was pretty certain about Viktor, even after the way she had dashed his hopes for a relationship with her. But the Santa Catalina Giant knew this country, and he was powerful, huge and ruthless. He would leave false trails and could elude them for days, and one by one, or two by two, he would pick them off. None of the men who would come looking for her stood a chance against this force...

Melissa moved her eyes from the big man and let them me-
ander the cave, studying it more thoroughly now that her heart
had stopped racing. It was in the shape of a rough horseshoe, the
back wall narrowing noticeably but still perhaps fifteen feet wide.
The opening of the horseshoe, which let out onto the cliff, was
probably twenty, and from what she had been able to ascertain
the floor would have had a steep slant toward the outside but had
been built up with a layering of logs and branches, on top of
which had been piled dirt and sand, creating a level walkway.

The eleven-foot ceiling near the front of the cave, blackened
by the smoke of many cook fires, curved up and outward over a
fireplace made with stone walls set in clay, sand and gravel. On
either side of it stood a large, forked stick with a slender metal
rod resting across it that would act as a spit for cooking meat.
There were several cooking utensils and vessels scattered about
here, some primitive, probably made by the giant himself, and
others obviously taken by raiding—other signs of which were numerous about the room.

There was a motley collection of glass jars near the fireplace,
containing what appeared to be salt and pepper and other spices,
also signs that the giant did not stay here all the time and had been
raiding the countryside. It was likely in that manner he had acquired a large cast iron cooking pot and a couple of metal pans, a
butcher knife and a cleaver which he had left dirty and lying by
the fireplace.

At the left rear wall of the cave, beads of water ran slowly
down two vertically meandering cracks and merged into a larger
one that continued to descend toward the cave floor. It was inter-
rupted by a shelf of rock about three feet high and varying in
width from three to four feet until it tapered off and ended about
mid-wall. There below the seep someone had carved a large
bowl-shaped basin into the top of the shelf, and it was brim-full.
The only constant sound in this place was the overflowing of the

water, with its steady gurgle as it ran over the side of the bowl, down the face of the shelf, then continued in a little rivulet to the front of the cave, where it fell over the rock face.

On the other side of the cave was a large bed. It was made of logs cleverly held together with rawhide bands. Having seen Tom repair his rifle stock with wet rawhide, she surmised that the Indian had done the same, as the rawhide seemed very taut and solid, much like bands of iron. Other, wider, strips of rawhide crisscrossed the frame, as she could see by the exposed sides of the log, and this was covered with furs of different animals. One that stood out in her mind was what appeared to be the skin of a wolverine, a famously vicious member of the weasel family which she had once studied with a close friend who had been doing his Master's thesis on the secretive beast.

Set into the rear wall were two sets of deer antlers and one probably of elk, which the giant used to hang odds and ends. There was a sheepskin vest he might use for winter, two metal canteens, and an old leather gun belt with a pistol still in the holster. She surmised that was probably more of a trophy than anything, for she doubted he could ever use it. He could never have fit his finger through the trigger guard even if he knew how to load it or had the powder and ball.

A rope also hung from the antlers, and below them leaned two axes and a couple of long spears, along with a wicked looking club whose head appeared to be made of a tree burl. A jumbled assortment of tools was also piled there, some metal files, wood rasps, a brace and bit with a half dozen wood bits, along with a heavy steel chisel and hammer. She also saw a blue jar of buckles, buttons, and some spools of thread with needles stuck in them.

Against the wall at the foot of his bed leaned more items, an extra quiver of arrows and another bow, along with some rawhide thongs and strips of leather that hung from pegs inserted in cracks in the wall.

Along with all of the other items Melissa made note of, she thought she recognized several things that had been confiscated from the cave of the giants. That was no surprise.

Seeming satisfied by what he heard or did not hear, the giant now turned back into the cave. His eyes fell on Melissa. Slowly, he walked over, seeming to measure each step for full, awful effect. At last, two feet away, he squatted down.

He was close enough that she could smell his male muskiness, his sweat mixed with other bodily fluids she didn't want to contemplate. His hair hung long and loose and greasy to almost the middle of his chest, held in place by a faded yellow band of silk cloth tied at the back of his head. This was the first time she had seen the man up close, and in the brief second she allowed herself to look into his eyes she noticed that they were a shocking shade of blue tinged with brown—like no pair of eyes she had ever seen before. They stared into and through her, reading her soul like the predatory eyes of a golden eagle she often stood to stare at in the Central Park Menagerie. She suddenly realized that his mouth was smiling at her, but there was no smile in his eyes. She looked quickly away, hoping that brief contact had not been enough to set the giant off in any way.

Melissa chided herself. It seemed so strange to call a living man a giant. She had spent so many hours as a child listening to her mother and father, and some of her teachers, tell tales of dwarves and trolls and giants. But it had all seemed so fantastic, so much the stuff of storybooks and scary tales told around the hearth. Never could she have imagined seeing a troll or a giant in real life. And now, here was one who seemed suddenly like both rolled into one...

Seeming to sense her fear, the huge man grunted derisively, then rose to his full, horrible height. He stood looking down at her, but she kept her eyes on the floor. Finally, he walked past her, and she turned her head and let her eyes follow him to the water basin at the far end of the cave. The giant kept a pan there with a handle on it, and this full-sized saucepan he used as a dipper. He immersed it in the water, lifted it to drink—and froze.

He raised his head. He stooped and set the pot on the floor, still full of water. He stepped once again to the cave's entrance, turning his head this way and that. Melissa could hear a grasshopper, somewhere in the jagged rocks and brush below. And the water gurgling down the side of the rock shelf. That was all.

But Death-Shadow, with his ears so much larger than hers, heard something more...

It was amazing how fast and agile he was. He whirled from the basin and in three steps was crouched in front of her. He grabbed the gag and raised it to her mouth, stuffing it in and tying it harshly at the back of her head. Then, as if for spite, he gave her head a hard shove back against the pallet of furs. He whirled and went to the back wall, where he grabbed his long quiver of arrows and slung the strap over his head and beneath his left arm. The quiver tilted at an angle to place the arrows in easy reach over his right shoulder.

He snatched his big bow and dropped it over his head and under his right arm so that its shaft crossed his chest like a bandoleer. With one quick look at Melissa, he took a few strides across the cave, took up his iron pegs, and started his upward climb out of the cave. In no time, Melissa was alone.

She listened intently, trying not to breathe. She thought a full minute had passed before she heard what had sent Death-Shadow out so fast: the muffled sound of horses walking and men speaking. Her heart started to pound. She was sure she heard the tone of Tom's voice, although she could make out no words. It was them! They were looking for her! Then the fear raced through her. The giant knew they were there... but did they know about him?

They were at great risk—because of her! The giant would kill them if he could—and she *knew* he could. No matter what she did, that might not change. But she could not have those men looking for her, risking their lives, if she was able to do something about it. She had to get out of there before Death-Shadow returned. There had to be a way, but how? One thing she knew: She was on her own. She doubted even Sam could find this over-sized eagle's aerie the giant called home.

Rolling over, she looked wildly around. She was so helpless! The giant had bound her hands so tightly they were almost numb. There was no way to slip out of these rawhide bonds. And her feet were the same. She looked over at the fire pit, where the giant had carelessly left his cooking tools. There was the knife. And the cleaver. But they were of no use to her. She couldn't have taken them in her numb hands even if she could reach them.

If she could only get her hands loose! Her desperate eyes scanned the cave. She had been in scary situations. New York City at night was not the safest place in the world. But always before she had known there would be policemen not far away, and generally she had at least one male companion with her if she was out in the city at night—or even in the mountains. Never before had she felt so completely alone and vulnerable.

Suddenly, her eyes came to rest on the pan of water the giant had set down. Like a bolt of lightning, an image came to her: Tom fixing his rifle stock by soaking the rawhide. *The water!* By soaking strips of rawhide Tom had made them as pliable as noodles!

With a surge of hope, she started wriggling toward the water pan. She had to reach it, and now. It took her half a minute of squirming like a disabled worm to reach the pan. Then she was there, and she reached back to put her hands into the cool water. There was a dull *tunk*, and for a moment she froze, not sure what had happened. Her hands had struck something, and she felt cold rush beneath her buttocks, where they rested against the sand. She had struck the handle of the pan and knocked it over! Her heart sank. And with it all her hopes. She was in the stream of the water that spilled over the rim of the basin, but it was not deep enough to do what she needed it to.

God, please don't let this be, she thought, and then she growled out loud, "I won't let him have me!" She cranked her body around and looked up toward the top of the basin. Three feet... She could make it. Struggling, first frantically, and then at last with controlled anger, she was able to stand up by pushing against the floor with her numb feet and sliding against the rock shelf. Finally, she stood at full height, leaning against the shelf.

It seemed so high, and her numb hands could hardly feel the rock. She eased forward so that her hands came out more horizontally behind her, then slowly lowered them. Even with her hands as numb as they were, she felt the cold water close over them, and her own bath of wet tears streamed down her face as she said a prayer of thanks.

Where was the giant? The rawhide was soaking. When she had seen it soak before, she had been with Tom. In his company, hours could seem like minutes. How long would it really take? These bands were so tight! She heard a dog barking—barking frantically, like he was trying to tell someone something. She recognized it as the bark of Crooked Foot's hound. She struggled at the bonds on her wrists. There was no give to them. She wanted to scream, but she couldn't. She tried to make a sound. Even in the cave it was muffled. They would never hear it above.

Suddenly, the barking of the dog started to get fainter. They were moving away! She heard a man's voice—unmistakably Sam's. Then Tom answered. She tried to scream again. Nothing came out, but if it had it could not have been heard over the furious barking of the dog.

She fought the rawhide. It was winning. The voices continued. Fainter. Fainter. *Fainter...* At last she could hardly hear them anymore. Then they were gone, and she was alone with the grasshoppers, the gurgling water, and the stillness...

Tears of frustration runneled down her cheeks. She tried to grit her teeth, which of course was impossible with the rag between them. She ripped at her bonds, and they held. But suddenly she felt a promising slip. She prayed again. She growled. She cursed the giant.

The bonds gave again. She prayed again. She jerked her hands, and the bonds held. But they were weaker. The water was working its magic.

She lowered her head, and for a long two minutes she forced herself to hold completely still. She listened to the trickling water, to the grasshoppers, to a swallow that dashed down the face of the cliff and called out its love of freedom.

Finally, she took a huge, lung-filling breath. Then, timidly, she began to twist her wrists. The rawhide was weakening with incredible swiftness. The water must be seeping deep into its pores. With one more breath, she threw all her strength into twisting her wrists and trying to slide one past the other. For one breath-taking moment the rawhide held, its last valiant stand. Then, with astonishing suddenness, it gave way.

Her hands were free! She cried aloud, and with the tears pouring out of her eyes she couldn't see. She swept them away with her numb hands and tried to jerk the gag out of her mouth. He had tied it too tightly. She hopped toward the fireplace and fell on her knees, grabbing the knife. Frantically, she reached back and cut the gag, severing a hank of her hair at the same time.

She started to let out a scream, then stopped. She couldn't scream. What if the giant heard her and the others didn't? He would come back on the run. Her last chance at freedom—her *only* chance—would be dashed. Sick inside to have to hold her voice when Tom was so close, she cut the bonds that held her ankles, then sat and massaged them until the feeling came back.

Then, taking a calming breath, she rose and walked with wobbly steps to the cave's entrance. She looked down at the ladder, and it seemed so far to the closest ledge below. From what she could see, it was only the first of a series of ladders. The others below it were more like real ladders, built with two logs for side rails. Each one rested on a separate ledge and continued down the cliff face to eternity. She took another deep breath. She had to keep her head. No matter what else she did, she had to keep her brain supplied with oxygen. She had only this one chance to escape alive. Her freedom was in her own hands.

As she had surmised earlier, she would not be able to negotiate this ladder with its long stretch between rungs. She went to the deer antlers and pulled down the long piece of rope coiled there. Scanning the room, she tried to decide what else she might need. She collected a canteen and filled it at the basin, then thought better of the extra weight and decided she must leave it. She pulled down the gunbelt and pistol. Her heart sank when she removed it from the holster to see how corroded it was. It would hardly cock, and it surely would not fire. She dropped it where she stood.

She heard a rock tumble off the cliff not far from her, and felt fear and desperation flow through her like ice water, or like some beast clawing at her vitals. Again, she took several deep breaths and felt better. She ran to take up the butcher knife at the fireplace again, and then she headed once more for the ladder.

As the vertical rock served as the ladder's rails, there was nothing but the far-spaced rungs to grab onto. With trepidation, she wrapped the rope around the first log. It was almost level with the cave floor. She evened up the ends of the rope, then lay down, and holding onto the rope, she swung out over the steep rock and let herself down to the next log. She reached it with a feeling of elation, a sense of power in herself. She repeated the process for the next seven or eight logs, trying not to look down.

She had never been more frightened, but the prospect of being caught again by the giant was far scarier. Then, at last, she came to the bottom of the ladder. It was the first time she had dared look down and study what lay below, and what she saw was nothing short of horrifying. The drop from the bottom rung to the rocks below it could have been no less than twelve or thirteen feet. It would be nothing for a man of Death-Shadow's physical prowess to let himself down on the bottom rung, holding on at arm's length, and then drop the last inches to the ground. For Melissa it was a different story.

But she had not come this far to give up now. And one thing was certain: She could not go back up.

With another heart-stilling breath, she tied a bowline with the end of the rope around that second rung from the bottom as she crouched there on the last one. Then, with gritted teeth, she held onto the rope and swung down until her feet were pressed against the cliff side.

As brave as she could make herself, she started to go down, hand over hand. She ran out of rope with her feet more than four feet from the ledge below.

Dreading all the other ladders that must lie between her and the valley floor, so endlessly far below, she took one last look at where she would land, and then she dropped.

It seemed forever she hung there in the air, and then the ground came up to meet her, and she went to her knees and rolled over. She found herself looking up at the cliff face, soaring high over her head. From here she could just barely see the top of the cave opening. With a sigh, feeling shaken but at the same time empowered by the first leg of her escape, she stood back up and went to look over the ledge. Sure enough, there was another ladder, this one looking much more broken and older than the first. Even at a quick glance she could see there was a place where it was missing one more rung than the other ladder.

Melissa Ford was a tough woman, as tough as most men in some ways. But she stood there and wanted to weep with frustration. Here she was, on a ledge on the side of an unscalable cliff, with her only rope hanging tantalizingly out of reach. No one knew she was here, and no one could help her.

All she could do was wait here for Death-Shadow, the giant, to find her...

CHAPTER THIRTY-FOUR

Melissa stood there for only a moment. Her despair was deep, but fleeting. There might be no way off this cliff side. She might indeed be here waiting for Death-Shadow when he came back, although she was not so sure it would not be better to jump to her death than to let him capture her again. Maybe she was in a hopeless situation. But she was not going to die knowing she had not done everything she could to survive.

With that thought, she turned and began to explore her surroundings. The ladder below her was not completely out of the question. It would take a little work and a lot of faith, but the chances were she could scale down it if she had to—if its strength held out. From its looks she didn't know if it had been used in years, even by the giant. She couldn't go back up. No question there. But... What about sideways?

She began to explore the rocks along the ledge where she stood now. To the left, it would be tough. Without some ropes and a few other tools of a mountaineer she didn't know if it would be possible. But to the right, it looked like there were enough smaller ledges and hand and footholds that she could make it along for at least twenty or thirty yards. And then? What if she were caught there? What if the trail simply ended? The deeper question was: Did she want to be caught *here* when the giant returned? All other questions came back to that one.

Melissa let her eyes trail along the precarious—albeit *imaginary*—path that led in a jagged upward line from where she stood. The cliff there was not vertical, at least not in all places—although parts of it actually hung out over the rocks below. But much of it stood at a sixty to eighty degree angle, and that was something. It would at least give her the comfort of not feeling like the rocks themselves were forcing her backwards.

Melissa thought of the voices up above. Tom, Sam, and probably Viktor would be there. Maybe Baron as well. They were close, and although the giant might see her first, she knew she had to take the chance. Those men might not ever be this close to her again. Her faith must carry her through.

One thing was on the woman's side: There was no dirt down here in which to leave tracks, or at least very little. Death-Shadow might be able to track her, but it would not be easy. That would give her time, as long as she moved fast.

With her mind made up, Melissa took one last look at the route ahead and then started along it, carrying only the butcher knife. The going was treacherous, but as she went she began to feel certain the way had been used for travel before. There were places where rocks seemed to have been removed by hand, to make the way smoother, and in spots the rock had notches in it that she could not imagine having been made by nature. This did not make it an easy path, but so far it was not impossible.

She made it sixty yards, always living with the fear of hearing footsteps behind her or the *whoosh* of an arrow before it slammed into her back. She tried not to step in any places where dust had collected, but with her hard boots she only had so many choices where to walk. Besides, at the moment it was more important to cover as much ground as possible.

She came to a large column of rock that she had been watching and dreading for some time before she actually reached it. The rock was her first major obstacle, and it scared her so badly that for a time she almost wished she had stayed back on the ledge.

After some study she realized there was a way around this side and the face of the rock column. But it was a forty-foot drop if she lost her footing, and the toehold she would be relying on was only one or two inches wide in places. The finger holds weren't much better. Then what if she reached the other side and found that her way did not continue? She would have to make her way back, and from there, back down to the ledge and to the precarious ladder. But she had come too far not to try.

With a deep breath, she stepped out against the column, hugging as tightly to it as she could. One slip, and she would drop to her death. She had no question of it. She moved an inch at a time. There were moments when in her fear she almost froze there like a statue to the side of the rock. But then somehow she found the strength to take that next step.

Maybe it was the fear of the giant, which was even greater than her fear of falling. Another step, another handhold. Her fingers were going numb from gripping so hard. She realized one fingernail was torn and bleeding, and she had left spots of blood on the wall. But perhaps it didn't matter. If the giant tracked her to this point she wasn't sure he could have negotiated this rock column as she was doing. Perhaps this horrifying obstacle would be her saving grace—if she made it across.

Another small step, and she was halfway there. She prayed silently. She wanted to rest here, but her grip would not last forever. And she had to know what lay around the corner. So she kept on.

She had to take a step of two feet to reach the next toehold, and for that brief second she could almost feel herself falling to her death. But she made it, and the grip she found with her right hand was solid and generous. For a few seconds she clung there, breathing hard, praying harder.

Now was the telltale moment. One more step, and her eyes— or at least the fingers of her right hand—would probe the far side of the rock chimney and discover if the way went on to complete her escape. She took that step, reached around the corner to find a bare handhold, and pulled herself over, and back up straight.

Slowly, she moved her head and let her eye peek around the corner. What she saw made her heart fall. There was a ledge there—a solid looking ledge four or five feet wide, and from it a dim trail seemed to creep up through the dusty rock that now was not nearly as steep as before. But in between her and that ledge was a chute—an empty chasm with no place to clutch or to put her feet. There were four feet of empty space between her and the ledge, and very little room to place her feet on this chimney to make such a jump.

Melissa froze. Oh, how she wanted to move. To turn back. To scream out. She could do nothing. She was frozen there, turned to a mummy like the giants. Her mind was blank, filled only with terror. Would it end this way? Would she ever see Tom again? Or New York?

Tears welled into her eyes, and she swore. Melissa Ford swore. It was something she never did, and it shook her. She gritted her teeth. If she was going to die, she was going to die in the attempt to save herself from a worse fate. The angels would herald her bravery. That was something.

Choking back her tears, she looked at the ledge, so far away. She stared at it, but only for a moment. Then she made her leap.

It seemed like forever she hung there in the air, the rocks so unforgiving far below. It was like many dreams she had had, of trying to fly—and failing. Then she felt her upper body slam into the front of the ledge, and without thinking about it her feet were churning. Rotted granite was breaking away from her boot toes, and she could hear the bits of it tumbling down and striking the rocks below. But her hands had fastened on the stubborn roots of a red madroño tree that grew out of the ledge itself, and she would never let go. She would choke the life out of the tree itself before she let it give her up.

She vaguely remembered rolling. She somehow recalled gripping the root until her fingers ached, and the feeling of sheer pain rushing through her upper arms. And then all was silence, all but the rapid, ragged rush of her breaths that filled her lungs with dust and the free air of a living human being—a human being who had conquered her worst fears and the biggest obstacles of her life and was alive to tell about it.

Melissa opened her eyes to see the blue sky above her. The cliff soared there, too, but not so tall as she had thought. No more than fifteen feet. And here she lay, exhausted, on a ledge that moments ago she had little hope of touching. She took one last lung-filling breath, then rolled over and came to her knees. Far below she could see the rocks that might have claimed her—that surely would have taken down a person who did not have God on their side. She sighed deeply again and wiped tears off her cheeks that she had not even felt come to her eyes.

Standing up, she found her legs were shaking almost uncontrollably. She turned and looked at the far side of the ledge, and the trail she had viewed from the rock chimney was not just a dream, but it did not seem nearly as clear as she had thought. It was there, and it had seen use in the not-so-distant past. By what, she did not know. She let her eyes track up along it, and her view of it ended within what she guessed was around ten feet of the top of the plateau. Could that be as close as it went? If so, it would be of no help to her. She took another deep breath, stifling a cough brought on by sucking in dust.

She had started to take a step toward the dim trail when she heard a noise. It was the sound of something clicking against rock. She threw herself up against the far side of the cliff, looking around for a place to hide. There was nothing here. She was completely exposed.

There was the noise again, someone or something coming down, not from behind her but in front. Had the giant taken a different way to get back to the cave? It wouldn't surprise her: Such a man would surely never take the same trail twice in a row if he could help it.

She was frozen in fear. She thought of the knife in her belt, and she drew it out and put it behind her back. More noise now, and louder, and then she saw beyond some rocks a movement in the bushes, and a rock rolled down an incline and then pitched over the cliff side.

Oh please, God, don't let it be him! she thought. Don't let it be him, not after all this. A shudder went through her and left her feeling weak and helpless. Her eyes were pinned to the place where she was sure he would emerge. And then she saw them.

One by one they appeared, two does, and then a young buck wearing two little nubs on his head. She realized she was holding her breath, and she let it out and took in two big gasps and dropped to her knees, resting her hands on them. This was almost too much for her. Her heart couldn't take many more of these events. As beautiful as the deer were, she would rather never have seen them.

And then she realized something of vast importance: If the deer had made it down this far, they were coming from some place and going somewhere else. That meant from this point the plateau was accessible to her, and probably the bottom as well, should she have need to go that way later.

With a surge of elation, Melissa lunged to her feet. The deer, now having made a turn in their path and passed down below her by ten or fifteen feet, paused to look back up at her. Deciding she was not a threat, they meandered down along that branch of the trail and disappeared around a bend. Melissa was already on her way up the path the way they had come from.

It was then that she heard the rapid hammer of rifle shots...

* * *

Just as the eyes of both Sam and Tom settled on that dense forest of juniper at the top of the ridge, and just as the chill touched both of their spines, the scrawny hound began to bay. Suddenly, the dog that had been so intent upon howling at the edge of the cliff, barked like it had a new scent and turned tail, heading at a long trot up toward the junipers. Sam and Tom shot each other a glance, then looked at the others, hefted their rifles, and headed out in pursuit.

The dog's enthusiasm did not wane as it neared the trees. If anything, it grew stronger. Viktor and Baron were both riding their horses, and far back behind them all came Crooked Foot, dutifully leading the rest of the mounts.

Sam scanned the trees carefully as he went. Now and then he looked over at Tom. He had never had any reason to worry about his partner before; he knew he could handle his end. But this time Melissa's life was on the line, and Sam recognized the deep soft spot Tom had developed for the woman. He had worried that that care would cloud his friend's vision. But Tom seemed as vigilant as ever. He had his rifle ready, and his eyes picked apart the deep green forest as carefully as any long-time scout. Sam nodded and continued on.

Now his pace was slowing. The dog had reached the trees, and he raced back and forth there a couple of times. It didn't look like he had lost a trail, but almost as if he had found two strong ones and was trying to decide which to take. That was Sam's signal to call him off. He yelled back to Crooked Foot.

The Indian immediately responded. He let out a strange, high-pitched whistle. The dog hesitated, looking back. It was obvious he wanted to go forward, but it was also evident that he had been carefully trained, and he knew what that sound meant. A second whistle. Again the dog looked back. Finally, lowering his head and his tail, he slunk back toward them. Several times he turned and looked back over his shoulder at the trees.

Baron was up near where the dog had been when he growled something back at Sam. Sam didn't hear him, but he could tell by his face and the tone of his voice that he wanted to go into the trees. Holding in his anger, Sam waved the man back to them. He made the same wide-armed motion three times before the entrepreneur finally returned. Viktor came on behind him.

The two of them pulled up in a swirl of dust a minute or so before Crooked Foot would have reached the partners. Sam held off Baron's angry questions until they were all together.

"You wanna go into them trees by yourself, Mr. Baron?" Sam finally asked, barely hiding his disdain.

"I said for you to come up," Baron retorted angrily.

Sam nodded, only half interested in the city slicker's words. "We need to all be together before we go in there."

"What if he's waiting for us?" asked Viktor.

"I'd bet a dollar he is," said Sam flatly. "That's the hell of it. I don't know that we have a lot of choice. That's why we need a plan. We all know he can pick us off one at a time like you'd shoot pickles in a barrel. But with all of us together he's going to have a hell of a time."

Baron nodded grudgingly. "All right then. What's the plan?"

With an embarrassed chuckle, Sam said, "I wouldn't call it a plan. Just togetherness. We'll form a line and start through there like you'd do a deer drive—only this time there won't be a bunch of hunters waitin' on the other side to shoot whatever we flush out. This time we'll be the brush stompers *and* the riflemen. And this deer might be shooting back. There's only two rules: Don't shoot toward where you think any of the others are, and don't *not* shoot if you see something suspicious in a direction where none of us would be. You might not get another chance. Make it count."

Tom set his jaw and pierced Sam with his eyes. Sam felt Viktor do the same. "What about Melissa?"

"You mean if she's out here?" There was a long pause. "Use your judgment, Tom. I'd sure hope she'd yell out if she's here. That big bugger won't be givin' free shots. But remember, we need him alive. With him dead, I don't know how we can ever find the girl."

Tom sighed and looked over at Viktor. From the big man there was an almost imperceptible nod to him. For some reason it made a wave of emotion well up inside Tom.

Sam swept the group with his eyes. "Crooked Foot, I'll take the dog with me. You hold the horses. And if that big cuss comes out of those trees, you shoot him."

Crooked Foot stared at his friend. His Adam's apple bobbed when he swallowed. They all knew Death-Shadow and Crooked Foot were acquaintances, if not friends. The Indian just smiled and patted the bow slung across his chest. His face was somber. He raised his hand and held out the end of the dog's leash to Sam.

The four riflemen turned with pounding hearts and started into the trees. The dog was now eerily quiet. He bent his nose to the ground and began sniffing his way in. The junipers were only average height, mere shrubs to Death-Shadow. But most of them were three to six feet over the tops of the hunters' heads, so although they were nothing like the massive ponderosa and Douglas fir above camp, it was enough to hide a giant. The sun pulsed down into this forest, yet in its own way it was as dark, and in many ways denser than the deepest northwest woods. Many times Sam had to rethink his route and go around a tree when two of them grew too close together. He prayed the others were keeping the same pace he was. This grove was only one or two hundred yards across, but it was dense enough that none of them could see anyone else the majority of the time. Once in a while Sam would come across a rock outcropping or a high spot, and he would pause there and get his bearings, looking around to see if he could spy the others. Every time, with patience, he found them, or at least some of them. The first time, Tom raised his rifle and nodded at him as he came into a bare spot. A minute later Viktor came through a clearing, caught him from the corner of his eye and touched his hat brim in acknowledgment. The first time he saw Baron the New Yorker was completely oblivious of him.

They moved on. The grove closed in, then opened, then repeated the pattern. They must be nearing the cliff edge, and they were quickly coming upon the tall rock outcrop that shouldered ten feet out over the tallest junipers and was frothed with a ragged stand of oak.

The air seemed to thicken. The tension closed over them. Sam's hair prickled on the back of his neck. His hands tightened on his rifle. They were fifty feet from that sentinel rock. Suddenly, a rifle barked to Sam's left. *Boom! Boom! Boom!* Sam saw a cloud of smoke drift out of the trees where Tom should be. He heard his partner yell, a guttural noise.

"He ran downhill! I might have hit him."

Sam pulled in a deep breath. His first urge was to go running through the trees, but where did he run? The hound started baying toward Tom. Sam stared that way helplessly, trying to decide which way to go. If they had been chasing *him*, he might have run one direction, but he would have shortly found a way to double back or at least take a perpendicular path. No smart woodsman-turned-prey would stick to one direction for long.

And then a monster materialized.

There he stood, up on the side of the sentinel rock. Sam was stunned. It was as if the giant had come from nowhere. He had an arrow nocked and aimed to Sam's right, and even in the excitement Sam noticed there was a stream of blood down his right leg, which was the leg that held most of his weight at the moment. So the wound couldn't be serious.

Sam's rifle was coming up. It seemed to take forever. The arrow left its owner's bow with a *twang*. In almost the same instant the huge figure was lunging to the left, and when smoke erupted out of Sam's barrel and the butt plate slammed his shoulder, the bullet sliced through thin air. So intent had Sam been on the shot that he didn't even hear its explosion.

He heard a strangled cry in the trees to his right. He cast a glance that way, but he ran straight forward, the dog baying as if he had gone insane and lunging against his leash. Sam knew he could be knocking on death's door, but he had to get up to where the giant had been and at least try to see if he had left a blood trail. Also, he knew the hound would pick up his scent from there.

He hadn't made it far before he heard a yell from the trees below and to his right. It was almost like a wail, a strange, heart-wrenching sound from deep in someone's chest. Sam slammed to a halt. He looked toward the rock, envisioned himself for a moment silhouetted there, a target for one of those big arrows. He took a deep breath and a step back.

The dog was still heaving against his leash, but Sam growled and yanked him back. Going on that wounded giant's fresh blood trail was a sure way to die. He knew better. Any Indian fighter knew better. And this wasn't Sam's day to die.

Slowly, he backed out, jerking the dog with him. He continued to scan the trees, but there was no more movement, no sound.

Once in a while a grasshopper would clack its wings, and he heard the distant crowing of a quail. Beyond that, the day was still.

Then he heard the anguished cry again. He didn't dare break his own silence, but he used that voice to track sideways through the trees. At last, he heard a scrape of gravel, and he whispered harshly, "Who's there?"

A broken, heavy voice replied, "Me—Viktor. Over here."

Sam made his way through the trees, and just before reaching where he thought Viktor would be lying wounded, he yelled out to Tom to join them. He couldn't leave his partner tracking the giant, thinking they were all still together.

When Sam cleared the last of the junipers and broke into the clearing, he lurched to a halt. There was Viktor. Sprawled down on his side in the rocks and grass and gravel. But Viktor wasn't hurt. He was lying with his arm under the head of Stuart Baron.

And Baron had the thick shaft of an arrow sticking out from the center of his breastbone.

CHAPTER THIRTY-FIVE

Melissa stared upward, her heart in her throat. The sound of the shots had faded down the cliff side, but their memory was just as strong in her head. What did they mean? Was someone hurt? Had they killed the giant?

Whatever significance lay in the sound of the shots, she could not stay here to ponder it.

She started up the steep, narrow trail, trying to step on the bigger rocks when she could. Partly, that was to keep from leaving sign in the dust, and partly because she would slide and lose ground on the smaller gravel. The incline of the path was drastic!

A couple of times she found herself bent over, grasping and clawing with her hands. There were bushes and clumps of grass here and there along the way, and sometimes they helped, but other times they broke off in her hands. She cursed them helplessly when they did. She had listened to Sam enough to know how important a sign the broken branches and blades of grass would be if the giant took to her trail.

Well, it didn't matter now. Her only hope lay in getting back to camp or in finding the search party somewhere above her. Let the giant track her, as long as she made it back to camp before he could make out her trail. She prayed for nightfall...

The trail leveled off now, then made a little downhill jog. With a quickening heart, her eyes scanned ahead to make sure it would rise again, which it did. She sank to her knees, sweating and breathing in gasps. She ran her sleeve across her forehead and took a deep, calming breath, then another. She had to keep her wits, had to keep oxygen flooding freely to her brain.

As she knelt there she noticed a big, black beetle traveling across the ground. She had watched it for several seconds when suddenly out of a nearby bush raced a black and white lizard. It sped to the beetle and fell on it. The struggle was fierce and short.

Melissa took another deep breath as the impact of the incident hit her. What if that had been a rattlesnake in the bush? Tom had also warned her about the tiny straw-colored scorpions that inhabited this country. And the giant centipedes and coral snakes. The lizard had been an important reminder: The giant was not the only menace out here.

Her eyes traveled up the trail a ways, and she knew she should get up and move. But it felt so good to sit there. Rest was what she needed. But she also needed Tom...

How wonderful it would be to see his smile and the twinkle in his eyes, and to have him softly take her hand in his.

She stopped and chided herself. She had to keep her mind on the business at hand. Yes, it would be nice if Tom were here, but he wasn't. She had only herself to rely on, and she had to move.

She started on and had almost reached the top of the trail, her heart starting to pound with the suspense of wondering what awaited her on top. A loud hiss startled her, and she jerked back. A snake had reared up beside the trail, its head emerging from its ring of coils. It had startled her, but there was no rattling noise, and no buttons on the end of its tail, and this was the long, slender green head of something besides a pit viper. The serpent gave another hiss, then dropped to the ground, glided around some rocks and disappeared.

Melissa steadied herself and looked upward once more. Again she had to remind herself to be more alert. She had walked almost completely past the snake before it made a noise, and she already knew the giant could be just as silent. She should have seen the snake before it made any noise. With that blunt mental nudge, she turned and scrutinized the area around her, down the cliffs and up to the edge that seemed so near. She carefully checked her back trail. Satisfied at last, she readjusted the knife in her belt and set out again.

Where was the giant now? Trailing her? Trying to ambush her friends? Neither possibility was pleasant to contemplate. Even the thought of seeing the huge man made her cringe. She still could hardly come to grips with the knowledge that he was real.

"Please keep them safe," she prayed aloud. Oh, how she didn't want to be the cause of anyone's getting hurt—or worse. She didn't like the idea of being used for bait, and that was exactly what she was right now. Curse Death-Shadow the giant!

It was with elation that Melissa made the last steep ascent onto the plateau. She was so happy she wanted to scream out. She ran out a ways from the cliff's edge, scanning the country for movement. Where were they? Where was Tom? Where had the shooting come from?

She began to walk briskly toward the high point of the plateau. She already knew the insurmountable cliffs that lay before her if she continued on in the direction where she and Tom had sat that long ago evening on the rocks. The path she would follow would lead her parallel to the cliffs, and for a while it would take her far closer to the giant than she had any desire to be, but there was no other way. She would just have to pray for darkness to fall and then try to make her way as quietly as she could through the dark forest and trust her faith in God.

Camp still seemed like an eternity away. She held her fear in check. If ever there was a time to be courageous, this was it. To give in to the worry that clawed inside her would be to destroy all the progress she had made. She could make it back alone. She had to! If the searchers weren't already headed back, they would have to soon. Shadows were growing long, and the sun was well on its way to a rendezvous with the western horizon. They could not stay out here after dark, not knowing what stalked them.

Melissa caught a flash of movement in the distant junipers. She stopped and stared, but now there was nothing. Then there it was again, something that seemed to bob up and down. Then another one appeared near it. Then another. Not daring to hope, but hoping all the same, she began to run to get to a high spot she could see ahead of her. Her heart pounded wildly, so fast and hard that it almost hurt, not so much from the run as from... that hope she was suppressing inside her.

Then it was clear. The three bobbing shapes were the heads and shoulders of men riding through the junipers! It was her friends! Had they seen her?

In another second she realized—they were riding the other way... They weren't coming, they were leaving! She filled her lungs and bent down, ready to throw all her energy into the loudest scream she could muster, even though the riders must be six hundred yards away.

Then she realized another thing, even more important. She couldn't scream. She couldn't make any noise at all. The Santa Catalina Giant might be just behind her, or just behind the next tree. He could be far closer to her than the riders. Melissa wanted to cry. It was all she could do to keep her emotions inside. She kept running and running and running, and when her legs were so exhausted she couldn't lift her feet she kicked a rock and stumbled, going down. She lay on her face and sobbed.

She was down in a little swale now, and she could not see the riders anymore. But perhaps it was for the best. It would only make her ache more if she could see them. They were gone. It was something she had to face.

Sitting up, she wiped a sleeve over her eyes and clutched the knife at her waist, making sure it was still secure. Then she took a deep breath and stood up, starting on. She would have to travel fast if she was going to make it even halfway through the deep woods before darkness fell. Once it did, she had no hope for what became of her afterward. She was only glad she would be hidden from sight of the giant.

Melissa knew she had to save her energy, but still she put herself into the fastest walk she could maintain and pointed straight for the head of the canyon. That would take her very near the place the giant had traversed in carrying her across the plateau—and dangerously close to his cliff-side lair. She cringed and clenched her jaw, looking in that direction. She had to be strong.

Suddenly, she felt someone watching her, and she froze. Her eyes scanned the plateau. They came to rest on one strange high spot about four hundred yards away toward the canyon's head. She knew in her heart who it was, and she clutched the knife handle. Death-Shadow the giant...

After all her work and struggle, he had found her at last.

The high spot that she knew was a head suddenly turned and began to bob off in the direction of camp, the way the others had gone. Melissa started and stared. It wasn't the giant! It was another of the searchers, riding a horse!

Without thinking, she started to run again. She ran for all she was worth. As she came over the next rise and could see a grand vista of the junipers that forested the end of the plateau and part of the canyon head, she stumbled to a halt. There was the last man she had seen, still at least four hundred yards away, but gesturing wildly in her direction. And he was facing two others!

One of the riders spurred his horse through the junipers away from the first rider. He was zigzagging in and out of the bigger brush, jumping the smaller stuff and only slowing when he had to maneuver through stands of juniper. He disappeared in a depression for a few moments, and she thought she heard the faint stir of hoofbeats. The third rider was coming too, more slowly than the first, and she knew who both of them were. Before she knew it a fourth man came back through the trees, and the last two headed toward her. Other than the first man, she could only see the other riders' torsos and their horses' heads, for the brush was too deep.

The hoofbeats grew louder and louder until they sounded like they would come right over her. Then, like a specter, Tom and his horse Cocky exploded up the rise Melissa was standing on. The horse veered to one side, and Tom was over the animal's side before he had a chance to come to a full stop.

The big cowboy almost knocked her backwards when he reached her, sweeping her literally off her feet and squeezing her to him. Melissa was laughing, and crying at the same time. She wanted to talk, and at the same time she wanted not to have to talk. Mostly, she just wanted to feel safe.

Tom didn't seem inclined to let the woman go. He had been sick, physically sick, thinking of what had become of her—what *would* become of her if she weren't found soon. He hadn't known if he would ever see her again.

He murmured softly, "Woman, I don't know how you got here, but I thank God you did." He released her at last, letting her feet solidly touch the ground. Then he took her hands in his and looked at her intently. "Did he... hurt you?"

She smiled, her eyes welling up again. It was all she could do to reply. "I'm tired, Tom. Half dead. But I'm all right. He didn't do nearly what he could have. I'm perfect now, with you. But... what about... *him*?"

"Gone," replied Tom. "We came to the edge of a cliff—had to be a twelve foot drop off to a ledge. He went over there, and there wasn't any more sign. He's got his own little labyrinth in here, Melissa. He could be anywhere."

Melissa closed her eyes, then steeled herself. "Well, we're back together now. I'll tell you all about his 'labyrinth' later. We have to get back to camp before dark."

"I'm glad you're safe."

"So am I. I was afraid you hadn't seen me," she said.

"It was Crooked Foot that saw you. He was hangin' back with that dog of his, and he came ridin' after us, all wild about seein' something. At first I thought he was daft. Then somehow I knew it would be you."

They had heard more hoofbeats on the rise behind them for a time, and now Sam came riding up and dismounted, dropping Gringo's reins. He strode up to the woman and brusquely threw his arms around her without warning. He broke away quickly and looked down at her, sweeping off his hat.

"Sorry, ma'am. But it sure is good to see you."

Melissa shook her head adamantly, her face all smiles. She grabbed Sam again and gave him another big hug of her own. "Don't you ever think of apologizing to me, Sam Coffey. It's awfully good to see you too. Thank you—for not giving up."

Sam grinned. "Not much chance of that. I reckon there are some folks down to camp who'll be anxious to lay eyes on you too." Her smile widened. "I'd offer you a ride on a real horse, sittin' behind me. But that rascal standin' there beside you might have different ideas."

Tom grinned at Melissa, then swung up onto Cocky, reaching down for Melissa's hand. He helped her up behind him, and then looked over at Sam, who just smiled and turned to lead the way back down the hill.

The woman threaded her arms around Tom's middle and laid her cheek against him, smelling his musky masculine odor. She didn't find the smell objectionable in the slightest—the opposite, in fact. She felt the dampness in his shirt, too. It was sweaty, but she didn't mind a bit. Oh, how happy she was to be back with him. Even with the giant still alive she felt secure now.

She was starting to relax when Tom spoke. "Melissa, there's somethin' I've gotta tell you. It isn't good news, and you need to know before we catch up to Viktor."

She was alert again. Her brow furrowed. "What is it?"

He hesitated, then sighed and went on quietly. "We ran into Death-Shadow up on top, at the head of the canyon. He... He killed Baron."

Melissa gasped and exclaimed "Oh no!" She was silent for a long time as they rode on, and finally she said in a whisper, "It was my fault. I'm so sorry."

"I never thought I'd say it, but I am too," Tom responded. "He wasn't the friendliest man I ever met, and he was awfully proud of himself. But there at the end I could tell he cared about you, once it got past his tough talk. He gave his life tryin' to get you back. I wanted you to know about it now, since you'll see him tied to his horse when we get to where Viktor is. I didn't want it to be too much of a shock."

There was a long silence, and then she replied, "Thank you, Tom. It certainly would have been."

They rode quietly for a time after that. Tom kept getting set to tell her some news he knew she would take even worse, but he didn't know quite how to say it. Baron had been a tough man, and little given to showing tender emotions. He was a hard man to like, on a day to day basis. Other than Viktor, Tom didn't think anyone had been close to him.

But Delbert Moore was another story. Tom was pretty sure Melissa had been with him for a long time, and he was a likeable young man. It was going to be a lot tougher telling her about him. For five minutes or so, he stewed about it, trying to think of just how to say it, after all she had been through. Suddenly he just felt tired. Tired through and through. Maybe he should leave that news for the Professor. But he couldn't. He was here, she was here, and she had to know...

When they reached Viktor and Crooked Foot, they were off their horses standing and waiting in an open area forty yards from the nearest cover. They weren't taking any chances on being caught unaware by the giant. The Indian broke into a smile when he saw Melissa. Viktor just watched her come, standing there and holding onto the reins of Baron's horse, where the limp bundle was folded over its back. Melissa slid off Cocky with a hand from Tom and walked to Viktor.

The big brawler's face was drawn and gray looking. He looked physically ill. They searched each other's eyes, and in his there was none of the old arrogance. There was only a profound sadness, and his demeanor was one she had never seen him display before. She stepped forward and hesitantly took his left hand in her right and closed her left one over the other side. "I'm so sorry Viktor, I know Mr. Baron meant a lot to you."

When the big man's chin started to quiver, the other men looked away. Viktor looked down for a moment, then forced his eyes back up to her. "He was like a father to me. He took me off the docks." Then he looked away into the distance and said, clenching his jaw to hide his pain, "That monster killed him."

Melissa nodded. "Tom told me." On an impulse, she leaned close and gave the big man a quick embrace. It was obvious he needed one.

He looked at her, shocked. Then he looked down again and ran a hand quickly across his eyes. He seemed to speak to no one in particular. "He killed them both, and now I'm going to make him pay."

Melissa searched his face. "Both?"

The big man looked up, confused for a moment. Tom had started to step forward, having climbed off Cocky, but before he could speak Viktor said, "Mr. Baron and Del."

A look of shock and disbelief spread like flame over Melissa's face. She stared at Viktor while the others stood as if caught in some crime. No one dared speak.

Finally, Melissa cried out. "Delbert?" She whirled to Sam and Tom, searching their eyes. "Del Moore?" She was stunned, and as Tom started to nod slowly she said, "Del is dead?"

"Forgive me for not tellin' you, Melissa. I was tryin' to figure out just how."

Viktor's face flushed. "I'm sorry, Melissa. I thought you already knew."

Still shocked, but gathering her wits, Melissa said, "It's all right, Viktor, it had to come out sooner or later. I just... I think I'd like to sit down for a minute or two."

Without a response from anyone, she turned and started to walk away. Then her knees buckled, and she plopped down cross-legged on the gravelly ground. Tears once more welled up in her eyes and began to run down her cheeks, and she brushed them away with her sleeve, staring at the dirt in front of her. Finally, she got her legs back under her and dusted off, then walked back to the others.

"What happened?"

"He was on night watch," Sam replied. "Death-Shadow shot him, right there in the dark."

Crooked Foot was standing to one side, one arm straight down and the other folded across his torso and holding onto it by the elbow. His smile was gone, and he looked dejected. No one seemed to take notice of him.

Viktor suddenly piped up: "How did you get here, anyway? Did he let you go?"

"No!" she shot out. She took a deep breath and looked around at them, then down at the ground, recalling the recent events almost too clearly. "We were in a cave he lives in on the side of the cliff. He heard you and the horses up above, and he went after you. I was tied up, but I got away down the wall and found a trail that came back up here."

She paused, then dropped her hands to her sides. There was so much more of the story, but it would have to wait. It was going to be a long time before she had the energy to recount it all, and at this moment she simply did not want to relive those memories.

At last, she said, "I want to thank all of you. It could have been any one of you there instead of Mr. Baron. I owe you all my life." She looked around and sighed. Last of all, her eyes fell on Crooked Foot.

She started to walk toward him, her heart swelling up inside. The smile she had for him was genuine, and her face was full of an unbidden love. "It was you who saw me. You are the one I really owe. Thank you." Without a warning she threw her arms around him. The shocked Indian could only stand there. When she pulled away, his face was beaming.

"Crooked Foot need to save woman more!" he blustered. Then he quickly held up the reins to his horse and said, "You ride. Crooked Foot walk."

She laughed, looking at him warmly. "No, my friend. Please keep the horse. I would feel very bad if you had to walk. I will ride with Mr. Vanse."

She started toward Tom, and on the way she had to pass Viktor. She looked up at him, and he looked over at Tom, then back at her. The hint of a smile touched his eyes, and she saw him faintly nod. Reaching out, he gave her shoulder a squeeze, then turned back to his own horse.

CHAPTER THIRTY-SIX

Melissa's reception back in camp was a joyous one for her, in spite of the aching in her soul for the loss of her friend Del Moore and the anguish of knowing Baron had died trying to save her life. It was good to see the Professor again, and Dowdy Ross—oh, how she had missed them! Alfredo Sanchez and his son Juan, and even old Guillermo—their smiles were so genuine and adoring. Quiet Wind, as taciturn as she often seemed, was the proverbial sight for sore eyes, and she couldn't help but give the old woman a big squeeze.

Surprisingly, since she and the old woman had never had much interaction during the venture, Quiet Wind was one of the most solicitous of her needs. She kept coming by and checking to make sure she was wrapped tightly with her blanket, while Ross brought her cup after cup of coffee, throwing them away if they cooled off too much and bringing new. The Professor stood over her or crouched before her or sat beside her, asking her way too often how she was feeling. And there sat Tom on the other side of her, his arm protectively around the small of her back.

Sam was sitting on the far side of the fire, and he kept shooting furtive glances that way, then dropping his eyes and shaking his head. Shouldn't it be obvious to everyone how they were smothering that woman? She kept looking desperately around her, as if for some escape, and there was none to be had. No one in that camp would have dreamed of leaving her alone.

Melissa's safe return was nothing short of miraculous, and everyone knew it. That gave good cause for their doting, but it was still too much. Sam knew the woman needed to be alone, to sit and contemplate what she had been through. And she was a woman, after all, with a woman's needs—she was going to need to cry out those horrible memories and the fear before she could really begin to recover from her ordeal. No one had ever, nor *would* they ever, consider Sam Coffey a lady's man, but he knew that much about women.

One thought occurred to Sam, as the smoke puffed and curled around him, and his coffee cup grew cool in his hands. He glanced up, feeling the sense of sudden revelation, and let his eyes settle on Tom. Then they went to Melissa, and it was one of those times that he caught her looking at Tom. The look now was different than with the others. Sam knew then: In spite of all the smothering, there was indeed one person the woman would have liked to stay beside her. The knowledge filled Sam's heart with a strange loneliness he had never expected. That one person was the man he had spent thousands of days riding beside, thousands of nights camped out with: his partner, Tom Vanse.

The looks in Melissa's eyes continued to get more and more desperate until finally she cleared her throat. She looked over at Tom, and her expression seemed apologetic. She said, "Tom, I need you to do me a big favor. Could you excuse the rest of us for a moment while I talk to them?"

Tom was obviously taken aback. After a moment, he said, "Sure, Melissa." He stood and walked off to the horses, hiding his feelings expertly.

When the man was gone, Melissa turned to the others, studying all their faces as they waited. "You have all been so good to me. No one has ever had a happier reunion. It is a girl's dream to be waited on hand and foot this way. I want you to know I love you all. But I need to ask something of you, and I pray you'll understand. What happened to me was very frightening. I have to say I really thought I would die, that I would never see one of you again. That terror and the relief of being saved has filled my heart with so many feelings I can't describe, and someday I want to be able to talk to you all about it. Right now, though, I just need to breathe. Please don't think I don't appreciate what you're doing. You are all so gracious to me. But... I wonder if I could ask you to let me have some time alone... with Tom."

There it was, finally out before them all. Sam had seen it coming, but he could tell by the looks on some of their faces that everyone hadn't. The Professor and Ross were especially shocked, but they did not seem displeased. Viktor was not there to hear it, as he had retired to his own tent immediately upon their return. His absence was conspicuous. He had a grievous loss in his own heart, and to all appearances had forgotten about Melissa.

Everyone gazed at Melissa, and after a few seconds they all began to smile. The Professor gave her shoulder a squeeze. They offered their last words of comfort, and last of all the Professor was left with her and hugged her close to him. "You do not have to wonder if we understand, my girl. We all understand completely." With that, he turned and walked back to the fire.

Melissa sought out Tom, and there he was, in the dim light at the horse picket line. Steeling herself, and glancing about, wide-eyed, at the midnight-black shadows, she walked out to him. His back stiffened as he heard her, but he didn't turn around until he felt her hand on his back. Then he slowly came around and looked down into her eyes.

"Tom, I need you," she said softly. He took her in his arms, and there in the darkness he held her tight.

The tears began then, softly at first. Then they came faster, accompanied by wracking sobs. Melissa cried and cried until there were no more tears to cry. Tom simply held her.

Listening beyond the sobs, his ears were keened to the night. There was no doubt in his mind that Death-Shadow would be back. Not only had they hurt him, but they had shamed him terribly by taking back Melissa. He would be back—for a reckoning.

So with great care Tom listened to the sounds in the darkness—the normal night sounds such as an owl, chirping crickets, or the scurrying of rodents in the grass. They had strung up their perimeter of tin cans so that if Death-Shadow tried to approach camp he would be heard. He listened for any ringing of the cans beyond the normal breeze. They had also set logs and rocks around, and dug foot-deep holes here and there at random—anything to trip him up and cause him to make a warning noise.

After Melissa had cried for more than five minutes, and her sobs were subsiding, Tom said quietly, "Would you like to sit?"

She nodded, and he led her over toward the cliff. Several of them had rolled boulders out that way to use for seats, and it was the only place other than in camp itself where they felt a measure of safety with a monstrosity such as Death-Shadow lurking out there in the darkness. There was little way the giant could approach them there without making some kind of warning noise. When they reached the slope, Melissa sank onto one of the boulders. She looked up expectantly until he did the same.

"I need to talk to you, Tom."

He simply nodded.

"I..." She paused and looked down at her hands, folded in her lap. "Oh, I'm sorry. I know I must look a sight." She raised her hand and ran her fingers back through her tousled hair.

Tom laughed. "You look a sight, all right. That much I'll grant you. But the fact is, right now I can hardly see you."

She looked up, and their eyes held for ten or fifteen seconds. The moon was bright enough that they could still dimly make out at least the shapes of each other's faces. Tom felt his heart flutter again.

"I hope I won't embarrass you, Tom. I truly don't mean to. But with what I just went through, I really need you to know how things are with me."

"I understand."

She filled her chest and looked up at him again. "Tom, you can be honest with me, I promise. I'm a big girl. What I need to tell you is..."

She paused, and Tom finally reached out and took her hand, giving it a gentle squeeze. "You can say whatever you need to. It's come down to that time. We're not far from leavin' this mountain."

Another deep breath steadied the woman, and she placed her hand on top of his. "Okay, I've held this back too long. After the first shock of what was happening to me wore off, when that... *giant* was carrying me away, I could think of only one thing. Just one: how much I wanted you to come after me—to come and save me from him. I knew Viktor was here, and the Professor, and Dowdy and Mr. Baron. I knew Sam was here, and I knew they were all very capable men. But it was you I couldn't get out of my mind. I knew I had to live—for you."

Tom did his best to keep meeting her eyes during the ten or twenty seconds after she stopped speaking. He thought he had been ready to hear whatever the woman had to say, but he was wrong. Perhaps the feelings she had just expressed had been living somewhere deep in his own heart. But it had been too much for him to dare dream. Here he was, a middle-aged rancher with very little to offer a high society eastern woman, and especially one with the looks and intelligence and charm of Melissa. He had come to know many days ago that there was a mutual attraction between them. But she had her world, and he had his, and he never could have believed that after the expedition was over anything would remain between them. Now that possibility had been laid in his lap.

At last, he swallowed hard. He squeezed her hand a little harder. "You went through a tough time, Melissa. And I'll understand if you find out later that... Well, that maybe you jumped too fast and were a little confused. But if you really mean what you say... I've only cared about one woman in my whole life like I do you. I never figured I could feel this way about a woman again, after my wife died."

He laughed suddenly and looked away, then back. "I always thought I was pretty good with words, pennin' poems and songs and such. But you make it so I can hardly breathe, much less tell you what I'm thinkin'. I don't know what will happen to us between this camp and Tucson. I don't know how serious that mad man is, and if he'll come after us. So I've got to tell you, just in case... I'm in love with you. I have been for a long time."

Melissa let out a long-held breath. "Oh, Tom." She stood abruptly, and he met her halfway, hugging her to him like he never wanted her to get away again. Tom didn't care what anyone in camp thought of the display of affection. Nothing could keep this from happening.

After their embrace, they stood holding each other's hands for a moment, and finally Melissa said, "What will this mean for us, Tom? Do you have any idea?"

He sighed. "That's been long on my mind, believe me. One or both of us is gonna have to make a hard choice if this is going to work."

She nodded. "Yes, I know. I'm a city girl, and you're a western man who likes the open spaces. Tom," she said suddenly. "Do you remember when we were with the Apaches, and the old woman gave me something?"

He nodded, thinking back. "I do remember that. I just figured it was something private, since you never showed me."

Reaching up with a trembling hand, Melissa reached to the back of her neck and fumbled with something. After a while, she brought her hands back around, drawing something from down inside her bodice. In the dim moonlight it shimmered, and she held it up. "It was this necklace. It's some kind of ancient gold coin, with a hole drilled through it. Tom, whatever happens... I want you to have this." She placed the coin, with a fine chain through the hole in it, in his big hand, and he closed it.

Before he could say anything, she said, "Tom, you know it's really not that far out of New York City to where you would be back in the mountains. Not mountains like these, but green, beautiful ones, where in the spring the creeks and rivers run full to the brim, and the waterfalls cascade at every turn. Where in the autumn the world turns into reds and oranges and golds that would have you so enthralled you would forget all about this country."

A deep, inevitable ache seeped into the pit of Tom's stomach when he heard those words. He let his eyes scan the darkness around him. Of course he could see none of it, but in his mind he could picture the rugged, broken canyons, the smeared look of the scattered evergreens against the far mountains, the sight of an azure lake in the midst of the desert. He could see the stately way the saguaro cactus pierced the sky, and their white-flowered tops glistening in the June sun. All of the harsh, spiked plant life of the Sonoran desert made an unlikely foreground for the panorama of the rose-enveloped ridges of the Santa Catalinas in fading afternoon light, and the unreal scarlet and gilded sunsets had been given as a gift to those who waited out Arizona's furnace-like summer days. He looked back at Melissa, and he was sad to say the words, but he had no choice. "A man don't easily forget this kind of country."

Melissa stared upward. He heard her draw a deep breath. "Tom, you said a few minutes ago that you're in love with me. I didn't say it back, but it's true—I love you, more than anything. I would never want to be apart from you. But I would be lying if I didn't say I knew it would come to this. You have your life, your wild-roving, free, devil-may-care life. And I have my structured one, my operas, my ballet, my scientific work with Professor Ashcroft. Neither of us would be happy if we had to leave what we love. You know it, and so do I. I think we always have."

He squeezed her arms. A desperate pounding had started in his chest. "Let's don't talk like this right now. What if... what if I come out there to New York? What if I come and see what it's all about? Do they let no-account drifters in your city?"

She laughed, her husky voice hiding tears that were very near the surface. "Drifters and worse, Tom. You would be one of the upper class citizens in New York."

"Then I will. I'll come out there. I promise. When this is all over, I'll hop a train and I'll just take me a ride and see what all the fuss is about. I'll climb some of those little hills y'all call mountains and maybe even go to one of those operas with you. It's like they say: It ain't over 'til the fat lady sings."

All Melissa could give in answer was a bear hug that threatened to drive the breath out of the man to whom she had given her heart.

*   *   *

That night the camp slept well, even Melissa. With two guards out at all times, and the string of cans doing guard duty of its own on that windless night, everyone enjoyed a sense of restful peace. But no one would forget that Death-Shadow was out there—lurking, brooding, wanting them dead.

In the morning, they sat around a big fire and sipped coffee, trying to avoid looking at the new graves beyond camp, where Moore, Baron, and Pistolito lay asleep. They had held a meeting over breakfast, and it was decided that immediate preparations should be made to leave. What they couldn't take would be left in the cave, and they would return for it later—for the most part, that meant the giants themselves. The Professor had decided to take out only three of them on this trip—the biggest three.

They knew one thing concerning Death-Shadow: He had been wounded. But they didn't know how badly. By Sam's one quick glance, and by the height of the blood he had left on the juniper branches, it was a low wound, along the outside of his right thigh. A flesh wound, probably—not a wound that would kill him, unless by infection. If anything, Sam figured it would make the giant even more anxious to see them dead. They had shamed him, and they had drawn his blood.

Sam was under no misconceptions. The Santa Catalina Giant knew they could find his home. He would no longer feel safe there. He would know he either had to find a new home, or he had to kill every last one of them to keep his secret on the mountain. And from the way Melissa talked, the cave was too ideal a hiding place to be relinquished lightly. So... why hadn't he tried to come after them in the night? What were his plans? Could he be hurt worse than they thought? No. He had made a drop of at least twelve feet over the side of the cliff. No badly wounded man could have done that. And the sprinkle of blood he had left when he landed was small. No, Death-Shadow was not hurt—not so much that he couldn't still kill everyone in this camp.

Sam also felt that the giant would be bent on getting Melissa back. Not only was it a slight to him that she had escaped, but he would have felt that aching in his loins that comes with the presence of a beautiful woman, especially to a man who has lived alone. Death-Shadow had not lain with Melissa, but Sam could not believe he had not meant to. It was a sure thing that he would want her back. He had claimed the woman as his own.

In camp, with their alarm system set up, and as long as whoever was there kept a rifle close at hand they would be as safe as anywhere. Even a giant couldn't survive many rifle bullets. So they would leave Ross and the Sanchezes there to guard the camp, its artifacts, and the animals. The rest of them would make one last trek to the cave and carry down anything the Professor couldn't live without until the next trip.

Everyone went armed now. Even the Professor had a pistol, which he had taken from Delbert Moore's belongings. Quiet Wind didn't own a gun, but she kept a knife in her moccasin top and a short-handled axe in her belt, in whose use she was deft. Melissa wore her .32 Smith and Wesson strapped around her waist. Before they headed up the trail, Sam came to her, carrying his saddlebag.

"You need something more than that pea shooter." He reached into his saddlebag and drew out the biggest brother of the Smith and Wesson Melissa carried. It was a .45 caliber Schofield. "Take this," he said. "I loaded it with six rounds, so be careful. And put them all here—" He slapped his chest vigorously, dead-center. "Don't hesitate, Melissa. Don't let him take you again. Shoot him like a rabid dog."

*   *   *

With their plans for the day set, and a desire to be headed off the mountain before noon, the little party trailed up to the cave. As they hiked, they began to hear intermittent grumbling over the ridge across the canyon. It was an ominous sound, but it seemed far away.

Left inside the cave were the giants, and some carefully cata-logued artifacts in stacks. The Professor picked through them and assigned a pile to each person who would be going down—except for Sam, who would be carrying his and Tom's rifles and keeping guard over them. It appeared they would be able to carry it all in one trip.

The Professor sighed and looked around the dark cave, hear-ing a mutter of thunder make its hollow echo in some far-off can-yon. He took in one last long breath of the cave's musty odor, a smell that would forever live with him. He scanned the blackened walls and sighed again. To a man like the Professor, it was like walking away from Christmas morning gift-giving on the last year that he would be allowed to believe in Father Christmas. He swallowed a big lump in his throat and stepped back out into the sunshine. Would he really ever see the cave again?

Clouds were huffing over the rim of the canyon, and a silver glow skittered across them, followed by a distant grousing of thunder.

The party had made it only three-fourths of the way to camp when the Professor gasped and turned around, a little curse escaping his lips. "I meant to bring some of those torches from the wall!" he exclaimed. "I would like to use them in my display."

Sam looked longingly toward camp, then back up the canyon. Against his better judgment, he said, "If you want them so bad, I can go back up. I don't think you'll need me this close to camp. Just keep a sharp eye out."

The Professor shook his head. "I want them, but you can't go back there alone. Take Viktor with you."

Viktor nodded on the instant and gave Sam a wink. He leaned down to deposit the things he was carrying beside the trail. Tom did the same, wordlessly. The Professor understood, and smiled. "All right. The three of you go back up together. Fetch at least six of those torches, if you would. Also, could you please look at the feasibility of making some type of wooden barricade to cover the entrance until we get back?"

Sam nodded. It was far too late to think about that now, but it was just as easy to agree.

The wind was starting to pick up and kick dust and sand around, and Melissa cut in: "Make sure you hurry. Look at those clouds."

They all turned to take in a huge wall of black thunderheads that were boiling up over the far ridgeline.

Tom whistled, casting a passing glance at Sam to see his reaction to the lightning-filled clouds. "We'll definitely step quick. If we have to, we might hole up in the cave 'til it passes over."

With that, they turned and headed back up, Sam's rifle swinging at arm's length, and Tom carrying his in the crook of his elbow. Back inside the cave, three of the torches had already been taken out of their brackets and were lying on the floor. Three others Viktor and Tom wrenched out of their holes. They took one last look around at the artifacts they were leaving. Without exception, all were items that they already had more than one of down below. And what would stay here could be easily gathered on one more trip—except, of course, for the giants themselves. That was going to be the chore.

As Tom started to turn away, he noticed the bow he had strung up and tried to shoot. That day seemed so long ago. It lay there with two arrows beside it, a symbol of a distant, mysterious past.

Going to the cave entrance, they peered at the sky. The seething clouds were halfway across the canyon, but possibly far enough off for them to make it back to camp before the storm hit. It would be safer inside the cave, but who knew how long it would last? There was no sign of the sky lightening up beyond the head of the storm.

"We'd better go back down," Sam decided. "Much as I hate to with that storm hovering over us."

"What about blockin' the door?" Tom reminded him.

"To hell with that. It would take another two days up here to cover it. The Professor wasn't thinkin' straight—just wishful thinkin'."

In agreement, they all started back down the mountain, stepping fast.

But they didn't step fast enough.

The first raindrops were just a warning. Lightning was abundant now, and thunder cracked and brumbled down the canyon, seeming to shake the earth to its soul. A whip of lightning started down the far sky, then seemed to explode into a dozen writhing, whipping tentacles that curled and snapped this way and that, up, down and to both sides, all at the same time. The following percussion was tremendous, and Tom saw Sam cringe and look wildly about. He would never completely overcome his well-earned childhood fear. How could anything ever wash away the fact that lightning had killed his family, right before his eyes?

Only seconds later, a flash rent the sky, and the *boom* of its voice was on its heels. The bolt of fire exploded an already half-dead ponderosa up the hill a hundred yards from them, throwing splinters and burning brands here and there.

Sam ducked and swore with great feeling. But he quickly got his senses about him, and even with the lightning flashing so fierce that they hardly had a second to think before the next thunder-boom, he got Viktor and Tom together. "I don't know much," he yelled above the howling wind and rain that pelted them like nails, "but I know how dangerous it is for us to be packin' this iron. Let's shuck our weapons and leave 'em under this bush, then get down there to that wide spot and take cover—pronto!"

The others agreed. They left the two rifles and all three holstered pistols under the bush Sam had pointed out and ran down the trail to the only wide place along the whole path. It was a grassy area, fairly level, and surrounded close in by oaks, with the wall of rock and the forest looming back beyond it.

They found that if they crouched on the far side of one large oak it kept most of the sideways-driving rain off them, and even what was landing on top of the tree had a hard time making it down through all the thick leaves to the ground. This was a particularly large tree, for its species, and it sheltered them nicely. In a way, it didn't matter, for they were already quite wet, but at least it wasn't running off them as it would have been had they tried to make it the rest of the way to camp.

Without warning, a heavy bolt speared down the sky and slammed into the canyonside opposite them. The percussion was almost instant, and Sam swore, clamping his hands over his ears. The thunder bragged and sputtered its way all along the canyon, echoing both up and down, and before it had quite faded another mighty flash lit them up from behind, and its explosion sounded almost as loud as the first. The thunder gods were having fun with Sam Coffey, damn them. But this time he would not be cowed.

The rain was splashing into its own lake bed now, spraying everywhere as it landed, sounding like a waterfall. The wind spun up the canyon, then would turn one way or the other, launching raindrops pell-mell. As suddenly as it hit from the west, the wind would then turn and come from up the canyon. But mostly it drove at them from straight across the way, and the trunk and heavy boughs of the oak kept them as dry as possible.

Like most dry mountain storms, this one ended quickly. It was there, flashing and splashing, booming and crashing, and then it was gone. The thunder still grumbled up over the hilltop behind them, and they could see a dim flash of light from time to time. Raindrops pattered about, sometimes carried by the wind, but sometimes falling straight down, for the storm in leaving had taken most of the wind along with it. Below, in the depths of the canyon, the creek was now raging, carrying with it loose debris, logs and even rolling some of the smaller boulders.

They listened to the fading thunder and the hollow echoes drift down the canyon, scuttling off rocks. The rain continued to drift down, and some of the drops were huge, but spears of sunlight crept out of the far clouds. The sun had counter-attacked, it seemed, and had the dark forces on the run.

With the rain still falling fleetingly, they kept to their shelter. They could see it would only be a minute or two before they could step out and start to dry. Tom was fascinated with the way the clouds rolled about overhead, changing size and shape, seeming at times like fantasy figures locked in combat, only to disperse and metamorphose into something else. They would be the subject of one of his poems before too long.

As for Viktor, he shut his eyes for a moment and drew in the mountain air through his nostrils. It smelled incredibly clean after the rain, and it had brought out the perfume of the juniper and pine. He was sitting there thinking of getting himself a broad-brimmed hat like the ones Sam and Tom wore. His small-brimmed bowler was fine in the city, but out here in the sun and rain a broad brim sure had its advantages. He might also consider purchasing a pair of tall boots to take home with him. Women seemed to like the mystique of the "Wild West." And he was growing to like it himself, in spite of the horror they had experienced on this lonely mountain.

Tom's voice, announcing that the rain had stopped, broke into Viktor's musing, and he and Sam looked out at the sky. The sun was out, and it was time to go down and get some dry clothes.

Sam stood up and stretched, then shivered involuntarily and said, "Let's go. Right about now I could use some of that paint remover Ross calls coffee."

They laughed, then picked up the torches and started back up the trail to where they had left their weapons.

They didn't make it far.

From the bushes beside the trail came a loud, low rumble, sounding no less dangerous than the thunder itself. They stopped dead in their tracks, and they stared in disbelief as he stepped from cover, the rumbling laugh still in his throat.

His eyes pinned them, full of disdain, full of hatred, but full of mirth. He had caught them—a man, a giant...

Death-Shadow!

CHAPTER THIRTY-SEVEN

Even in all their glimpses of him, mostly distant and fleeting, they had never imagined the giant more menacing and powerful look-ing. There he stood, towering over them, his huge, thick legs braced against the trail, the right one with a white cloth tied around it, crusted with dried blood.

It wasn't horrific enough to see him standing there, but in each hand he held a rifle, and slung around his massive neck were Viktor's shoulder holster and both Sam and Tom's gun belts.

He stared at them with a wicked smile of satisfaction and an-ticipation, savoring the moment. They stared into his half-human eyes, which appeared blue surrounded by a ring of brown. It seemed twenty seconds they stood there, all of them frozen.

Sam broke the silence, letting out an involuntary rush of breath. It was as if someone had hit him in the stomach. Without thinking, he said, "Look at the size of that belt knife." Tom's eyes dropped to the weapon. He said nothing, but he could see why Sam had made the comment. It was like a small sword.

"Cover your forearms," said Viktor suddenly. "He can't use them guns—his finger's too big to fit in the trigger guards. But he can sure use that knife, and if we don't have some protection on our forearms he'll make short work of it."

Squeezing their torches between their legs, all three of the men peeled off their jackets and wrapped them around their left arms as a shield. Death-Shadow watched them silently, a good deal of what appeared to be amusement remaining in his eyes. As they finished, he looked down at their weapons. One by one, he turned a little to the side and flung the rifles over the cliff behind him. The partners cringed. Viktor licked his lips, his eyes flickering over the big man as thoughts raced through his mind.

With his hands now empty, the giant slid the gun belts off over his head and looked at them disdainfully just for a moment, as if they were no more dangerous or useful than dead flowers. Then he turned to the side and threw them high into the air, where the four of them could watch them plummet for some time before they disappeared over the side of the cliff after the rifles. They could hear them strike bottom long after they left their sight.

Viktor's face settled into hard lines. Then, without warning, he charged.

The attack took Death-Shadow by surprise. How could so small a man attack *him*? He was three feet taller than this man, and hundreds of pounds heavier! He had just started to turn back to them, and he saw the "little" Vik Zulowsky come at him with amazing speed. Off balance, the giant swung a fist that would have been devastating had it connected. Viktor ducked beneath it and retaliated with a whack of his torch across the giant's shin.

The huge man let out a gasp, and pain etched his face. The sound of the torch's strike had been loud enough to sound like the shinbone had fractured, and the Indian doubled up. This brought him down nearer to Viktor's level, and he was quick to take advantage of it. He stepped in and pivoted on his left foot, delivering a powerful side kick to Death-Shadow's nose and face. There was a sharp crack, and blood streamed from the giant's nostrils.

Viktor didn't pause to admire his work. Dozens of fights in dozens of taverns and side streets had conditioned him for this moment. Of all the fights of his life, this one was the most important. He had to move in for the kill.

He swung to his right and delivered a second kick to the left side of Death-Shadow's face. The huge head snapped back, and he would have fallen over had he not succeeded in putting out one hand to catch himself.

The look on the giant's face as he lurched back to fully erect was one of stunned disbelief. His upper lip was split, and a nasty cut on his left cheekbone bled down toward his jaw. One eye was starting to swell, and his lip was beginning to puff up already, and bleeding as well. Blood had dripped down on his chest in twin streams, and he painted a horrible picture. By the look in his eyes, he was still trying to comprehend the sudden turn of events.

The entire counter-attack had taken place all within the space of little more than five seconds.

Viktor realized the giant's physical power. Even hurt, he was enough to kill them all. He couldn't be left with any weapon to augment that power, especially if Viktor could use that weapon himself. So Viktor lunged in and ripped the knife out of the Indian's sheath. If he could drive it through the giant's heart...

Death-Shadow slapped Viktor's hand with the sound of a whip, and the knife went flying and slid over the cliff's edge. The giant went to grab his opponent as Sam and Tom started forward.

Viktor slammed the big man's hand on the knuckles with his torch, peeling back the hide. Death-Shadow jerked back his hand. Viktor punched him in the middle of the breastbone. For a moment, the Indian seemed shaken—but *only* for a moment.

Even as Viktor's torch was swinging at him again, the giant let out a roar and caught his feisty opponent in the chest with a mighty backhand. The blow struck Viktor hard, knocking the air out of his lungs and sending him tumbling across the ground.

The New York brawler rose to his knees, gasping for air. The partners were closing around Death-Shadow, but before they could even react, he spun on Sam and struck him a blow to the side of the head, sending him to his knees. Tom came in and flung a hard right to the giant's kidney, but it only seemed to anger him more. He grabbed the cowboy and struck him twice in the chest, then shoved him away. Tom landed on his back, dazed, staring up at the sky.

The enemy Death-Shadow really wanted now was Viktor, who had just turned his head to look at him. Viktor had hurt him. He must pay!

The giant felt his face and grimaced. He spat blood and started toward Viktor. Viktor had been so shaken by the blow to his chest that he was helpless to do anything as Death-Shadow reached him and grabbed him by the right upper arm. Then he took his left thigh in the other hand, and he straightened up until all of Viktor's two hundred sixty pounds was in the air, high over his head. Now he would end this fight once and for all.

Death-Shadow turned and started for the cliff as Viktor bawled and started punching and kneeing him with his free fist and knee. It was at the last moment when Viktor saw the arrows in the quiver on the Indian's back. Reaching out in desperation, he grabbed onto three of them and yanked them out of the quiver. In almost the same motion, he drove them as hard as he could into the giant's trapezius muscle, right at the base of his neck.

The giant stopped, paralyzed. He let out a sound that was a combination of a blood-curdling scream and a roar of pain, frustration and rage. He spun around as if to escape the pain, but then he turned back to the cliff. There was one sure way to stop this little fiend he had latched onto...

But Viktor was too fast for him. With his free hand, he reached down and grabbed a big handful of the giant's hair. Let him throw him off the cliff now! They would die together.

Death-Shadow realized the predicament he was in. He could neither throw the big man off the cliff nor down to the ground now without causing severe damage to his own scalp. He lurched away from the cliff's edge just as Sam was coming to his knees.

On reflex, he kicked Sam hard in the chest and knocked him onto his back. Then, as he felt Viktor let go of his hair and slam him in the cheek with another tremendous blow, he shut his eyes against the pain and threw the little fighter as hard as he could.

Viktor landed on his side but rolled with the fall. Even if it was the worst fall he could remember taking, he was still Viktor Zulowsky, the fightin'est man in New York City! He scrambled to his feet just as he saw Death-Shadow jerk the bow from around his neck and draw an arrow from his quiver.

It was run now, or die. Viktor ran. He gave the big man a wide berth and took off sprinting down the hill, his pain forgotten. All he could think clearly was that he had to dodge back and forth as much as possible, or that big killer was going to sink an arrow in his back.

With the other arrows still sticking out of his trapezius, Death-Shadow nocked his arrow and raised his bow. By now, Sam and Tom had recovered enough to get to their feet. Sam picked up his torch and smashed it down across the huge wrist that held the bow. The arrow flew wild, whistling harmlessly down into the canyon.

Death-Shadow growled in anger and frustration.

Thwarted at every turn!

He threw his arm around, aiming low as if he expected Sam to duck. But Sam didn't duck, and the blow took him in the shoulder, sending him reeling. It was a blow that if it had taken him in the head as intended might have ended the fight for him.

Tom ran up behind Death-Shadow and leaped up to grab two hands full of hair. He dropped with all his body weight, jerking the big head back and pulling him over backwards. As the giant was toppling, Tom maneuvered to one side to keep from being crushed. He wasn't about to wrestle this behemoth if he could avoid it.

The giant slammed into the ground, and Sam stepped back in and hit him over the head hard enough to break his torch in two.

At almost the same time, Tom stepped in and kicked him in the chest. The giant lunged up, amazingly fast, and reached out to catch a handful of Tom's shirt. He started to jerk Tom toward him, but Tom was doing his best to pull in the other direction. There was the sound of ripping cloth, and with another backward step by Tom he was left wearing half of his shirt. The only part left to him was the collar, back and sleeves.

In disgust, Death-Shadow threw the material on the ground. Tom and Sam were standing together now, and he stared at them through his one good eye. Then, with little effort, he stooped and retrieved his bow, the arrow still nocked to the string. With a snarl, he reached back and yanked the three arrows out of his trapezius, their tips covered with blood. Tom and Sam had started to back toward the brush, where they hoped they could outmaneuver him.

A grimace of pain crossed Death-Shadow's face as he stared at the partners and shoved the arrows back into the quiver on his back. They stood facing him, weaponless except for jackknives in their pockets, which might as well have been quill pens, for all the good they would do against this juggernaut.

Tom dared a glance back toward the oak trees and the mountain slope. He was reminded of what he didn't like to know. There was little place to hide there, after the first few yards. Then it turned to rock again, and the mountain would be nearly impossible to climb with Death-Shadow behind them. He stood now between them and the camp, and the only way to run was back up to the cave.

Had Viktor made it to camp? Maybe help would be on its way. But it would be too late. The bow was coming level...

"He can't get us both, pardner," said Tom in a low voice. "We've got to run for it. Ready?"

Sam replied, "He looks kind of wobbly to me, maybe he'll miss."

"Yeah, and maybe a tree will fall on him."

Sam's lip curled. "It's now or never. Been good knowin' you, Tom."

Tom nodded. "Same here."

Then a shot rang out, and both of them turned to look down the trail, as did Death-Shadow, in vast surprise. There crouched Viktor. He hadn't left at all! He was holding his little boot gun, a .41 caliber Remington over and under, in one hand, steadying that wrist with the other hand.

The shot had missed, fired too quickly. And it was too far for the little gun anyway. But Viktor obviously didn't want to come any closer. He aimed carefully as they looked on, and the second shot rang out. This time the giant winced and growled something unintelligible. He dropped to one knee, then lunged back up and looked down at his thigh, where a little round hole had appeared. With a roar, he turned his bow once again on Viktor.

The big brawler wasn't waiting around to see the results of his shot this time. He had used both of his bullets, and the only way to save Sam and Tom was to go for help. He took off down the trail, nearly falling a couple of times, trying to run in a zigzag pattern again to keep from taking an arrow. It worked, too, for the one arrow the giant flung went wide of him, and then he was moving too fast and erratically for a decent shot.

Viktor heard the arrow strike wide of him. He had bought himself another life! He ran as hard as he could. He had to make it to camp. He had to bring back help. The lives of Sam Coffey and Tom Vanse were in his hands!

*   *   *

The giant whirled back toward Sam and Tom. They were gone! He looked quickly around, and then he saw them. There was no place to hide, where they were bound. They had taken advantage of Viktor's disturbance and were halfway up the trail. He started after them but cringed in pain and almost went to a knee once more. He cursed the fighter and his little pistol.

Jerking the cloth band from his head, he tied it around the wound on his leg and looked up the trail at Sam and Tom. He could take one of them from here, even if he could no longer out-run them.

He took another arrow from his quiver, one of the ones that had wounded him, and nocked it. At the critical moment, his loose hair blew into his face and blocked his vision, and he missed the shot. But the partners heard it hit, and the sound spurred them on harder.

Death-Shadow roared and started after them. He paused and made as if to fire after them, but then he shook his head and raged on, making good time in spite of his limp.

*   *   *

Once Sam and Tom saw Death-Shadow go down, they figured it was now or never, and they broke for the cave. Tom yelled something about the arrows they had left behind in the cave, and that was enough impetus for both of them. Those arrows might not have been much protection if used as hand weapons instead of the missiles they were intended to be, but they were better than nothing. And, those failing, there were always rocks. It wouldn't be the first time in history a giant had been taken down by a well-placed stone!

Neither Sam nor Tom was used to running, not in a day and age when good cowboys never did anything on foot that could be done from horseback. And the steepness of the trail made it that much more of a challenge. But the surge of energy racing through them at the moment gave them an edge. Even so, it was the leg wound from Viktor's derringer that saved their lives.

They were halfway up the trail, with Sam twenty feet in the lead, when Tom looked back for the first time. Viktor was no-where to be seen now, and Death-Shadow was coming up the mountain looking bigger than a freight horse. Yet the .41 slug must have sunk deep into the muscles of his thigh, for his gait was ungainly, and several times he had to reach back with his hand and actually jerk the leg upward. It was a pathetic picture, a man of Death-Shadow's physical prowess reduced to such means. Tom, however, could dredge up no sympathy.

Taking several huge breaths, he turned and started after Sam, who had continued on, unaware that his partner had stopped. Thanks to Death-Shadow's wound, Sam reached the cave a hundred yards before he did. Tom, stepping up his pace in desperation, was fifteen yards behind. By the time he lurched into the cool shadows, Sam already had an arrow in each hand.

Before Tom could catch his breath, Sam was throwing a plan his way. "You take one of these, and I'll take the other. I'll stay on this side of the cave, you stay over there, and when he comes in we'll attack from both sides and drive these into his ribs as deep as we can. Or better yet, I'll go for the kidneys, and you go for the belly."

Tom gasped, trying to speak. He had looked to the sides, at the great width of the cave entrance, and he shook his head. Finally, he leaned down and put his hands on his thighs, then sucked in a deep breath. "It won't work! He'll see whoever's on that side before he gets near enough to walk in." He had to pause to take a few more breaths, during which time he whirled and looked down the trail, then swore vehemently. He turned back to Sam.

"Another fifty yards and he'll be here. Come on!" He ran to the wall of the cave, and now that his eyes had adjusted somewhat to the dark he was able to snatch the big bow off the floor.

"What are you gonna do with that?" Sam shot out. "You tried to shoot it before!"

"I don't know, damn it!" Tom looked around frantically, as if some other worthy weapon would simply materialize. "What if we could somehow both hold it and shoot together?"

"We can't!"

"Then how about one of us holds the bow and one shoots?"

Exasperated and desperate, Sam laughed. "Yeah. Maybe he'll see us try that and die laughing."

Tom stared at his partner. They were both going to die here if they didn't think of something fast. Neither of them would be alive five minutes from now, and they had come too far to give up. Then a thought dawned on him. "Remember when I told you about that article I read in *Harper's?* About that South American tribe that used a big bow like this and shot with their feet?"

Sam scoffed. "You don't have a chance! How long do you think they had to practice to be any good?"

"What other chance do we have?"

"Fine!" Sam growled. "Get on the floor." He ran to the cave entrance, looked out, then collected four rocks that would weigh two or three pounds each. Tom took the two arrows and went far enough back in the cave that he would be in deep shadow when Death-Shadow first turned the corner.

Sam brought his rocks to the back wall with him, but well off to one side of Tom, where the giant wouldn't have them lined up like two ducks. He took his stance with the rocks, leaving Tom sitting on the floor, trying to position the bow in the notch of his boot heels and balance it. He had an arrow nocked.

Tom shot a frightened look back at Sam. This was it. Sink or swim. Do or die. Perhaps do and then die anyway. Impulsively, he said, "You've been a good partner, Sam."

Sam just grimaced and spat. "Been good callin' you my friend."

Tom leaned back and raised his legs. He was easily able to elevate his aim or lower it and could twist his body left or right for windage adjustment. He took the string under-handed and gave it a try. It was stiff, but he immediately knew he would have the strength to pull it back enough to be more than effective. It was aiming that was going to be tough. Without any practice, he was at a loss as to where to hold.

"Hold low," said Sam. "Way low. You always hold lower than you think with a bow and arrow when you're close up."

Tom looked at him doubtfully. Taking a deep breath, he relaxed and eased the pressure off the bowstring. Who knew how long it would be until the giant showed up? And then—what if he *didn't* show? What if he had gotten within yards and then decided to try some other tack? Well, that was all right with Tom, too. But damn the big bloody demon! He'd better make a move soon if he was going to make it! This kind of terror was something a man shouldn't have to suffer for long.

Many thoughts went through both of their heads in that minute that they waited. Sam thought of Nadia. Tom of Melissa. Perhaps that was inevitable. Tom thought of the possibility that if Death-Shadow came around the corner with an arrow already nocked and his bow drawn, he could still let fly with an arrow even if Tom hit him dead-center. It wasn't a comforting thought, but it was why Tom had set himself somewhat to the side, and well into the darkness. If he was going to play David to this Goliath he had to have every edge.

Thinking of that age-old story, he also thought of his faith. He said a silent prayer. *Please, Lord, let my aim be true. Don't let the string or the bow break. And please don't let him see me first.*

Then it appeared... A shadow slowly glided across the ground toward the entrance to the cave. The killer was just outside. Tom's heart started to race. *Calm down*, he told himself, but the sweat was trickling down his cheeks, and his hands were moist. He didn't even have time to dry them.

Sam crouched in the shadows, a big, round rock in each hand and two more at his feet. His years with the Tarahumaras might pay off now. He had spent hours throwing rocks at targets and at small game. He would need every ounce of the strength he had developed and every bit of his skill in aiming. He had played baseball with some of the cowboys on one ranch in Texas, and they were in awe of his power and his aim. God help him now. He was going to need it. He said a silent prayer of his own.

The shadow outside had stopped and was still. Sam swore. He knew what that meant. Death-Shadow was standing there with his eyes shut to adjust them to the dark inside the cave. He swore again. One advantage—gone...

*   *   *

Back in camp, they were trying to clean up after the big storm. It had raged through and done more surface damage to the camp itself than the earthquake had done. Two tents were down, and the top of one tree had given way and fallen way too near the horses. Baron's mount had snapped its tether in fear and charged down the mountain. Of course it would come back, once it realized it was alone and got over its fear. But if the tree had fallen much closer it may no longer have been alive.

Ross was stowing his Dutch ovens in a pack when he looked up and saw Viktor charging down the trail, and he heard him start yelling. The words were unintelligible, but the look on Viktor's face was plain, undisguised terror.

The camp froze.

Melissa came stumbling out of her tent, staring up the mountain toward Viktor. Why was he alone? Where were Sam and Tom? She ran out a ways toward Viktor, feeling her face tight and tingling in her fear. The others stood frozen.

"He's got 'em!" Viktor yelled.

His face was white, even after running all the way down the mountain. He charged inside his tent and ran back out holding Baron's Ballard rifle. The strain of the run seemed to catch up to him suddenly, and he gasped for breath, looking up the mountain. Between breaths, he said, "Death—Shadow... he's got... got Sam and Tom... He'll kill 'em!"

It was Melissa's worst fear coming true. Her gaze flew up the mountain. She knew she could never make it, never be any help at all. But... She shot a glance over at the line of horses, hoping beyond hope. Yes! Alfredo Sanchez had saddled up his mule, planning to go after Baron's horse before it got too far away. She looked down, and there was the .45 Smith and Wesson Sam had loaned her, still belted around her waist. She looked back up at the saddled mule. There was no time to think, only to decide.

On the run, she snatched up the mule's reins while Alfredo stood there in dismay. She fairly leaped on board, astride, and wheeled the animal around. Viktor had started back up the hill now, going slow because of his lack of wind. She raced past him, and could hear him and Ross yelling at her. She had glimpsed Ross with a rifle, and she knew he would shortly be on his way too. But they were on foot. They would be no match for her speed. She was going to reach Sam and Tom before anyone... except, perhaps, for the Santa Catalina Giant...

*   *   *

Outside the cave, the shadow budged, and Tom, in near panic, drew back the bowstring partway. He started to raise his feet again. Following Sam's advice, he planned to sight straight at the giant's belly. That way, if he shot low it might still get him in the groin, and if he shot high it was in line with his heart, his neck, and his head. The shadow moved again, and then, like an apparition, there was the end of the giant's bow, then the right side of his body.

Chills raced over Tom. This was their one chance. He knew it more than he had ever known anything in his life. If his aim wasn't true, Death-Shadow would kill them both like pesky ants. Did Death-Shadow know they might have weapons here? Would he expect to have to defend himself again? They would never know those answers for sure...

CHAPTER THIRTY-EIGHT

Melissa was well ahead of the others. In spite of the precarious trail, especially in the two spots where it was only a matter of one slip between her and an agonizing death on the rocks below, she was racing the mule as hard as she dared, and as hard as she could make that wisest of pack animals move. Viktor's last words hung in her brain: "He'll kill you, Melissa!" But she couldn't wait. That was Tom up there. Tom, and Sam, who had risked everything to save her life.

*   *   *

The bowstring was starting to cut into Tom's fingers, even at half-draw. "Come on. *Come on!"* he whispered fiercely.

And then he was there, silhouetted like a magnificent statue.

The Santa Catalina Giant stood framed in the cave entrance, bigger and more horrible than any nightmare Tom had ever known. Lying on the floor as he was, the giant looked even bigger, as imposing as a grizzly bear, and heavier than many.

Tom drew the bowstring back. He held it with both eyes open, centering on Death-Shadow's belly. The giant's arrow was also nocked, but it wasn't yet drawn back. It started to come up with frightening speed even as Tom let out half of his breath.

God, please let this arrow fly true...

As smoothly as he could, he released his fingers. A thud... a gasp... The sounds were mingled with a strangled cry of desperation. The big figure staggered back into the sunlight. One of his eyes was swollen horribly shut, but the other was full of shock and surprise.

Until that moment, Tom hadn't realized he was holding his breath. He let it out in a gust and took in another, refilling his lungs with fresh air. He fumbled for his second arrow. The giant was not going down! He dropped the arrow and swore, reaching for it again. A rock flew past from the side, but Death-Shadow was still alert enough to step to one side, and it sailed out into space and dropped from sight. Sam's second try struck Death-Shadow in the left biceps, and he roared in anger.

Tom could see the arrow where it had gone through the Indian's left side. Only the fletching was visible from the front.

Tom heard Sam yell: "You did it, Tom! Shoot him again!"

The giant had drawn another arrow from his quiver, and he nocked it before Tom could. Tom's yell came out almost as a scream. "Look out!" At the same moment, he rolled, and Sam dove to one side. The arrow struck the floor where Tom had been and skidded along the floor until slamming and splintering against the back wall.

The giant reached and drew another one just as Sam was bending down in desperation to grab another rock. But this time he would be ready for them to move...

*   *   *

Melissa screamed as she saw the giant let go of his arrow, aiming into the cave. She knew there was nowhere inside to hide. He had killed Sam or Tom! She screamed again, making the mule shy. Her heart sank, and a huge weakness spread over her. She heard herself screaming, and it was as if it came from somewhere else on some other part of the mountain. "God! Please!"

Suddenly, she was angry, very angry, and her strength came flooding back. This man had kidnapped her, terrified her, held her captive. He had killed two of her friends, and now probably a third. She was not going to let him continue.

She was only twenty yards away, and this place in the trail was nearly level. She slid off the mule, but his head was pointing out over the canyon, so she had to run all the way around behind him to gain sight of the cave. As she did, she drew Sam's pistol.

She lurched to a stop next to the mule. Her view was clear. The Indian had fitted another arrow to his bow, but now he stepped out of the cave's entrance, and to her horror he turned to face her. She gasped, momentarily stunned. The giant was covered with gore. His hair was in disarray, and his face almost unrecognizable. He moved like a man badly hurt. Then she saw the arrow in his side. Confused, she stared. Who had shot him? He was the one with the bow!

There was no time to contemplate those questions. The big man was raising his bow now, aiming it at her. Her scream had drawn his attention, and in his desperate drive to kill something, she became his target.

She raised the .45, aimed and fired. Years of practice with her father paid off. She knew she had hit him. But he just stood there. She fired again, and the mule shied and slammed into her. She lost her balance, and then, as in a dream, she was falling. She knew it, but she could do nothing to stop it.

She landed jarringly on her side and rolled. She clawed at the ground, trying to stop herself. She came to her knees, dazed, and realized she no longer held the pistol. And the giant was drawing another arrow!

*   *   *

Inside the cave, Sam and Tom saw Death-Shadow disappear from view. They had heard Melissa scream, and now a shot exploded. Soon, it was followed by another, and they thought they heard Melissa cry out. In fear, Tom leaped up, dropping the bow, which was useless as long as he was standing. He ran to the cave entrance and carefully looked out at the big man. Sam rushed up beside him, holding another rock.

The giant still had the bow in his hand and another arrow fitted to it. But somehow he looked like he was just barely hanging on to it. His mouth was open, and he gasped for air.

* * *

On the trail below, Viktor had stopped four hundred yards below Melissa. He could go no farther. He was beat. He dropped to his knees on the trail. There was no place to rest the rifle barrel. He would have to rely on what he had thought of as his vast strength, which at this moment was failing him.

He had two cartridges held between the fingers of his left hand, in case he was offered more than one shot. But he couldn't count on that. He raised the big rifle and peered through the brass scope. Sweat ran into his eyes, and he swiped at them angrily, swearing. When his eyes came into focus through the telescope again he noticed the arrow protruding out of the giant.

"What the hell?" The sound of his own voice shocked him.

Then Death-Shadow started to raise the bow, and he drew back the string. He was battered, he was bloody, and he had an arrow stuck through his ribs, which made no sense at all. But his reserves of strength were vast. Death-Shadow had probably killed Sam and Tom, and now he was going to kill Melissa, too...

* * *

Death-Shadow was going to kill Melissa. The words of warning rang through Tom's head for only a second before he left the comparative safety of the cave and ran. He would drive the giant over the cliff if he had to go over with him to do it!

A shot exploded, reverberating up and down the canyon. Tom lurched to a halt as he saw the giant's whole body jerk. The bow and arrow clattered to the ground, and the giant grabbed his head with both hands. He seemed to hang there momentarily, as if frozen. He began to teeter, and he slowly turned around, facing the canyon.

Then, like a mighty pine, the giant called Death-Shadow fell forward.

He hung at the cliff's edge, frozen in time and space. Just for the briefest piece of a second, but one that seemed like eternity.

Then he toppled over the edge of the cliff.

Tom cringed as he heard the body hit the rocks below...

Melissa was standing there with her mouth agape when the giant went over. She looked up to see Tom, and Sam came out beside him. Both of them were staring toward the cliff, as if unaware of her presence.

Dazed, with tears streaking the dust on her cheeks, the woman walked stiffly the rest of the way up the hill, where Sam and Tom had approached the edge and were looking down. She stood behind Tom and reached out to touch his sleeve. "Is... Is he gone?"

Tom heard the words, and although he knew Melissa was there he was stunned. He wheeled around and threw his arms around her almost savagely, kissing her hard on the mouth.

Melissa started to cry out loud, and Tom just held her. Finally, she whispered, "I was so afraid I had lost you."

"No such luck." He kissed her softly on the forehead. "You're gonna have to do a lot more than that to get rid of Tom Vanse."

She raised her head, stepped back, and smiled while gazing intently through her tears into his eyes.

Tom grinned as a pleasant feeling of warmth and peace flowed through him. They had been through hell, but they were here together now.

Viktor had made it up the hill, and not far behind him came Ross, his rifle clenched in his fist. The rest of the party arrived one by one, until all of them were there in front of the cave entrance, all sucking for air. Everyone had made the climb three times faster than ever before.

Quiet Wind was standing at the edge of the cliff with Alfredo, Juan, and Guillermo. Ross and the Professor stood near Melissa, pawing over her like a lost child. Tom looked down at the Ballard rifle in Viktor's hand. "Damn good shot. I owe you."

Viktor looked at the cowboy for a long time, seeming somewhat dazed. Finally he held out his hand, and Tom took it and squeezed hard. They looked into each other's eyes, one fighter finally understanding another. "Evens things up for Baron," Viktor said at last. "You don't owe me a thing."

Tom looked over at Melissa, putting his arm around her shoulders. He grinned at Viktor but spoke to Melissa. "You should have seen Viktor. Darn'dst thing I ever saw—like a one man army."

Viktor was beaming, and a big grin split his face. "You cowboys did all right yourselves." He glanced over and nodded at Sam. "Something strange, though—I swore I saw an arrow sticking out of him."

Tom sighed and told about the old bow, and his shot of a lifetime. Crooked Foot was standing nearby, and the look on his face was one of mixed emotions. Once, his chin quivered, and he looked out over the canyon. He was the only one who would not go to gaze down at Death-Shadow lying there below, to make sure he was gone.

Melissa caught the Indian's sad, bewildered look, and she walked over and put a comforting hand on his shoulder. For his pride, it was the wrong thing to do, as it made tears well up in his eyes. He gave a quick shake of his head. "Not good him kill people. No good. Better him gone."

Melissa looked over sadly at Tom, then Sam. She said, "He was your friend, wasn't he?"

Crooked Foot looked down at the ground, seeming to study his moccasins. "Sometimes... him—*he*—not nice. Hurt my dog. Hurt me. Say not good things."

"But he was your friend." Melissa gave his shoulder a rub.

Crooked Foot nodded, his face sad. He looked out over the canyon. "When you go, just dog left. No friends."

Sam looked over at Tom, and his partner met his eyes. They had been together many years. It wasn't hard for them to read each other's thoughts. Sam pictured the menagerie of hands back at their ranch—Cuidado, the Reeses, the Sanchezes, and Cholla. What was one more stray?

He looked back at the Indian. "Tom and me have a pretty nice place in the valley down below. You got a home if you want to come ride for us."

After taking a moment to make sure he understood the words, Crooked Foot raised his eyes. He glanced back and forth between the partners, making sure both agreed. "Bring dog, too?" he asked finally.

"Why not?" said Sam. "We got every other stray in tarnation."

A grin stretched Crooked Foot's face almost in two.

"Can't be cowboy without horse."

"You'll have a horse," Tom agreed. "But you ain't no cowboy. You're still an Indian. A good Indian."

Crooked Foot shook his head adamantly. "No, you remember? I know what they say. Only good Injun *dead* Injun. Me cowboy. Good cowboy."

The first real laughter in days rang against the back wall of the cave of the giants.

Sam looked toward the canyon and noticed that Professor Ashcroft had walked over and was standing on its brink, staring downward. He stayed there for quite some time before Sam stepped away from the group and walked to him. The Professor's back stiffened a little as he heard Sam's boot scuff a rock, but he didn't look over. In silence, they stood there, listening to the droning sounds of conversation behind them as the New Yorker's eyes left the giant and swept the heights of the canyon slowly.

"What's your next big adventure, Professor? After all this is over."

The Professor looked quickly at Sam, making his first conscious show of knowing someone was with him. He sighed long and low, and at last a little laugh escaped him. "I honestly don't know, Sam. How does a man follow a discovery like this? Retirement? I mean, nothing could ever match this. Nothing in my life before it has come close."

"Sure. I understand that."

"I do know one thing," the Professor went on. "I have a strong feeling there is something more in this place, something of great value—in a worldly sense. Once these giants are gone and this cave is empty, I won't be back here, Sam. You and Tom will be free to do whatever you choose up here, with no interference from anyone in New York." He looked meaningfully at Sam.

Sam cleared his throat. "Professor, before you go any farther I have to tell you something. That second hawk's eye Baron was so heated up about, it—"

The Professor quickly held up his hand. "This mountain holds many secrets. Those who discover them discover them. Please understand what I am saying." He paused and bored Sam with his eyes. "I came here looking for this cave, for these artifacts, hoping beyond hope that the giants would still be here. I found the makings of my wildest dreams in these mountains. That is all I came for. But you—you and Tom—you came here because you were hired to do a job. Yet you stayed against all odds. Why? Not for the money, because it was very little in the face of what you were up against. No, you stayed because you cared. You cared for people. It is only because of you that Melissa is alive. And I feel it safe to say that if it weren't for you and Tom *no one* from this camp would be alive. Not one soul. And what you have offered to Crooked Foot, just an Indian, to most people... That might seem small to some, but in reality the humanity of your selfless gesture is tremendous. It may surprise you to learn that Mr. Baron and I were authorized to go as high as five hundred dollars each if we had to to procure two good guides for this expedition.

"There could have been no better guides than you and Tom. No better guides, servants, protectors... and friends. Mr. Baron is gone, and along with him any argument. You will each have that five hundred. And I must tell you that I have no desire to be told one more word about that... *worthless* hawk's eye. I am going back to New York City bearing the fruits of an archeological expedition beyond anything we could have dreamed of.

"But I am also taking with me the information given to me by Stuart Baron that as far as we know there is no mineral wealth left in any obvious diggings in these Santa Catalina Mountains. I am an honest man, Sam. Please don't put me in any position where I have to lie to my backers, because that I am not sure I could do. As I said, you and Tom are free of any obligation to me or those who back me. Please use that freedom wisely."

Sam nodded. He understood. Professor Preston Ashcroft was handing him and Tom a gift much more vast than anyone could know. Even Sam did not know for certain the wealth of silver and gold left in this canyon. But he did know one thing: The giants sealed in that cave had died while they were still working a productive mine. And Sam Coffey and Tom Vanse had good, strong backs and arms.

Tom walked up then with his arm around Melissa and looked searchingly at Sam. He could see that something important had passed between his partner and the Professor, but he didn't question him. There would be plenty of time for that.

The Professor looked down again at the form of the Santa Catalina Giant, his body crushed and limp on the rain-wet boulders.

A shiver passed through him as a warm, determined breeze threaded its way up the canyon, picking up and carrying Death-

Shadow's spirit home, to a faraway, ancient land where giants never die...

THE END

Author's note

With the astounding popularity of the first novel about the ex-
ploits of Sam Coffey and Tom Vanse, *Yaqui Gold,* it seemed only
natural to pursue these two characters on further adventures. So
when Clint Walker came to me in 2004 with the idea of this book,
I could not very well turn it down. Through a series of unfortunate
events, Mr. Walker made the decision not to pursue our partnership on this book through to publication, and we released each
other from any obligations in regards to it. To my last knowledge,
he also had plans for pursuing his own version of the story, in
which I only asked that I not be named in connection due to large
differences of writing style with which my writing did not mesh.

It is important to note that while with *Yaqui Gold,* Mr. Walker
and I had an equal part in planning the story, around his original
premise, I did all of the writing. However, in *Canyon of the
Haunted Shadows,* Mr. Walker in every way put his skills into
plotting and inventing scenarios that will keep the reader on the
edge of his proverbial seat to the test. I took part in working out
a few of the scenarios, and as per our agreement did all of the
actual writing, but the majority of the ideas in this book, the twists
and turns, plots and sub-plots, were Mr. Walker's, and I cannot
take credit for them. I have been informed by fans of the televi-
sion show *Cheyenne,* in which Mr. Walker was the star, that there
are certain episodes from which much of this book is taken, but
that is a claim I know nothing about. I do not know anything about
the series beyond the first few episodes, so this claim stands to be
proven or disproven by the reader.

In working on *Haunted Shadows,* I chose to set the story in
the Santa Catalina Mountains, north of Tucson, Arizona, because

it is an area with which I am intimately familiar. I have spent years studying the wildlife and plant life there, as well as the terrain and the ways and legends of the native people. With little extra work, I was able to deal with the kinds of plants and trees, the species of rattlesnakes and larger wildlife that populated those mountains in the 19th century. Even the earthquake which takes place in the book was an actual occurrence, on the exact date when it takes place in the book. The wildfires that were set off by the quake, as well as everything else documented in that part of the book, are part of recorded Arizona history.

The giants of the Santa Catalina Mountains, as far as Mr. Walker or I know, are fictional. But the background from which they were taken is very real, and there is a much vaster history of gigantic peoples throughout the world than most people would ever imagine. It was with much intrigue that the research by me and Mr. Walker unfolded the stories of giants throughout the world, and throughout history. I hope you, the reader, will be as fascinated by this history of little known facts as Mr. Walker was up until the time of his death and as I have become.

Happy reading!

Acknowledgments

Other than the research on gigantic people of history, which Clint Walker did, I was able to turn up most of the research in this book on my own. But I gladly acknowledge all of those people who have helped in past books, because without the stores of knowledge gleaned during their research and writing this would have been every bit as large and convoluted a project as any book I've written before.

I do need to give a special thanks to Grace Katterman, of Tucson, whose experience in archaeology and in such subjects as transporting fragile items like mummies out of rugged mountains was indispensable. She has also provided a much-needed oasis for rest and refreshment over my years of research in the Tucson area, and her friendship has meant the world to me and my family.

Thank you to Jeffrey and Trisha Reese, for letting me use them as characters for a cameo appearance. And thank you to the authors, the actors, the directors, and the film producers of the past and present who have inspired me to want to bring more stories of the West to life for hungry readers, present and future.

Thanks most of all to Clint Walker, for asking me to write this book with him and for spinning such a wonderful tale, to which I had merely to put the words. I only regret that our writing partnership had to be dissolved and that we cannot both be listed on the cover of the book, the way it should have been. Mr. Walker was an intelligent, unique, and generally kind person to whom I do not believe Hollywood ever did justice. I hoped that one day he would finish his own version of this book as well, but alas, it was not part of the final plan, I suppose. It would have been interesting to compare the two in finished form.

About the Author

Kirby Frank Jonas was born in 1965 in Bozeman, Montana. His earliest memories are of living seven miles outside of town in a wide crack in the mountains known as Bear Canyon. At that time it was a remote and lonely place, but a place where a boy with an imagination could grow and nurture his mind, body and soul.

From Montana, the Jonas family moved almost as far across the country as they could go, to Broad Run, Virginia, to a place that, although not as deep in the timbered mountains as Bear Canyon was every bit as remote—Roland Farm. Once again, young Jonas spent his time mostly alone, or with his older brother, if he was not in school. Jonas learned to hike with his mother, fish with his father, and to dodge an unruly horse.

Jonas moved to Shelley, Idaho, in 1971, and from that time forth, with the exception of a few sojourns elsewhere, he became an Idahoan. Jonas attended all twelve years of school in Shelley, graduating in 1983. In the sixth grade, he penned his first novel, *The Tumbleweed,* and in high school he wrote his second, *The Vigilante*. It was also during this time that he first became acquainted with Salmon, Idaho, staying toward the end of the road at the Golden Boulder Orchard and taking his first steps to manhood.

Jonas has lived in six cities in France, in Mesa, Arizona, and explored the United States extensively. He has fought fires for the Bureau of Land Management in five western states and carried a gun on his hip in three different jobs.

In 1987, Jonas met his wife-to-be, Debbie Chatterton, and in

1989 took her to the altar. Over some rough and rocky roads they have traveled, and across some raging rivers that have at times threatened to draw them under, but they survived, and with four beautiful children to show for it: Cheyenne, Jacob, Clay and Matthew.

Jonas has been employed as a Wells Fargo armored guard, a wildland firefighter, a security guard for California Plant Protection and Inter-Con, and police officer in Pocatello, Idaho, where he calls home. He is now retired after almost twenty-four years of proud employment as a municipal firefighter for the same city of Pocatello and works full-time as a private, armed security officer for Federal Protective Services, under contract with the security company Paragon.

One of Jonas's greatest joys in life is watching his second son, Clay, become a recognized writer of much talent in his own chosen field, that of fantasy and science fiction, with his current series *The Descendants of Light*. There is no greater compliment a son could give to his father than to follow in his footsteps.

Books by Kirby Jonas

Season of the Vigilante, Book One: The Bloody Season
Season of the Vigilante, Book Two: Season's End
The Dansing Star
Legend of the Tumbleweed
Lady Winchester
The Devil's Blood
The Secret of Two Hawks
Knight of the Ribbons
Drygulch to Destiny
Samuel's Angel
The Night of My Hanging (And Other Short Stories)
Russet
A Final Song for Grace

Savage Law series
1.   *Law of the Lemhi, part 1*
     Law of the Lemhi, part 2
2.   *River of Death*
3.   *Lockdown for Lockwood*
4.   *Like a Man Without a Country*
5.   *Thunderbird*
6.   *Savage Alliance*
7.   *Dark Badger (forthcoming)*

Yaqui Gold series
1.   *Yaqui Gold* (co-author Clint Walker)
2.   *Canyon of the Haunted Shadows (co-author Clint Walker)*

Legends West series
1.   *Disciples of the Wind* (co-author Jamie Jonas)
2.   *Reapers of the Wind* (co-author Jamie Jonas)

Lehi's Dream series
1.   *Nephi Was My Friend*
2.   *The Faith of a Man*
3.   *A Land Called Bountiful*

Gray Eagle series (e-book format only—forthcoming in print)
1.   *The Fledgling*
2.   *Flight of the Fledgling*
3.   *Wings on the Wind*
Death of an Eagle (e-book and large format softbound)

Books on audio

The Dansing Star, narrated by James Drury, *"The Virginian"*
Death of an Eagle, narrated by James Drury
Legend of the Tumbleweed, narrated by James Drury
Lady Winchester, narrated by James Drury
Yaqui Gold, narrated by Gene Engene
The Secret of Two Hawks, narrated by Kevin Foley
Knight of the Ribbons, narrated by Rusty Nelson
Drygulch to Destiny, narrated by Kirby Jonas

Available through the author at www.kirbyjonas.com

Email the author at: kirby@kirbyjonas.com or write to:

Howling Wolf Publishing
1611 City Creek Road
Pocatello ID 83204

Made in the USA
Columbia, SC
08 November 2024

45798108R10259